The Institution

Terra Dime

THE INSTITUTION. Copyright © 2009 by Terra Dime. All rights reserved. No part of this book may be used or reproduced in any manner whatsoever without written permission except in the case of brief quotations embodied in critical articles and reviews. For information e-mail TheInnClub@yahoo.com.

This is a work of fiction. While names of actual historical figures have been included to frame the narrative, all other characters and events are the product of the author's imagination.

FIRST EDITION

First printing, May 2009

ISBN 978-1-44214-285-5 (pbk.)

*This book is dedicated to mindful thinkers
with the audacity to transcend hope...and paradigms.*

TO PURCHASE THIS BOOK GO TO:

TheInstitutionBook.com

The sneakiest form of literary subtlety,
In a corrupt society,
Is to speak the plain truth.
The critics will not understand you;
The public will not believe you;
Your fellow writers will shake their heads.

— Edward Abbey

PROLOGUE

On July 22, 2040, Jerome Raines died peacefully in his sleep. It was the one and only thing he ever did without a fight. As an author and cultural critic he was fearless. He had balls when it wasn't fashionable to have balls. Society endured him for awhile. Sunny, on the other hand, loved him. On her way out, she turned and took one last look at Jerome lying silent and still. No more words to write. No more ideas to share. It was a grim day indeed. Using her shoulder as a stop to muffle the sound, she proceeded to close the door on critical thought. She did so quietly in the way a delusional system had taught her to. It was not acceptable to disturb those who were going through the motions of living.

Back in her darkened room she began to cry. She had held back to spare Jerome. And she would hold back again when the Nurse showed up later in the morning to help Sunny with her mental issues. There was much to cry about. While his death was a tremendous loss, it was no more debilitating than facing the planet's diminished circumstances. Knowing that we were on the brink of extinction was overwhelming. The link between human survival and that of forests hadn't resonated with the smartest species on Earth. At least, not in the way one might expect. Back in the 1980s, when the Interior Secretary of the most powerful country in the world alluded to a connection, it was with a gleeful fatalism that pretty much summed up the human experiment. *"After the last tree is felled, Christ will come back."* In recognizing that forest eradication would usher in a new era, sadly, he was ahead of the curve. Not when it came to the bit about Jesus though. He was a no-show. Unconscious, middle-aged, white men willfully engineering our demise remained an enduring trait of "civilization."

Sunny stared vacantly out the window. Lamplight illuminated the sweeping driveway leading to the entrance in the main building. Patients had not arrived by that massive front door for many years and they hadn't ever left that way. In fact, it was rare for a new patient to be admitted at all. The Faith is Truth Institution attended to a vanishing breed. All the action these days was through the back door, in body bags. A dwindling contingency bothered with the patients out here at the end of the road. That was especially true of relatives. Most likely it was they who recognized how sick their loved ones were and had them committed. Over the years the families had drifted so far apart in ideology, it was impossible to have a conversation that didn't turn contentious. Visiting parents or spouses at this facility meant coming to terms with how deep-seated and incurable their mental illnesses were and that was more than relatives could bear.

Twenty-eight years ago, when mental health came to be defined in less expansive terms, the Institution was recommissioned. After initially operating as a tuberculosis clinic, it had been closed for decades when the new opportunity arose. A completely self-contained facility, it was selected to receive patients from both Canada and the United States. Early on there had been some interest in the good work they were doing. But that had changed. Other than heated debates about what the facility cost to maintain, the Institution was virtually forgotten. The funding was in no danger of ever being terminated though. Unlike a host of other mental patients who had been cut loose to fend for themselves, this was a segment of the population no one ever considered releasing. And that meant Sunny would not return to either of the places she considered home. All that was left for her was to wait, and to watch the river slip silently past the Institution.

While standing there lost in thought, a way to eulogize Jerome took shape. Where they met years ago was a metaphor for his whole life – eyes wide open, shouting at the top of his lungs, yet unheard above the roar of the machine. Why had she not thought of that before? He would have laughed at that analogy. She wished she could go to him and tell him now. That was going to be the most difficult thing to bear – the loss of that mutual connection that had sustained her. It was both immediate and eternal.

BOOK ONE

THE MIND IN MOTION

Stretched out in her attic bedroom in Nelson, Sunny had only to pry her eyes away from the pages of her book to catch a glimpse of Kootenay Lake narrowing into the Kootenay River and heading west and then south towards the USA, her father's place of birth. In 1970 Samuel Owen Day successfully dodged the draft by fleeing north from Washington State into British Columbia. His actions were what defined her family. At nineteen years of age, without confiding in anyone, he packed his few belongings onto his back and walked across the unprotected border region around Metaline Falls into a country that while geographically adjacent was politically miles apart.

Sunny's father eked out a living any way he could but his primary occupation was backcountry outfitting and guiding. It was what brought her parents together. During Sam Day's very first summer in British Columbia he guided Kathie Wetherington and her friends into Valhalla Provincial Park. It was a weeklong adventure for a group of girls from Victoria. It was life altering for Kathie. Although she returned to Vancouver Island that autumn to attend the University of Victoria, the whole college scene paled by comparison to the real life adventures she could be having in Nelson with Sam. She lasted one year before dropping out and moving to the hinterlands where, by comparison, she lived like a pauper. It wasn't until Sunny was college age herself that she came to realize what her mother had given up for Sam and for her as well. Not that Kathie ever indicated sacrifice on her part. Sam had simply been this larger-than-life character. Before she knew it they had a baby and the adventure quit being a temporary diversion with which she could shock her friends.

Sunny's parents loved to talk about her first hiking trip to Kokanee Glacier when she was only a few months old. She liked to think she could remember clinging to her father's warm, sweaty back and falling in love with nature. It was all so vivid for no other reason than her parents' memories had become hers. How she pictured their lives and the cool things they did was not arrived at impartially. Like most young people, she was heavily influenced by her parents' perception of reality. She learned to ski shortly after she learned to walk and she could identify the elements of an ecosystem before she could name her body parts. By the time she entered first grade she had received a type of education most of her peers would never access.

It was during the summer of 1985 that the old Simpson place underwent a transformation of substantial proportions. Sunny's parents were concerned about a renovation of that magnitude going on at the end of their street. They mulled over the likelihood of the town becoming gentrified as its popularity soared with outsiders from cities like Vancouver and Calgary. Carpenters, roofers, and painters worked on the home around the clock. Once one of the grandest residences in Nelson, it had become dilapidated almost to the point of no return. While the previous owner was alive the maintenance on the sprawling three-story Victorian had been deferred indefinitely. However, the Shelbys – the new owners – had plenty of cash due to a death in the family and were committed to fixing the place up. They wanted to be moved in by September – the start of the school year. Mr. Shelby had been hired out of Vancouver to assume the position of Principal at the High School.

At the age of fourteen, Sunny started to become aware of who she was and began to deal with that. She might have remained unconscious a while longer if she hadn't made friends with Kim, the Principal's daughter, during the Nelson period. While there were some similarities between Kim and Sunny that made them destined to become friends, there were significant differences that ensured it would be short-lived. It was, without question, the baby bird incident that brought about their friendship.

***

Sunny finished tying her shoes and headed out of the locker room. She started running hard across the playing field, slowed down to ease her way through the gate, and then got onto the footpath that rose sharply to the old railroad grade. Once she reached that trail she turned right and challenged herself to catch the rest of the cross-country team who had a several minute head start. It was unavoidable when Ms. Paulson's English class was the last period of the day. As a teacher, she loved to stretch her students' minds with literary analysis. That day, it had been *Animal Farm* and even after the bell rang she was still casting pearls of wisdom about how "power corrupts and absolute power corrupts absolutely."

Most of the students couldn't stand Ms. Paulson. Conventional opinion was that she took stories too seriously and when it came to grammar her love of prepositional adjectival phrases was over the top. But Sunny did not share this belief. Ms. Paulson had passion and insight but most of all she was brave. She dared to stand up in front of a bunch of teenagers and express something more than the superficial. That she would challenge them intellectually and emotionally was a compliment.

Sunny told herself to stop thinking about school. She really wanted to enjoy the sounds of an early spring afternoon. First, she screened out the rise and fall of her own breathing and made it drop away. Next, it was the soft thump of her feet striking the trail. When she became aware enough to take in the slightest rustle, everything opened up. Wind in the trees, the scrape of a squirrel finding higher limbs, and birdsong filled her ears. As well as something else. Human voices that were angry and defiant. Around the next corner, in a small clearing, were two boys, a girl, and a Grey Jay. The bird was flying frantically overhead, back and forth between the trees, swooping and squawking. The boys strutted around, sticks in hand, like they had accomplished something of consequence. The girl was down on her knees cupping something in her hands and sobbing.

Recognizing the Principal's daughter, who was also on the running team, Sunny stopped. "What's going on?" she asked before realizing that what she held were the smashed bodies of baby birds.

"These little jerks knocked their nest out of a tree and then beat them to death."

Reality had slipped unwelcome into Kim's life. Chances were she wouldn't be seeking any more thanks to the discomfort this small dose of truth had inflicted. Unlike Kim, Sunny was well-versed on what little value human beings placed on nature. Her parents had made sure of this. She wasn't going to cry around about such things for the rest of her life. She intended to do something about it. Defending nature, that would be her life's work. But still, even knowing what she did, Sunny couldn't help but stare at the boys as if they were a couple of sick puppies.

"Why would you do such a thing?" she wondered out loud.

They turned their backs on Kim and Sunny and began to saunter away. "We were just having a little fun. What's the big deal? They're just BIRDS after all."

It was one of those understandings we have at an early age. They were such young boys. Eight years old or so and they came from good homes. Already, they had determined their relationship with the natural world. How exactly did they come to it? Had it been spelled out? Had their parents sat them down one day and told them that non-human life didn't matter? Or was a lesson that explicit unnecessary because the subliminal understanding was everywhere? Sunny wanted to run after them and scare them so badly that they would think twice before doing anything like it again. But she knew that was behavior that fell outside of what was acceptable.

Kim had found the nest and was gently depositing the lifeless birds into it. "I want to take them home and bury them," she said.

"Maybe that's not the right thing to do," Sunny suggested. "Let nature handle it. I'm not sure how it works but I feel we've interfered enough."

"But wild animals will come and eat them," she cried. "It's awful. I can't bear it."

"I was taught that nature's way is the best way."

She seemed to think about what Sunny said while the tears continued to flow. "Okay," she agreed. "But I'm going to place them under those shrubs over there where they're not out in the open."

After she attended to that, they left the clearing together and began to run. So worked up were they, they ran the six-mile course at a race pace without even noticing. While they ran and talked, Sunny thought about how to handle the Grey Jay situation. She decided to write a letter to the editor of the local paper to see whether the community thought the boys should be held accountable for their actions. The outrage and condemnation in response to her letter exceeded her expectations. The insistence that the boys be appropriately punished raged for several weeks before it was decided they should perform community service at the animal shelter. This small success left Sunny with the impression that the strength of a person's will could make a difference. And, by working within the system, with the tools that were available, she could impact the adult world in a meaningful way.

At a young age, Sunny cared deeply about environmental issues. She placed her trust in the future of the environmental movement. There was momentum. Awareness was on the rise, or so it seemed. In the mid-1980s we felt our destiny was to live lighter on the land. In the end, her environmental career followed along a similar path to the baby bird affair. She would make her living being there after the fact, to dole out punishment to the kind of people those boys were destined to grow up to be.

Once school let out for the summer, the two new friends spent time running on the trails and doing speed work at the track. And they came to avoid spending time with Sunny's family. Instead, they did things like watch movies in Kim's bedroom. It was inconceivable to Sunny that a teenager would have her very own television. They had no television at her house. Her parents were philosophically opposed to it. Kim's parents were not philosophically opposed to anything. Mrs. Shelby let them drink pop, read teen magazines, and lounge around by the pool all day. Sunny did not read a single book that summer. She was educated in a different way. In the midst of all the fun and excitement, Sunny became aware for the first time that there was more than one way to see the human world.

Hanging out with Kim's family was so easy. They didn't challenge her in any way. They didn't talk about anything controversial. Everything for them was exactly as represented in the mainstream. They had faith in the goodness of the western way, in boundless human ingenuity, and in technologies that would erase limitations. There existed no ulterior motives, no conspiracies, and no man behind the curtain. It was obvious to them that human life was getting better and would continue to do so. A discussion to the contrary was out of the question and they could not contemplate that any other household had the conversation either.

Terra Dime

Because Sunny was self-monitoring she prevented herself from saying things that would make the Shelbys uncomfortable. Kim, however, was very uncomfortable at the Day's shabbily-furnished rental house. Most of the time she had no idea what she was eating or what they were talking about except she was vaguely aware that the things she valued most in life were being criticized. After coming home, she would ask her father what a Plutocracy was or who Howard Zinn and Noam Chomsky were. Or turn to her mother in hopes of having the mystery of greenhouse gases unraveled. But her mom and dad were way out of their element as well. They found it shocking that a girl who seemed as normal as Sunny could have such unusual parents.

It was a one-of-a-kind summer for Sunny. Overall it was a blast. How could it not be when you had a friend with a swimming pool? One of their favorite things to do was to practice diving. They would go at it for hours. Sunny didn't mind that she wasn't good at everything in the way Kim was. That may have been another reason why they got along so well.

"No, you're still not jumping up high enough," Kim scolded. "Let me show you again," she said climbing out of the pool, all 5 feet 10 inches of her, and striding down to the deep end. With her toes curled around the end of the diving board, she threw both arms into the air, and bounced once. Getting maximum spring out of the board she entered the water with legs straight and toes pointed perfectly. "See, it's easy," she exclaimed as soon as she broke the surface.

"I don't know what I'm doing wrong. It sure looks easy when you do it. And yet, you keep telling me I suck." She called out to Mrs. Shelby who was stretched out on a chaise lounge painting her toenails and asked if her diving was as bad as Kim said it was.

"Oh I'm sorry dear, I wasn't watching," she answered diplomatically and then changed the subject. She asked Sunny if she would like to join them when they went to Expo '86.

Two weeks later they all loaded into the Shelby's snappy Chevy Blazer and headed to Vancouver. Going on vacation with them turned out to be nothing short of hedonistic. They stopped wherever and whenever Kim wanted. Nothing was off limits – ice cream, milkshakes, potato chips, chocolate bars, greasy hamburgers, even the music of the teenagers' choice.

The Institution

It was a contrast to Sunny's mother's diligent packing of nuts, fruits, vegetables, and filtered water. Her family didn't have the money to spend freely. On their road trips they either listened to the CBC or took turns reading to each other. Her mom and dad believed firmly in turning every available moment into a learning opportunity. The pop culture was sure to turn young minds into mush.

Once they got to their destination, the townhouse on False Creek was the biggest surprise up to that point. It was the property of some past associate of Mr. Shelby's and Sunny's first impression was that it was grand. Given the fact that she hadn't even stayed in a Motel 6 she couldn't claim to be an expert. It seemed to her that if the fridge was stocked with items like caviar, Brie, and champagne, chances were it fell in the upper range of Approved Tourist Accommodation. For Sunny it was her first opportunity to venture into a magical world that was completely foreign to her until that year. They ate three meals a day in restaurants. It was always the Shelbys' treat, as her small amount of spending money designated for the trip would not have gone far.

The 1986 World's Fair in Vancouver, British Columbia was highly regarded. In view of how the early part of 1986 was marred by two disasters – one of horrific proportions – it seemed amazing that humanity mustered the enthusiasm for a fair. In January, it was the Challenger space shuttle manned with the "lucky" schoolteacher who won the opportunity to be the first civilian in outer space. It barely made it off the launching pad before disintegrating. In April, the Chernobyl nuclear meltdown blanketed the planet in radioactive fallout. It was a catastrophe too heinous for the average person to comprehend. The irony of two superpowers being humbled in such dramatic fashion was lost on the crowds. The Challenger and Chernobyl incidents were forever linked in Sunny's mind. They provided a taste of how deadly a combination economics, hubris, and certainty can be.

There were moments from that Expo trip she would revisit throughout her life. Experiences like sitting at a waterfront table on the patio of Bridges Restaurant watching the kind of people she hadn't known existed moor their yachts. An endless parade of the happiest, most beautiful people she had ever seen walked past on their way to formal dining. And they had impeccable timing too. When the nightly fireworks began at dusk, they were back out on the water enjoying the display from the best seats in town.

And then there was "The Scream Machine" – the roller coaster that had a futuristic rocket ship quality about it. That provided the most memorable experience of all. For years she would be puzzled by how an hour of waiting could take on a lifetime of relevance. Kim and Sunny had bought the tickets for the ride and were already in line when Kim chickened out. She announced that since rides made her sick, it was likely she would throw-up if she got on this one. No amount of pleading on Sunny's part could convince her of any other outcome.

Kim was already on her way out of the line and Sunny was about to follow when the guy in front of them turned and said, "You're welcome to ride with me."

Sunny didn't know what to say. It was close quarters in those cars. She would have to sit all snuggled up beside him. The thought of this gave her the creeps.

"Go ahead Sunny," Kim said. "You're dying to ride on this thing." And with that, Kim left her.

Sunny moved up beside him. She was at that age when she couldn't help feeling awkward and uncomfortable. He was one of those boys on the verge of being a man. And this made her self-conscious. They were about the same age but his voice was deep and his limbs were very muscular. He had hair on his upper lip even. Strangely enough he didn't engage in the usual small talk. In fact, he didn't talk anything like other boys. He didn't ask her name or where she was from. Instead, he made some thoughtful observations. The kind, that in the future, would come to be known as his unique style.

"You know a Special Category Exposition is supposed to be great to attend because it gives young people like us a sense of what adults are working on. Especially in a case like this when the theme is transportation and communication. With a slogan like 'World in Motion – World in Touch – a Celebration of Ingenuity,' I was expecting to be wowed. I did a little reading up on transportation before I got here. If history is any kind of guide, it shapes everything. So, if we were smart about it we could set our

The Institution

course. I mean, wouldn't it be great if the future looked so hopeful you couldn't wait to get there?"

After he said that, he did a verbal about face. "Of course, the bad thing about attending a World's Fair is you might get a sense that the people in charge have no vision for the future. That would be unsettling, don't you think?"

Sunny felt herself put a little off center by these remarks, mystified by how it's possible to be more aligned with a total stranger than everyday acquaintances. And that was why she told him what she really thought. "After the first day, I figured out there wasn't anything educational here. This is pure entertainment. And that's what people want. They want to feel good about themselves on account of all the wonderful inventions that have come along."

"So these fair goers don't actually care about the future? They're not interested in the overall value of our contraptions or where it's all leading? The amazing number and array is where it's at?"

"It must be something like that. Transportation systems don't have to take us anywhere important and they can still be called transit. I'll bet most miles are spent on the same worn stretch of road day after day. Look at this roller coaster we're waiting to ride. All that twisted metal defying gravity. This is the most futuristic vehicle on site and it doesn't actually go anywhere. And what about the Parachute Drop? Wouldn't you say that's a way to get from way up high to way down low in a hurry? That gets my vote for Rapid Transit. And those really loud boats that race around out in the harbor several times a day – Noisy Transit. Let me see, what else? What about the McBarge? That's like Fast Food on a Slow Boat to nowhere."

He laughed at that, already liking her sense of humor. "You didn't mention the General Motors' prototype," he said. "There's no way you could have missed a car with a navigational system and a mobile phone. That can mean only one thing. Twenty years from now, people who are so stupid they aren't capable of reading a map are going to be driving around lost while talking on the phone. That can't be good but it's the future so get used to it. I agree with you, if I don't think about the big picture, there's lots here for me. Transportation and communication all around. Wait a

15

minute, what about the Northwest Territories' exhibit? That one explored the downside of our easily getting into places that used to be off limits."

"Well there's always some crazy group that takes things too seriously. I'm guessing most people like that exhibit. It's tolerable to have one fringe group in the mix as long as they don't get carried away with anti-progress nonsense." She sounded exactly like her dad.

Sunny couldn't stop herself from talking so starved was she to say what she was thinking. "As far as the pavilions go, the U.S. and U.S.S.R. seem to be committed to space travel. And some of the lesser known countries have some really nice photos to entice tourists to travel to their lands. It's going to take some serious air transport to pull that off. Coming from B.C., I've been led to believe there is nowhere else in the world as scenic as this. But I saw the pictures of Thailand and now I'm not so sure. That's a beautiful place. That's beside the point, though. The point I really want to make is there is no reason to be confused about the message you take away from all of this. There are only two. One, everything we're ever going to come up with for getting around here on earth has already been invented. And two, but don't dismay, we are seriously trying to figure out how to increase our presence in outer space."

The crazy part about her going off like this was she hadn't realized she'd been thinking these thoughts at all. The Shelbys were not the kind of people you discussed things with. When she was around them, she knew to see things only as they were meant to be seen. Anything else would not come across as healthy curiosity, but as negativity, which was not a virtue by any measure. It struck her that she had spent the last few months coasting. Worse yet, she had been making a concerted effort not to think in order for the Shelbys to find her agreeable.

She stole a sideways glance to see how he was taking in what she had just rambled on about. He appeared to be mulling it over. At least he wasn't laughing at her like she was the biggest dork in the world.

"If what you're saying is true – and I think it is – that means all we can look forward to is business as usual, no change, more of the same. It's likely this extends way beyond transportation and communication and that's awful to think about," he quipped. "The forces that brought us this far won't permit us to take a different direction. What opportunities does that leave for people our age?"

"Just whatever it takes to keep it all going, I guess. My dad would blame it on the rich and powerful who run everything and stop innovation." Sunny also knew that her father wasn't one ever to question his own ways. "But it's more than that." She didn't know how to put it into words though.

He turned away from her and scanned the crowds moving around the site. "I wonder what all these people are thinking? I'm fifteen years old, troubled, and disappointed. Shouldn't the adults be insulted?"

Sunny thought about the Shelbys. They weren't stupid people. They just weren't thinking people. And because of this they weren't troubled or disappointed and they certainly didn't have a sense that this Exposition was an affront to their intelligence. There were other forces at play here and she still couldn't come up with the words.

He had something to say on the subject though. "I think most people are kind of like walking zombies. We're alive but our senses aren't sharp, our minds aren't active. It's like you said, we want to be entertained, not engaged. In a way we're like complacent, domesticated animals that are not at the top of our game. We've lost our edge, our basic survival skills. Isn't that what we're really talking about here? The ability to analyze our situation, come up with an honest assessment of where we've been and where we're going, and then make adjustments if our long-term chances of survival don't look so good. We don't know how to do that."

"It might actually be worse than that," Sunny responded, thinking about how bad it made her feel not to fit in. Which was why she had been going along to get along for the past year and finding that everyone liked her a whole lot better when she was like that.

"We don't exactly have a culture that encourages people to question whether there's a better way. Talk about a way to be made fun of. School provides the perfect example of how much better it is to be popular. The fear of not being liked is a powerful de-motivator, don't you think?"

"So we've created a culture that doesn't value critical thinking. How bizarre is that?"

Smiling while she said it, she agreed that it was bizarre. And that what it really meant was if we were going to accomplish anything of any

Terra Dime

value, we were going to have to force ourselves to make some unpopular choices. Now that she had gotten over her initial shyness, she couldn't stop looking at him and wondering about him. He was such a serious guy. Sunny was serious too but she adjusted accordingly. You wouldn't catch her trying to engage in a meaningful conversation with the in-crowd at her school. How did he get by? His lack of guile was kind of ironic because that could be seen as an important survival skill as well.

"Since we're on the subject of critical thinking, want to hear where I think the future of transportation lies?"

"Sure." As she said this she forced herself to look him square in the face and felt herself blush at the way he looked at her so intently. There was a lot of heat in his dark eyes.

"It came to me when I was looking at that 'Highway '86' that was built on the site. At first glance it's a four-lane freeway for pedestrians covered with a bunch of different modes of transportation frozen in time. Which is kind of weird in itself. I mean, why would anyone want to be walking on a highway? I thought it was supposed to mean something and that I was missing it. The way it rises out of the ocean – it could represent the Evolution of transportation. It could even be a metaphor for Evolution, period. If that were the case, it's peculiar that the highway doesn't go anywhere. That would mean as far as we're concerned, Evolution is over. And there may be some truth in that but it's not very inspiring."

Sunny couldn't help but comment even though she knew he wasn't finished. "Let's face it. If the adults recognized that we had a way to go before we reached our full potential, they'd have produced a fair that was meatier than this one."

Before continuing, he laughed again at the way she deciphered everything. "Eventually, I realized it was nothing more than a literal highway. I felt cheated because someone got paid to create something that was a whole lot less than it could have been. But it did get me thinking that the concept of transportation is too literal. The way it stands right now whole lifetimes are wasted going back and forth when they could be spent moving forward. The futility of that should be obvious. Let's face it; how people get around doesn't really matter if they are just as uninformed at the end of the trip. What if mobility morphed from being important on a physical level to being important on an intellectual one? Or, say we focused our energy on finding a way to advance human character. Those are the areas where we're most deficient. Doesn't that sound more powerful than moving bodies to and fro? Yet with all these countries and corporations represented here not a single one had the inclination to challenge us in that way."

At this point Sunny couldn't take her eyes off of him. She began to feel self-conscious in a different sort of way. Who was this guy? He sounded destined to advance a new theory or something. "You know what you ought to be when you grow up? A philosopher." She caught herself immediately. "Wait a minute, maybe that was a stupid suggestion. Are there any modern day philosophers? You don't exactly hear about them. If there are, they mustn't be getting nearly as much respect as a guy like Socrates."

"From what I understand 'there is nothing new under the sun' when it comes to philosophy. I think we're supposed to believe, like many things, that everything has been decided. We're not supposed to waste our time pondering the 'why of things.' We're supposed to get jobs and be productive members of society."

"For real?"

"I think so."

"Well I don't get that at all. How could a few people who lived 2,500 years ago know more than we do now? There weren't nearly as many people and there were no nuclear weapons. But that didn't mean things were great then either. They had a system based on slavery. In place of science they had all these weird superstitions. They didn't even know how the planet worked. If they were unaware of all those things, why should they have the last word on philosophy?"

"It's safe that way. I guess it's possible that over the last 2,500 years we aren't any wiser because we truly aren't capable of it. What's more likely, though, is it's not encouraged because it would turn everything upside down."

"You have all the answers, don't you?" she said flippantly, before realizing that he was seeking the strength to explore many questions that were swimming around inside his head.

Terra Dime

His face registered embarrassment while those big, unpretentious eyes of his tried to figure her out. "I hope you don't think I'm a jerk. Sometimes, I want to tell someone what I'm thinking. I guess I can come across as a know-it-all."

Sunny's own awkwardness evaporated when she realized he was looking to her for encouragement. "I wasn't making fun of you. You're different and I like different."

"You do?" he said, as if this were astonishing. Suddenly, something occurred to him. "Sonny's an unusual name for a girl. Is it short for something?" he asked.

"Sunshine – it's not S-O-N, it's S-U-N. And you'll never guess my last name. It's Day."

"Sunny Day," he said in awe. "What a great name."

"The name thing can be embarrassing so please don't go on about it."

"Are your parents hippies or something?"

"Yes they are."

"Cool. This is a first. None of my friends back home in Oregon have hippies for parents. That's where I'm from, by the way. I'm here with my family but we're driving back tomorrow," he told her. "What's it like having hippies for parents? I'll bet it's not all it's cracked up to be. I'll bet there's a downside."

She got tired of being singled out in this fashion. This group her parents identified with was the most interesting thing about her life. He was the first ever to allude to there being a downside to having hippies for parents. Not everyone would agree the drug thing was a downside, but for her it was. In his younger days her father had done LSD. He talked about a dimension few could see. He was one of the lucky few – so he said – whose mind had become elastic enough through the use of hallucinogenic drugs to be able to enter this other world. He heard voices, saw things coming out of the walls, frolicked with the Gods in exotic places. He was convinced that it was possible for properly trained individuals to be in two parts of the world at the same time even though they were thousands of miles apart and he knew of at least five of his previous lives. He could explain away all his bad thoughts and behavior as vestiges of an earlier existence in which he was acting out an unresolved scenario. Sunny's mother was a little less fervent in her metaphysical beliefs but she was working on it through meditation, coupled with marijuana assists, in order to attain the same level of consciousness that her husband enjoyed.

When the discussion in her household turned to this, Sunny grew cold. The analytical part of her was clear on this subject. Her father had not opened his mind. He had shut down its capacity to get beyond a perception that came to him in a drug-induced euphoria. Developmentally, he remained frozen at the place those drugs had taken him. For him, there would never be anything more concrete than that experience. She had no doubt that he was seeing something and that he believed in the authenticity of the visions but it was just as likely that the chemicals had tricked his mind into believing that what he saw under their influence was real. But she could not tell him this. He claimed he was at a higher level of consciousness and that gave him special insight.

Her dad offered on many occasions to drop acid with her so that she might also "open her mind." He would get teary-eyed when he spoke of how beautiful a drug LSD was and how taking it had been the most important thing he'd ever done. It was obvious the strength of his belief. This was Sam Day's religion. He had faith in illegal drugs and their ability to help a person see reality.

It was the same with marijuana. She felt that he was addicted. She knew it wasn't supposed to have that effect but it did on her father. He was stoned from morning to night. Always trying to find a way to relax his mind and searching for the opening into a dimension that was preferable to the one in which his family resided. What was real? What was false? At that point she had more questions than answers. No right wing conservative could have conceived of a more effective anti-drug program than the one her parents inadvertently concocted. In spite of their drug reassurances and proposals to get high with her, Sunny was clean, squeaky clean. She had to be. She was the only adult in the family.

"It's like not having parents at all," Sunny finally responded. "I've never been told what to do. I've never been disciplined. I'm just supposed to know what the right thing is. That isn't to say I haven't learned a lot, especially from my father. We talk all the time. My dad feels so strongly about things, I think it's hard for him to stay sane. He's seriously opposed to some standard stuff. And he doesn't give up on them either. He gets as worked up today as he did twenty years ago. Do you know what I mean?" Sunny said, looking over at a stranger who she sensed was similarly inclined. It was the underlying principles of conventional life that they questioned.

A moment later they were crammed tightly together in the way she knew they would be. She saw how his knees came up much higher than hers. She took in his muscular thigh, the length of his calf, and the tan along the top of his foot where it disappeared into a deck shoe. The roller coaster was exhilarating in one way but it paled next to the overall feeling of buoyancy when the ride ended. He was quick to get off the ride. Eager to help her out, he offered his hand and as he did she watched his biceps flex with the effort of lifting her. For little more than a second she felt the heat of his skin and then it was the smell of his hair that disabled her.

When he was very close to her he said, "That was fun. Would you like to go again?" And she couldn't answer. All she could focus on was how he hadn't let go of her hand. He held it longer and tighter than he needed to.

"I'd love to," she said once she could breathe again. "But we're supposed to meet Kim's parents in about five minutes. We're going over to the Canada Pavilion for the afternoon."

"Can we meet later?" he asked, trying not to let desperation creep into his voice.

"Sure," she said. "Let's see…We should get back to the Skytrain Station about five o'clock. I'll look for you over by the Canada Portal. Say under the giant hockey stick?"

"What if we miss one another?"

"We won't." Now she could see Kim checking her watch and scowling. "Look I'm sorry. I've got to go. They'll be waiting."

Sunny could hear him call after her. All she caught was, "By the way my name is Jerry..." The end of his sentence was drowned out by the noise and she completely missed his last name as she and Kim took off running and dodging the crowds. When the four of them finally arrived at the Canada Pavilion forty-five minutes later, her heart sank. There was a line a mile-long outside. There were lines inside. And just when they were about

The Institution

to leave and she calculated being about fifteen minutes late for her rendezvous, the Shelbys decided not to head back to the main Expo site right away but to eat dinner in Gastown. As much as she wanted to object, Sunny knew she couldn't. So they waited outside of a restaurant in yet another line for their turn to eat. It was eight o'clock by the time they were back on the Skytrain approaching the Expo Station. She tried to look nonchalant as she searched frantically below for a glimpse of him.

"What is the matter with you?" Kim finally blurted out in frustration. "You have barely said two words in the last six hours. Ever since you went on that ride you have been so weird. Are you sick or something? I told you that ride would make you sick."

But Sunny couldn't explain what had happened. Last year she had known only of her parents' world. Then, she had entered Kim's. And it had seemed exciting for a while, in an unchallenging kind of way. Another door had been unlocked. In this other place there was potential, or at the very least, the hope of another way. Best of all, was who else would be there. This was not something she could share with these people. It sounded hokey even to her.

Sunny responded with the answer Kim was looking for. "That must be it," she agreed unconvincingly. "My stomach is upset." While she spoke her eyes never left the window.

"What are you looking for?" Kim asked.

"Just concentrating on keeping my dinner down," Sunny lied as she glanced toward the proposed meeting place. She spotted him alone right where he said he would be. He had waited for three hours. The knowledge of this was crippling. Then a man, a larger, older version of him approached. They spoke and she saw Jerry nod his head in agreement. His father ruffled his hair, put an arm across his shoulder in a parental gesture that said he loved his son and couldn't stand to see him hurt. Trapped in the Shelbys' world, she couldn't shove her way to the exit and chase after Jerry and his dad. She could only watch as they stepped into the crowd and faded away.

Everything about the trip lost its luster after that. By the time they returned to the townhouse, Sunny thought it had diminished in their absence. The rooms seemed sterile, the furnishings cheap in that trashy sort of way that doesn't stand the test of time. The Shelbys were up for watching one of the dozens of videos in the collection but Sunny managed to convince them she didn't feel well enough to give it a try. She gave a sigh of relief when she was able to disappear alone into one of the three bedrooms, the one she had been so enamored with just that morning. While she got ready for bed she heard them popping corn in the microwave. Later, she envisioned Mrs. Shelby curled up on the couch, Mr. Shelby stretched out in the recliner, and Kim lying on her side on the floor completely engrossed in a mediocre film they had all seen before.

When she pulled back the comforter in the desert southwest motif and slipped between the sheets, she thought the whole room's color scheme was beginning to look dated. She felt the sheets chafe against her skin when she reached for a book on the nightstand. For fifteen minutes she scanned the pages and failed to absorb a single word. She thought about what had happened and tried to think intelligently about what it meant. She had always known it would be just a matter of time before she got interested in boys. But why that boy? Her imagination embarked on another kind of wild ride conjuring up all the possible scenarios under which they might meet again. And once she had run through all of those, she was left to wonder if the feeling was mutual. And if it was, did he have enough information by which to find her? And would he try? All of these thoughts were running through her head in the first giddy hours after their brief meeting when everything seemed possible and likely. It was only hours that separated them – not a lifetime of choices and commitments.

Having had no prior experience with this sort of thing, she didn't know whether this was the way adolescent crushes always felt or whether it was more than that. She felt like she had seen a glimpse of who she wanted to be. And that someone belonged in a place full of bright, decent people who were aware. She wanted to know a place that valued quality people. She wanted to live in circumstances where critical thinking wasn't a fringe activity but the prevailing one. Was that too much to hope for?

Oh, she didn't know what she was seeing. But whatever it was, the best thing she could do for herself was to be surrounded by people who demanded that she be more than she was, not less. Never less. Otherwise, she would quit growing and would have nothing to contribute. Recognizing

The Institution

this at her age felt like an important step – one that had the power to stay with her. It was the messenger responsible for triggering this round of emotions that she would cling to the longest. She would think of him often throughout her life. She would revisit their conversation and mull over the significance of their having run into one another that way. Instead of the memory diminishing over time it seemed to grow more vivid.

And she thought of him when she and the Shelbys pulled up in front of their rental house in Nelson a day later to find all her family's possessions out on the sidewalk. They had been evicted. She thought how much better it was this way. He would never really know who she was or where she lived. Had she not been so eager to escape to the Shelby's house that summer, she would have been aware that her parents were having financial problems. The Shelbys were horrified by the spectacle of eviction. Her father did paint a forlorn picture sitting on the sidewalk with a tiny pile of personal belongings on one side of him and a large collection of marijuana plants on the other. Sunny had reconciled that this was the way her father augmented his income a long time ago. The Shelbys were less amenable to the situation. It was an excellent time to start over, and within days, fate handed them a big surprise. Sam Day's mother died thus affording them the opportunity to take possession of her home in Silver Falls, Washington. After seventeen years in self-imposed exile her father decided to make peace with his country.

Just as the Shelby's world had been an eye-opening experience for Sunny so was moving to the U.S. It was true her father had railed hard and often about the differences between Canada and the United States, but Sunny didn't appreciate what he meant until she was in the middle of it all. It was during the Reagan years when she and the U.S. became intimately acquainted. As President, he shifted the country into a more consumptive frame of mind. By telling people they didn't have to cut back, he became a national hero. Americans liked being told they were doing everything exactly right. They especially liked the part about how the only thing that made sense was to keep doing it, only more recklessly. In response, consumption ratcheted up a couple of notches. The consequences, however, lagged by several decades. They were foretold but not believed. Holding the view that it was "morning in America" in the 1980's ensured that it would be twilight thirty years later. Initially, it was this spread of conservatism that alarmed Sunny. Until she began to see Conservatism as a different strain of the same disease. Her concerns grew to include the values on which the whole human system was based, political and otherwise. Unsustainable consumption was not widely accepted as cause for concern. The time to make adjustments came, and then it passed us by while we searched for someone else to blame. The way we are inclined to do.

Sunny discovered that it's possible to care as much about the mountains, rivers, and forests of a foreign land as it is your own. The wind in the pines at their new home in Washington State sounded as good to her as the wind in the firs back in British Columbia. Silver Falls, the waterfall in the heart of downtown for which the city had been named, struck Sunny as the perfect centerpiece the moment she lay eyes on it. The only thing missing from this idyllic natural feature were the salmon. Dams on the Columbia had thwarted their ability to spawn in the Silver River. It was thrilling for her to think about seeing them making their way over the falls again. It would be a dream come true to be responsible for something like that.

For a while, things were okay for Sunny's family. Because there was no mortgage on their recently inherited two-story craftsman bungalow, the Days did not need to make much money to survive. This was a good thing because making money was not something they excelled at. Not being someone who could bear to work indoors, Sam Day found employment at an area ski resort during the winter months and with an outfitter during the summer. It was inevitable though that Sunny's father would eventually draw upon his B.C. Bud connections to smuggle pot into Washington. In the summer of 1990, when he was supposedly guiding a group into the Pack River Wilderness he was arrested on the shores of the Kettle River loading fifty pounds of pot into the family Subaru.

Sunny loved her father. She knew he wasn't a bad guy. He just had these beliefs about certain things that didn't always coincide with the law. He didn't think marijuana was as potent or harmful a drug as what the pharmaceutical industry was hooking the general public on. It was hypocritical that because the dollars those sales generated were part of the

GDP they were looked upon favorably while operating outside The Economy made one a criminal. And he hated hypocrisy. The connection he failed consistently to make was that it didn't matter whether the pharmaceutical industry was a more insidious drug pusher than he was, and that the Food & Drug Administration was also culpable in turning people on to the products it approved, he was going to jail.

He put on a brave face about the whole thing. He went so far as to indicate it was no big deal. He'd been arrested before during protests in the Vietnam era and for other acts of civil disobedience, mainly to do with developers and their penchant for trashing prime wildlife habitat. But this wasn't like those other times. This was a five-year sentence he would not live to see the end of.

***

Dr. Doug Marsh passed on the information about Jerome Raines' death to Nurse Darlene Hannon in the early hours of the morning. Darlene was indifferent to the news and responded as such. "Surely it was to be expected. The human body isn't meant to survive the kind of trauma his did. He was living on borrowed time."

"Nevertheless, the other patients will take it hard," Dr. Marsh explained. At some deep intuitive level he knew that Jerome's death would take the wind out of the sails of most of the patients. "They saw him as their spiritual leader," he continued. "As difficult as it is to attribute spirit to such a delusional group, you'll have to find a way to show respect for their loss as you go about your rounds."

Darlene's face screwed up in disgust. She didn't know how she could show her patients any more compassion than she already did. "What was the deal with Jerome Raines anyway? Was he considered a good writer at one time? From what I've heard, his books were that same drivel all our patients are obsessed with. Lies, all lies." Of this, she had no doubt.

"The one thing they are not in denial about is the amount of power he once had. He could really stir up the masses. Forty, fifty years ago people liked to get worked up about the most inane things." It made them both shudder to think about wasting time reading or writing such negative crap.

Terra Dime

Neither one of them wished to give it another thought so Darlene searched around on the nightstand for a diversion.

"Here," she said, placing one of Doug's little blue pills between his lips and following up with some water she also kept handy by the bed. She lifted his head from the pillow so he could swallow easily. Once the medicine began to work its magic, he'd be up for spending another couple of hours the way they'd spent the last two. Come tomorrow, even that bunch of neurotics she attended to couldn't keep her from smiling.

After the pharmaceutically enhanced extra innings, Darlene managed to squeeze in thirty minutes of sleep before the alarm sounded. She attempted to disentangle her legs from his. With his face buried in her heavy breasts, Dr. Marsh let out a sigh of contentment. She tried to lift herself from the bed without disturbing him but he clung to her large body for warmth. Finally, she worked her way free and began to get ready for work.

In the shower she turned off the water and reached for a towel. When she tried in vain to wrap it fully around herself, she cursed the laundry staff for having shrunk another one of her possessions. At the mirror she examined her teeth for cavities before popping a pill in her mouth. She had "Dry Mouth Syndrome" and her lack of saliva caused tooth decay. At the age of twenty-four she had already received several dental implants. The tooth fortifying maintenance drug that was rectifying the problem caused hardening of the arteries so a blood thinner had been prescribed. These were in addition to the high blood pressure and high cholesterol medications she had been on for years. Because the active ingredient in the high blood pressure drug was known to cause liver malfunction, part of her morning ritual included obtaining a urine sample on which she performed a diagnostic test. She also screened herself for high blood sugar since it had been determined she was borderline diabetic. Gout, once the scourge of kings, was now commonplace. Hers was being managed and she was happy for that because left untreated it was a debilitating condition. She felt fortunate to be living in a time when the miracles of modern medicine appeared limitless. These thoughts went through her head as she pressed her fingers to a sore spot on her abdomen that she suspected was her gall bladder acting up.

The Institution

"Thank goodness," she said out loud as she checked herself out in the mirror, "I'm such a picture of good health."

When she returned to the bedroom, Dr. Marsh was lying naked on his stomach with the covers in a heap beside him. Just seeing him there made her want to crawl back into bed and go at it again. She thought about pleasing him all day long and she thought about it even more on the nights they weren't together. She tried to satiate him in every way imaginable so that when he left her bed he didn't have the energy or imagination for anyone else. With the cocktail of libido-enhancing drugs he had access to it was an impossible task but it made her feel better to think she was doing something for her cause. She suspected that he performed the same sexual athletics with others after overhearing a couple of nurses comparing performance reports on a guy whose moves sounded a lot like Doug's.

Darlene reached into the closet and removed the pastel pink skirt and matching plaid smock from her collection of uniforms. It was the least institutional of the approved outfits the nursing staff wore to go about their duties. True to her word she intended not only to act but also look compassionate. As she buttoned her smock in preparation to head out the door she was torn between duty and the proximity of Doug's bare bottom. But then she thought about how hard he worked. How worn out he must be after an exhausting night attending to a dying patient.

In reality, he hadn't attended to Jerome Raines at all but had been notified by another patient of his death and gone to his room to confirm the obvious. But Darlene was more interested in manipulating the facts to match what she *knew* to be true than in the facts themselves. His was a thankless job. There were few rewards when it came to mentally ill patients who could not give him the respect he deserved. Outside this Institution, in private practice, an MD and Psychopharmacologist of his stature was appreciated. It would be more gratifying to be prescribing to normal, rational people who didn't wish to suffer.

Quietly she left her room and walked through the tunnel system connecting her living quarters with the rest of the Asylum. On the elevator, as she ascended above ground, she considered her patients and decided to switch up the order in which she attended to them. With one less to see she could spend a little more time counseling the remaining ones. Invariably, they would be acting out in response to Jerome Raines' death. Determined not to procrastinate on the most difficult chore but to get it over with as quickly as possible, she entered the elevator in the east wing and punched the third floor button. When she arrived outside the room numbered 308 – instead of 306 where she usually began her rounds – she took a deep breath, tapped briskly on the door, and prepared to be greeted with contempt.

"Instead of being born again, why didn't we simply grow up?" It was this patient's mantra and was always delivered in exactly the same tone, from the same spot in the room.

"Hi Sunshine," Darlene chirped in her perkiest voice. "How are we feeling this morning?"

The patient inspected the Nurse clinically, as if she were a pathogen under a microscope, before losing interest and turning back to the window. She did not look at Darlene when she spoke although the bitterness was directed her way. "Another one of us gone. We're dropping like flies. Soon you and your doctor friend will be out of a job."

How she knew about Dr. Marsh was a mystery. Darlene was certain the rest of the staff was in the dark but somehow the patients knew all about it. There were a couple of others who also liked to let her know at every opportunity just how perceptive they were.

Darlene ignored the reference to her and Doug and said, "I was sorry to hear about Mr. Raines. Would you like to talk about it? How do you feel about his dying?"

The patient's tone was more malicious than usual. "You mean do I feel worse about his dying than I do about being locked up in here? Or do I feel worse about his dying than I do about everything else that is dead right outside this window? It rates pretty high in the misery. Once I've decided how high, I'll be sure to let you know."

Sunshine was definitely Darlene's most difficult patient. She was so angry about everything. And that anger seemed to manifest itself in what lay outdoors. There was no easing her distress by putting her in a room without a view. They had tried that. Regardless of how much it pained her to see out, it pained her more to be denied the negative stimulation. That's what kept her stirred up and alive.

Darlene walked over to the window and stood alongside her patient. "I see the lavender is blooming. Oh, and look, the lilies are opening up. What do you see Sunshine?" She asked this as if it wasn't a question she had posed dozens of times before.

If this wasn't mental cruelty, what was? Placing a perfectly sane person in a compound overlooking a phony garden and then regularly asking how it measured up against a history of genuine outdoor experiences was mean-spirited. Sunny's eyes traveled up a lamp standard that hovered over the garden. Its ultraviolet head was one of a dozen that had started duplicating dawn about 4:30 and continued to throw shadows that mirrored a real mid-summer morning.

"I'd rather talk about what I don't see," the patient responded.

Darlene shifted uncomfortably. She hated listening to this rant but she knew it was her job as a Psych Nurse to let the patient talk.

Sunny was tired and irritable. She had barely slept. When she had awoken, it was with her arms stretched above her head reaching for the sun. Before she remembered that there was no sun. It was a persistent inner clock, a solar memory that had stirred her. "I miss the sun. I miss the feel of it on my face," she said. "I guess it's still up there hidden behind that thick layer of cloud. It doesn't do us any good anymore does it?"

"It doesn't do us any harm though either. With those patches of skin cancer that have been removed from your nose and cheeks I would think you'd be grateful not to be experiencing it."

"The sun was not always our enemy. We did that. You know that don't you?" Whether the Nurse understood about these things was unclear. When the conversation reached a juncture like this she would either jump to something completely unrelated – quite often something that made no sense at all – or engage in militant optimism. Disconcerting and annoying at the same time, it proved effective in keeping discussion superficial.

"It's lovely not to be susceptible to the vagaries of climate. Orange groves in the British Columbian Province of the Americas – now that's progress. When I was a child the food supply was riskier than it is today. I didn't like that one bit you know. And since we're talking about progress, from what I've heard the InterCoastal Water System is about 75%

complete. Soon we'll be ensured a safe, steady supply of desalinated water," Darlene stated proudly.

The patient doubted a public works project of that magnitude was happening on the outside. But Darlene talked glowingly of it all the time.

"And while we're on the subject of safety, look at what happened to Mr. Raines hiking around in the wild like that. You can't tell me the earth didn't used to be a very dangerous place. It's much safer now. And safer is better, I tell you."

The patient could feel her blood pressure rise into heart attack territory. Waves of anger washed over her. She wished she could get to the point where she didn't care. The key was to become a detached observer. Physically outside the whole business now, she had more work to do in order to be removed emotionally.

"Do you say these things to piss me off? Do they give you pointers on that in your training? Antagonism 101, is it? What to say to those in your charge to cause the maximum amount of anguish. I guess it's possible it was covered in those rhetoric classes you're all so proud of having taken."

Darlene peered innocently at the patient, utterly in the dark about what she had said to cause such a reaction. She was being optimistic was all, proving the human race was more resourceful than anyone could have imagined. It wasn't just the living by artificial means in a controlled environment. What was most impressive was a way had been found to make believe this was enjoyable.

From the window, little more than a narrow strip of river could be seen. The region's sole source of fresh water was shrinking. According to the "experts" this was nothing to be alarmed about. Over the previous decades, the evaporation of the river had generated an unexpected opportunity. Water shrinkage had produced vast swaths of prime real estate. It provided a place to go for those whose homes had become submerged at the coast. For a time everyone had been ecstatic that yet another law of the natural world had been broken. There was new land being made. And, at the same time, human values had not been turned upside down. Waterfront property remained a desirable acquisition right up to the moment when it was inadvisable to go outside.

After the patient reflected on this she said, "In the early part of this century, when I was a young woman, I was surrounded by people just as smug as you. They too forfeited the whole notion of critical thinking and living consciously much the way you have. I'm pointing this out in case you have some distorted notion about the uniqueness of what you're saying. Yours has always been the dominant perspective. We built a whole civilization on it, in case you didn't realize."

Darlene cocked her head to one side. "I'm afraid I don't understand you."

"Well let me make it a little clearer. You're completely uninformed. What a weird twist of fate that someone as ignorant as you would end up watching over me," the patient blurted out in frustration.

A visit with Sunshine often ended in an outburst like this. Darlene didn't blame her though. It wasn't her fault. She suffered from a form of delusional dementia that produced these psychotic episodes. Her chart explained how she came to be this way. She was born in 1972 to a couple of hippies. From what Darlene could ascertain these hippies had been an evil lot that launched an assault on the human need to expand habitat and increase standard of living. It took decades to rid the world of their punitive environmental and human rights laws. It was her parents who warped her with their violent protests and their condemnation of war, government, and other vital Institutions. They hadn't even given her a proper name. She was the only "Sunshine" Darlene had ever heard of. And worse yet, her first name had been picked because it complemented her last. A woman with the name "Sunny Day" had called Darlene ignorant.

Darlene pitied this patient more than all the others. She patted her shoulder in a gesture that said as much. The reaction was almost violent. The patient's thin, lithe frame was out of the chair with lightening speed. They both looked over the other's face in the most peculiar way. While the patient searched for the Nurse's mind, the Nurse assumed the patient was trying in vain to locate her own mind, the one she had lost. One of the two women was blank through and through.

Sunny opened her mouth to speak but decided against it. Accepting the futility, she moved as far away as possible and asked to be left alone.

Terra Dime

***

Everyone at the Institution called him Saint Paul. The title was in snide deference to his past career as a Methodist minister. He poured tea for Darlene from an antique pot into a delicate porcelain cup, also of another era. The way one hand curved around the handle and the other secured the lid as the pot tipped seemed orchestrated and ritualistic – almost religious in nature. This was not the case. In fact, his notoriety had come when he abandoned his religion.

For a guy who wasn't in his right mind, he wasn't edgy and intolerable. A visit with him was a very civilized affair. Darlene appreciated his not trying to convert her to his way of thinking. She especially liked the way he asked her lots of questions and they always ended up talking about her. On that morning, sitting across from one another, comfortably sipping tea, he asked about Sunny.

"So how is she doing?"

Darlene was bewildered. "How is who doing?"

"Sunny."

"Oh, same as usual. Mad about everything. Why are you asking?"

"Because of Jerome, of course. They were very close, you know."

"Closer than the rest of you? I thought everyone had a strong attachment to Mr. Raines."

"They were in love." Now that he was gone, Saint Paul didn't see any reason to keep their relationship secret. He had tired of hearing about Darlene's vacuous life. She was blissfully clueless about many things. A lesson in love was but one in a full curriculum of courses that would improve her greatly.

Darlene pondered this for about a second before saying, "That's impossible. He was a cripple."

"I think there was more going on with the two of them than thrashing around between the sheets."

Darlene's face registered more confusion. She couldn't get past the notion of how you could have sex with a man who didn't have control of his legs in addition to a whole host of other functions. She was quite sure it was impossible. If you couldn't have sex with a man, what on earth would you do with him? She'd already decided that when she got a little older and it was time for her to have a hysterectomy so that her female organs didn't become diseased with cancer, she was getting one of those pumps installed that would keep her juices flowing. Men, which meant sex, would still be an important part of her life at eighty years of age – or so she envisioned.

"Well, then, they weren't lovers," Darlene stated confidently. "At least not in the logical sense."

Saint Paul's face broke into a broad smile. Logical and Darlene were not two words that would appear in a sentence he constructed. Over the last couple of years, she had been a constant source of amusement. Sadly, despite his best intentions, it seemed another day was going to pass without her learning anything. Since obtaining her nursing degree, there had been a sort of governor on her brain keeping knowledge safely at bay. Darlene was not any different from her peers. Supposedly smart people went to college to be trained for a particular line of work, got a job, and never learned another thing. It was as if over a four-year period they spent all the intellectual capital they held in reserve and then never again had the where-with-all to earn more.

He considered when she had been born, 2015 at the earliest. So she would have known nothing other than the Christian Conservative Party that had ruled for the last twenty-eight years. Back around the Year 2000, universities dedicated to religious fundamentalism began to spring up unnoticed by the general population. While many people were wringing their hands over the regime that was in place, the religious right was implementing a plan for the future. Their mission was to graduate presentable young fanatics to infiltrate the Senate, Congress, Supreme Court, and eventually take control of the White House. Theirs was an anti-intellectual platform based on distrust of science in favor of literal belief in a myth – a slave religion – glorifying the meek for kowtowing to the strong.

The importance of the anti-intellectual component could not be overemphasized. Saint Paul had always believed that faith was the opposite of reason. When the Christian Conservative Party came to power he saw that faith was more hobbling than that. It was the opposite of truth. The Party began their reign during the Second Great Depression and some of their moves came right out of the playbook of the 1930s. Instead of

Terra Dime

initiating public work programs to fix the nation's aging infrastructure or building quality structures in the national parks, they refurbished all the point-of-interest highway signage, museum exhibits, and state & national park educational presentations to adhere to the story of Creation. Since a literal interpretation of the Bible meant the earth was a seven-day project less than ten thousand years old, they had quite a bit of history to rewrite. The CCFT (Christian Contractors for Truth) of the 21st Century were very busy boys. When their handiwork was finished, roadside signs explaining complex phenomena such as glaciating had been replaced with biblical ditties. Ditties about God looking down on the third day over this vast expanse, envisioning a glistening pool of water, and making it so. And, of course, God was pleased and He saw that it was good. Mustn't forget about that. Those same words seemed to make it onto every one of the signs. The CCFTs didn't care much about originality in their work.

The Christian Conservative Party's concern for reeducating the adult population paled next to their efforts to make sure the young were educated properly right from the start. Darlene was a product of that school system. She was unaware of the abbreviated nature of her knowledge and understanding. There was no nice way to tell her that she didn't know anything, and even if he tried there was no hope of the message getting through. It was better just to ask another question.

"I'm sure you didn't think of Jerome the same way we did. How did you see him?"

Darlene wasn't sure she should respond to this in view of what her honest answer would be. It wasn't ethical to disparage one patient to another. And she didn't know whether the rule changed once someone died. Mr. Raines had loomed large in her life as well, in a negative sense. Truthfully, she had been terrified of him. Entering his room played out like Little Red Riding Hood alone with the big, bad wolf. He had about him the chill of a predator. Darlene and Mr. Raines had been natural born enemies and she couldn't imagine why.

"He was some kind of snob. I don't know what kind. Intellectual, elitist, something like that. He wasn't like you. He wouldn't give me the time of day."

The Institution

Saint Paul knew exactly what she was referring to. Jerome's discourse had been controversial, argumentative even, completely foreign to a modern human being. He didn't do small talk, which meant they couldn't converse. Not much wonder she hadn't known what to think of Jerome.

***

Paul was an oddity within the Methodist Church practically from the day he was ordained. His sermons were non-devotional. They were almost always about how to be a decent human being and that included showing reverence for the planet. He didn't preach this as a way to get into Heaven but as an end in itself. Paul was more affected by flowers bursting into bloom than he was in the whole business of salvation. In all honesty, he couldn't see life on earth as something anyone needed to be saved from. If, as a young man, he had understood his feelings better he would have joined the earth ministry. That was the calling he heard above all others. Until he was forty-five years old he thought feelings that were inexplicable had to be religious. And he felt certain that God had something to do with it. He continued to think this even after he asked other ministers about their religious experiences and none of them could relate anything remotely similar. He clung to the notion long after his days in the ministry robbed him of his innate spirituality. He quit believing in 2004. It happened in a Portland, Oregon bookstore.

The store was packed that night. That was to be expected he supposed. What else could people do in such a rainy city over the long winter months? He assumed the crowds were there because of the author he had come to hear. Someone who was giving a reading on a book about faith. Religious faith was big that year. It became part of the political discourse after our Christian nation embarked on another Crusade in the Holy Land. Paul was in Portland attending a conference for Methodist ministers. On the third and final day he left the Convention Center early, jumped on the MAX, and headed downtown. After several hours of wandering around in the rain, he was ready to get indoors for a while. He remembered something about an author reading that had been advertised in his conference packet. Since the book in question was religious, he anticipated running into some other conference attendees and getting together for dinner afterwards. More than an hour early to hear the Reverend J. C. Brooks discuss the merits of one of the Psalms, he was just in time to get a seat for an author who had attracted a large audience. He took a chair in the front row having absolutely no idea who Jerome Raines was and what his book, *The Left Behind Paradox*, was about.

A man in his early thirties, who was dressed casually, came up the aisle and took his place at the front of the room. He began by telling them not to expect too much from him in person. "I'm a lot better with the written word than the spoken," he said.

Paul was aware instantly that there was something different about him. He had a genuine quality that permeated the crowd, affecting Paul as well. It made them receptive to what they were about to hear.

"It's much easier to wow a reader with your insight after the tenth rewrite," he kidded, but Paul didn't believe it. Not from this guy. He had such a solemn, thoughtful way about him. When he did eventually smile, it too, was engaging.

"Let me start by saying that frustration with humanity's learning curve drove me to write *The Left Behind Paradox*. After listening to the same discourse year after year at both the political and public level, and the only difference I was able to discern was that the dialogue was getting less sophisticated, this concerned me. But it also made me curious as to why this might be. What forces are preventing us from not only doing the right thing but also from seeing what it is?

"The whole religious construct called Creationism, or Intelligent Design, or whatever other term might be in vogue next season, has regained popularity in recent years. There appears to be no end in sight to the swelling hordes wishing to substitute what is scientifically proven with mythology. It's a very sad thing too because Creationism is a static story, whereas Evolution implies life forms that are constantly adapting and advancing. My wish for us is both to discover and apply our potential. We must quit looking elsewhere for meaning.

"*The Left Behind Paradox* encompasses more than the obvious religious absurdity. The one that amounts to religious fabrication promising

The Institution

deliverance from a world made uninteresting by religious fabrication. From that point, the paradox grows, of course. While we fear being physically left behind, it is doctrine and dogma that prevents us from moving forward. Denial of Evolution is a death wish. In the absence of Evolution, we don't stand a chance. So to look to Creationism for guidance is a wish for human life – and possibly all life – to end. And that takes the paradox to yet another level. Because, after all, isn't 'The End Times' really what Christianity and the story of Creation are all about. Revelations is the culmination. If we were to evolve into something other than simple-minded little lambs destroying our life support system, the whole notion of The Second Coming wouldn't have its sales appeal. This is why Evolution, both the reality of it and the belief in it, truly is the enemy when it comes to western religion fulfilling its destiny."

Ouch, Paul thought to himself. He looked around surreptitiously, thankful no one in the audience knew of his occupation.

The author continued to speak. "What I sense is the unfinished business of Evolution both for the species and culture as a whole. I'm excited about the concept of a new human condition but that can only come to pass if we are willing to let go of what we currently are. The human condition should not be a predicament. But that's what it is. And that predicament gets more depressing with each passing year to the point where people in the know are giving up. In order to advance the human condition, we have to become conscious enough to advance ourselves. That doesn't mean I'm endorsing spiritual enlightenment as a way essentially to cop out on trying to improve circumstances on the ground. Contrary to what the drug manufacturers and the self-help gurus are promoting, finding a vehicle for escape is not an answer. The task at hand requires our full attention. It's Evolution of mind, spirit, and civilization that we must address."

Whenever anyone mentioned Evolution, Paul's ears perked up. He didn't know how you could believe in the Bible in a literal sense and Evolution at the same time. He hated to be asked about it. As a Kansas minister, he was entrusted with preaching the Bible verbatim to a closed-minded congregation of Midwesterners that, for the most part, thought only in literal terms. He could picture how indignant they got at the mention they had a little ape in them. Low level humans who had barely attained the first step on the personal development ladder, unaware of how many more rungs there were to reach for. A unified force convinced of its superiority and not bothering to look up to see how far they might climb. We couldn't be whole if our only connection to the land and other creatures was through conquering them. There was so much more to life than the web of human beings. There was so much more to wish for than the birth of white babies of European descent, but you wouldn't know it from Sundays at Paul's church.

"In our current state, we are a restless species. Instead of being alert to our surroundings, we are constantly looking for that next new thing. There's a very good chance we ache for what was lost, an intrinsic passion, that had to give way so we could endure civilization.

"I do not want to romanticize the lives of our hunter/gatherer predecessors. I also want to make it clear that I am in no way advocating that we return to that state. What I would like to consider is the possibility that we lost a way of seeing or being that served us well. With that in mind, I am going to read a couple of pages from *The Left Behind Paradox* in which I explain the way our current predicament may have unfolded. These pages are a philosophical musing on my part about what we left behind. Ten thousand years ago, population pressure forced us to submit to a sedentary, agrarian, hierarchical system to increase our chances of survival. Losing the freedom to move at will, filling our days with repetitive mundane tasks, and suddenly being bossed around had to have been a painful part of the bargain. We wouldn't have accepted domestication easily. New stories, fantastic beliefs even, had to be created to make a lousy situation look good. And it remains the same today. The cultural stories will continue to grow more far-fetched as our options decline."

He reached for the book and flipped to a page he had marked and began to read. "Early man may have had a certain kind of awareness that sensed the energy, the blood, the life pulsing through his surroundings. He was connected with the essence of being alive, the wonder of his environment. He was a piece of a dynamic evolving system until there were too many people. At that point, he had to find a way to manipulate first his surroundings to accommodate everyone and then his mind to be

The Institution

pleased with the new arrangements. He lost something though. The world blazing with intensity, the way he had always seen it was left behind.

"The new sedentary living arrangements led to fixed viewpoints and a need to feel certain. He had to believe it was preferable to be stationary and powerless under a hierarchical system than to be free to move on. For as long as the population continued to grow, there was no other way. It was necessary to convince everybody they were happy and free. Self-knowledge had to be left behind.

"That didn't solve the problem of the lack of immediate reward that had crept into daily lives. There had to be something grand that lie beyond the drudgery of daily living – an afterlife, a heaven, or a spirit world. Delusion on an individual basis turned into cultural delusion on a grand scale. The static construct of Creationism replaced the adaptable possibility of Evolution. Reality was left behind.

"Throughout the ages there are bright spots. Philosophers are born, great works of art created, music is conceptualized and composed, science flourishes. There is an enlightenment period. Industrialization arises, technology moves to the fore but it is not accompanied by updated living arrangements, something beyond the civilization of yesteryear. We remain in the Dark Ages when it comes to conjuring up a more satisfying way to live. The opportunity for a New Renaissance left behind.

"The longer we remain set in our ways, fixed in our certainty that this civilization we created is the best it could ever be, the more difficult it becomes for us to conceive of anything else. So hardwired after decades of seeing the world one way, we don't adapt. We aren't incorporating life experience into an evolving self. And that rolls into the larger cultural picture as well. No matter how improbable the future looks, we continue to support the status quo. Thousands of years of potential, the opportunity for the species to enter adulthood left behind.

"Satisfied by the material goodies this civilization offers we begin to forgo our weightier expectations. Eventually, those same expectations no longer exist for us. We're a human assembly line – conceived, born, indoctrinated, put into production. And yet many signs of uncertainty appear to us. We are restless, edgy, unsatisfied almost to a person. We are missing something. We look for it everywhere. At some level we have an

Terra Dime

inner knowledge. Call it an awareness of the unfinished business of personal Evolution. The true miracle of existence left behind."

When the author quit reading and went on to explain that he felt Evolution was not only the reason for life but also the meaning of life, he was whisked off the stage rather abruptly. There was some nebulous explanation by the bookstore manager that the speaker had run over his allotted time and the next author was ready to begin, but Paul's watch did not bear this out. No one got to ask questions and he didn't have the opportunity to explain how to advance human Evolution. It was a peculiar way to treat him, but no one in the audience objected, including Paul. No one knew that the manager of the store was a fundamentalist who didn't believe in Evolution and didn't wish to know about human potential. In the early years of the divide that eventually engulfed the nation, we were too stunned to react. That was the time to fight, before alternative viewpoints were prevented from being heard, before they disappeared.

Paul left his seat. The author's message drifted around the room as well as inside his head – a generalist's perspective of conditions as they were, not as we believed them to be. A growing gaggle of expert nincompoops had drowned out this viewpoint until it was practically extinct. Jerome Raines wasn't looking at mankind from a position of specialized self-interest. As a result, he wasn't small-minded and shortsighted. He could see the long view, as if he were another species observing man from afar, and reporting impartially on his findings. Paul's tendency to resist new ideas before discussing them at length with other clergy was overridden by a feeling that there was truth in what this man was saying. While listening, he had felt the nudge of inspiration, a kind of mental joy come over him. The prospect of seeing anew excited him like nothing else. That was when he absorbed stimuli like a sponge soaking up every last drop into an expanding self. It was this great wholeness he felt, this light that filled him until he was practically bursting, that he had come to believe was God. But he was beginning to realize it wasn't that at all. It was something quite different.

He was no longer interested in sitting through the next author's treatise on religion. Aligning himself with someone bright, not the dissector of a single verse from the Holy Bible that meant absolutely

The Institution

nothing, was what he wanted to do. He had become an automaton who recited the same stories year after year, pretending they were the answer to everything. And he was ready to quit. He found the table where Jerome Raines' books were displayed and thumbed through the collection. At thirty-three years old, he had already published three nonfiction works that seemed to be building towards a comprehensive philosophy. While the earlier books put forth many social questions and concerns, his most recent book explained the obstacles in our culture, how they had come about, and why we did not have the intellectual capital to fix them. It was this author's conviction that every civilization has built-in prejudices – inarguable beliefs – that are mistaken for facts. And it is these beliefs that are the root of the problems that eventually cause it all to crumble. It was in this that Paul saw his own culpability, recognizing immediately what was at the core of his uneasiness. The Institution that employed Paul was responsible for advancing the untenable position that human demands take precedence over the existence of everything else. It was all there in the religious teachings. The Creator of the universe made us in his image and He gave us dominion over the planet to do with it as we please. And that if we went along with the doctrine and dogma, there was a prize called Heaven waiting for us and it was far better than Planet Earth anyway.

The Methodist minister from Topeka, Kansas, the state that had the proud distinction of being the first to bring Creationism back into the public school curriculum, bought all of the books, waited in line to have them autographed, and then began the process of deconstructing his life. Losing interest in his career would have slipped by unnoticed if he had been a carpenter or a lawyer but as a minister it was everybody's business.

***

"*Instead of worrying about saving our souls, we ought to be worried about saving our asses.* That blasphemy came over the Canadian airwaves during an interview on the CBC with one of America's own I'm afraid. Liberal, author, intellectual snob, environmentalist wacko, America hater, and now blasphemer Jerome Raines gave that stunning summary of his

Terra Dime

latest book, *The Left Behind Paradox*. Those were his words, ladies and gentlemen, not mine.

"Seeing that he hails from western Washington, that Godless portion of the state where liberals run rough shod over the good people of the rest of that region...Well, no need to depress my listeners further with a rehash of the consistently dismal voting record of the liberal wackos on the west side of the Cascades. Not when we have something as precious as some soulless elitist telling the rest of us that the state of human souls is not something we should be concerned about. Not when the souls of fish and birds and trees are in jeopardy. Not when, according to this Jerome character, our hunter/gatherer ancestors were more aware than we are today. Aware of what, I ask you? Where the best berry patch was?

"And you know what else? All those fears we mortals have of those small things like say another terrorist attack, or getting sick, or losing our jobs and our houses and going hungry, and yes, getting into the kingdom of Heaven, are not valid. They are nothing compared to the terror we ought to experience once we realize how ignorant we all are. Like, say when we try to wade through a book like *The Left Behind Paradox* and don't agree with such profane ungodliness.

"We know all about the liberal media that has virtually taken over this nation of ours, but what about the book publishers? Now I'm not one to advocate censorship or the burning of books but why in the name of God is this stuff on the shelves? It serves no purpose except encouraging civil disobedience. The United States is the envy of the world. People continue to immigrate here, don't they, legally and otherwise. They aren't being forced and neither is Jerome Raines being forced to stay. He's the worst kind of American. Enjoying the freedoms of our system while at the same time talking it down. I can't even put into words how much I hate guys like this who are so unhappy they won't be satisfied until everyone else is as miserable as they are. And believe me, if we let these guys keep criticizing our way of life, that's exactly how we will all end up. People will lose confidence. These liberals will bring the whole thing down around our ears. And then what – squalor on a global basis? Isn't that what these liberals want, equalization, a race to the bottom? Not on my watch!"

The Institution

That was how Conrad Tilton began his talk radio program, *The Conradic Equation*, the day before Jerome was scheduled to appear in Silver Falls to promote his latest book. He invited callers to weigh in on this dire circumstance, which, of course, they did. The recommendations included everything from a complete overhaul of the education system to ensure points of view such as this author's never surfaced again, to implementing a "scarlet letter system" that would prohibit certain writers from being published and, hence, stop the spread of such vile points-of-view.

And, it was this vitriol that made Sunny's book club so eager to attend the reading. It didn't matter that Karen was the only woman in the book club who had read *The Left Behind Paradox* or knew what Jerome Raines' writing was about. She hadn't recommended their reading it because she wasn't sure how the devout Christians in the club would feel about the author's disgust with the widespread belief in the Rapture, End Times, Revelations, and such. Their rather tame discussion of *The Da Vinci Code* had caused two women, one Catholic and one Nazarene, to quit the club. His naming religion as the ultimate command and control system that held us back ought to get some of the ladies really excited. On that evening, all they thought they needed to know was any author who was an enemy of Conrad Tilton, the meanest of all right wing talk show personalities, was a friend of theirs.

Liberals in Silver Falls were a small contingency. And they stuck together, all two hundred of them. It wasn't unusual for every single one to show up when a celebrity who was more than certain to criticize the current political regime gave a speaking engagement. Speakers would often comment on how strange it was that such a large group of people read the same obscure books and watched the same alternative programs. What they failed to understand was the audience was not a cross-section of Silver Falls' population. They were anomalies desperate for a kind of stimulation they were denied in that city's daily life.

It was lonely for anyone not of a conservative bent during those years. There was no escaping it. At work it was radios belching out Conrad Tilton's three hours of hate. In homes, it was an endless all you can eat buffet of Fox and CNN. And to top it off, passions continued to run high after the November 2004 Elections. A segment of the population was almost insane with anger over the outcome. That people could be that dumb once was bad enough, but twice? That was either willful or woeful. It was hard to know which was worse.

The spin Mr. Tilton put on the book and the author himself – because he wouldn't be satisfied without launching a personal assault as well – was repulsive. In a reasonable society nothing would come of a shrill man of limited intelligence labeling a writer's work vile. A man whose only claim to fame was tearing down people who actually had good ideas would not fool an informed public. But alas, we lived in a society that rewarded this kind of behavior handsomely, turning him into a multi-millionaire with clout. There were no more dreaded crosshairs than his because once he fingered you every conservative in the country would start gunning for you and that was about fifty percent of your fellow citizens.

It was into this environment that Jerome Raines was plunged upon his arrival in Silver Falls in February of 2005. Because he was an author of some notoriety the reading was held at the Masonic Temple so as to handle the expected crowd. The book club met on the street out front that night. Sunny hadn't gone home first but instead had arrived directly from work as they intended to get together for a drink and something to eat afterwards. The lower level of the auditorium was already full when they entered. Rather than fight the crowds for a seat, they headed up the stairs to the mezzanine.

The crowd was disproportionately of a certain age. The conciliatory "silent generation" that had the misfortune of being born between two argumentative overrated groups each convinced of its exceptionality. Reconciling disparate expectations was a role that had been forced upon them. A smattering of other ages, mainly young, made up part of the audience. Across the aisle from where the book club found a group of seats together, a couple in their teens was enjoying that early blush of idealism – quite unaware that soon it would be wrung out of them. As to be expected the misfits who quit caring what society thought of them long ago had shown up. Another, even smaller contingency recognized something was amiss and had come in search of an answer that would turn everything around and make it right. Who wasn't in attendance was most telling.

The Institution

Society's mainstream of working parents, professionals, and soccer moms were out on the Interstate, in the shopping malls, wandering the aisles of big box stores, or plopped down in front of television sets. They were too busy to get up to speed on the long-term prospects of their living arrangements.

The ladies in Sunny's book club sat chatting while waiting for the place to fill. Other than a tall stool in the middle of the stage, there was nothing else to look at. The man who eventually walked across that large stage was similar in age to Sunny and her friends.

"This stool is here for two reasons," were the first words out of his mouth. "One is obvious," he said, as he pulled the stool beneath him and sat down. "The other is to keep the right wing lions at bay should there be an additional ambush planned for this evening." This was, of course, a reference to Mr. Tilton's disparaging remarks about the quality of the author's soul and it set the tone. The room exploded with laughter and clapping.

The author seemed familiar to Sunny. As she watched and listened, she searched her memory for why that was, until he smiled. With that, came instant recognition. Jerome Raines was the guy she met at Expo '86. The guy she knew only as Jerry. Seeing him again was not something she had prepared for. She hoped she would never be expected to deal with the promises she made to herself that she hadn't lived up to. The paralysis the two of them once observed as being built into the system had, in fact, worked its way into her life. So much so, that she was afraid to take a single unconventional step. It wasn't something she had thought of in those terms until that very moment when she saw what had become of him. That she could so freely admit something like that was, in itself, out of character. It was a consequence of how he affected her. Jerome Raines' world was the mountain she planned to climb but she settled for lower ground. When she failed to reach higher, she lost her way. And she didn't find it again. Once her dad died, she quit believing that a personal code mattered. Her expectations were remade. Everything that was an impediment to peace and comfort evaporated.

***

Terra Dime

Immediately following her father's incarceration, Sunny's maternal grandparents took a more active role in her life. If they had not provided financial assistance, circumstances would have been bleak for Sunny and her mother. Sunny's mother was an artist. Sculpture was her medium and although she did sell her pieces occasionally, she had never held a steady job. With Sam Day out of the picture the Wetheringtons began to make plans for Sunny's education. Magnanimous in their generosity, they offered to pay her tuition if she lived with them while attending the University of Victoria. Back over the border she went. This time to Vancouver Island and into the molding hands of unfamiliar relatives who were nothing like her parents. Having seen how their daughter and son-in-law mucked up their lives, Pete and Pat Wetherington embarked on reshaping Sunny in their own image. Realizing that making something out of their granddaughter would be no easy task they got right to work the morning after her arrival.

"You know what dear?" Grandma Pat called from the kitchen. "Grandpa Pete and I were mulling over your first name last night and we came to the conclusion that we should change it. Not legally right away because we'd probably need your mother's signature for that but come up with a nice little nickname for now."

Sunny took her nose out of the book she was reading, placed it on the footstool, and mustered the courage to enter the kitchen. She pulled out one of the metal stools with the ornate backs and had a seat. "What's wrong with my name?" she asked.

"I'm not sure how to say this. It says so much about your parents, too much as a matter of fact. As soon as anyone hears that name they're going to know you're the product of a couple of sixties' children."

"You mean hippies? What's wrong with that?"

"It could prejudice people against you. Hippies don't have a positive connotation in all circles. We want to make sure that you get every opportunity and that no doors are closed to you. We understand your grades are good. We would like to see professors and future employers focusing on those, not your name. Would you like some tea or coffee dear?"

"Do you have anything herbal?"

The Institution

"No. Either coffee or black tea will have to do around here."

"I have a special drink I brought with me. Let me get that," she said, springing off the stool. She rushed down the hall and into her bedroom – perfectly decorated in a wildlife motif that was all the rage that season. Ducks and fish and trees and ponds in shades of green, blue, and maroon, everywhere. From her own private attached bath, she retrieved the rooibos off the counter. She didn't have any complaints about her sleeping quarters that was for sure. But this name change thing she wasn't sure about.

Too bad it bothered them so much, she thought as she looked at herself in the mirror. Sunny wasn't one to spend time worrying about how she looked or what she was called. Her mom and dad were great ones for concentrating on what was internal not external. And she had a flashback to the World's Fair four years ago when someone looked at her with adoring eyes and was wowed by her name. Sunny hadn't thought of him in recent months so she wondered why she was remembering him now. It was the beginning of a mental pattern triggered whenever she succumbed to forces stronger than she was. But she didn't know that then.

"Who do they want me to be?" she whispered to someone who wasn't in the room.

"Sarah is a nice name, wouldn't you agree?" her grandmother said when Sunny returned to the breakfast bar and had the hot drink in front of her. "I think whatever we choose it's best if it starts with an 'S' so your initials don't change."

"If you want to call me Sarah that's fine with me," Sunny said between sips. She had resigned herself to letting them have this victory.

"I'll call the university tomorrow and have it changed on your records."

"You don't have to go to that much trouble," Sunny protested. She was appalled that her grandmother was going straight for the permanent fix. "I can make sure everybody knows my nickname right from day one."

"That would be too confusing. Believe me, it will be better this way. Pete, we've agreed on Sarah," her grandmother said as he appeared through the double doors of the master suite that was the entire north wing of their new house.

"That's great. I'm glad to hear you solved that name issue so easily. How about her curriculum, have you had a chance to discuss that yet?"

Something passed between the two of them. Sunny decided it was a baton. "What about my curriculum?" Sunny asked, bracing herself, but for what she didn't know.

Pete took up the cause. "We couldn't help but notice that your core curriculum is lacking in courses that will help you obtain a Law Degree. Why are you taking all those classes like environmental studies, biology, sociology, psychology, philosophy, even? Don't you think a Business Degree would be a better base?"

"You do know that it's Environmental Law that I'm interested in, right? That's why the sciences are important. As far as the liberal arts, I think I'm going to be better at my job and a better all around person if I understand people and society as a whole." She didn't go into her wish to have a personal philosophy. That was a visceral desire brought about by a chance encounter she couldn't begin to explain to a couple who didn't wish for her even to hold on to her own name.

"No, we didn't know that. What do you intend to do with an education like that?" Pat asked cautiously, unsure if she really wanted to know.

"I'm interested in protecting the environment. I want to work for the public good by prosecuting corporate polluters." Sunny, now also known as Sarah, said this without considering her grandparents would be incensed.

Another baton pass. "Well, you know, Sarah," Pete tried to say kindly, "that's not where the big money is made. Defending large, deep-pocketed corporations against prosecuting attorneys and accident-prone litigious parties is where the big money is."

Through the French doors that led from the breakfast room out onto a great swath of flagstone, the patio furniture and flowering potted plants seemed to go on and on. Beyond that, blue sky, ocean, and evergreens. A pair of bald eagles stretched their wings and lifted gracefully from the red limbs of a gnarled Arbutus that rose from the bank below. Would there be any point in telling these people that she didn't want everything they had? Wouldn't they be smug that once she had the opportunity to live in an enclave overlooking the Saanich Inlet, she wouldn't be satisfied with less?

The Institution

Sunny gripped her warm mug a little tighter in an environment that was growing colder by the minute. If she didn't make it through the first day here she'd be deemed a failure by all measures, even her own.

"You're right," she said, calmly on the outside while kicking and screaming inside. "I should consider my future career from that angle. But even if I go to work as counsel for say a mining operation, I should know how the other side thinks. I will need to be well-versed and well-armed when it comes to the environment so that I can respond to the myths and shatter them," she said glibly enough to make her grandparents proud.

Just when they were beginning to relax and think she had a future after all, she screwed it up by asking whether they had a bus schedule. Both of them tensed up all over again. "Why do you need one of those?" Pat said suspiciously as if she had heard her granddaughter ask where the condoms were stashed.

"Why to get to school of course. There is bus service out this way, isn't there?"

"Yes, but it can't be very convenient and it's probably not safe. You don't have to take the bus anyway. We have an extra car you can use." Of course they did. What successful two-person family wouldn't have a spare, insured automobile lying around for this kind of emergency?

To say the years Sunny spent with her grandparents were all bad would not be a fair accounting. At some level, she wished she could accept the life they laid out for her. She was envious of how uncomplicated their views were on what constituted an ideal life, and how hard they defended those beliefs. They weren't troubled by hypocrisy and were not aware of their lack of perspective. There was either a right or a wrong way to live and their financial success proved theirs was the right way. Whenever she expressed an opinion that conflicted with their life plan, they would roll their eyes in that dismissive way that was full of hidden meanings. That simple gesture informed her they had heard it all before and she was just plain wrong. She was too young to understand the ways of the world but one day she would grow up and grow out of her peculiarities.

Sunny's Grandpa Pete was one of the owners of a successful architecture firm. At least, that was what she thought until she worked in the accounting office the summer after her first year at UVic. Everyone in

Terra Dime

the family assumed the firm was making a truckload of money, including Grandma Pat. Their lifestyle would make you think so anyway. Even Sunny's limited fiscal experience told her the company was screaming insolvency. They didn't have adequate cash flow to service the company's debt, not if they intended to make payroll. To solve this cash shortage, they often kept and then spent the payroll taxes collected from the employees, instead of turning them over to the government. Consequently, they owed hundreds of thousands in taxes, interest, and penalties. This didn't prevent the four principals from pulling down their six-figure salaries and living like successful entrepreneurs. It struck Sunny as being so odd. Not only that this was the way her grandfather ran his business but also how he didn't mind her knowing about it. She came to the conclusion that he thought he bore no responsibility for the firm's financial woes. To hear him talk you would believe some nefarious phantom was making the business decisions. It was not the company's structure, the lack of a business plan, or the day to day operations that contributed to the deficit. It was the economy, the employees, bad luck, and a draconian tax code that were to blame. With that kind of ownership philosophy she knew that nothing was going to change. After one summer of taking calls from irate creditors, she begged off working there for the remainder of the time she lived with her grandparents.

When Sunny returned to Silver Falls in 1993, upon completing her third year at UVic, she realized her father was really sick. After scheduling a visit at the prison, she knew he was going to die there. His illness had been kept secret from her. The usual reason for doing that was rattled off. In view of how close she and her father were, the rest of the family decided it was best not to distract Sunny from her studies. Another thing she noticed when she arrived back in Silver Falls was how changed her mother was. During previous visits she had been Sunny's confidante and sympathized with her about living with Pete and Pat. One Christmas, when her mother spent the holidays with them, she and Sunny sat up late into the night discussing how difficult they were. Sunny explained to her mother that she had never totally understood about the hippie movement and about being anti-establishment. It dawned on her that it had been born out of frustration with people not of a certain age, but of a certain mindset that couldn't imagine another way. Success, in their terms, was a shallow sphere of accomplishment but one the establishment clung to mightily. Sunny found herself driven nuts by the certainty of people. She had begun to see that certainty was the all-important element on which the system functioned. At the time Sunny was discussing these things with her mother it seemed she understood what she was saying and appreciated her insight. Now she was quick to come to her parents' defense. Now she would listen to none of these criticisms.

But that wasn't the worst of it. What was more troubling was that over that four-month period she refused to go with Sunny to the prison. This did not slip by Sam Day. He was bewildered by this abandonment on the part of his wife. For him, his relationship with Kathie and his role in society had not changed. Either he hadn't been paying attention or had chosen to ignore his wife's increasing disillusionment with their alternative lifestyle. What Kathie had once seen as exotic about Sam now reeked of stubbornness and an unwillingness to adapt. Personality traits appealing at twenty seemed fool-hearty at forty. These were the unspoken thoughts that had taken root recently. On her mother's behalf, Sunny lied to her dad. She was so embarrassed by her mother's neglect and so saddened by her father's broken heart, she didn't know what else to do. And then, she pretended not to notice that he was dying so they wouldn't have to discuss it and both could be spared the emotional trauma that talking about his death would bring.

Lying was the theme of that summer and it didn't get any better in the autumn. Back at school in Victoria, her grandparents were careful about what they said so as not to give away what they were thinking. The truth of it was that everyone knew what the other was thinking. Sunny knew that her grandparents and mother were experiencing a certain kind of relief at the prospect of her father dying and they suspected she was attuned to this. That winter, when she got the call she'd been dreading, she grieved alone as anticipated. This was the thing that got to her the most. Not the loneliness of it, but how she'd known instinctively this was the way it would be. Her father had threatened them in many ways. It was this discomfort he caused that made his transgressions unforgivable. The least of them was what he'd been arrested for. When Sunny failed to confront her family with their indifference, it caused her to agonize over who she was. The independent agent she wished to be or a complicit member of a society that felt threatened by dissenters of any stripe.

Sunny pondered these things alone in her room. A common thread of unrest and dismay ran through her schoolwork – in particular, her psychology papers – and it did not go unnoticed. Her psychology professor took a personal interest in her. In his words, he found her "fascinating and refreshingly unique in a sea of cookie cutter youth that had occupied seats at his lectures." And vulnerable, deliciously vulnerable. For there was no doubt, Professor Leonard Peyton somehow learned of her father's death. Someone might have told him in passing. Another student perhaps. There was a slim possibility that it had not factored into his deciding she was fair game. A very slim possibility.

In later years, when Sunny reevaluated this period in her life, she became less willing to give Professor Peyton the benefit of the doubt. Unlike in those first few months after the whole sordid affair became public, and in order to get through the humiliation, she convinced herself there had been some feeling for her on his part. He hadn't been lying about everything, had he? Right down to the hours of conversation and the many times he told her how he really liked her. No, *admired her. Thought about her day and night. Could barely get through the week without seeing her.* He hadn't been lying about all those things simply for sex had he? Could getting her into bed – the conquest of another student – spur that much deceptive energy? It was difficult to know and impossible to fathom.

There was a certain familiarity in Professor Peyton's Psych class that didn't exist in her other courses. The subject matter, Developmental Psychology, had something to do with that but there was also a disarming quality to Leonard Peyton. He put students at ease, drew them out, and before they knew it they were discussing things in class that were very personal. Sunny noticed when he began to take more than a passing interest in her. He watched her constantly. His eyes kept finding hers during lectures and she could tell he was attracted to her. Flattered by this, she began to enjoy writing Psych papers as a kind of personal communication. Sometimes adding a handwritten page at the end, in which she would question something like the nature versus nurture debate, and whether it

The Institution

was one of many examples of post-modernism run amok. Or she would extol the genius in Maslow's Hierarchy of Needs and speculate on how much self-actualization to expect over the course of her life. The best part was getting back the papers and reading his thoughts on what she'd written and his suggested reading list to further her understanding.

Running along Dallas Drive after class one drizzly afternoon in January, Sunny was presented with the opportunity to get to know him better and after mulling it over she decided that there was no harm in it. He had been in front of her for most of the run. She caught glimpses of him on the straight stretches and saw the distance between them had narrowed over the last mile. As she approached the entrance to Beacon Hill Park, she drew even with him and said hello.

"Are you intending to show off and pass me?" he said. "You look fast."

"Not if it will impact my grade," she responded. "And I'm not that fast. I tried out for the UVic cross country team and didn't make it."

"That's too bad." A couple of seconds later he said, "You could always run with a group of second string runners like me. I belong to a small running club. We meet Saturday mornings here at the park, run between six and fifteen miles, and then go somewhere for breakfast. You're welcome to join us. I'm not the fastest of the lot so I'm sure someone could keep up with you."

Once she took him up on the offer it seemed for a while as if she had done the right thing. Of the dozen or so runners in the club no one else was tied to the university. She loved to sit across the table from them afterwards and banter back and forth. For so many years she'd been a solitary runner who had forgotten what it was like to run in a group. How quickly you got to know a person when you ran alongside him and did nothing else but talk. This sudden camaraderie caused her to develop needs she thought she'd left behind. Something happened to her. The strength of her personality waned and she began to feel much as she had back in the spring and summer of 1986 when she and Kim had been inseparable. Wishy washy and without convictions, she wanted to fit in, be liked, be one of them.

On one Saturday morning in early March when she pulled into park, there was only one other car in the lot. Through the torrents of rain

Terra Dime

bubbling off the pavement she could see it was Leonard's Infiniti Q45. As soon as she came to a stop, he jumped out of his vehicle and got into hers. "Are we the only two crazy enough to venture out in this you think?" he said from the passenger seat. He was looking boyish with his neon yellow running cap pulled down low over his forehead. A few brown curls were already escaping out the sides and back.

"It would be unusual if no one else showed. These are die-hards after all."

"Well, maybe so, but even die-hards have their standards and this evidently," he gestured towards the streaming window, "is beneath them."

"Bunch of wimps," she said defiantly before starting to laugh. "I don't know about you but I'm going for it." She reached for the door. "What do you think? Are you up for getting wet?"

"Sure," he answered as he lifted himself out of the car and turned to face her across the roof. "I'll bet you have your heart set on doing the long course, don't you?"

"I was seriously considering it. Look at it this way, we won't get overheated," she pointed out as they headed east along the seawall toward Oak Bay. Even the golf course that ran along both sides of Beach Drive was empty that morning. A situation that happened but a few times per year.

As they ran through the old neighborhoods largely invisible in the steady rain, he told her he was from Mississauga, Ontario and was in awe of this part of Canada and doubted he would ever leave. He was thirty-four years old, had never been married, and lived alone in a 1920's bungalow three blocks from the ocean. He liked to windsurf when the weather was better than this, and read or run when the weather was like it was that day. He listened to jazz, drank good wine, and collected it as well. His philosophy for life was not to take oneself too seriously. Above all else, he liked to have fun and being too serious could be an impediment. He said he brought this up because she came across as being awfully serious for such a young woman. And, if she were like that her whole life, she would regret it. While he was pointing this out, she was already regretting how little fun she'd had. This was before his idea of fun crystallized. Right at that moment, what he said made perfect sense.

The Institution

She had only to take a peek at her life to conclude that it wasn't thrilling. She had acquaintances but no real friends. Dates yes, frequent lovers, no. As it was, relationships left her empty. And this made her resolute. For it didn't seem prudent to keep setting herself up to be so disappointed. She had begun to feel that someone with more to offer than "the same old crap" didn't exist. And this scared her more than her inability to meet him. The thing about it was that if she had to put into words what she meant by more than "the same old crap," she wouldn't know where to start. But she did know that it mattered. Whatever was missing mattered a great deal.

"What are you planning to do after university? Do you think you will live in the U.S. or Canada?" Professor Peyton asked.

At that time she had every intention of staying north of the border. "I have three more years after this. I'm going after my Law Degree. Then, if I can find a job, I'd like to stay in Canada. While I may not have a complete personal philosophy yet, I have determined that whatever I turn into, I will be more like a Canadian than an American."

He laughed at that and said, "That's probably a good thing. But why Law School? You don't seem like a lawyer in the making."

"Environmental Law – I'm not interested in a career as an ambulance chaser. Stewardship of the land is my first love. I want to make things better."

"And you think the law will provide that opportunity? Aren't you an idealist."

"I learned from my parents that protesting isn't the way. That gets you nowhere except in trouble or considered a nutcase."

"You might want to consider hiding out in academia. Merely talking about how things ought to be with others who are intellectually equal works out well. That way you can deceive yourself that the majority of the population wants what you do, and that given a choice they would seek wisdom and spend their lives in enlightened pursuits. Delusion, now that's an excellent choice," was his sarcastic reply.

Sunny looked over at him and rolled her eyes. "That's awful. Are you really that cynical?"

"That's for me to know and you to find out," he teased. "I could be playing devil's advocate with you. It's a discussion I've had many times and over the years I've played both sides of the argument. Your mission, should you choose to accept it, is to decide which side I'm truly on."

Sunny thought this was a legitimate challenge. She knew about passion, both ill and well placed. She had little or no experience with indifference and the amorality it spawns. It didn't seem compatible with intelligence.

The rain did not let up. If anything, conditions worsened. They splashed through puddles two inches deep. By the time they neared the end of the run their shoes were waterlogged, their hair looked plastered on, and their shorts and T-shirts were dripping. "It would be nice to get a coffee and a bite to eat somewhere after this. What do you think?" he asked, knowing full well she wouldn't wish to be seen out in public soaking wet.

"Are you crazy? We can't go to a restaurant like this. We're going to have to get out of these wet clothes."

And then casually, as if he hadn't planned in advance, as if he hadn't been thinking and scheming about it throughout the run or for weeks even. "You know, I don't live far from here. We could shower and have breakfast at my place."

That was how it started. That was the critical moment when she should have said, "No, I think I'll go straight home today," not "That sounds good. I'll follow you over." Because once she got to see how he lived, she was even more intrigued. Pulling into his driveway, peering through a jungle of foliage, she got her first glimpse of a Cotswold cottage wrapped in Boston ivy and she began to disintegrate. What he had created was a fantasy. She was aware of herself stepping into the pages of a fairy tale. It felt just like that every time she approached his property and what went on inside did not disappoint either. It had that same surreal quality, perfection in every detail. It was the big things that were missing but she would only discover those by chance. So enchanted was she, it did not occur to her the improbability of a single man who didn't specialize in seduction having on hand the provisions he pulled out of the pantry that morning. Sitting together in his breakfast nook lifting the champagne flute

The Institution

to her lips, the first rays of sunlight broke through the clouds striking the stemware and punctuating the moment. It was a memory that lingered.

"Just think, Sarah, if we had waited we could have run in the sunshine."

Thanks to her grandparents he knew her only as Sarah. They had created an alter ego for her. She made no mention of her real name. It wasn't Sunny who spent her Saturdays for the rest of the spring and into summer with Professor Peyton. It was Sarah. And make no mistake it was only Saturdays. Never once another day of the week. If she wished to know the truth that would have been her first clue. The very next weekend, after they made scrumptious seafood fettuccine and sucked back a couple bottles of New Zealand Sauvignon Blanc, he wrapped his arms around her and said he wanted to make love to her. It wasn't Sunny who willingly followed him up the stairs to his bedroom, but Sarah. Sarah, blind and bold.

But the dreams she had while in his bed could only belong to Sunny. The guy she referred privately to as "Expo Jerry" continued to occupy a part of her mind and during those restless nights, he occupied her body as well. He had never shown up in the night, in that way before. Prior to that, he was nothing more than an innocent memory, or every now and then, a passing thought about what had become of him. The ill-advised relationship with Professor Peyton brought him to life. Over and over again, she would awaken so turned on it would take Leonard but a minute to bring her sexual satisfaction. Naturally, he attributed this to his being irresistible. Sunny was deceived in much the same way by his desire for her. Before she was in possession of the facts, she thought she had some very special talents. The ease with which he could be turned on turned out to be more demoralizing than complimentary. While he was telling Sunny of the uniqueness of his attraction for her, he was anticipating his next tryst on Monday night. When the story broke it was made clear that even Leonard rested on Sundays. The headline in the paper was classic: *The Six Coeds of Leonard the Lech*.

As it happened, Sunny was the one who was caught in the act by Friday's girl, who having left something at his home the night before returned to retrieve it, found the door unlocked and proceeded to be disillusioned. It was Sunny who saw the look of horror on Kelly's face when she stepped in on them in the middle of yet another rainy afternoon. From Leonard's vantage, from where he administered to Sunny in the most delightful way, he could not see what was about to unravel around him. He thought it peculiar when Sunny stiffened and scrambled away from him until he heard a shrill voice, unexpected and unwelcome, in the midst of his bliss. And Sunny's humiliation was absolute when he turned to confront the disturbance at the door, fully aroused and fully exposed. Granted it was unpleasant for Kelly to catch her lover doing the deed with another. Being the other woman wasn't first-rate either.

Sunny sized up the situation and felt a sinking realization about what she was involved in. She recognized the furious Kelly from last semester's Psychology class. They also shared Leonard Peyton in his capacity of professor. The intense sobbing made Sunny wonder what lines he had been feeding Kelly in order to evoke such feelings of betrayal. It was unfortunate that she was the one to discover Leonard's active sex life, for she behaved like a woman scorned. The fury was classic in its strength of purpose. While the shameless Don Juan pleaded his case to the surprise visitor, Sunny gathered up her clothes and left the room unnoticed.

She neither saw nor heard from Professor Peyton again. And she missed him. She wanted to step back into his house and relive the fairy tale. Leonard knew how to live and he was accomplished in some other areas as well. He knew about good food and great wine. He had excellent taste in music. He had excellent taste, period – right down to the 450 thread count linens on his bed. He was never dull, constantly impressing Sunny with how much he knew. For him every day was a celebration and sex was an event. He did not cut corners when it came to life's pleasures. From the moment he disarmed her at the front door with his delight at seeing her, until many hours later when he would get up to walk with her to that same door, sleepy and only partially clothed, Sunny was purring like a kitty over a bowl of cream. And she wanted nothing more than to believe that what went on in that cottage once a week was how it appeared. She wanted to believe in the fantasy.

His appreciation of her was no deeper than the fondness he felt for a bottle of good wine. Just as it existed for the pleasure of his consumption

The Institution

so did she. And just as there were plenty more bottles equally as worthy at the store, there were plenty more just like her in the dorm. He had the mind without the ethical compass and one was meaningless without the other. Leonard talked such a good story. In the abstract he was a caring individual. He talked hypothetically about the ideal society while in reality he was not interested in societal change – not when his personal life was such a perfect fit. It took years for her to understand that the trenches of academia were overflowing with social warriors who were not interested in victory. Trench warfare had too many perks.

Leonard had proven his hypothesis. It was an impressive demonstration that was thoroughly convincing. Humans, even intelligent ones like her, prefer to live in delusion when doing so is pleasant and self-serving. Before she ever had the opportunity to fight for what she professed to care about, he showed her why she shouldn't bother. Might she have been a better person if she learned that lesson later in life after expending a little effort, rather than before? Who would she be if she hadn't accepted his offer of strawberries, croissants, and mimosas? So absurd as to think that the public wished to know the truth and if given the facts would behave ethically? Thanks to the professor, Sunny knew early on that position was untenable. Whenever she thought of those Saturdays in 1994, she remembered how incurious she could be when she was the one enjoying the good life.

Sunny had time to consider this. Once Professor Peyton's secret life – and by extension hers – became public fodder, all familial funding by Pete and Pat was suspended and Sunny returned to Silver Falls to live with her mother. She did not enter Law School that autumn as planned. She spent the next two years as a pink-collar worker at a law firm doing menial tasks for arrogant attorneys, waiting for acceptance at a university, obtaining student loans, and trying to figure out what had happened to her mother. She had wiped away all memory of Sam Day. After his death, the very first thing she did was get a legal name change. She was Kathie Wetherington again. Kathie Wetherington prior to meeting Sam. It was as if he had not existed. She did not reminisce about him the way you would expect a mother to do with her daughter. Any reference by Sunny was cut short. She no longer did any of the conscious things she used to do. Recycling,

61

gardening, making bread, even reading had been done away with. She lived a pre-packaged, microwaveable-entrées-consumed-in-front-of-her-new-television, kind of lifestyle. The only real food she ate was prepared by her daughter. And this was on rare occasions because she spent few days and even fewer nights in that Silver Falls' bungalow where Sam Day grew up.

When Sunny was at her weakest and most vulnerable, her mother decided she was tired of being a mother. She would prefer second-wife status instead. Surprisingly enough, the new man in her life was politically conservative. This was post 1994 *Contract with America*, when the neo-cons reared their ugly heads. Emboldened by newly found congressional success, they were a confident, belligerent lot and Gordie Goodman was a textbook example. He was the only man Sunny had ever met who made enough money to be a Republican. And he had his heart set on marrying Kathie Wetherington.

Over a year and a half period Sunny lost both parents. One was a literal death and the other figurative. Her mother was diagnosed as depressed and sustained what was termed "mental health" through a daily dose of meds. Sunny liked to believe the romantic liaison with Gordie could not have been possible without the pharmaceutical boost. If this way of thinking made her feel better or worse she wasn't sure. On one hand, it provided her mother absolution in that if she weren't under the influence of some mind-altering drug, Gordie Goodman wouldn't have gotten a second look. On the other hand, it was disconcerting to consider the popularity of a drug that in her mother's case simulated a frontal lobotomy. That generation of anti-depressants was the latest in a long list from cocaine in the early 1900s to amphetamines and major tranquilizers in the 1950s. Each had been similarly touted in its day as the best thing since sliced bread. And safe too. It remained unfashionable to suggest that anger, anxiety, and hopelessness were appropriate responses for sentient beings forced to live in distressing surroundings. It was more convenient to mask the way we think than mend the way we live.

As their relationship waned, Sunny became more objective about her mother. She saw how malleable she was. Hours were spent thumbing through the pages of *Cosmopolitan* and relating to a world of scantily clad nubile youth to which she did not belong. If she could be coerced into identifying with the *Cosmo* gals, she could be talked into anything. After years of watching her mother live by a certain code, it caught Sunny off guard to hear her object stridently to points of view she had defended for the better part of her life.

This change in attitude was reinforced on an early summer evening in 1995 when Sunny placed an after-dinner cup of tea beside her mother and joined her on the porch. The lawn needed to be cut and the flowerbeds weeded. She would do it the following day. It was unlikely her mother would spend two evenings in a row with her. As she stood up and began pulling spent flowers from the hanging baskets her mother flipped a page of the magazine and said, "Gordie and I are getting married."

"You're kidding, right?" Sunny responded, more incredulous than she intended.

"No, I'm not kidding. Why would you say that?"

"Well, let me see. Perhaps, it's because Gordie's a no-mind. He's the kind of guy you and I and dad used to laugh about. He's a walking, talking propaganda machine. He knows squat. He's embarrassing. How's that for starters?"

"In view of your trouble in Victoria, you are hardly one to be touting good character judgment. It seems to me that you were willing to overlook some major character flaws in order to spend time with someone you found urbane. It's nice to be with a man who has resources instead of some starving student or an aging hippie. I wonder how willing you would have been to accept the terms of your relationship with Professor Peyton had he been a poor, uneducated man? You and I, we're more alike than you think."

Sunny had thrown down the gauntlet. She just didn't expect her mother to reach for it with such a vengeance. It surprised her how completely their relationship had changed. Prior to that moment, the two of them had not discussed the incident to which she referred. There had not been a passing expression of interest in how her daughter, given that it was not in her character to get tangled up in the sordid, found herself in such a situation. And no concern about her emotional state. She knew Sunny well enough to know that she was serious and proud and had to be smarting.

Terra Dime

It wasn't as if Sunny came to her conclusions about Gordie Goodman dishonestly. Her initial introduction and subsequent conversation had been positively freakish. It was the moment she began to wonder whether it was an isolated incident or a systemic deficiency that enabled such a clown to be so successful. Her father hadn't been dead very long and she was a little edgy about her mother taking up with someone. That said, she didn't expect his response to a discussion about gays in the military to be:

"Do you remember the fifties?"

"No, actually I don't. I wasn't even born yet," Sunny responded.

"Man, weren't the fifties great?"

He had this peculiar habit of not being able to follow the thread of a conversation. He did not talk with you but at you in rehearsed sound bites that may or may not be germane to what you had said.

"I just told you I wasn't even alive then," she said sharply enough the second time that it registered.

"Oh that's too bad." He gave her a look that showed just how sorry he was for her. *"You'll have to take my word for how great they were."*

And to her horror, she knew exactly why he was enamored with that period. *"Wasn't that when the poor and blacks and women and gays knew their place? Is that what you're nostalgic for?"*

He licked his lips while he reminisced about how delicious it had been. *"You have to admit things were a lot less complicated then. Everyone is all confused now. They don't know what to think."*

"Thinking is quite a burden. You might try it sometime."

He proceeded to boast of his ignorance – a human right he defended vehemently. *"Yeah, well, no one can accuse me of being an intellectual."*

"I would certainly go along with you on that," Sunny said agreeably.

It was the only thing they ever saw eye to eye on. Over time, he learned to be less forthcoming with Sunny. But his was a sentiment shared by other successful members of society. There seemed to be a direct correlation between those who had amassed power and a wish to return to earlier periods when the distribution of wealth, health, and knowledge was less egalitarian. She would come to be dismayed by the simultaneous effort to turn back the clock. Politicians chipped away at the social advances hoping to return us to a pre *New Deal* era. Ownership by the wealthy elite

The Institution

began to resemble the days of the robber barons. And the religious conservatives, with their war on science, pushed us even further into the past towards the Dark Ages of pre-enlightenment.

"Mom, he owns a bunch of fast-food franchises. He's gotten filthy rich peddling junk food. It's hard to get excited about his contribution to society."

"You know what I'm sick of? Not having the good life just because of a bunch of silly principles. By all measures that matter, your father was a loser because of his. I'm not going to follow in his footsteps and I recommend you don't either. Look what you're planning to do with your life – torment good people, prevent them from improving their lives over a stupid set of environmental regulations. What species are you anyway? A human being or a fish? You are just like your father. You have a screwed up sense of loyalty. Instead of caring what happens to the planet, why don't you care about what happens to people?"

Nothing more was said on the subject. Starting the very next day Kathie spent the rest of the summer at the lake, was married the weekend following Labor Day, and honeymooned in Italy. And beginning that winter, and for many winters to come, her weekends were spent at Gordie's ski condo. Kathie Wetherington had back the life she forfeited more than twenty years before. Once her mother remarried the estrangement between mother and daughter grew. It took on a life of its own and became bigger than the both of them. For Kathie, just talking to her daughter meant not shaking free of her first husband's influence. For Sunny, a sense of isolation was all she got out of any contact with her mother.

Sunny opted out of Law School. Her stint in the attorney's office confirmed that the law was not a discipline in which to effect change. Nothing flourished there except the egos of the two partners at the top who did virtually nothing other than make sure their underlings were 100% chargeable sixty hours per week. Six days a week in a sweatshop was not her idea of living, so she started working towards her Masters Degree in Environmental Science & Regional Planning at Washington State University, with the idea that she could find employment with one of the public agencies. She didn't really want to go back to school but by that time the educational benchmark had risen. A Bachelors' meant nothing in her chosen field. An advanced degree was her only hope of bettering her employment prospects.

***

Sunny forced her mind back to the Masonic Temple in Silver Falls where Jerome Raines had the attention of everyone in the audience. Applause was erupting around her followed by whistles and catcalls. Some words had been projected onto a wall at the back of the stage. She tried to quit thinking about herself and instead focus on what he was saying so that she could get a sense of the path he had taken. It wasn't long before she saw how different the route she'd chosen was from his.

Let us admit the case of the Conservative
If we once start thinking
No one can guarantee where we shall come out,
Except that many objects, ends and institutions are doomed
Every thinker puts some portion
Of an apparently stable world in peril
And no one can wholly predict
What will emerge in its place.
— John Dewey

Let us consider this
When faith in an era that is not all that great
Is a deterrent to creating a future that truly is,
All is lost
For there is peril in fighting the same battles,
In wrangling over minor issues,
In the standing still
While lying arrested, silent, and ready for discovery
Is the unfinished business of Evolution.
— Jerome Raines

The Institution

Jerome came across as unassuming but if the audience knew what was going on inside his head, they would find his assumptions unflattering. Although the crowd responded favorably to the words placed in front of them, Jerome doubted there were many out there that really understood what he was suggesting. He had come to the sobering conclusion that educated men and women did not believe in Evolution. As a tool to describe the past, yes. But as an implement to be employed when it came to the future of civilization, no. It appeared that even champions of the theory did not believe that further Evolution could improve their own faculties or life choices. The majority, especially the "successful" majority, thought it had all been decided satisfactorily, in favor of human beings in their current form, living under the present system. Because this perception was accepted at such a fundamental level, it seemed an obstacle we weren't equipped to overcome. Seeing oneself as the pinnacle of Evolution was just as debilitating as not believing in it at all.

"For the record," he said, "there will not be an official response to our favorite radio celebrity's critique of my work. He so thoroughly proved my case that the obstacles to advancement are overwhelming, I'm tempted to hang up my pen right now and rest on my laurels. Yesterday, Mr. Tilton acted the role of the laboratory rat and proved every one of my points conclusively. It was nice of him to do it, really. The one thing I did decide to do in honor of Conrad Tilton was change tonight's reading. This is my last stop on my book tour and I think I have been handed an opportunity too rich to pass up. I have always enjoyed these words of John Dewey's. They capture the essence of conservatism and the feeble way its followers cling to all things good or bad as long as they don't have to change. I wanted to take his words a step further, however, to give a sense of how discouraging this way of thinking really is.

"Last night I jotted down some lines that I hoped would be equally descriptive in framing the type of environment in which passive minds thrive. I prefer to use open-minded and closed-minded as opposed to progressive and conservative because they better define the differences. However, it should be noted that progressive and conservative ideologies are closely related. Progressives have strayed so far from their origins that it's difficult to think of them as truly progressive. That term, that once had everything to do with making strides in the areas of knowledge and independence, is now little more than a belief in material accumulation – something that is a cornerstone of conservatism as well. I like to use the term active-minded to describe the mindset that will enable us to move forward.

"After being flayed by Conrad Tilton, I reflected on what he said. Two things struck me. The first, of course, being that he has an audience at all. Seemingly sane people, people we live with, work with or worse yet work for, identify with him. The second, is that things are so twisted around I'm the oddity, not him and his way of thinking. I know Evolution is thought to be random but not bizarre. And it would have to be some kind of peculiar twist in human Evolution that would bring us to this point where you are ridiculed for wishing to improve the human condition. Shouldn't it be the other way around? Shouldn't the guy who makes a living, a very good living as a matter of fact, discrediting anyone who wishes to see us reach our potential, be the one laughed off the radio? If your whole livelihood depends on convincing people that black is white by attacking anyone who articulates the truth, why are you even a player? Mr. Tilton, and a certain segment of the population, is nostalgic for a time when it wasn't fashionable to question. In their view the greatest problem we face is liberals, environmental wackos, and do-gooders painting a bleak picture and getting the general public all worked up.

"Contrary to what Conrad Tilton believes there is nothing morally superior about being ignorant. Doubts and a desire to improve civilization should drive us. What is he defending anyway – the one right way of living and thinking? Does he fear the release of human imagination in that it might picture another way? And that could lead to our leaving behind certain ethical, political, and economic beliefs on which western civilization is based. That is just another piece of the paradox. For him, leaving any part of our system behind is too awful, too futureless to comprehend. For me, failure to do so is.

"The belief in Creation. What a static view it is – so dismissive of the possibilities. Cause for hope in the mindless, cause for despair in the mindful. The Bible is a very good accounting of human nature at the level of human development of those the Bible speaks to. The insidious message is that this is what we are and all we'll ever be. And as mere mortals, we're not to question the wisdom of the Good Book and the mysterious ways in which it keeps us infantile. Remaining infantile will be our lot in life unless we accept that we did evolve and that we wish to continue to do so. The Bible gives the impression that we don't have the potential for this. We can make it our goal to prove the Bible wrong in its static view of humanity. As it stands now, it appears we wish to prove the Bible right in its pitiful assessment of the human being.

"This is my final thought for the night. In literature, there is one story that we depend on both to illuminate and console. Over time, we have found countless ways to write it. Aldous Huxley's *Brave New World*, George Orwell's *1984*, Ray Bradbury's *Fahrenheit 451*, Ira Levin's *This Perfect Day*, and Kurt Vonnegut's *Player Piano* are a few examples. It is a story based on our desire for independence from the predominant means of control. We seek freedom through a variety of means – the quest for truth, personal growth, enlightenment, or salvation. The root of the appeal of religious prophets is in that same capacity to transcend dysfunction. What's most interesting is that it's a second paradigm story. By that, I mean a narrative that took root during the last ten thousand years. It's an acting out, an internal revolt, to the freedom we forfeited when a burgeoning population forced us to accept human domestication. As long as we are under command and control with no means of escape, this will continue to be The Story. Without the will to solve the predicament The Story portrays, we won't have a less distressing reality on which to base a future tale. This lack of will is not serving us well. Writing creates the illusion that literary heresy alone is sufficient to bring about change. How many more years before we realize that we're going to have to do something more? The third paradigm story has yet to be written. I cannot say for sure the gist of its text. But what I would like to see is a New Story that doesn't depict anguish, but instead, is an expression of joy."

He gave the audience the opportunity to ask questions. As Sunny listened, she wondered why the bright boy who made such an impression on her back in 1986 had decided to wage a battle against civilization, as we know it. Static living arrangements, hierarchy, religion, our education system – all wrong. They had led to our living in a modern day Dark Age in which meaningful innovation had stopped. We were painting ourselves into a corner from which we might not emerge and we were culturally and evolutionarily dead. She could tell that he imagined something much better than our current circumstances. But she had lost her imagination, so it felt like nothing more than criticism of her life.

Jerome fielded questions for a good hour and a half, before he called it quits. Sunny was taken aback by what he was asked. It was as if he were perceived to be a guru who had all the answers. It made her wonder what people were looking for. Answers, or the next Messiah? It also made her uneasy for fear that if he didn't deliver, the audience would turn into an angry mob and be upon him. But more surprising was that there didn't seem to be a scenario he hadn't considered. And she couldn't help but be impressed by this.

Before the book signings began, she mentioned to her friends that she knew the author and would like to wait around to say hello. They took one look at the crowd waiting for the same opportunity and told her they'd meet her in the Lounge at the recently renovated Silver Falls Lodge. Once they left, Sunny did not join the line, but instead positioned herself by the exit. That he had attained some kind of celebrity status made her feel funny about waiting for him. Increasingly so, when she heard the last of the stragglers. They were also seizing the opportunity to talk to him alone and sounded so sincere in their devotion. Finally, the last four filed past and out into the cold night. A few minutes later she could hear his footsteps coming down the hall. He rounded the corner into the foyer and she watched him approach the small flight of stairs above where she waited. He still hadn't noticed her. She went into a panic wondering what had possessed her to wait around like a groupie. What could possibly be gained by it? And more realistically, what were the chances of his even remembering her?

As he reached for the banister, he glanced up and they made eye contact. She couldn't register in that split second what the look on his face meant. It was now or never. She spoke his name uncertainly. "Jerry?"

He kept walking her way until he reached the landing and was close enough for there to be no mistake. "Ah, it's you. Sunny Day," he said.

No one had called her that for many years. She was struck by a brief recollection of who she used to be. "Eighteen and a half years late but I finally made it to our rendezvous. Actually, I was there three hours late, in time to see you leave. A lot of good that did."

Just when she thought she was going to embark on a round of nervous babbling he stated matter-of-factly, "That doesn't make me feel very cool. I always hoped you didn't know how long I waited. I was taken with you. When you didn't show up I figured I'd come on too strong and scared you off." He shrugged at the thought of his fifteen-year old boy self.

No pretense. He was as she remembered. "No, it wasn't that way at all. The family that I was with had other plans for me." And she left it at that, preferring to keep her dignity intact.

"I have to admit I haven't read your book. I didn't have a clue who Jerome Raines was before tonight." She went on to explain why she had come.

He looked disappointed at that admission. "Books," he corrected her. "There have been more than one."

"You've managed to draw the ire of the most radical conservatives in the country. That must concern you."

"Not really. They're not critics I respect. How could I take those who know so little seriously?"

"Because their followers don't care what they know. They're ideologues. They create a truth and then they manipulate the facts to match. Anything that conflicts is turned into a lie. I got the distinct impression that Tilton and his fans thought writing books should be off limits to people like you."

"That's why I decided not to respond directly. I don't want Conrad Tilton dumbing down my message any more than he already has. There is no winning with a guy like that. All I can do is cut my losses, scratch my head, and wonder how one terrorist event spawned so much sickness. People you thought you knew changed overnight. Some became religious zealots, some militaristic, some downright stupid, and some, all of the above. I listen to the mainstream dialogue and I can't believe it. Now, secularism is talked about as if it is an unacceptable backward thinking. I thought it was religion that was backward. How did the rules get changed so fast? I thought we all agreed that a Theocracy was not a progressive form of government. Our response to this crisis was an eye-opener as to how backward we really are."

"It has to do with this whole political shift in the country," she said. "In the last few years, friendships have either been made or lost based on where people fall politically. I don't think it will last though. Things will get back to normal."

Whatever that was, Jerome wondered, while she continued to talk. He believed we kept reaching increasingly important junctures and were running out of opportunities to find the right course.

"In the meantime, you should be concerned about the attention you got this week. If I were you I'd lay off religion. No good can come of it. And besides, people have a right to worship anyway they see fit," Sunny said with the conviction of an open-minded liberal who believed that anything and everything was a-okay.

It occurred to Jerome that he was wrong to assume that her thinking had moved forward along the same line as his. It was beginning to sound as if this weren't the case. There was a distinct possibility that she was frozen in time, or more disturbing still, she had regressed.

"There are many obstacles that prevent us from envisioning a better human experience. Religion is one of them. I won't ignore it because talking about religion makes people uncomfortable. Talking about population control makes people uncomfortable too, but we're doomed without it. Religion is so irrelevant to me it was a challenge to get up the enthusiasm to write about it. Expending energy on something I expected educated humans of a certain level of intelligence to have moved beyond, was not something I had any intention of doing. Yet, I can see what's going to happen. Religious fundamentalism will have its day again. We are going to have to relearn that same silly-assed lesson. Have you listened to that generation behind us? They're all gaga about their religious convictions as if they're forward thinking in their spirituality. They don't appear to know we've gone down this road before and it ends in disappointment."

"I guess I'm a little surprised by what you have all your energy focused on. And by how stirred up you are."

The Institution

Not nearly as surprised as he was by how she wasn't perturbed. What he was seeing and hearing had brought about a precipitous decline in his expectations. As little as five years ago, he had not intended to write anything like *The Left Behind Paradox*. When the Year 2000 neared its end he had almost finished writing a completely different book. One Sunny would have found more to her liking. And then there was the election followed by the terrorist event. Overnight, what he had written became completely irrelevant. The country was less equipped to deal with the challenges that lie ahead than he imagined. And he had thought himself sufficiently pessimistic. With a keen sense of inevitability, H. L. Mencken had foreseen a "moron" President and a moron had definitely made it to the White House. Plus, it was all too obvious that as individuals we were developmentally several stages below where Jerome thought we were. He had to speak to the existing intellect not some future mode of thought that was nowhere to be found. That meant he had to scrap his earlier manuscript along with his illusions and start anew. *The Left Behind Paradox* was his reaction to conditions on the ground.

"Now I know I'm at a loss since I didn't actually read your book, but it sounds as if you're advocating some major changes. Revolution, is that what you want? Because if it is, you're going to get locked up or worse."

"No, you've got it wrong. I don't want revolution. That's just more of the same left to right, pendulum-swinging, no-progress ideological change that leads nowhere. That's what I'm hoping we avoid. What I'm suggesting is the alternative – Evolution, mainly cultural." The irrelevance most people assigned to his ideas was beginning to wear on Jerome. A little support from someone he once connected with would have meant a lot.

He put his bags down on the floor because they were heavy and he realized they could be standing there awhile. "Honestly," he asked, searching her face for a clue as to what she had become. "Is this where you thought we would be in 2005, the new millennium, under the leadership of a man who talks directly with God about evildoers? Government policy reduced to endless warfare that pits Christians against Muslims?"

"Oh that's just this President. Next election, when the Democrats get back in, everything will be better."

73

"But we just had an election. He won. As difficult as it is for me to understand, a majority doesn't have a problem with what's going on. There's something terribly wrong when this is what a so-called advanced democratic system gets you. The Democrats are only marginally more palatable. It could even be worse when they're back in power because all the progressives will be lulled into believing we're back on the right track and we won't be."

"I don't see that. Everything was going along fine before the 2000 Election. And it will be fine again once 2009 rolls around."

"It will? You didn't think so back in 1986. What happened to you? Your idealism, I mean?"

"Isn't being realistic part of growing up?"

"Or is it something you convince yourself of when being oblivious is personally beneficial?" She looked shocked when he said that. He hadn't meant for it to sound as harsh as it did, but this was the last stop on a lengthy book tour and he was running out of patience. All across Canada and the United States he heard the same platitudes word for word. The bottom line was no one was willing to consider meaningful change. Nothing advanced beyond the theoretical. His attempts to connect with strangers in order to find common ground had left him frustrated.

"Look, it isn't just you. Collectively, we've quit believing there is something better. We lost the desire to envision anything beyond this. Tell me, do you know any idealistic youth that want to change the world? That is, someone other than the Evangelicals we just talked about, who think it will be accomplished through religion. What about your co-workers? Any of them wowing you with their insight?"

Day after day Sunny listened to her coworkers discuss, with wistful longing, the next vehicle they were purchasing or the new plywood palace they made an offer on over the weekend. The number of garage bays or the color of the vinyl siding was a decision they believed had awesome consequences. Their awareness did not extend beyond the moment, the monthly payment, the madness of it all. And this was at an environmental agency. With a reputation for being unselfish, forward-thinking individuals, this was supposed to be the cream of the crop, at least according to liberals. Sunny herself didn't know what mattered anymore.

The Institution

"We're too busy making sure the regs are enforced at the Department of Ecology. That's where I work. We ARE making a difference though. I'm more effective working within the system. No one listens when you're too far out on the fringes. I promised myself a long time ago that I wasn't going to follow that route. I still care. I'm just not willing to draw attention to myself and be some sort of broke oddball."

"Is that how you see me?"

"Well, I'm sure you're not broke. You have been published more than once. But surely with your mind there would have been a place for you in the conventional world."

"Why would anyone want to fit into the conventional world?" The strangest look came over his face. "You're disappointed in me, aren't you? You think I'm wasting my talents. That's unbelievable." He paused while he thought for a moment. "What do you have – a Masters Degree?"

"Yeah, in Environmental Science and Regional Planning."

"Why did you go to college?"

"To get a job of course."

"Why Environmental Science? And why a Masters?"

"That's where the jobs were supposed to be. It was a relatively new field and I thought there was going to be a lot of work. First in mitigation since Industry had left behind so many environmental messes. And then with the shift towards protecting the environment, clean industry would mean new systems designs for existing plants. I thought clean energy and renewables would be on line in no time at all. That was an area in which great strides were to take place. As far as the Masters, once I finished my Undergrad it was clear my best chance for steady employment was with a public agency. There is no getting hired without an advanced degree."

He kept staring at her as if he were expecting something more and when she didn't come through he made the connection for her. "So after thirty-five years of debate in this country over whether the environment matters or not, you spent six years in university so that you can make sure Silver Falls' good corporate citizens don't dump more than their allotted share of pollutants into the Silver River. Which, according to everything I've read, is dying. In fact, it's one of the top ten most polluted rivers in the entire U.S. If you're okay with that, fine, but I was hoping we'd be doing better than that by now. I've gone a step further and come to a conclusion. Our civilization, the one the masses have complete faith in, is not up to solving those kinds of problems. It can't solve them because it's based on screwed up fundamentals. I haven't spoken to anyone who is receptive to taking a serious look at those."

"Jerry, trivializing what people do for a living in that way will only make things worse. We'll all be demoralized, depressed even. We need to feel like we're useful."

"No, we need to BE useful and in order for that to happen we're going to have to grow up and face the facts. We're not all babies, Sunny. We can do this."

"But why would we want to? We have so much. It seems to me we have more to lose than to gain."

"If you're not mindful enough to see beyond your own individual existence then you may not get what I'm saying. At this point you may have to take my word for it. From my own experience, I can tell you that gaining wisdom, insight, awareness, or whatever you wish to call it, is heady stuff. It is far more gratifying than wandering around in an unconscious material fog. It's the difference between being a master and a novice. Initially, there is bound to be some pain associated with really seeing. It turns conventional thinking on its head, but there is also an inner comfort in the going forward. Like when you realize you've outgrown a childhood friend. There is relief in escaping their prison – the prison of a static mind. We're going to have to take that concept further and outgrow civilization at the point it is right now. Only then can we make it better. Is that really so bad, so radical that you're not even going to consider it?"

She had been looking for that same easy, effortless connection they had before. That was what she had hung around for, but it wasn't to be. She hated to see herself as plodding along day after day. But how could she defend a system that was so bad it had to employ watchdogs like her to make sure untreated oil, fertilizers, chemicals, and human waste weren't dumped into the river or toxins spewed into the air?

Her tone changed to one of resignation. "You're right. We should be doing better by now. So why aren't we?"

The Institution

"We talked about one reason already – education. Schooling produces consumers who can find jobs. Which really means conforming so we can fit in to what the marketplace has to offer, which isn't very much. Because you were able to find a job, you believe the system works just fine. In fact, if our material lives are super gratifying then our inner mind, the best part of us, dies."

She looked at him and winced. There was awareness in that instant that she abandoned the best part of herself years ago and he knew it. What could she say to distinguish herself? That she lived in a really big house, that she skied every weekend, that she had a brand new Hybrid? This would be an obvious indictment of how happy she was with the way things were. It made her uncomfortable that her mind began running over her assets, adding them up so to speak. It was an automatic reflex. She was a product of this culture after all.

Other than some vague hope that the salmon would once again leap over the falls in the Silver River, Sunny didn't imagine a different future. As a teenager, she got it in her head that getting the salmon back would be a great accomplishment. She now knew it would be great because it was impossible. Even if by some miracle the environmental movement managed to breach some dams on the Columbia, as soon as the salmon hit our warm oxygen deficient waters they'd be floating belly up. And if that didn't finish them off, it would take an even bigger miracle to see them through tons of waste on route to the lake upstream. That lake happened to be a Super Fund Site, although, you wouldn't know it to hear the local developers talk. There were many changes that needed to take place before there was hope of salmon recovery. The whole ecosystem was a mess. Soon the environment would be so thoroughly degraded that human life would be in jeopardy. Then all environmental concerns would vanish. Getting to that point frightened her, until she thought about it a moment and came to the conclusion we were already there. Her loss of idealism was evidence of that. Hadn't it been about keeping it going at any cost for a very long time? Wasn't that what technofixes were for? In fact, wasn't that what she and Jerry realized back in 1986?

Six years of post-secondary indoctrination had rid her of that wisdom. Sunny's "education" amounted to little more than a certification to be gainfully employed and actively participating in the lifelong process of acquiring assets. Like scores of other students pouring out of universities across the country, her days of learning anything of value, if they ever began, were over. She became a different person after obtaining her Masters Degree. The paralysis of prior investment worked its magic on her. With so much time, money, and energy sunk into obtaining employment within the current system, the status quo was something that benefited her directly. She couldn't remember how she saw the world prior to obtaining advanced education. She did know one thing. She was not nearly as critical as she once was. What used to incense her now passed barely noticed. There was a kind of pragmatism that held her in its grip and made her accepting of what she knew was unsustainable. Upon graduation, her focus shifted to supporting the Institutions that were in place. The environmental solutions that were part of her curriculum were temporary patches at best. All they did was stem the flow of faulty thinking that was at the core of everything. What else could an education system offer when its purpose for being was to perpetuate the beliefs under which we lived – and itself – in the process?

"So why is it that you're not stuck in the routine, working for the man, no original thoughts in your head?" she asked.

"I didn't feel I had a choice. That whole Expo thing got me thinking differently. It was the first time I realized that the people in charge, the adults, didn't know what they were doing. That hadn't occurred to me before and it changed everything. With the mainstream Institutions stuck in a paradigm spin cycle, I was forced to become an independent scholar."

Sunny felt fourteen and in love all over again. She looked into his big dark eyes and remembered how mentally engaged and fearless he'd been. These were traits that mainstream culture frowned upon and it took courage and determination to retain them.

He reached out and squeezed her arm. "It was nice to see you again," he said. "But I must be on my way. I have to get to the train station where I will probably sit all night waiting for a train that may or may not come. Believe me when I tell you this, it's much easier to be a hypocrite."

"Would you like a ride over there?" she asked, not ready to let him go quite yet. "It's on my way."

"If you don't mind that would be great. I wasn't looking forward to walking carrying this heavy thing," he said, pointing to one particularly large bag that Sunny guessed was full of books.

When they were in her car and working their way through downtown, he said he had a confession to make. "I tried to find you after Expo. I want you to know that. I looked in Canada but you were nowhere to be found. You moved to the U.S. That didn't exactly make things very easy. And you changed your first name. That really was tricky on your part. I guess I should be calling you Sarah."

"It's not what you're thinking. Changing my name was not my idea. It's not even legal. But has it ever stuck."

He continued, "Anyway, remember this was all pre-Internet. Once it was invented, I did periodic searches but it wasn't until you began working for the environmental agency that I located you. By that time you were married and it seemed best not to make contact."

"So you knew that I lived in Silver Falls. That's why you weren't all that surprised to see me."

"Guilty as charged. I don't like to lie."

She confessed too, before she could talk herself out of it. "You know I thought about you for years. Scenarios about how we would run into each other again were constantly running through my head. I finally convinced myself that I was half crazy." She paused to consider just how much she should reveal but then decided to plow on. "I guess it's good to find out that we were both kind of doing the same thing. Except that might mean we're both insane."

He flashed that great smile at her. "I'm not that sick. It's not like I voted for The Idiot President or anything like that. A little unwell, maybe?"

Sunny laughed. "It's still madness to feel the way I did after spending an hour talking to a complete stranger. Especially now, knowing that if we were to be meeting for the first time today, we wouldn't feel the same attraction at all."

He raised his eyebrows at her and looked genuinely surprised by this admission. "Is that what you think?"

She pulled up to the curb in front of the station. "I'm not so vain to think the disappointment isn't a two-way street." And she felt bad about it

79

too and fully intended at that moment, while in his presence, to do something to broaden her perspective.

"You shouldn't put words into my mouth. As I said before, it's not you personally. I'm disappointed with what this system does to people," he explained. "Even the very best ones, like you." He had one hand on the door handle as if he intended to leave and not look back. Something compelled him to stop and look at her in that way he had that was completely open and honest.

"The real Sunny, she's still in there. I know she is. There may come a time when it hurts more to keep her locked up than to set her free," he said tenderly.

The sadness closed in so quickly she couldn't think of an adequate response. He removed his bags from the trunk and walked away. For Sunny, watching him go was like before. She was pinned to her seat by a force she couldn't overcome, in much the same way as she was back in 1986. Powerless to say how she felt and terrified to go after what she wanted. Growing up had changed nothing. She was still unwilling to act on her own behalf.

Sunny remained outside the train station long after Jerome disappeared from sight. She thought about how she had admitted to being infatuated with him. That was a big step for her. But she had downplayed his role. He was literally the man of her dreams. Sunny had been preoccupied by a memory right around the time she met and married John. Alone, and in the dark, she indulged in more disquieting recollection.

***

There was a long stretch, between 1995 and 1999, when Sunny's life amounted to work and school with some running thrown in and virtually nothing else. Except at night. Nighttime was something else all together. The dreams had grown increasingly erotic and she was very attached to them. In those first few minutes after she awoke, she was convinced it had really happened. She didn't think it was her imagination that the taste of his lips was upon hers. As the day wore on she would shrug it off as an immature attachment that she was going to have to get over. It occurred to

The Institution

her that she was consumed by work and school and that she was lonely. If all that passion of hers wasn't eventually channeled elsewhere, some guy she met briefly back in 1986 would remain the only man in her life.

When the dreams persisted after she secured a job at the Department of Ecology, she began to notice something else. Who she was while dreaming about him was a different version of herself. When she was younger and focused on living up to her potential, she loved that person. As she became more culturally indoctrinated, the dreams were an uncomfortable reminder of who she wasn't. She interpreted them as the product of a barren love life – not as the symbol of personal discontentment that they were. Sunny didn't know fulfillment could be found by less conventional, internal means. That was why she didn't look elsewhere. What she became obsessed with was finding romance and she ended up making her situation worse, much worse.

In the late summer of 1999, a small pain in the ass led to a really large one – a 5'11", 180 pound one to be exact. One morning in August, while she was out on the trails running, a shooting pain in her buttocks stopped her dead in her tracks. Sciatica forced her temporarily towards some alternate forms of exercise. A co-worker suggested she join an outdoor recreation club of which he was a member. She took his advice and began to participate first on bike rides and then on backpacking, skiing, and kayaking trips. She could not have found a more homogeneous group than the Trekkers. They were all professionals, recreational enthusiasts, and recreational snobs. Their philosophy was that unless you were recreating seven days a week, you weren't living. And it would also be safe to say you were dull. It was fun for a few months. There were no romantic entanglements before Sunny's desperation with being single went into full swing. It happened when John Morris, who was going through a divorce, joined the group. And he was in a pathetic state on that first trip as he tagged along for skiing in the Methow Valley. It had been Sunny's experience that people in a state of malaise gravitated towards her. It wasn't a trait she cultivated but nevertheless she had a way about her that encouraged people to spill their guts.

The snow began before dawn. By the time Sunny got to the Safeway parking lot on the west side of downtown an inch of snow coated everything. She pulled alongside the only other vehicle in the lot, a white Suburban, even though she didn't recognize the driver. The Thule carrier on top made her think it had to belong to someone in the club. She stepped out of her vehicle and put her head back to look up in wonder at the disorienting flakes floating sure and steady through the sky, landing on her face, covering her hair and shoulders, and transforming the world.

The warning tone signaling the keys were in the ignition began to sound as the door of the Suburban opened and she looked over as the driver emerged. She did not know him. "I assume you're one of the Trekkers," he said.

"Yes." She extended her hand. "I'm Sarah Day." It still didn't sound right whenever she said it. The number of people who knew her as Sunny was a contingency of about four. There was no going back on the name now, so the first words out of her mouth in recent years were the same lie.

"John Morris," he said giving her hand a brief shake. He looked around in a preoccupied way and wondered out loud whether anyone else was coming.

"Oh they'll be along," Sunny said. "This is closest to my house. That's why I'm so prompt. Is this your first trip with the Trekkers? I've never met you before so I'm guessing you recently joined."

"Yeah, I did, but that's not to say I'm a novice skier or anything like that. I was just looking for a new group to hang with." His eyes caught sight of a Forerunner and a Subaru turning in and he looked relieved. They were closely followed by a Blazer and an Explorer.

By the time all the jockeying of ski equipment and bags and coolers took place, Sunny found herself the sole passenger in John's vehicle. She silently questioned whether this was the best use of carpooling resources or if the two of them were being set up. So much for curling up in the back and reading the way she usually did. On that trip, she was forced to engage in small talk and it became increasingly personal as they got closer to their destination.

John Morris was going through an experience that was affecting his self-esteem in a very negative way, so he wasn't giving off his usual macho signals. On that morning in January, he was raw and vulnerable in a way that was appealing. For four hours he talked freely and she listened to what

The Institution

was going on in his life. It was such a one-sided conversation because there was more going on in his life than there was in hers. By the time they got to the first small town outside of Silver Falls, he told her he was in the midst of a messy divorce and that he had two children, aged six and nine. As they rolled through Grand Coulee, he was explaining how his wife had a relationship going with a mutual friend of theirs for years, and that he had only learned of it around Thanksgiving.

"It was the worst holiday season of my life," he said sadly. "I couldn't believe it. It was such a shock."

That he had no inkling his spouse was unhappy with him meant one of two things. It was possible his wife had failed to mention it, but more likely it was one of many things he didn't hear her say. The significance of his bewilderment did not register with Sunny on that day. When she looked over at the thoroughly broken man, she did not question his pain or his true nature. It didn't occur to her that she was not seeing the real John, the one who had disappeared in a temporary period of soul-searching introspection and that once his confidence returned so would his hubris. And that the real John might not be a very good match for her. None of those thoughts crossed her mind as she reached across that great expanse of front seat and touched his forearm.

"I'm sorry," she said. "It sounds like the worst might be over though, don't you think?"

"I hope so," he told her. "I wonder if you ever get over something like this or are you bitter and suspicious for the rest of your life?"

While he was talking there was this little voice in the back of Sunny's head going WARNING, WARNING, DAMAGED GOODS – BEWARE. But she was in no condition to heed the message. She was a twenty-seven year old woman in the company of a sad thirty-five year old man who was in serious need of a good woman to restore his spirits. They were both sports-minded people without attachments who were embarking on three days of winter recreation in paradise. They would be sleeping in the same cabin, drinking a lot of wine, and to top it off she was starved for male companionship. All of the clichés predicting the inevitable applied.

Upon arriving at their destination in the Methow Valley, the Trekkers got right out on the trails for cross-country skiing. After a few hours,

Terra Dime

Sunny split off from the rest of the group. Compelled to get back to the cabin to work on dinner so there would be something to eat when everyone finished up for the day, she cut her own skiing short. At least that was how she begged off joining the rest of them on the East Loop Trail. A more accurate explanation was she felt the need to pace herself when it came to group activities. She had become more of an introvert over the years and had to take her exposure to people in increasingly smaller doses. This was not something she could tell her extroverted companions. Nor could she explain how being outdoors and alone in this great expanse of life – silent and dozing under a layer of snow – brought her inner world alive. She craved that feeling of aliveness and connection above all else.

The flurries turned to snow showers and the wind kicked up. Snow accumulated on her skis where she stood at the edge of the forest feeling the joy inside. Minutes passed before she readied herself, tugging her hat down, adjusting her eyewear, and zipping up her collar for a fast final mile out in the open on flatter ground. As she veered off the main track and onto the trail that led to the log cabin she calculated how much time she had to work on dinner before everyone showed up. When she first joined this outdoors club, the other members gave her grief about the elaborate meals she prepared but they had come to accept that for some reason, that was thankfully foreign to them, she enjoyed cooking. Now they asked only to be briefed on the menu so they could anticipate dinner.

Sunny snapped off her skis, stepped up on the porch and brushed the snow from her hat and jacket. She stomped around dislodging what she could from her pants and boots. The way it was coming down, like it would never end, was perfect, she thought to herself as she went inside. Snow enveloped the rooms. To her left she caught swirling flakes in the square windows on either side of the fireplace. Straight ahead, as well as to her right, two sets of glass doors and transoms framed the wintry scene like a work of art. Above her, snow piling up on the skylights bathed the room in a kind of winter storm white out. To call this a cabin was a gross misrepresentation of the facts. It was a five-bedroom, four-bath log palace. The kind of place it seemed a shame to rent and then not spend any time in. As soon as she laid eyes on the kitchen that morning she pictured herself standing here watching the snow through the wood windows. Alone with her thoughts, she would have her way with the various ingredients. Chopping vegetables often proved to be more gratifying than mincing pared down language. She knew this was a bad attitude but it was not one she came to through lack of trying. Hundreds of fruitless attempts to engage her peers had brought her to this point where she was sick to death of talking about nothing. The gulf between what we should be discussing and what we were was staggering.

Sunny's knowledge about environmental issues put her in a unique position. What she had neither expected nor been able to overcome was her lack of credibility. People tended to disregard everything she said as the ravings of a lunatic. The amusing part was that she had yet to share with a crowd such as the Trekkers how bad things really were. Her disdain for the consumer culture and its inability to make any environmental connections whatsoever was something she kept hidden from a group who acquired new gear, not as-needed, but on an "annual, new and improved model" basis. There were many more millions just like these folks who comprised the hollow cultural core of modern times. They believed they couldn't live without a cell phone, a perfectly appointed house, the latest in electronic gadgetry, and a late model SUV. They did not have the imagination for anything else. If you wished for something more meaningful, there was no place for you.

Sunny rummaged around in her bag for dry clothes. Once she had pulled on some jeans and a sweater, she got to work in the kitchen after uncorking a Riesling and giving herself a generous pour. Out came a cutting board, a knife, bags of vegetables, and numerous jars filled with ingredients she prepared the night before. She got started on the appetizers – Asian Stuffed Mushroom Caps and Spring Rolls – so they would be ready when everyone returned. That would help ward off starvation before the main course, the Thai Curry, was ready to eat. She hadn't been at it for very long when she heard a heavy step on the porch and looked up to see John Morris unsnap his hood and then run his hands through his hair. Unaware that anyone was watching, he checked himself out in the window, gave his head a toss until he was satisfied with his appearance, and then tugged aggressively at the door. Sunny frowned and turned back towards the stove, not letting on that she had seen him arrive.

Terra Dime

When she heard the door open she spun back around in time to watch clumps of snow dislodge from his jacket and fall onto the wood floor. "You're back early," she said. "I wasn't expecting anyone for at least an hour."

"I got to thinking that you shouldn't be out there skiing by yourself. You might get lost or something."

"Really? Well you don't have to get too concerned about me. I'm not stupid, you know."

"I really started to wonder when I didn't catch up with you. I thought I would since I didn't turn around that long after you did. You must have caught a good tail wind."

Sunny rolled her eyes as she reached for her glass. He continued to stand there while the snow from his clothing plopped onto the floor and melted into a pool. She remembered thinking how he operated like he was in a trance or something. Back then, though, Sunny gave him the benefit of the doubt assuming he was preoccupied by his current circumstances. It did not occur to her that he was sleepwalking through life.

"Would you like something to drink?" she asked.

"I think I'll get showered up first. I'm kind of cold," he muttered as he traipsed unconsciously through the puddle of water that surrounded him. He proceeded to track it around the corner and up the stairs.

Half an hour later, catching his image in the mirrored dining room hutch as he passed woke him up long enough to put his hands in the side pockets of his wide wale cords and strike a pose. Sunny watched the preening with amusement and it did not register that someone this pleased with himself was not a candidate for personal improvement.

"How about all this snow?" was the first thing he said to Sunny as he pulled a Kokanee from the fridge.

"What if this were the last year that it snowed? I think about that a lot lately. Sometime within the next two decades, we will see the last low elevation snowfall. Of course, we won't know it at the time. It will be like Peak Oil and seen for what it was a decade or so after the fact."

She liked to throw things like that out there, to get a feel for where someone was at. She was feeling increasingly uneasy about where humanity was headed and how much of the support system would crumble around us. Unless you were intentionally ignoring it, Global Warming had to be real to you. There wasn't much discussion yet about Peak Oil, but there would be. Getting our "advanced" civilization to face the end of oil was going to be a Herculean task, even though a rudimentary understanding of the biology of the planet made it a simple fact. It wasn't about reason though. It was about faith or fantasy, which was essentially the same thing.

He didn't let on that he heard her. Without skipping a beat he said, "I think we should drive up to Loup Loup tomorrow and go downhilling. The conditions will be excellent."

"Either way is fine with me – cross-country or downhill. The plan, though, was downhill the day after tomorrow. I don't know how flexible the group is," she commented while she scooped the last bits of avocado onto the rice paper, turned in the ends and wrapped the contents snuggly into place. With the appetizers complete, she began snapping the ends off green beans.

"So where do you work?" she asked, aware of the lack of easy dialogue between the two of them and again attributing it to his preoccupation with all the negative stuff that was going on his life. It surprised her that it hadn't come up on the drive here but then their conversation had not touched on a range of topics.

"Oh, I'm the Controller for a company called Precious Pieces. Prior to that I was with Big Falls Forest Products."

"What's Precious Pieces? I don't believe I'm familiar with that company."

"We make fine china for children. They're great collector items. Bound to be worth a lot of money some day."

Fine china for children, Sunny thought to herself. *What next?* "Those sound like two very different places to work."

"Not from an accounting standpoint. They're both production-oriented and that means cost accounting. That's all that matters to me."

"How long have you been there?"

"Not very. I started in April of last year so as you can well imagine everything was about getting prepared for Y2K. Thankfully, we got through that okay. I imagine this year will be different. It won't be all about crisis mode."

Terra Dime

She was surprised that there was a local manufacturing company she hadn't heard of. Her job required she know about that type of facility. "So are these 'collector items' manufactured here in Silver Falls?"

"No, not exactly. We have a team of designers here. They're produced overseas."

"And I'll bet the majority of the sales aren't generated in the country they're made in, are they?"

"No, of course not. These aren't low-end trinkets that the Chinese can afford. They're an investment for people of means to make for the children in their lives."

"I get it. Kind of like Beanie Babies for the rich."

That brought a furrow to his brow, as he was unsure where she was going with comments like those. "How about you? Where do you work?"

"Department of Ecology," was all she was able to say before that mind elsewhere look came over him. He was gripping his beer tightly with one hand while he picked ferociously at the label with the other.

"Yeah, I really think we should go downhill tomorrow. I like downhill better than cross-country. Cross-country is a lot of work. Plus, I have some of those new radial skis I'm dying to try out. They are going to be soooo sweet."

Seeing John the way she came to, it was difficult to reconcile the passion that engulfed them that weekend with the reality of their marriage. For he and Sunny were polar opposites in every way that mattered. He was the enemy of thought, of ideas, and of internal growth. He was the anti-Zen.

Sunny struck him as an amusing diversion, so different, so passionate about doing the right thing. She talked in an excited breathless manner, as if there were so many issues she cared about she might forget to mention one if she didn't blurt them all out quickly and with enough force to emphasize their importance. Half the time he had no idea what she was talking about. John was the kind who was proud of not having learned anything new since 1988, the year he graduated with an Accounting Degree. He often said this without embarrassment and with no awareness of how appalling an admission like that actually was. Politics, cultural trends, the future, were all things he couldn't talk about coherently. That wasn't to say he didn't have strong convictions about all of those things, plus a great deal more. Whenever he was pressed to articulate his points of view, he was unable to do so. He just knew that whatever he felt in his heart to be true, was fact. Discussions with him always began and ended there because he was so hostile when it came to defending the illogical. Unfortunately for Sunny, that weekend when he made his first impression, a brief bout of insecurity made him come across as mild-mannered.

For the rest of the weekend, she didn't want to know what was on his mind anyway for fear it might detract from his physical presence, which was quite superior to his mental. It was a gap that did not narrow over time. In the coming years, every time he opened his mouth, she wished he hadn't.

***

Sunny pulled away from the train station and drove over to the Silver Falls Lodge just in case some of the book club members were still waiting for her. It was pushing nine o'clock when she entered the Lounge to find Karen was the only one who remained. She had read all of Jerome Raines' books and that was why she was the one who chose to hang around. It certainly wasn't because the two of them were close because Sunny didn't know what to think of Karen. She appreciated that it was good to have someone in your book club with an alternative perspective. But her views were so radical it was hard to believe there was any truth to them. What Karen succeeded in doing was making everyone uncomfortable and that wasn't what the ladies were looking for.

Her manner was conspiratorial that night as if she could see the future and Sunny wondered what it was she was seeing. Because Sunny hadn't yet arrived at the conclusions she would later embrace, she had a tough time understanding what Karen was telling her. Sunny tried but at that point they weren't speaking the same language. Karen prodded her by explaining how there were few opportunities for personal growth in conventional life. In the absence of a trauma of some kind – death, accident, or illness – to wake us from complacency, epiphanies most often took place when we were in our thirties.

Terra Dime

"If a person ignores, or is immune, to the signals, he's destined to remain a dullard," Karen said. "It's as if that's the length of time it takes – thirty years give or take – for the brain to become hardwired. It's the final moment of elasticity before every slot in the brain takes the data it has been provided up to that point and memorizes it for life. It gets brittle after that. It won't budge to make room for advanced code that might read the data better. And then before you know it, you're in your fifties and you're a flippin' freak. You've had the same worldview for so long and you've spit it out in exactly the same way so many times, you sound like a moron. Even when presented with evidence to the contrary, you can't incorporate it. You're virtually retarded. And it's not a liberal versus conservative thing, although that's the way we like to label everything these days. It's as difficult, possibly more so, to get someone who believes in liberal causes to think differently. Normally, those sorts feel they're already sufficiently enlightened. They aren't any better at seeing the disappointing results of the policies they endorse because they feel so good about the spirit in which they acted."

The three glasses of wine she had already consumed by the time Sunny arrived made Karen more animated than usual. This was not an area in which assistance was needed. Karen's natural enthusiasm was greater than Sunny was comfortable with. "You have to read Jerome Raines' books," she said emphatically. "I hope you intend to do that now that you know who he is. They are not like anything I've ever read. They're scary at the start because they destroy many notions that you might be comfortable with. But they're worth it in the end."

She took her praise even further when she told Sunny, "I don't want to be over-the-top here about his writing, but his words open your mind in a way that sets you free. All the while he nudges you, as the reader, to discover what is intrinsic, outside of popular culture, and beyond what we have come to believe through education, indoctrination, or whatever. What he asks you to wrap your mind around, you can feel it happening as you read."

It was an amazing endorsement. Karen couldn't emphasize enough that when the opportunity to grow is presented it should be seized. And still Sunny wasn't willing to let that shift happen to her. She knew without giving it more than a moment's thought that she could not heed Karen's message. It wasn't in the cards for her to change her priorities if she wished to stay married to John. She consistently chose remaining married over making other commitments that would be more agreeable to her. And she did this without fully understanding why. She realized early on that if she didn't let go of much of her environmental and fiscal responsibility, their marriage would be a battleground. And so, she had acquiesced. For what? It wasn't as if she adored her spouse and wished for nothing more than to make him happy. She was uncomfortable with John regardless of how often it had been impressed upon her that he was a good mate in an educated, hardworking, dependable kind of way. It was what he sucked out of her that she hated. Over time, it had become increasingly difficult to ignore all he had taken from her. It hadn't been enough for him to stop her dead in her tracks. He had also managed to give her a good shove backwards.

She and her husband worked hard for everything they had. The way they spent, they could forget about doing anything else. Not long after they married they sold her bungalow even though she owned it free and clear. It had been too modest for John's tastes. Now they rattled around inside a 6,000 square foot mini-mansion in the prestigious Highland Terrace area, plus they had a lake cabin and a condo at the ski hill. They needed both their incomes to pay for it all. She told herself that she loved her job and she was doing good work for the Department of Ecology. Good, environmental work.

Sunny's mother and second husband thought John was the greatest. She was the odd one out. There was no support from her immediate family, not through the good times and certainly not during the bad. She dreaded having to listen to their versions of what was right or wrong, good or evil, or whatever was the popular way in which to frame their deeply held beliefs from which they never wavered. She fretted about getting together over holidays. On such occasions, Sunny remained in the kitchen for much of the ordeal – limiting her exposure to ten or fifteen minutes. And she could forget about being true to herself because that would mean the most horrendous arguments. Sunny accepted that reasonable discussion with family members was out of the question. None of them had learned the art of fair fighting. It was her husband she blamed primarily for the insults that were hurled her way. She found it difficult to overlook the tone he set and the way he dismissed what she had to say both when they were alone and in the company of others. He had made it okay to attack in a very personal fashion. He declared open season on Sunny every chance he got. And when it was open season, well, everyone brandished a weapon.

As long as they didn't discuss anything controversial everything was okay. Politics, religion, the environment, and a whole bunch of social issues were taboo. Some of these she had learned the hard way. Politics, for instance. John's party affiliation, even in the face of overwhelmingly destructive policies, also never wavered. They hadn't been married very long when on the eve of the 2000 Election she watched in horror at what she thought was going to be a victory for the Democrats turn into a win for the Republicans and then become an unknown. While she let her disgust at this turn of events be known he grew quieter until she realized he wasn't agreeing with her. In fact, he was livid with her characterization of the Republican candidate. The talking strike lasted until the Supreme Court decided in favor of the conservatives and then John was gracious in victory.

The September 11th terrorist attacks of the following year flushed all of John's insecurities to the surface. With the U.S. flag wrapped tightly around him, it was hard to fathom the place he went to after that. But for her, it was best described as a neo-conservative purgatory where she was forced to live through the daily horrors of right wing talk show bullies. He identified with those people. So much so that just being in the same house with him scared her in ways she didn't like to think about. She watched him day after day tune into the most radical newscasts and recite the lunatic ravings as if they were truth. He became a God guy in a big way and his religious fervor had not abated. In addition to watching the Evangelicals on television he also began attending church regularly. He was so eager for the Rapture, he sat in his Lazy-Boy tuned into the Fox News Network "fair and balanced" reporting while waiting to be sucked up into Heaven. He had no doubt that he would be going while his wife and others of her ilk would be left behind. According to John, she was a heathen and he was a chosen one brimming with true Christian values. Unprecedented terror at the hands of Jesus, whose anticipated mean streak during the Second

Coming was highly anticipated by literal-minded folk everywhere, would be just punishment for non-believers like her. Fortunately, Sunny's exposure to all of this was limited due to his travel schedule. John's employment took him out of the country more than 50% of the time and that made life tolerable.

She remained convinced that her lack of curiosity about John prior to making the decision to marry him was for the best. If she had held out for all the qualities she was looking for in a man, she would be thirty-two years old, single, and statistically speaking stand a better chance of being struck by lightning than marriage. It made perfect practical sense to hook up with a man who enjoyed the same sports, didn't it? That gave them one thing in common. That's all you needed, wasn't it?

Terra Dime

BOOK TWO

THE ACQUISITIVE SPECIES

Toward a Civilization that Values Acquiring Wisdom over Possessions

---

As Darlene passed the elevator that would take her to the staff dining room, she checked her watch. It was fifteen minutes early for lunch break but that was within the Institution's range of tolerance. And she was so tired and hungry. This job of hers was hard work. As mentally exhausting as her rounds were at least they hadn't robbed her of her appetite. Her heart began racing as she rode the elevator knowing she would have her choice of seats and wouldn't miss one minute of her favorite daytime drama. The longest running program in history, it was celebrating its seventieth year in grand fashion. All manner of bad behavior had been paraded across the screen in recent months. She could barely wait for each new episode. It made Darlene giddy to think about the generations of women who had watched this program, and like her, had been moved by what was going on in the lives of the characters.

When she reached her destination, the elevator doors appeared to ripple as they lost their hard shape. They gave the illusion of turning into a thatched bamboo screen opening up into a tropical paradise. A soft, velvety trade wind perfumed with jasmine ruffled her hair. The sound of surf drew her eyes to the window. In the near distance was a lively little village. People were on the streets going about the business of old-fashioned living. Whimsical stucco structures in pleasing pastels meandered along a steep stretch of cobblestone to the water's edge where dozens of sails dotted the sea. A couple of brightly colored birds flew past before perching on a coconut palm in the center of the room. A red Macaw clinging to the back of a chair shifted from one foot to the other and spoke melodiously for her benefit, "Don't worry, be happy," it said over and over again.

The Institution

It was so realistic that her sensible shoes looked out of place on the clay path that skirted the dining room tables in this new "mood room" – one of the ever-changing collections of plasma window treatments the Institution purchased. Once a way to throw hologram images onto indoor spaces was discovered, life improved measurably. With the aroma therapy and sound effect add-ons, the whole package was sublime. So much better than what the British Columbian Province of the Americas had to offer.

Right now, if she were actually looking out the window, her senses would be assaulted by denuded hilltops to the north. The forest that once extended for hundreds of miles was long gone but the pulp mill's decaying smokestack remained. It still rose high over the river valley, although, it had been idle for ten years. But that didn't keep old-timers from reminiscing about the days when it spewed out thousands of pounds of fumes. This olfactory assault was often referred to as "the smell of money" and for a time the city had been drenched in it. Darlene – as her parents before her – considered the early 2020's as the glory years. This was when loggers came from all over to ensure that fire and disease did not decimate the forests before they had a chance to harvest them. Once it quit freezing in this part of the world, the devastating bug infestations made felling the forests a necessity. The whole region prospered when the logging industry was given carte blanche to take care of it all. And they were very efficient in their work. When there wasn't a tree left unturned, the loggers moved further north to take care of the boreal forests. Places like Alaska, the Northwest Territories, and the Yukon also had an opportunity to enjoy the boom.

Recognizing the urgency at the front end of their awesome responsibility, the logging industry – and the policies that supported it – was slightly remiss in thinking through the back end. The massive reforestation effort that ensued was a complete failure. Every seedling died. The climate was wrong for what they planted – too warm, too dry, not enough oxygen, and eventually not enough sun. Who would have thought conifers could be such a temperamental species? But they were. The best scientists in the country, using the most advanced technologies, were working on the problem though. It was just a matter of time before they came up with a genetically altered seedling that would thrive under current conditions. Once those were planted, they would gain a foothold in no time at all.

"Hey Darlene, how's it going today?" Sue called out from the buffet serving area.

"Oh, okay I guess. Been working hard though. This job of mine is hard work. My gout's been giving me a little trouble this morning too. I'm thinking I'm going to have to get my meds increased again. That will be the third time don't you know it? But what else am I to do?" she lamented in the manner of the unlucky victim whose lot in life is to bear a tedious list of diseases.

"Hang in there girl," was the comfort the server offered. "What can I get for you today? You need to keep eating good. Keep your strength up."

Thick hunks of meat sizzling on the grill caught Darlene's eye. "How about an ADAM Rib Eye Steak and some mashed potatoes and gravy?"

"Would you like some carrots and broccoli to go along with that?"

"No, I'll pass on those. You know the way vegetables make my acid reflux act up."

The opening bars of her soap opera's trademark music were blaring by the time Darlene took a seat. She adjusted one of the four screens on the entertainment-square in the center of the table and increased the volume on the headset. The e-squares that popped up in every public place were the greatest invention. They were marriage and friendship savers. People were freed from having to stare at one another across a table and be reminded of how little they had to talk about. Plus, the entertainment could be personalized so no one was forced to watch someone else's idea of a good show.

Darlene's heart fluttered in anticipation of today's episode. Friday had been a cliffhanger. It had been an agonizing weekend waiting for this moment to find out who at the orgy had given Teresa AIDS. She had her money on Bobby. He was kind of a slimy, free-spirited character who had never fallen madly in love with a single one of the divas he played opposite. This was a guy who did not know how to bare his soul. And to top it off his relationship with God was shaky at best. Scummy.

The rare meat was so tender it yielded easily under the steak knife. This ADAM was as good as the last. He'd been cloned repeatedly right

The Institution

there at The Faith is Truth Institution for going on fifteen years. The ratio of lean to fat was perfect; the marbling of each cut consistent from animal to animal. There were no surprises when it came to the quality or quantity of their meat products. Same with the produce. Cloning, hydroponics, and artificial sunlight had improved everything. Hunkered down over her plate, mesmerized by the discovery that none of the other orgy participants tested positive for AIDS, Darlene pondered that some aspect of Teresa's life had been kept secret from the viewing audience. This usually meant a new character was about to join the cast.

Dr. Marsh and his associates passed Darlene's table without glancing her way. She wasn't offended by this. Regardless of how the night was spent, his ignoring her during working hours was to be expected. She knew the rules of the system and she always played by them. Dr. Marsh was close to the top of the Institution's hierarchy. She was not. That made her inferior, but if she were lucky sexual privileges traveled down the chain in her direction.

Once the doctors had loaded their plates with food, they headed for the far corner of the cafeteria where their conversation would not be heard. They were all a dither with the latest breakthroughs from the pharmaceutical industry that were about to hit the market. Each of them held a piece of paper in his hands; kind of like a fresh sheet you might find at a seafood restaurant, listing the day's offerings. Or, as in the world of horse racing, an insider's key to the hottest picks entering the gate.

"This is the greatest weight loss drug to hit the market in thirty plus years," Dr. Marsh exclaimed while his chubby fingers slathered two pats of butter onto a yeast roll and then dipped it like a ladle into a pool of gravy. "On average, test patients lost fifty pounds. And when they quit the drug they gained it back. So how great is that? They'll have to stay on it for as long as they want to stay thin, or in other words, for the rest of their lives."

"I don't see why you're so ecstatic about it. It's not like it's something that needs to be prescribed in this environment. The patients aren't the ones with weight problems around here," Dr. Scott pointed out while looking around the table at his colleagues' plump, florid faces conscious of the feel of his own roll spilling over the waistband of his slacks.

"It's not like I intend to work here forever," Dr. Marsh shot back, thinking longingly about the opportunities that lie outside the Institution. He couldn't stop fantasizing about the prospect of shedding fifty pounds without lifting more than a finger simply to pop a pill into his mouth. It was the stuff that dreams were made of.

"None of us will be working here forever – twenty-five years tops and then this little blip in the story of mankind will thankfully be over," one of his other colleagues threw out. "It's just that Weight Loss Enablers have proven historically to have significant side effects."

And he was right to feel cautious. Pharmaceuticals for weight loss had been one of the Achilles' heels of their profession. Heart problems in the previous century paled next to the last generation of Weight Loss Enablers (WLEs) that hit the market in 2005 to rave reviews and wide acceptance by an obese population. They were now known to have caused widespread Alzheimer's. That generation of WLEs ravaged the brain so completely those patients were spared a long life. With any luck at all, the general public's memory being what it was, that unfortunate episode would have already slipped their minds. Evidently, it had slipped Dr. Marsh's.

"The clinical tests are conclusive," he said excitedly. "All carrot, no stick." Yet another new wonder drug was about to take the population by storm.

***

Darlene wore a much happier face when the afternoon rolled around. Nothing perked her up quite the same as watching her favorite daytime stars battle through a litany of personal problems that made hers look tame. Visiting with Heather Holmes immediately afterward struck her as the perfect way to bring herself down slowly before finishing up with the less fascinating patients. Whenever she knocked on Mrs. Holmes' door it seemed that something was missing. There should be a big star smack dab in the middle. That was what she was after all. An actress, albeit an old one. At the age of 81, she was the most senior patient. Her narrow shoulders were rounded, back stooped from the weight of her most valuable asset turned liability.

The Institution

Her mother and a brother had also been movie stars. It was her mother who had been the most famous of them all. She had been another one of those crazy activists who fought for a whole range of causes – peace, the environment, civil liberties, nonproliferation. Sometimes, too passionately. Back in 2003, in the lead up to the 2nd Iraq War, she was arrested for civil disobedience. The irony of the whole thing was she was playing the role of the President of the United States in a television series at the time. According to Mrs. Holmes, she played it so well that a public disillusioned with the real leader of the free world tuned into the program every week and was wistful for her brand of leadership. The anti-liberal supporters of the real President were disgusted by this kind of disloyalty. By that time the media was controlled by big business which profited from war. Because they helped to install the party in power, a lot of pressure came to bear. When she was released from jail the producer of the series, who her mother had always respected, told her she was an embarrassment. Gripped by fear of plummeting ratings and the potential loss of advertising dollars, he suggested that being fired up and angry all the time was no way to live her life. He followed that up with a quick, uneducated diagnosis of depression and recommended she take something for it.

Right around the same time a popular author – Heather wasn't sure of his name anymore, but she thought it was something like Cretin – wrote a novel poking fun at the environmental movement and more specifically her mother. He killed her off in a hideous fashion. A fantasy brought to life on paper for everyone to read. It was supposed to be fiction, but there was no mistaking whom he was writing about. Being liked was way too important to her mother. She hadn't realized that people saw her like that. That the book would go on to be a tool of the conservative anti-environmental movement – and be quoted from by a member of Congress in setting actual environmental policy – took the anti-intellectual crusade to another level.

Her mother became inconsolable. Wouldn't listen to a thing Heather had to say so convinced was she there was something wrong with her. And it certainly wasn't difficult to find a physician eager to agree and eager to prescribe a little something. Anti-depressants, Serotonin Selective Reuptake Inhibitors (SSRIs) to be more specific, became part of her daily regimen. And those pills were powerful. Her personality dissolved in that chemical stew she was prescribed. Heather wasn't quite sure who inhabited her mother's body at the end, because it wasn't anyone she recognized. Unable to enter into conflict there was no discussing anything meaningful with her. In a matter of months, she was fully docile. She went from being an energetic intelligent woman to a disengaged shell who eventually drowned herself at Malibu. The rest of the world thought it was an accident but Heather had wondered about her mother's whereabouts. She had been the first to arrive at her beach house and the one to destroy the suicide note.

Most of the time this was the kind of thing Mrs. Holmes liked to talk about. Darlene preferred the rare instances when she would become nostalgic about her early years as a stacked, blonde, primetime heartbreaker and then she and Darlene would leaf through photo albums and newspaper clippings. On those occasions, the old girl would pretend she wasn't interested in revealing the more intimate details of her young life. She would wait for Darlene to ask whether she had "knowledge" of this bulked up piece of flesh in the cut-off jeans or that hunk with the mesmerizing eyes. They both knew what kind of "knowledge" she was getting at. After putting on a grand performance in which she blushed and tittered, explicit details followed. So far, Darlene had struck gold with every one of the photographs, finally coming to the conclusion that she only kept pictures of men she had affairs with. They were less than half way through the stack. When it came to lovers her memory was as impressive as a little black book dying to be read. It was great fun. That was the way Darlene saw it anyway. Heather would have said that half of what she told the Nurse wasn't true and there was a very good reason for why she spoke to her of these things. It was all she could understand.

On the day after Jerome Raines' death, she was fixated on telling a story that was new to Darlene. "It all started with a piece of fan mail," Heather explained, flipping through the pages of one of the albums hoping to find what she was looking for. "It was from a man who had been writing to me for twenty-plus years. Pure idolatry and he had it bad. I looked forward to hearing from him. He seemed harmless enough. Garth Gum – a dentist if you can believe it with a name like Gum – from Fort Wayne, Indiana. It probably surprises you that I would bother to read a letter like this but I was hoping it would raise my spirits. What with being dumped by

The Institution

Ricky and my career going through a soft patch, I was a little desperate," she confessed.

"I was middle-aged. There wasn't much for good roles out there and once they quit producing *Hot Days, Sizzling Nights* things languished a bit. I could always count on Garth, my most faithful fan, to tell me what I wanted to hear. He liked to lament how I was being passed over for starring roles by young upstarts who didn't have a fraction of my talent. That was what I was counting on. That's not what I got.

"Ah, here they are," she said, triumphantly waving a newspaper clipping and several yellowed sheets of paper around. "The only other time Garth had been pissy with me was about my third marriage. That had been less than three years earlier. At that time, he tried to persuade me not to waste my time with such a homely, temperamental, egotistical producer as Ricky (the Rickster) LeCadeau who had a disastrous track record with women. But you know how that goes, I thought I was different from all those other women. How original," she grimaced crinkling her nose, signaling she had caught a whiff of something stinky.

"As an aside, do you happen to know what le cadeau means in French? The gift. And he was sure the name was more than a coincidence. The end of my marriage was what precipitated this particular piece of correspondence from Mr. Gum. I was feeling so low that it made more of an impact than it should have."

Darlene interrupted, sure she could guess the contents. "So did he write just to gloat and to say I told you so?"

"No, not at all. My loyal supporter had gone through a transformation it seemed. I could tell something was amiss as soon as I began reading. The tone was different, new and improved. And he thought it was time for me to go through a transformation as well." Heather hung on to the letter but placed the newspaper clipping in Darlene's lap. Two longhaired blondes of disparate ages, both blue-eyed under heavy black lashes with matching sets of perfect teeth and twin plunging necklines stared up at Darlene. One was in her twenties, the other her forties. The story was about how one was soon to be the recipient of a new but very used husband. The other was surrendering this well-worn groom. The younger of the two women was fresh and pert and of course delighted with this seduction and all the affairs that were yet to come. Heather, on the other hand, came across as bored and beat-down.

"It's a given that I would have looked better with a more mature style, but this is a particularly bad picture. I didn't look quite this horrible. Although, the dentist from Fort Wayne seemed to think I did. He thought it was time to grow old gracefully, so to speak. I've kept the contents of this to myself all these years because it was so painful to see the truth, my truth, laid out so starkly in his letter. Take my word for it, when even rabid fans are leaving you behind, it's time to grow.

"There's no need for you to read the whole thing. I'll paraphrase for you. Basically, what he had for me was a big batch of pity. He wanted to let me know how sorry he felt for me. He referred specifically to how awful it must be to feel that I had to keep bleaching my hair and wearing it in the same long style, slathering on the makeup, pouring myself into tight clothes that made me look cheap and older than my years. He wrote that I was a beautiful woman who should find the nerve to comport myself in an age-appropriate manner and quit worrying about the antics of infantile men like the one I was being dumped by. Mr. Gum thought I would be happier and more attractive if I followed this advice and that I would land better acting roles as well.

"He was right you see. But it was the coincidence of the timing that was so strange. Any other time it wouldn't have landed up being a catalyst. On the day I opened this letter, I was looking for something. I can see that now. That's why everything began to sink in rather than bouncing off without leaving an impression. And then once I opened up, I saw things differently. I started noticing what had been there all along. I made connections I'd never made before. I grew up. Those next few weeks became magical."

Darlene picked up the old photo of this now elderly woman and held on to it. "His words seem a little harsh. You looked pretty good to me," she said wistfully while some foreign sense of her own image tugged at her.

"Good for one thing and that was about it. You should be impressed by something more than that."

It was the kind of putdown that slipped by Darlene. She was now fixated on the sight of her ankles, flaring out and over her white oxfords.

The Institution

For a fleeting moment she was aware of every square inch of herself. Involuntarily, her hand reached for her throat where it fingered three chins before she moved it away. The patient took note of the confusion. For a second she had the strange sense of sitting across from an altogether different person. A silent seed of doubt had slipped through, furtive and ticking. In the next instant Darlene settled back into her own reality and all was well again.

Heather continued with her story. "The reason I referred to the timing was I left the next morning for Vancouver Island to stay at an Eco Spa."

"What on earth is that?" Darlene asked.

"You know, a place to relax, to be out there in nature. Do some kayaking, hiking, reading. No televisions, no pollution, just slow food, luxurious accommodations, the ocean, and old growth forest right at your doorstep. Plus, this particular resort had a yoga/meditation component, as well as a full schedule of speakers who specialized in personal growth. It was very exclusive," Heather finally said, trying to find something that would impress the Nurse.

"It sounds boring. Why would anyone pay to go to something like that?"

Heather remembered why she didn't make a habit of torturing herself trying to explain to a human of today the ways of the past. But on this day, she wanted to have her say. "I know it's hard for you to believe but people thought nature had merit back then. We were misguided so we did a poor job of showing our affinity, but at least it was there."

"Yeah, but what about that other stuff? What was that all about?"

"I was looking for something. With my mother gone, I felt I had to pick up the slack. She'd always been the one keeping me informed. For years I had let her do the work for the both of us. As a matter of fact, I felt quite smug that she was doing the work of two or three; therefore, I had a pass to do nothing. It was my wish to get off my ass and get involved that caused me trouble with Ricky. As you can see from his choice in women, Ricky was in a rut." As soon as she said it she couldn't keep from giggling. "No pun intended, by the way. He simply liked his women young, built, blonde, beautiful, and nothing more."

Terra Dime

***

When the pilot dipped the wing, she got her first glimpse of the Olympic Peninsula that included Mount Olympus, Hurricane Ridge, the historic seaport of Port Townsend, and the relentless plume of smoke rising from the mill at Port Angeles. As he leveled the seaplane, she saw the near perfect cone of Mount Baker rising through wisps of cloud. Over the Strait of Juan de Fuca, an oil tanker plied its way east and even from this distance Heather was struck by the enormity of the vessel.

And then they were over the southwest end of Vancouver Island. Immediately, she was struck by how lush and green it was below. But before she knew it, invisible topography under great stands of evergreens met massive inland scars of scraped hillsides. The gnarled remnants of vegetation scant on soft clay banks. Here, the lay of the land was plain to see. Flat spots that turned to slippery slopes descended into sheer drop-offs all crisscrossed by logging roads. The pilot watched and waited for her to comment on these, so that he could give her his "good for the economy" speech, and put her in her place. She was her mother's daughter after all and her position on clear cutting climax forest was well known. But Heather knew better than to get him going.

The clear cuts turned to miles of beach stretching out beneath the floats of the plane. From up above like she was, the ocean was without definition, all white squiggly lines disintegrating on the sand. The Sound, her destination, came into view just as the plane began to descend. The water's hue turned deep and rich; the surrounding land remote and mysterious. As the seaplane skidded across the surface the troubles that had dominated her thoughts for weeks, slipped away. She was overcome by the vastness of it all. She could see herself as she never had before – a minute dot clinging to life on a tiny planet floating in an infinite universe. The whole imagery, that she was capable of it, shocked her. And she felt something else. Some gear shifting anticipation that moved her senses to a different level.

It was so big – the sky, the forest, the glassy water reflecting it back. Distracted by the beauty, it took a second to see they were making their way towards a dock jutting out from the shore. As she continued to take it all in,

The Institution

the Range Rover that would whisk her through the forest to the Spa eased its way out of the wilderness.

"Looks like your ride has arrived," the pilot said. Other than to point out some geographic features along the way, these were the only words he had spoken since leaving Seattle. So torn was he by how beautiful and famous she was, along with the added burden of her politics that were in direct conflict with his own, he didn't believe they had anything in common. Their shared humanity was not enough. And so the time was squandered. Before he knew it, she and her belongings were loaded into the waiting vehicle and gone from sight.

All was quiet when the SUV came to a stop alongside steps leading up to a boardwalk that seemed to run for only a short distance before disappearing into deeper forest. "This way," the driver said as he stepped onto the wooden path. She followed him along planks floating through ferns so rich in color she was aware of their being alive. Their fronds danced and shimmered with something intangible. When they came to an intersection, they took the one that wound its way to the left, the one marked with a sign labeled *Zen View Suite*.

"This is it," he said as they approached the rear of a white canvas structure. An inauspicious arrival, unlike the usual scurrying about upon her appearance at an exclusive resort. It had the look of a prospector's tent nestled inside decking constructed with railings of gnarled branches that had been gathered from the surrounding forest. She was speechless when he pushed open the low curved gate and unlatched the flap of a door. She got her Zen views – the kind that did not lay it all out in a single frame but enticed with greater possibility. A fraction of the Pacific framed in one transparent panel, the peeling russet bark of an Arbutus in another, and a rocky outcropping peeking out from below in a third. Heather walked over to the bed and fingered the gauzy fabric that cascaded from the canopy. She couldn't help herself. It was something out of *The Arabian Nights*. She found the opening and poked her head inside while running the palm of her hand along fine silky pillows in shades of purple and orange.

Knowing what she was thinking, the driver said, "They're not silk – they're bamboo fiber. We try to be as environmentally aware as possible."

105

"Bamboo, really? They're exquisite." When she turned around the anticipation of spending time in this place showed on her face.

"I think you like it here. Am I not right?" he stated.

She nodded in the affirmative. "I like it a lot."

He showed her the composting toilet and explained how only ecologically-sensitive soaps and shampoos could be used in her private outdoor shower. But he saved the best for last when he led her onto the front deck. "These steps lead down to a trail that will take you to the beach. You can stop there or you can follow it for about a hundred-mile round trip. I don't recommend you do that alone, though, and you'll want to be here for dinner. The Chef is preparing West Coast Paella tonight. There will be tapas to start. All sorts of delicious dishes. The kitchen has smelled fantastic all afternoon. Sunday is a fun, get acquainted kind of night since it's when a new round of guests arrives. I hope you won't miss it."

"Oh no, I'll be there," she said easing into one of the deck chairs no longer able to restrain herself from enjoying the suite. "That is, if I can drag myself away from this spot."

"Would you like a glass of wine? There is some waiting for you in the fridge. I'd be happy to pour you one," he offered.

She was still looking around in wonder when he returned. "I've never been in a climax forest before," she explained. "Unbelievable."

"It is mesmerizing. I'm not looking forward to the end of summer. Going back to school, you know. I'm really going to feel the loss."

"Where is school?"

"Back east – McGill."

"Can't you come back next year?"

"No," he said and the finality of it was disheartening. "I'm entering my fourth year. Time for me to go out and get a job. Sit behind a desk for the next forty or fifty years. I can hardly wait."

"There doesn't appear to be any good choices, does there?"

"Oh I don't know, your choice of occupation looks good."

"Until you get to a certain age. Then it suddenly turns on you."

The look on his face was one of complete disbelief. There was no way, given the opportunity, that he wouldn't jump at the chance to change places with her. He placed a tray on the table at her side.

"This is a B.C. Guwertztraminer. I hope you like it. I also thought you might be hungry so I brought out some flat bread and a vegetable paté. Both are made here at the resort. And I sliced up a peach as well. They just arrived from the Okanagan region of B.C. and they pair perfectly with the wine."

"Why thank you. I believe I'm going to sit here and relax. The unpacking can wait 'til later."

"Unless you need something else, I'll be on my way."

Over the next two days, Heather spent hours attending what were termed personal growth sessions. Meditating, exploring the metaphysical, trying to discover the road to spiritual enlightenment, that sort of thing. She'd heard it all before, given that it was all the rage those days amongst the Hollywood crowd. It always left her wanting though. There was something fundamentally lacking in those messages. It was the same old escapism. An icky kind of make-believe in which you sought a way to convince yourself you would live forever. What difference did it make whether it was Heaven, Shangri-La, or reincarnation? From what she had seen there were myriad ways to escape. Drugs, alcohol, gambling, television, vacations, second homes, and overspending came to mind. All sorts of entertainment to block out the human condition. That reminded her of the title of a book she'd seen on a shelf somewhere – *Amusing Ourselves to Death* – wasn't that the truth.

Heather decided what she really needed was a break from the same blather she'd been hearing back in Southern California. The stuff her contemporaries spouted off about, as if they were in some higher state of consciousness, which she rather doubted. On the third day of her stay, while the majority of the guests attended their sessions, Heather slipped down to the beach at dawn and with some effort lifted a kayak into the water. This wasn't something guests were supposed to do alone. Protocol was to tag along with another group for liability and safety reasons. But she had done it their way yesterday and it hadn't been the experience she was hoping for. It had been mainly honeymooners. First and second, as well as third-time-arounders all in a self-proclaimed state of wedded bliss. The babbling on and on was not only exhausting but also demoralizing. It was so late by the time they got going, the water had ruffled up with an onshore breeze making the paddling tricky and the visibility poor. They missed all of the promised wildlife sightings the brochures raved about.

She intended to make up for that. Currently, the conditions were perfect. In water smooth and glassy she was sure to spot something. She paddled towards the north side of the Sound in the opposite direction from the one taken the day before. Meandering along close to the shore watching it change in character from the sandy stretch in front of the Eco Spa to steep rocky ledges. It wasn't long before she spotted a head barely above the surface surveying her from a short distance away. Other curious heads popped up to join his. She knew they were otters when they began to dive, one after the other, long shiny tails propelling them into the depths. Before she turned around and headed back to the Spa she saw a sea lion doing the breaststroke off the bow of the boat. She heard him blow rhythmically as he swam a straight line in her path before slowing and then turning over to take a closer look, his flippers hovering above the water like helicopter blades. And when she was sure she had seen her fill for the day, a line of porpoises looped along the surface parallel to the kayak, so close she wondered if they were aware of her proximity. As if in answer to her unspoken thought, one broke away from the pod and rolled onto his back so that she could see his face lifted out of the sea, looking over at her, the curve of his mouth giving her the impression that he was smiling.

By the time she was back at the Spa undoing the skirt and jumping out of the boat, she was flying. Her T-shirt was soaked in sweat from the pace of her paddle. She looked around for someone to share the experience with but the beach was deserted. Tired, she struggled to get the kayak out of the water and back where she found it, having to set it down several times along the way. With that task completed, she turned back toward the Sound still tingling with the thrill of her encounters. It was then that she realized she wasn't alone. Someone sat beneath a rocky outcropping partially shaded by the hill leading up to the Resort. Although he did appear to be engrossed in his pen and paper, it surprised her that he hadn't offered assistance while she battled with the kayak.

He looked up as she approached. "Looks like you were first one out this morning. I'm not used to anyone getting a head start on me."

"Your late start? Is that why you didn't drag yourself away from what you're doing to help me with the kayak? I can't believe you sat here and watched me struggle like that. You probably got a good laugh out of it."

"Oh no, the progress I'm making with this," he pointed to the tablet he held in his hand, "would not suffer from an interruption or two. I was afraid you'd be insulted if I offered assistance. You might think I was insinuating you're a weak woman who can't get by on her own. It's hard to know the right thing to do in every circumstance, don't you think? Sometimes I have no idea. But I thought that if I left you alone you'd figure it out. And you did."

"You think too much," she stated. "What are you working on anyway? Are you an artist?" she ventured a guess.

"A writer."

"Really? What kind of stories do you write?"

"Not stories, actually. Non-fiction. I guess I'm what you would call a cultural critic. I write about humanity, civilization, the why of things. What I'm working on right now though has really got me stymied."

"Writer's block. I've heard about that."

He was trying to be cool about this lull in mental breakthroughs but it was starting to wear on him. Until recently, he could count on a passage in a book or a conversation or one of his own thoughts to start a chain reaction. His mind would open wide and reach until he was so aware of everything he could sense his brain expanding into new territory. During stretches like those, when his mind felt exposed, he saw a direction to take. New connections were made. The thoughts and ideas that flowed made him prolific for years.

"It's more like ideas block. That's much worse," he responded. "I've never had it before."

"These things you say you write about, they sound heavy. Have you actually been published?" she asked, suddenly realizing that he was only about thirty-five years old and might be full of it. It wouldn't be the first time some loser tried to ingratiate himself with her.

"Uh huh, that's why you haven't seen me in the dining room. I'm not a regular paying guest. I'm here to give workshops and to lend a certain cerebral cachet to the place. Mention how the resort provided an indispensable venue for putting together the text of this current masterpiece." Again, he indicated the barely used tablet for emphasis.

"Man, what are you trying to write about that's got you so freaked out? Maybe you should get in one of those kayaks and take a paddle around. But don't expect me to help you get it into the water," she teased. Heather went on to explain all that she had seen that morning and how it had done wonders for her. "I can't remember a time in my life when I felt so satisfied. It might relax you a little too. You know, so you can think."

"Believe me I've tried. I live on the water full time in Washington State. It's been my experience that I do better with my thinking and writing when I'm surrounded by the worst circumstances. Sometimes it doesn't pay to be too content," he explained. "You see, what I'm trying to put into words is a concept for the future. A civilization beyond what we have right now. Something palatable and sustainable. Something people would be excited about."

She looked completely baffled. "For real? That's what you're thinking and writing about? Not much wonder you're all messed up."

"It occurs to me that civilizations are like living organisms. They lose their vitality, become ill, and eventually die when not provided some kind of nourishment. Ideas, vision, goals are the food of advanced civilizations. We should expect to atrophy without them. And we appear to be withering in the most extraordinary, very public way. Have you listened to the news lately? Entertainment, politics, our whole culture is a human freak show."

It occurred to her that he did not realize her role in the entertainment portion of that freak show and this surprised her more than his writing project. She was not offended by his honest disgust. Hers was a superficial, opportunistic way to make a living. She had come to grips with that a long time ago.

"What's your name by the way?" she asked.

"Jerome Raines, or Jerry if you like," he answered extending his hand. "And yours?" He asked her this because he really didn't know.

"Heather Holmes." Still no recognition of her super star status. But his name did ring a bell with her. "Wait a minute. Jerome Raines? Didn't you get into trouble a while back with that kooky right wing talk show guy?"

The Institution

"That was me. He didn't like one of my books. It was *The Left Behind Paradox*. I questioned whether people ought to be more concerned about being left behind in the wisdom and understanding departments rather than missing the boat on being sucked up into Heaven." It struck him how he kept butting up against this same obsession in various guises. Again, it was all about literal transport. In this case the belief in an actual leap into Heaven in lieu of an intangible, conscious shift in perception that is heavenly.

"It was what I said during an interview on the Canadian public radio station that got him worked up. He must have a crew of minions out there waiting for someone to say something he can seize upon. The funny thing is that it was completely non-scripted. I spent years writing that book and it was disparaged for a line that wasn't even in it."

"Please, refresh my memory about what you said."

"Instead of worrying about saving our souls, we ought to be worried about saving our asses."

"Ah yes, we sure can get worked up about the silliest things. What a waste of energy." Heather laughed, remembering the brouhaha that had ensued. She was sure it made the entire talk radio circuit, late night comedy shows, everything. "That was a great line. I'm definitely going to get my hands on that book now. So, do you have a title or an outline for this new book of yours?"

"The working title is *Turning on the 'digm*."

"Turning on the Dime? Like a sharp change in direction?"

"That's part of it. It has a double meaning. It's apostrophe D-I-G-M," he said spelling it out. "You know, like paradigm. Turning away from the current paradigm and creating a new one," he sighed. "I thought it was good."

"No, it is clever. I would have got it if I'd seen it written down. Honest." And she continued to stand there waiting for him to say something more. "So are you going to elaborate?"

"I'm not sure where to start. It's hard to explain because I don't know where *you're* coming from. That's the difficult part. Knowing how much to assume someone knows."

111

"Explain it to me from your perspective. Don't worry about how uninformed I am. I can always ask questions. Besides, good ideas can be like good food and their appeal is universal."

"Well, you see, in addition to writing non-fiction, I also read quite a bit of it too. What I've noticed is that all these authors, me included, are excellent at identifying problems. Where we seem to fall short is solutions. My thought was to approach this book differently. Devote one chapter to what's wrong and nine to recommendations for making life better instead of the other way around. It seemed like a good idea at the time."

"But it doesn't any more?"

"I now realize why authors generally don't take this approach. There are no solutions within the current model so that means almost everything about our lives would have to change. Think many people are going to want to hear that? This is the only time I can remember feeling concerned about how I will be perceived after a book is published."

"My mother always used to say and I quote, 'If you're not making people uncomfortable, you're not doing your job as a citizen of the planet.'"

"There is something indelible about putting ideas like this onto paper. Someone will think to attach some sort of 'ism to the concept. Most likely socialism, ala Upton Sinclair. Once you get labeled it's hard to have any credibility after that. I'm prepared to insert a disclaimer explaining this is the best I can come up with at my current level of development, but I'm hopeful that further personal Evolution will improve my perspective. That's in case I'm embarrassed about my naiveté in the not too distant future – like when the critics go after me."

"It sounds like you've already thought it through and come up with some sort of solution. Is it only fear that's preventing you from putting it onto paper?"

Jerome did not answer her right away. Instead he asked, "Have you ever noticed that you can tell what someone values above everything else by his version of utopia?"

She smiled at his unfamiliarity with what most people were thinking about. If he wished to be blown away, she could provide thousands of pieces of fan mail substantiating the meager range of human thoughts. "No, I can't say I have considered that." And then she eased herself down onto a huge log that had washed up onto the beach sometime in the distant past. The sun was well up over the hill behind them now. She stretched out her legs and leaned back to soak up the morning rays and the foreign territory this conversation was now entering.

"Did you ever read *Atlas Shrugged*?" When Heather indicated she had, he continued. "Ayn Rand's utopia as envisioned by her character John Galt was based on industry and business. She believed the economic money making machine left to its own devices will do what's ethical. Technology will save us, that sort of thing. It's a great coming of age story when one is heading out into the workforce for the first time all idealistic. It is stunning in its ignorance of power and greed though."

"Hmm, I see what you mean. Like my mother. Being that she was first and foremost a new-age deep ecologist, her utopia would be an egalitarian, granola-eating, birkenstock-wearing, Gaia-protecting, living-off-nature kind of place. Everything else would be secondary. I'm not sure anyone would even sit down to a cooked meal. Their ideal day would be little more than wandering around feeling the energy in places that were sacred."

"I don't believe I would thrive in that environment. First of all, I don't like the word sacred. It conjures up images of religious figures giving their blessings to places they perceive as having merit. Personally, I feel the whole planet is something to be revered and should be treated as such," Jerome interjected.

"How differently we would behave if we felt that to be true."

"There's the religious view of the Promised Land. It has the flock following a very specific code of moral conduct as written down in a book and interpreted by some sort of spiritual leader. A community incurious and under control looking to the heavens for happiness. Even in the more spiritually advanced religious sects, there is this element of seeking a specific set of breakthroughs on the way to enlightenment. It's preordained. Our destiny as human beings has already been written. The common thread running through religious utopias is achieving everlasting life through a connection with the Creator. They are all based on human self-love, narcissism so pronounced that a single species believes anything as wonderful as Planet Earth could only have been created with them in mind.

"And what about survivalists," he continued. "Ever met any of those? I know people who dream of a return to primitivism as the ultimate reality. Back to the hunter/gatherer stage, as if caveman represented humanity in its highest form and that we can't do any better than that. They want no civilization of any kind. All that we have learned, all the beauty we are capable of creating is meaningless. We would be better off if all the great inventors, writers, thinkers, artists had never been born."

"Yuk, I hope you've come up with something better than that." That particular Utopian vision gave her the heeby jeebys something fierce. Some Cro-Magnon clubbing her over the head and dragging her back to his cave. No thanks.

"If what you say is true, there must be something shaping your view. What do you value above everything else?" Heather asked.

"You're right. There is something. And that's one of the things that bothers me. I've always prided myself in being an informed, well-rounded generalist with an understanding of how it all works. Wrapping your mind around the complete system makes you whole. Once you do that, you realize there are certain beliefs – economic, political, moral even – upon which western civilization is based, that are going to have to be rejected. In suggesting we have a flawed belief system, I'm exhibiting a prejudice. In choosing which of our cultural blind spots are holding us back, my own prejudices come into play. By reaching the conclusion that it is imperative some significant cultural Evolution takes place, I am again making an assumption based on personal prejudice. It's obvious the lion's share of the population doesn't share my concerns."

"That doesn't mean you shouldn't write it. I don't imagine the general public was begging for a 'Theory of Relativity,' do you?"

"That was different. There's something about suggesting to people that they examine their lives. They will dig in and justify the most inane behavior. How about *Ishmael* by Daniel Quinn? Ever read that?"

"Oh sure, I remember when that was all the rage. My mom lived and died by that book."

"Then you're familiar with how he portrays Mother Culture. How convinced we are that the beliefs we share about our own history are real. What it means to be successful, who we fear, admire, all trickles down from

The Institution

that. It is lore on which our civilization was built and on which it depends to continue in the same fashion. We are defenders of the lore, not defenders of the truth particularly if the two aren't one and the same. We're very adept at finding ways to keep the whole thing plugging along when lifestyles depend on it. It's changing course that we don't do well. Just before I left to come here I was reading that NASA intends to have a permanent human colony on the moon by 2024. From there it will be much easier to explore Mars and points beyond. In addition to a space program it was also being touted as a commercial enterprise. There will be construction and service opportunities with all those human beings living in outer space. Think of what will go into simply keep us alive and happy in a place where we can't breath without assistance. We're supposed to believe that it will all be worth it because of the whack of natural resources waiting to be extracted. The article was sincere in its pronouncement that this represents the only chance of a future for the human race what with Global Warming and other catastrophes awaiting us. This colonizing of space, this extension of our bad habits into other realms, was portrayed as more logical than rethinking the way we live so that our prospects here on earth aren't so bleak. If there has ever been a more telling case of our being a bunch of one-trick ponies who are doomed, I haven't come across it."

She couldn't keep herself from laughing. "Sorry. Can you imagine what it would be like to discover oil on the Moon and then transport it back to Planet Earth? What would we do? Reconfigure spaceships into huge oil tankers? Or would we drag big barges of the stuff back to our thirsty planet? The best though is picturing pipelines snaking throughout the solar system. I can see what they mean by business opportunities. Discovering oil in outer space would be an economic windfall. Can't you just picture it? A 'big as Texas' mindset on the moon and beyond?"

"No, you've got it wrong. We won't be dragging any of the stuff back here. Once we've stripped the earth of its natural resources, it will be of no use to us. Look at the way we treat the planet. Obviously, we have no allegiance to this place. We'll be abandoning 'the third rock from the sun' in droves. We'll probably have to come up with a lottery system to handle the demand to leave. I could already sense the disdain, or maybe desperation is a better word, in the tone of that article. There was this

115

underlying urgency to cut our losses with this planet and get enthusiastic about a new one. The human being can be fixated on the afterlife, a second life, or a new life in outer space. What we don't have is a burning desire to create a life we don't have to escape from, right here, on good old Planet Earth. I don't know how to generate that kind of desire."

"Ah, so now we're to the real reason you're sitting there with a big pad of empty pages gripped in your hand. You don't think there's any point. You've already written the whole thing off."

He did not answer the question directly because giving up was something he was trying to avoid. "There's another reason why this talk of space travel has resurfaced – civilization exhaustion. There's a growing anxiety about the future. Surely, even this lousy government is aware of it. The thing is, if the government could do something to stave off the looming collapse, it wouldn't. The powerful people, the ones who got them elected, don't want anything to change because they're getting richer by the minute just the way things are. Which leaves few options other than creating a diversion. Get the voting public focused away from Planet Earth where all the failures are staring them straight in the face. Every leader knows, when you're way over your head in big problems, it's best to focus on something completely unrelated, insignificant, and doable. We have made it to the moon a time or two before. At least I think we have," he said in honor of the conspiracy theories surrounding that accomplishment.

"There's another added bonus with this space travel thing. The general public won't believe how close the planet is to running low on oil if the government is willing to squander millions of barrels of the stuff. We'll be less inclined to demand alternatives which the government also can't come up with."

"Can't or won't?" Heather asked because according to her mother it had always been a question of won't. She firmly believed the alternatives and the technology were there. It was big oil or big business preventing it from getting to the marketplace.

"Can't. We are living on ancient sunlight, millions of years worth. And by the looks of things we're going to blow through those millions of years of stored energy in about one hundred and fifty years. We've built a whole way of life, a whole way of thinking even, that cannot function on a lesser energy source. We designed for the most powerful and adaptable. How are we going to scale back when 95% of our manufactured goods depend on it? Food production, food delivery, modern medicine, construction, transportation, everything. And all these educated people we've been cranking out of the universities for decades, most of them aren't even willing to discuss it. Every generation says either one of two things; 'As long as it doesn't run out before I die,' or 'they'll come up with something' without understanding that we solved the easy stuff a long time ago. What's left is way over our heads."

"If I were to believe what you just said, I'd have to completely change the way I see the future. I grew up believing it would only get better. We'd be living so long and so well we would be overwhelmed with the leisure hours at our disposal. Call me naïve, but I thought war, especially over religion, would be a thing of the past. And to be honest with you I thought we would already have colonies on other planets, we would have found life in another solar system, and we'd be zipping around like the Jetsons. Cancer was supposed to have been cured, spinal cords repaired, and life expectancies would be in the neighborhood of one hundred and fifty years."

"I hate to be the bearer of reality, Heather, but none of those things has happened."

"I know. But I haven't thought much about the things that haven't gone the way they were supposed to. It's going to take me more than five minutes to adjust. Not for one moment have I considered a diminished future. Even my mother who ranted around about environmental degradation didn't believe we wouldn't find an answer. Why do you think that is?"

"Did you know it takes between eight and thirteen years for a child to learn everything he needs to be fully indoctrinated into our civilization and function adequately. Around that time he quits absorbing information about the finer points, the ones his parents are unaware of, the ones he's not curious about. From that point on, even though there's a wealth of information to access and plenty to be gleaned from what's going on around him, it starts to bounce off. His personal philosophy and his worldview are set. He knows everything he needs to survive – not to improve, just to survive. It helps to explain a few things, doesn't it? Like the immaturity of our popular culture and the circular nature of concerns and conflicts. Revisiting the Wall Street excesses of the 1920s strikes me as redundant. As does modern youth wishing to recreate the 1960s right down to the bell-bottom pants, tie-dyed shirts, and drug culture. Ditto for war of any kind. And the fact that raping and pillaging continues to factor in to every conflict, how low is that? Behavior *that* bad, you'd think we'd have left behind. But we can't, because the same thirteen years worth of knowledge and understanding keeps getting re-circulated. We are being led by politicians, dictated to by corporate executives, and sadly yes, making love to spouses with the minds of thirteen-year olds. It makes the task at hand seem futile."

"I can vouch for the thirteen-year old spouse," Heather offered. "And his propensity for do-overs, at least in the marriage department, is legendary. But wow, to think that a philosophy as immature as his determines our direction is not reassuring. So what is the answer – more education?"

"I hesitate to use the word education. A bunch of politicians will jump on the bandwagon eager to argue that we need more engineers and scientists and such. And then throw billions of dollars at it. That's not what I'm talking about. Spitting out more experts in a narrow field won't help and that's all we'll get with our current education system as it is geared towards specialization. All it does is leave us unable to think critically outside a narrow area of expertise. It teaches young minds to be satisfied doing repetitive tasks, conforming, following orders. The current education system encourages status quo thinking."

Heather was now hunched over with a big frown on her face stealing nothing more than glances at him out of the corner of her eye. Jerome was attuned to this change in body language. "You're looking at me as if you're uncomfortable with what I'm saying," he said. "Why is that?"

"Education is all we have. It's the great equalizer, isn't it? I don't want to be back like we were a few hundred years ago when only a select few received an education. Women will be one of the casualties if we return to the past and that concerns me."

"Do you think there are only two choices – the past or the present?"

The Institution

"I don't know of anything else. I don't have that vision thing you're talking about. Come on, give me a break. Even the President and the three branches of government don't have it. How can you expect me to?"

"Do you think there's any chance we're all products of a failed education system that taught us a version of the past, prepared us to fit into the present, but fell short when it came to encouraging us to envision a system with a future?"

"I suppose you could be right, but it's really hard for me to think about it in that way. And I don't want to be seen as an ingrate. The system has been good to me. I can't see how it could be any better than it is right now. You go to school so you can get a job so you can have food on the table and a roof over your head. I know I'm not the smartest person in the world, but I'll tell you what, another way just doesn't jump out at me."

"You're right about that, education is a means to an end. And that end is not advancement of the species as it would be under ideal circumstances. It's about creating personal wealth and a robust economy. That boils down to a means to maintain our system as it stands right now. Ironically enough, all the emphasis on material wealth has not translated into freedom from worry about being cold and going hungry. In the most affluent nation in the world, the majority is a month's pay away from being on the street. That seems peculiar to me. The fear of not fulfilling our basic survival needs still consumes our lives. The whole notion of the human condition conjures up the same hopeless image year after year. I guess at some point we're going to have to ask ourselves: What exactly is the long-term plan? Are we going to keep recycling those same eight to thirteen years of cultural beliefs indefinitely? Or are we going to make an effort to liberate ourselves from cultural insanity?"

By this time Heather had grown very quiet. He had moved way beyond her frame of reference. Although he was still speaking English, the thoughts were foreign, so she was unable to translate them into a familiar lexicon. What he was saying should be important to her, but it wasn't for the simple reason that she did not know about it. There was no bringing it all into focus when the prevailing cultural lens had a blurring component built right in. It was the obstacle Jerome had not figured a way to get around.

"I really do want to know what you think," he said. "You're helping me get a sense of how what I'm writing will be received. That's a knowledge I tend to lack. I can't help but feel that when you're talking about education you're defending it in its purely idealistic form. Is there any chance you're repeating a standard cultural line and failing to incorporate what you're really seeing out there? We have spent thousands of years educating ourselves. Are you impressed with our progress, popular culture, political discourse? Has our education system produced citizens up to the task of preventing the crash we now appear to be waiting for like a bunch of deer in the headlights?"

As far as progress was concerned, she lived a gilded existence. Her life was a series of parties and vacations. When it came to popular culture, that was the key to her lifestyle. Her views on politics had been so shaped by her mother; she couldn't honestly pass them off as her own. But there was something about education that she did wonder about. She had a niece and two nephews who were at various stages in their schooling and professional careers. As much as she tried to be happy for them, their prospects made her uneasy.

"Hmmm, I think I see what you mean. It's difficult to let go and be honest with yourself. There is something I've found peculiar lately about post-secondary education, but I haven't wanted to consider it. Every year it seems more schooling is required just to provide for the basics. Twelve years used to get you better than subsistence, but now sixteen years is necessary, actually thirty-two if you consider two parents working, to ensure food and housing. That means we're investing more to get less. When an advanced education provides only the basic needs, that's not a very good trend is it?"

"No, it's not. The more sophisticated a society is, the more likely individuals are to support systems that don't necessarily improve their own material circumstances as long as their basic needs are met. Or in other words, the more developed you are, the less you demand for yourself. We can't expect citizens to make that leap when they're in constant fear of being destitute. So you can see how education quits being about improving the human condition and becomes tailored to fit the marketplace. Contrary to what some loud-mouthed analysts say, the marketplace doesn't always give us what we need."

"I know how members of my family make a living. I'd be lying if I didn't tell you how boring it sounds. In Southern California, the freeways are clogged with people driving back and forth to work everyday and I wonder what they're all doing. It's overwhelming to think about all those people striving to earn a living and to think about how much we need just to get by."

"You're right about the jobs we're doing. The ones we're spending sixteen to eighteen years in school in order to perform. They are boring as well as repetitive and meaningless to boot. If you don't believe me on this, try going to a High School Reunion. More shocking than how old and fat everyone is, is what they're doing for a living. Talk to your peers who were the most impressive in their early years. The ones you thought might change the world are now kept occupied designing bedpans, moving pixels around on a screen, or performing administrative functions they can't begin to explain. That's far more depressing than a few wrinkles and a bit of blubber. Why aren't we lamenting that the spontaneous abortion of both mind and character is a prerequisite for earning a decent living? Have you seen the latest list of fastest-growing jobs over the next few years? It's enough to make you cry.

"Ever wonder why we prefer fantasy over reality and why we are all caught up in creating drama? Or why we favor reliving the same programs, the same sporting events? All that tradition crap. They're all coping mechanisms to deal with the boredom. And yet another irony of our culture is that our potential is far more fantastic than any religious story or contrived excitement we've cooked up.

"But culture's a dictatorship and not a benevolent one at that. It packs a powerful prejudicial wallop that's blinding. It can change values in the blink of an eye for better or worse. Biological Evolution meanders along at a snail's pace, but cultural Evolution can turn everything on its head overnight. Culture is about believing in a certain set of truths regardless of their actual merit. If we decide a new set of truths is where it's at, how we live right now goes out the window. It's as simple as that."

Terra Dime

Heather was intent on not being offended. His criticisms were not directed at her personally. The whole mainstream culture disillusioned her as well. So it seemed silly to defend a way of living as if it were perfect. Western civilization was based on economic growth and she knew, in her mind, it was finite. There was nothing to defend. It was the other thing he said about our true nature that intrigued her. She had not considered that some of our urges are biological and some are cultural. Or that culture could be used as a tool to shove humanity in a direction that was beneficial biologically. It wasn't easy for her to articulate any of this.

"Is improving the quality of man really possible? Can we change the future by choosing a different set of values today? I've never thought about it that way before. I've thought all along that human nature is what drives everything but you're saying it's human culture and it can be changed. *Change your values, change the world.* What a great slogan. Instead of Victory Gardens to win a war we could have Victory Values to save our asses." She thought she was pretty funny if she did say so herself. "I don't mean to be flippant. I'm easily amused. I've been married to three different dullards. What can you expect?"

"Three?"

"Not all at the same time."

"But still, that's a lot of husbands. You're not that old."

"It's not so many. At least not in the circles I travel. Thanks for noticing that I'm not that old. Now can we change the subject? My choice in men is very boring, believe me."

When Jerome looked towards the Sound he noticed clouds had moved in. Nothing more than a wedge of sunlight lay across the water. He looked back at the blonde woman seated beside him and wondered why she was still sitting there listening to him and hadn't left already. It occurred to him that he shouldn't strike up a conversation like this whenever the mood struck him.

"I'm not boring you to death, am I? If I am, tell me, and I'll go away."

"No, not at all. I'm interested. You've probably saved me having to read a dozen books with what you know."

The Institution

"It's better to read the book for yourself," he said. "But here's something I didn't read. This is my own. I know this is going to surprise you, but I have a theory – one of many. This one concerns your level of immersion in the mainstream culture. If you have a toe in it, just enough to keep track of the temperature, you're alright. Only up to your knees, you're weighing the conditions before taking the plunge. Waist-deep, you're drowning and it will take a powerful life preserver to pull you out, so you better be worth it. Fully immersed, don't even bother with Search & Rescue, you're already gone."

"That's it – only four categories? I think I'm somewhere between the knees and the waist. With just the right kind of flotation device I know I could be prevented from sinking further."

"It's doubtful that you'll be put to the test. I think we're destined not to reach our potential as a species. We could have used all the years we've spent educating ourselves for a moment such as this, but instead we're going to squander it. That's my prejudice. I favor a scholarly solution, a scholastic option. I favor creating living arrangements that enhance behavior, creativity, and thought. Two of the really major differences between us and the rest of the animal kingdom are the size of our brains and these."

He held out his large hands, palms open. "It might not seem so right now but there are better uses for these than checking for e-mails and sending text messages. I want to be part of a curious, doubting, not quite so self-satisfied population that instead of rattling on about how great it is attempts to become wonderful. I would like to be surrounded by people who are secure enough to see our civilization as a work in progress, know the future lies in personal and cultural Evolution, and be okay with that. I'm talking about activating our minds. There is no excuse for being willfully ignorant. Not to apply knowledge and understanding when they are most needed is completely inexcusable.

"The moral of the story is we learn only to increase our standard of living. We do this at the expense of quality of life, quality of discourse, of life period. At some point, I'm going to have to face that we'll never be more than we are right now. Sometimes I sense this impatience all around me. Like the whole planet, possibly the universe, is holding its breath waiting to leap forward, waiting on us. And we're out of time."

"Does that mean you're not going to bother with the book? Somebody has to do something, don't they?"

"No, I'll write the book. But it won't make a difference. I'm afraid the need for change has already exceeded our desire for it by many decades."

"Seriously, I'd be willing to make changes in my life if they would translate into something meaningful like no one ever having to lose his life, limbs, or mental health in a war again. I'm ready for a change. And I can't believe I'm the only one. Listen to this. I can come up with a bunch of different ways to say it. I'm Sick of Spending, Maxed out on Meaningless, Tired of the Titillating, Bloated on the Banal." And just when it looked like she was on a roll that had no end in sight, she gestured with a nod of her head towards a man at the water's edge who had been trying to get her attention for several minutes. "Pissed off by the Primitive," she said rather loudly because she didn't care if he heard and knew he wouldn't get it if he did.

He had noticed the guy watching her for the last five minutes and up until then she had either not seen him or pretended she didn't. Jerome, on the other hand, hadn't been able to take his eyes off the slack face and moist, loose lips that quivered with expectation. He was single-minded in his purpose, sneaking up on unwitting prey. His was a mind emptied of all human qualities. A wish to DO her was the extent of his humanity. Jerome would be willing to bet money that if that guy got Heather cornered, he could scream, throw stones, turn a hose on him and he would not retreat.

"So what do you think? Biologically, culturally, or educationally deficient?" Heather asked sweetly.

"All of the above. I think he's managed to get by without soaking in even the requisite eight years."

"Got any suggestions about what to do with the likes of him?"

"No need to be snide, Heather. There can't be that many out there like him."

"Jerome, there are hundreds of thousands of guys just like that. Believe me, I know. Guys like that are my life." A pained look passed over her face and she turned away so he wouldn't see it. He took that opportunity to look at her more closely and it dawned on him that she was more than beautiful. She was exquisite. And there was something vaguely familiar about her. He bounced that thought around for a couple of seconds but couldn't come up with who she was. The more he delved into the human prospect, the more insurmountable it seemed. Some were left behind at their own behest, some by circumstance. But yet Heather, who evidently had first hand knowledge of the worst of the human condition, was at least willing to engage in a dialogue about cultural improvement. She had to have made that impartial step outside her own individual existence to talk with him about such things.

When Jerome looked again, the yahoo with the tan skin stretched taut over rippling muscles was still hoping to will her over his way. The guy was an energy sucker. All conversation had stopped and they both felt as if they were sinking. Heather stood up making sure she was at an angle to the beach so she could see out of the corner of her eye any quick movements from that direction. Jerome watched her instinctive body language with some distress.

"Look, I better be getting back to my room. I think I've missed breakfast. I don't want to miss lunch as well. It's been nice talking to you," she said. "Sorry about the creep. I imagine he'll leave as soon as I do."

"That's what I'm afraid of. Let me walk you back. I don't think you want him knowing where you're staying and that you're alone."

"Thanks. And please accept my apologies for the interruption. You're never going to get any writing done at this rate," she said as they crossed the beach with Jerome shielding her from a product of what we were certain was the most sophisticated, advanced civilization there ever was or ever could be.

***

"Surely you're not ending the story there?" Darlene asked after Heather lapsed into silence. Her eyes were fixed on a distant corner of the room but what she saw and remembered had turned inward. She let out an odd little sigh. It might have been of pleasure or regret. Darlene couldn't tell, but the suspense was killing her.

"So what happened next? I mean after he walked you back to your tent. Did you make good use of that bed, the Arabian one with all the netting around it? What was he like?"

Heather shook her head to indicate NO.

"NO you didn't do it or NO you won't tell me about it?"

"NO, we didn't make love."

"You didn't? I don't understand that at all. I thought that was going to be the whole point of the story. I have to say I'm disappointed. Usually, your man stories are better than that. I'm not sure why you bothered to tell me this one at all."

"I told you the story because he died last night. I thought you might be interested in knowing what he was about. And I guess I wanted to remember as well."

"Like when you got back to your tent he didn't even try to jump your bones?"

"He was too young for me."

"That never stopped you before."

"He wasn't like any of the guys I knew. It was complicated. Jerome's head was full of ideas but the one thought he failed to have was how appealing he was."

"So you were hoping he was going to make a pass at you weren't you? And if he had you would have had your panties off in no time. Isn't that right?"

Heather frowned at Darlene's imagery. "Have you ever loved so many parts of a person that the physical act of making love as we humans know it would not be nearly as sensuous, as say, sharing a thought?"

Darlene didn't know what to say to that. Of course she hadn't had the kind of experience Heather was talking about. It didn't exist except in the minds of old, sick people. Up until today, she hadn't thought this patient was much different from herself and her contemporaries. Now it was plain to see why she had to be committed. And yet, as she finished up her rounds, she couldn't get Mrs. Holmes' voice out of her head talking about the love of thoughts and such. The notion that some old woman knew something Darlene didn't was confusing, but it persisted. That crazy little seed kept poking around trying to put down roots. But not for long. As the end of the day neared, Darlene had swept aside all doubt.

She headed once again for the cafeteria and a hard earned coffee break and prepared herself for the last of her rounds. Coming to grips with Dr. Michael Sayer's frame of mind presented a challenge. On this day she wasn't up to it. How he could call himself a doctor was beyond her. His opinion of the medical profession was unethical. Listening to his version of the history of modern medicine was disturbing. It didn't matter that he couldn't practice any more. Once a physician took the Hippocratic oath his role was to save human lives and to ease pain and suffering without question. She'd never known of a medical professional to behave otherwise. She didn't understand the whole notion of personal philosophy. Imagining things differently, questioning our ways and then taking it to another level and questioning whether we were capable of seeing things the way they really are. How had he put it?

"We aren't curious enough to have any concept of the truth."

What did all that mean?

Darlene tried to understand Dr. Sayer more than she did the other patients because of the MD attached to his name. One night, early in her relationship with Dr. Marsh she had gone so far as to ask Doug about it. While they were lying in bed she let her guard down, started talking way too much, and asked him the same question that had been posed to her earlier in the day.

"Do you think the patients are physically healthier than we are?"

When Dr. Sayer made this observation, she had gotten defensive and denied that it was so. She hadn't given it another thought until later in the day when she began swallowing her daily regimen of maintenance drugs. Between pill #4, the purple one that she couldn't remember what it was even for and pill #5, the green one that she knew was a blood thinner because it was the most recently prescribed, she stopped and thought about what Dr. Sayer had said.

"Healthy people don't need to gorge themselves daily on pharmaceuticals to survive. Any drug that focuses on one condition impacts another part of us in a negative way. Each aspect of our health cannot be

looked at separately, not if we want to be truly well. It's where the medical profession went wrong right from the start. That whole reductionist way of thinking got us into the mess we're in."

Darlene didn't know to what he was referring when he said things like "the mess we're in." Everything seemed fine to her. But she did have first hand experience when it came to medicine and that was why her curiosity had been piqued enough to ask her lover, Dr. Marsh, the question. It was an instant antidote to the afterglow they'd been basking in.

"Of course they're not healthier than the hospital staff. Where would you get an idea like that? Never mind. Don't tell me. I know where – Michael Sayer, MD, right?" The cooing tone he typically used when he was in her bed and urging her on to sexual bliss had turned cold.

"I didn't take him seriously or anything. I know he has some issues about maintenance drugs and that's why he tries to make me feel guilty about the few I take. You see, he thinks that's significant, given that he's more than fifty years older than I am," she explained awkwardly, wishing she hadn't brought up any of this and fearing the worst type of reaction. Doug would be turned off for the night and she had her heart set on another ride.

Dr. Marsh was cutting in his response. "You talk too much. There is no reason for you to be telling the patients intimate details about your personal life. I hope you're more discrete when it comes to other matters."

"But Doug," she protested. "I don't tell them anything. They just know."

"Well that's impossible. You must be providing information without being aware of it."

She was miffed by this accusation. "I don't see how. Half the time it doesn't seem we're talking the same language."

"Look, the next time Dr. Sayer tries to brainwash you with his antiquated diagnoses you tell him any meds you've been prescribed are to prevent disease. As long as we keep addressing your health issues as they come up you will avoid any full-blown diseases. Soon, we will be living in the 'End of Disease Times.' You mark my words on that. This latest 'First Line Defense' family that is being tested right now is the best yet. It blows the last two generations away. There is relief on the horizon for conditions

The Institution

we didn't even know were conditions. I thank God everyday to know that within my lifetime, discomfort will be a thing of the past. And I strongly suggest you start doing the same." The more Dr. Marsh talked about it the hornier he got until Darlene could plainly see that one last ride was going to be a reality. She hadn't lied there a moment longer, but instead turned happily to the matter at hand.

Dr. Sayer was so far off the conventional medical rails, it was eerie. From what Darlene could piece together he had to give up his practice because he offended so many patients. He spent the last years of his career as an Emergency Room physician because discourse with patients was reduced. As a GP, he refused to prescribe medication if he thought a person didn't need it. His patients weren't very accepting of this and would be less than satisfied if they left his office without a prescription in hand. No one was happy about being cheated like that. If he told patients it was better to let what they had run its course or suggested a lifestyle change was in order, they didn't listen. They called him a quack and threatened to find another doctor – one who was freer with the pharmaceuticals.

This only served to make Dr. Sayer more disillusioned with both the medical profession and the pharmaceutical industry. Was it all a corrupt, money-making machine that had a vested interest in not finding cures? Offering perpetual treatment was what really generated steady income. The more he thought about it, the more convinced he became that good health, should it come about, would deliver a devastating wallop to the economy. He did not have to look any further than oncology to see the nation's GDP would be severely compromised if people quit needing cancer care. Whole careers had been created to cope with a single disease. Physicians specialized in cancer. Technicians were trained to administer radioactive substances for diagnosis and treatment. And where did those radioactive materials come from? Nuclear reactors, of course. We had to have reactors in order to produce isotopes for chemical therapy. Entire hospitals were built to treat patients with this dreaded disease and although the rate of death had declined, the rate of incidence was up, way up. Within one century it went from 5% to 50% and in 2005 he predicted statistically where they would be right now – 100%. He had also anticipated the complacency with which this grim indicator of human health would be met.

Terra Dime

The dialogue shifted in the 1990s toward management of disease through pharmaceutical chemical warfare and away from finding cures. And no one seemed to notice. In 2006, on the 25th anniversary of the detection of the HIV virus that causes AIDS, Dr. Sayer read an article that drew attention to the lack of progress being made in finding a cure. He was struck by how dismayed one of the researchers was about the scope of the failure. This guy had been working on it right from the start, for a full twenty-five years, and in his opinion they weren't any closer to understanding or curing the virus. This was not the success the researcher expected. Early on, he and his colleagues were cocky about having the thing solved in as little as five years.

Michael Sayer began to count off the number of discoveries in the 20th Century that struck him as markedly improving human health, and he could come up with only one – penicillin. Thanks to indiscriminate overuse, humanity was getting close to turning out the lights on that one bright spot. Once his curiosity was aroused, he found reams of information and opinions on the subject of medical breakthroughs. He saw the graphs depicting the steep decline in meaningful advances as compared to dollars spent on research. He agreed with the conclusion that human beings had solved all the easy things. What was left was too difficult, particularly if we kept approaching research in such a specialized, market-driven way.

In 2007, the public had the opportunity to vote on the greatest medical breakthroughs since 1840. Sanitation came in at number one. Rounding out the top five were antibiotics, vaccinations, anesthesia, and DNA, but sewage systems won. Perhaps that's what happens when the general public gets to weigh in rather than just the specialists. From a pure numbers standpoint, the public probably got it right. That didn't stop the medical experts from scoffing at sanitation being awarded this much prestige, claiming the stem cell breakthroughs that were on the horizon were going to make this sewage pronouncement look silly in years to come. Evidently, they weren't interested in reviewing studies outside their narrow field. If they were they'd be plagued by the same doubts as Dr. Sayer. He wondered whether any of those same experts noticed that none of the top five medical accomplishments had come about in recent years. He was further convinced of the difficulty of the problems left to solve.

The Institution

This disappointment of his began taking shape long ago when he realized that our way of life was making us sick. It was impossible to cure diseases we were creating. Not if we were unwilling to change. Modern medicine was about developing drugs and procedures to address man-made health problems. Our health would improve in tandem with the environment and the quality of our lives. And that was not on the horizon, only more chronic diseases, at earlier ages, for a greater number of people. It made the whole discussion about affordability a joke. Mopping the floor with the water running required a medical machine operating around the clock simply to keep pace.

Sometimes he would be overcome with guilt about how hard he was on his profession. The broader issue was that we did not see ourselves as part of a larger whole. We fought that reality by compartmentalizing everything. The medical industry was but one example of how we had succeeded in paring down every aspect of our lives into a separate specialty. Each function of living relegated to a particular time and place. The lack of fusion had become debilitating. He saw how this failure extended beyond the world of medicine. It was also true for healing the ills of the whole human predicament. There were some lethal contagions – mainly ecological – that were spreading fast. Dr. Sayer laid blame on the doorsteps of the Institutions, and more specifically, the hierarchical system under which everything operated. And with that, he was overcome by a sinking feeling that as a species we had gone as far as we could under these arrangements.

Quite possibly it was a conditional response. Many people experienced something similar after the United States elected The Idiot President. Although Dr. Sayer was Canadian, he was aware of how en masse there was this collective head scratching about what went wrong. This was accompanied by a fearful weighing of future problems, with such a weak link at the top. The very fact that he was elected and surrounded by over-achieving cronies pointed to the possibility that political figures, the most senior corporate officers, and the entire elite that determined the direction of our world had not been placed through merit. It began to look more and more as if the converse could be true. That turned the hierarchical command and control system into a joke. More ominous though, in an increasingly complex world, it foreshadowed disaster. And that got Michael Sayer enthralled with complex versus distributed intelligence and whether there was a way to combine the two so that we could move forward to the next level of understanding. Failure to do so, in his opinion, meant the near-term collapse of civilization.

Once he began to search for a general sense of what was happening, his most basic beliefs were shattered. The nonfiction he consumed regularly cited sources he also felt compelled to read. Internet searches linked him to bloggers and authors, some well known, some just well informed. And they, in turn, introduced him to alternative perspectives. There were smart people out there who did not have much of a stake in the status quo. They had a different reality.

During this period of discovery, one author's work kept popping up. He read the first of Jerome Raines' books, *The Mind in Motion,* and found the words like music, as he was so in tune with the spirit in which they were written. Next, he read *The Acquisitive Species – Toward a Civilization that Values Acquiring Wisdom over Possessions*. He thought of his own family and friends and considered how much happier and energized they would be if they could find it within themselves to make that leap. *The Left Behind Paradox* was more reactionary than the others and the author apologized for this. The book could be summarized by the quote, "Instead of being born again, why not just grow up." But Jerome Raines was on the mark in tackling biological, religious, and cultural Evolution, and more specifically, how they intertwined. We seemed to be unable to remove religious fundamentalism from our repertoire of solutions, especially when we were in a state of fear.

What would it take for us, as a species, to reach adulthood? For Michael, that was the million-dollar question. He recognized what was happening to him. He was moving towards adulthood. No matter how difficult the experience was at times, he was sure of one thing. He did not want to go back. The way was forward.

It was *Crisis, What Crisis? – How "Advanced" Civilization Bickers While Earth Burns* that introduced him to the perfect storm of economic and environmental catastrophes that were building. Gloomier than the rest of Jerome's books, it addressed the whole banking system including the issues of debt, both individually and nationally, usury, fractional lending, and the perceived value of the stock market. It segued into education's role as a tool of corporate indoctrination and the growing dependency on large Institutions as natural systems failed in the face of an expanding human population. Global Warming and Peak Oil were also addressed. It was the first time he had read anything about the fallout that would take place once the world had used one-half of its oil. Supply would begin to contract when demand was at its highest and every barrel coming out of the ground from that point forward would be more costly to extract and of diminishing quality. The commodity that contributed to every component of daily life would be on the way up in price while it was on its way out. And there was no substitute. It was the mother of all issues. Once he wrapped his mind around what it meant – a post-industrial Stone Age unless certain adjustments were made – he was obsessed for a while reconsidering everything he had been led to believe about man's future. Jerome Raines was not the only author during those years to write about it. It was a hot topic but it didn't materialize in the way it was predicted to. Ecological failure was the bigger attention grabber.

Well before that event took place, Jerome published two more books. *In Praise of Climate Change*, and the one that caused him the most trouble, *Turning on the 'digm*. The first of these was a plea to his fellow man to wake up, open his eyes and mind, and be receptive to meaningful changes in our civilization. We were overshooting all the natural systems to the point that we were dependent on a manufactured existence and maintenance of the status quo. It was a strange phenomenon that modern man had reached the point where he could look out over eighteen lanes of highway or yet another subdivision gobbling up precious farmland and not see environmental degradation and loss of a food source. Instead, he saw survival in a faster commute, in land development, and in overpopulation.

By that time, Jerome had grown harsh when it came to the environmental movement's desire for the whole western way to continue, as long as it was powered by bio-fuels. He didn't see 5,000 square foot McMansions sporting solar panels and Hybrid cars as a plan with a future. The general reception was lukewarm when it came to tweaks like those and downright chilly at the implication of a contraction in our living arrangements. In his book, Jerome referred to vision as a two-step process. In order to see how we might improve our future prospects, we had to be realistic about our current circumstances. We failed consistently to be realistic. The average informed citizen didn't think in terms of civilization adaptation, although, this was what had to take place. He wrote about how unlikely it was that a Socrates, a Jefferson, or an Einstein would receive a fair hearing should one of them be alive in our times. He saw this disdain of critical solutions as the defining ailment of the period. So appalled was he at the level of discourse from all arenas, he believed that ours was a civilization in its terminal stage that had lost its ability to recognize truth. For when it came to seeing there was trouble all around, we were unable to reach a consensus that this was the case. We couldn't get past the debating stage, which he saw as a process that failed to change a single mind. It only served to prevent action.

And then came *Turning on the 'digm*, striking a chord with an even smaller audience. A huge failure. He shouldn't have written it. If he had heeded his own observations about vision being a two-step process, he would have accepted that since he had not been effective in getting past the first step with *In Praise of Climate Change*, there was no reason to go to the second. The public wasn't looking for anything new. The pain of clinging tightly to our way of life may have been getting to him, but most of the population was feeling no such discomfort.

When Jerome Raines arrived in the Emergency Ward at Vancouver General Hospital on October 12, 2012, Michael Sayer was the attending physician. Having followed this author's career so closely, he knew the name and the face as soon as he saw them. His spine had been damaged in what was termed "a hiking accident." He would not walk again but that wasn't the most serious of his injuries. It was the harm to his internal organs that would not allow him to know another day free of pain.

In the years that followed, Dr. Sayer questioned why he had fought so hard to keep him alive and wondered in whose interests he acted. Jerome Raines was a mind to him; not a body, possibly not even a man and he couldn't bear to see that mind extinguished. He once rationalized that the world would be worse off for the loss. But now he knew better. The world wasn't better or worse off because of any one man. It was worse off because of man in general.

***

Darlene sighed heavily as she polished off the last of the Coconut Cream Pie. As she scraped the remnants from her plate and licked the tines of the fork repeatedly, she continued to prepare mentally for the very disturbed Dr. Sayer. She was sure the worst assortment of patients had been assigned to her. It was because she didn't complain enough and when she did there were a couple of older nurses who weren't very sympathetic about her plight. They could really dig in their heels when it came to changing up the patient mix. In a staff meeting, they had all but called her a whiner and then proceeded to relate stories from the early years of the Institution. Back then, they used to try to help these crazy people by providing them with the means to see reality. If these veteran nurses were to be believed, then Darlene really couldn't argue with them. Their jobs had been horrific. Finally, it was decided the patients were too far-gone for rehabilitation. It was all about keeping them quiet now.

Her brief respite was over. She pushed herself away from the table and headed for the elevator ready for the next onslaught. Dr. Sayer surprised her on this day in the same way Mrs. Holmes had. Normally not one for histrionics, he launched into a personal account of his first meeting with Jerome Raines. It was only partially true, of course, but Darlene would never be able to convince him of that.

"Mr. Raines sustained his injuries in a fall," she stated confidently.

"I was at the hospital when he was brought in. I know exactly what his injuries were. He didn't exactly *fall* into the Canyon."

Doctors may get off on intimidating nurses but it wasn't a ploy Darlene appreciated, particularly when the doctor in question was a patient. "Look, I've seen his chart and that's not what it says. He was out hiking alone in some God-forsaken place and took a tumble."

"His chart was written that way to cover up what really happened."

"Well I don't know anything about that. I just know that's not what it says."

"Since I know you would never be curious enough to ask why someone would want to cover up the facts surrounding Jerome's accident, I'll volunteer the information. By the way, didn't you ever wonder why the name on his chart is Jason Reimer yet everyone who knew him prior to his being admitted to this Institution calls him Jerome Raines?"

Darlene wanted to put her hands over her ears and scream, *I don't want to know*, at the mere threat of his telling her something she didn't want to hear. As far as the name thing, that had been explained more than adequately to the medical staff. Jason Reimer was his real name. Jerome Raines was the pen name under which he authored all of his books. Given the content of those, it was easy to see why he wished to be anonymous. When it came to the other disclosures, Dr. Sayer wouldn't be able to rest without sharing them with her. She didn't know what was with these people and why they thought every Joe Blow on the street needed to be aware of everything. She did know, however, that too much information was a burden meant only for those who wished to be tormented. If it wasn't necessary to get by, why bother with it? As much as she felt like cowering in the corner until he was finished, she stood her ground while he gave his version of a sequence of events he couldn't erase from his mind.

"The damming and diversion of the Fraser River, multiple damming actually, was the last environmental battle ever waged. There was nothing left to fight for after that."

At school, Darlene learned of all the wonderful projects that came to pass once the whole protesting, civil disobedience thing came to an end. She knew how nostalgia skewed memory making it untrustworthy. That explained Dr. Sayer's distortion of the early years of the 21st Century as the end of something precious rather than the start of a promising new era. His was the old way of looking at things. And because she was so sure he was wrong, she only half-listened. And he spoke out loud only half of the time. It was for his benefit that he remembered. All else was a hopeless cause.

Dr. Sayer considered how much had changed. It didn't seem so long ago that the Fraser River supported the largest salmon runs in the world. In 2012, at 820 miles, the Fraser had the distinction of being the longest, most powerful, free-flowing river left in North America and it remained that way up until 2020 when construction of the first two dams was complete. In

The Institution

view of what happened in the first half of the 20th Century to the Columbia, whose headwaters were not very distant from those of the Fraser, it was miraculous that it took so long for its power to be fully harnessed.

It was one of the issues that should have concerned us – our increasing dependency on artificial systems for survival. Corporations controlled all aspects of our food and energy supplies from monopolization of grain and vegetable seeds to heating fuels. With the decimation of every wild species and forest ecosystem, we inched our way closer to total dependency. For some reason, the average person couldn't make the connection between the destruction of the land base brought about by population growth and the loss of independence.

Prior to the Fraser River proposal, there had been a concerted effort to make Canada more homogeneous with its neighbor to the south. The Government of Canada had been carting out the small rate of population growth as troublesome for quite some time. By the first decade of the 21st Century, the whole dollars and cents of it were beginning to strike fear into a baby boomer generation on the brink of retirement. Dr. Sayer was struck by how Canadian citizens felt the need for additional population. Smart people, caring people, seemingly environmentally aware people had convinced themselves that there was no link between exponential growth, environmental degradation, and a low quality of life. Like most places, Canada's cities were exploding in size, condominiums were popping up all over the place, the highways were in gridlock, the land was being raped, the water polluted, and the people were looking fondly at it all and saying it's not enough, we need more. It made him wonder what everybody was seeing, other than the hope that their share of Social Insurance and Canada Pension Plan benefits made it to their pockets. Canadians thought of themselves as more enlightened than Americans. From a political standpoint Canadians were more critical of their leaders. Environmentally, Canadians talked a good game. But when it came to living arrangements, consumerism, driving habits, and financial expectations, Canadians were identical to Americans. The failure to recognize this was astonishing.

Might it be that it was a detriment to border a country – the "whipping boy" U.S.A. – that was consistently a poor performer? However one defined the mood of the moment, the North American Union became a reality and the timing was perfect to push through the Fraser River dam projects. Just as it had been in the previous decade when the Whistler Sea-to-Sky Highway project – a perversion in its own right – blasted its way through the hills above Howe Sound to the glee of a nation hell bent on making it easier to drive. And drive we did. We were buoyant as we sped along careening blindly but sure the way was straight and clear, collectively squealing with delight in that weightless moment before it dawned on us why the wheels were spinning effortlessly. There was nothing firm beneath them. Nothing but fumes and shiny expectations and no sense that even at full throttle, we wouldn't get there any faster if there was no place left to go.

More importantly, the United States and Canada needed the electrical power and the water to keep their economies rolling along. The U.S. had the weaponry to bomb Canada back into the Stone Age for not doing what it was told. It was in everyone's immediate interests not to oppose the North American Union's new Assistant Secretary of State.

"We concluded that the life cycle of wild salmon was too difficult for human beings to work around. Those needy fish had unreasonable environmental expectations. There was a general consensus that on a finite planet it was unconscionable for one species to be incapable of adapting. The dams ensured the Fraser River salmon met the same fate as fish populations throughout the world. In the following decade, there were no wild fish left in any of the oceans. And still no shift in our development patterns or our consumption practices. A staggering lack of imagination when it came to our living arrangements," Dr. Sayer explained to the Nurse as if he thought she cared.

"Oh well," Darlene responded. "It's not as if there aren't farm-raised fish being produced for us to eat. I've never understood the big deal about the wild stocks. They weren't as reliable were they? I mean you couldn't count on the quality or the fishermen even catching what you wanted for dinner for that matter. It all sounds so unpredictable."

"I was thinking of it more from the marine mammal perspective. You know, the whales and walruses and such. Wild fish stocks mattered to them."

The Institution

"Whatever," Darlene said dismissing that point of view as irrelevant. "I don't bother myself with that sort of abstract thinking. I'm more concerned about what shows up on *my* plate."

"Yes and it shows too," Dr. Sayer said, succumbing to his lower instincts. He was unable to comprehend why someone of her size would brag about her appetite.

"What's that supposed to mean?" Darlene exclaimed defensively, sensing by his tone that she should be offended.

"If you insist that I state the obvious then I will. You're awfully fat for such a young woman. Have you ever considered cutting back on the food and getting a little exercise?"

She was exasperated. No one had ever said anything so stupid to her before. "Don't you understand that people are bigger than they used to be. It's got to do with nutrition being better and food more plentiful. We're getting more out of our food than ever before."

"That's the story is it? You're getting something extra all right. More fat, growth hormones, or possibly it's all the pharmaceuticals you and your contemporaries are taking that are puffing you up like inflated balloons. Whatever it is, it's not natural." Even while Dr. Sayer was saying this he wondered why he was doing so. It was mean-spirited on his part and incomprehensible on hers.

Darlene thought about Sunshine, a woman more than forty years her senior. How trim and quick moving she was. And that picture of Mrs. Holmes. Was that how women looked way back when? It didn't seem possible. Why she didn't even look human she was so puny. Except for the chest, of course. Although Darlene wouldn't say it out loud, she was looking forward to the day when the last of this group that had come to be called "The Troubled Generation" was gone. They were such downers. Angry all the time, they didn't know how to love life. That made her think of another unpleasant conversation – one she had with Jerome Raines. After being completely disgusted with something he said, she had taken it upon herself to point out this deficiency that, in him, was very pronounced. How he responded was as peculiar as everything else about him.

"The point of living is far more complex than whether each human being is happy with his individual existence. There is plenty of evidence to

suggest that people are concerned with their individual existences to the exclusion of everything else. The better question to ask is whether we care about anything other than our own immediate satisfaction. Things like the planet, for instance, on which all life depends."

How could they have missed the point of life? Every last stinking one of them. Indifference was not that difficult to understand. Given that it was the key to personal happiness, it made no sense to Darlene why they wouldn't make the effort. She looked at her watch and saw that she was finished for the day. Then, quite sincere about her priorities, she pointed out to Dr. Sayer that she must leave now because she didn't want to be late for dinner.

***

Darlene may have flaunted her intention to tie into another meal. It might have been said out of habit or spite but that was not what she did. Alone in her room, she began experiencing an odd sensation in her head. There was this relentless gnawing, this impression of gnashing teeth chewing through brain matter. She considered going to the dining room as she always did at that time of day. If she were missed, someone could come looking for her and the last thing she wanted to explain was why she was hunkered down in her room. There was no explanation other than she felt odd.

She rocked in her chair and tried to calm herself. Her heart raced and her ears rang. Before too long she was clammy with sweat and her mind hurt like crazy. It wasn't her head. It was definitely her mind, aching as it turned over, losing the battle with inertia. Then something let go and it all came rushing at her. A whole lifetime of data that had been glossed over was suddenly significant. She closed her eyes to better focus and considered whether she was dying. Could this really be it? Her whole life flashing in front of her.

After floating for so long in a fog, the clarity was blinding. The first thought that entered Darlene's mind was that she didn't know the half of it. As she looked around her windowless bunker, it occurred to her that this place and her patients may not be what she had been led to believe. The

The Institution

words they had spoken earlier in the day were sharp and clear in her mind. In retrospect, Darlene felt the power in them, true human passion, the kind she did not usually have the capacity to see.

And what about herself? She looked down at an expanse of thighs still clad in pastel pink spread the width of her rocker. Lifting her lower legs, one at a time, she inspected her calves and ankles. Big as tree stumps, they were. She didn't have to squeeze her middle section to know its size. She was well aware of the roll extending from below her breasts to her waist where it was met by another more impressive chunk of fat. She got up, went into the bathroom, and looked at her face.

"Oh my," she moaned. Darlene didn't look anything like she thought. How long had she been sporting those chins anyway? It didn't require much imagination to picture herself shoving food into her mouth. Those chubby cheeks puffed full with each ravenous bite, hungry for the next meal before she'd even pushed herself away from the table. She steadied herself at the sink while she shook with grief. Why had she let herself get like this? How could she have not noticed? But more troubling than that, why was she suddenly able to?

Her mind leapt away from herself to Doug and the prospect of his coming around tonight. Sniffing around was more like it and it shocked her that this was the imagery that came to mind. For whatever reason, she no longer wanted him. He was a fifty-year old bully. Anyone could see that.

She walked back into the living room to hear someone shuffling past her door. She froze in place and willed whomever it was to keep moving. But then she told herself not to worry about it. The only person who came to her room was Dr. Marsh and he wouldn't be seeking her bed tonight. He was here last night. How many nights had she lied awake waiting for him the following evening? A hundred or more? Tonight he would be with Cynthia, tomorrow Susan. It was up in the air after that. He had never spent two nights in a row with a single one of them. That's the way it had always been. This night she was certain of it. In the same way she saw more than a kernel of truth in what the patients in her care had been telling her.

***

Terra Dime

Early the next morning, before anyone else was moving around, Darlene entered the elevator and ascended from the lower underground portion of the building to the upper floor. She grabbed a respirator from the bin closest to the exit and placed it over her nose and mouth. As long as she were properly outfitted with the right gear, it was safe to spend small amounts of time outside. Like most of her generation, Darlene didn't do it much. She exited the rear of the Institution and walked out onto a deck that at one time was nestled amongst the pine forest, but now dangled above barren hills. The reason that most stayed indoors was plain to see. The commanding view the deck provided of the river flowing toward the sheer wall of intricate rock formations was not that impressive. For one thing, there was now more riverbed than river and the water was an unappealing gunmetal gray. Without plant or animal life, oxygen, blue sky, and sunshine it wasn't all that nice out here. Everyone was supposed to be convinced that what had been created indoors more than made up for what had been lost. On this warm summer morning, Darlene had her doubts.

To the northwest, as far as the eye could see, were sand dunes. Someone could argue that they weren't technically sand dunes but it didn't take a Psychopharmacologist to see that was the direction it was going. With the forest a thing of the past, the winds had scoured this landscape for a decade and a half. The result was a rippling sea of silica.

"It's the frickin' Sahara Desert," Darlene murmured into the breeze that was gaining in strength.

With that, another memory was triggered and another connection made. It could also be attributed to Jerome Raines and that surprised her. When asked yesterday, she had no recollection of anything meaningful passing between the two of them. She thought he had barely spoken to her but that wasn't the case. It was the way he said things, seemingly out of the blue, that she hadn't understood. She was now willing to bet that he hadn't said a single thing without a reason. In view of the feedback he received, why had he bothered?

"Did you know the Romans were responsible for creating much of the Sahara Desert?"

When she looked at him like she was thinking, what kind of fool do you take me for, he followed up with, "No, I read it somewhere. Much of the

The Institution

Sahara was once rich land. The Romans farmed North Africa. Usual story. Their empire outgrew its land base. They had to look elsewhere for arable land to grow food. So they cut down all the native species on the other side of the Mediterranean, planted crops year after year, denuded the soil, and then eventually the desertification process began. You know what's odd about that? Lots of people didn't believe it when alarm about the widespread destruction of our natural systems was expressed. There was this certainty, in some circles anyway, that nature was so resilient it would find a way to repair itself no matter how degraded. If there is no such thing as a point of no return then why is the Sahara still the Sahara? I guess it's possible that fifteen hundred years isn't enough time, but I can't help but wonder how long we're talking about. Chateaubriand said it best, 'Forests precede civilizations and deserts follow.'"

And how had Darlene responded to this knowledge he tried to share? With a clever snort, no doubt. She could see why he had chosen to share these tidbits. Just as clearly as she could see there wasn't a tree lurking anywhere in the distance. He had been hoping to spark something. And it did have that effect now. It sparked the question she should have asked. *Deserts followed us on our way where exactly?*

The wind stiffened. Coming straight out of the north at fifty miles per hour it tugged at the sand swirling it in all directions. Gritty particles were already clinging to her skin and trying to work their way into her breathing apparatus. But she wasn't ready to go inside yet. From the direction of the livestock building she could detect the groans and cries of various animals and it sickened her. She knew what went on over there and had ignored it. She had taken enough biology to know that when living creatures were forced to grow in two months to a size that would normally take two years it was a brutal process. Sometimes bones would break, stomachs split, organs explode.

Through the glass of the Institution's bubble gardens she could see inside to where tree fruit and vegetables were illuminated under grow lights. The clear rounded tops glowed against the sickly yellow monotone of cloud cover that hung low in the sky. Thick clouds sat just like this day after day, barely moving and rarely releasing a drop of rain. Had life of any kind really existed out here on its own, in the wild, without human

143

assistance? She had no memory of it. All she had were holograms and coffee table books. And with that thought she grew sad. An emotion she had never felt before.

Darlene made her way back through the building anxious to see Saint Paul. He was the one with whom she felt most comfortable. Under normal circumstances she would not see him two days in a row so she switched visiting times with another patient. After realizing how strange the situation in which she found herself was, she decided to act immediately.

"I didn't expect to see you today." He looked startled when she entered his room. A thick sheaf of hand-written pages was quickly placed face down on the end table and then covered by a picture book.

"I don't know where to start," she said, easing into a chair that faced him. "Let me just say this isn't an official medical professional to patient visit. It's a social call and anything we say is off the record."

"You look so serious. What's happened?"

"I don't know how to explain what's going on. It's something up here," she said pointing to her head. "Like a veil has been lifted. Everything looks different. I look different. In focus, you know what I mean?"

He looked at her curiously not sure what to think.

"This morning when I woke up I started thinking. I tried to piece together the stories you've all told me over the last year. The more I thought the more excited I got until I was almost bursting with the thrill of tracking clues and trying to figure out what it all means. I've never been able to think like that before. Hold a thought. Put it together with another thought. Make a connection. It was a strange experience."

"When did this start?"

"Yesterday afternoon while I was talking to Mrs. Holmes, I began to feel strange. Once I was off duty, it really hit me hard."

"You haven't told anyone else, have you?"

"No, I've been avoiding the other staff because I'm guessing that whatever's happening to me isn't supposed to be. And if they find out, they'll make it stop. Listen to me, talking in terms of 'they' just like a conspiracy theorist."

The Institution

Saint Paul didn't know how to respond to that. He liked to imagine that thinking was addictive and once people knew how it would be no easy matter to reverse the process. But that was ridiculous. It happened all the time. Usually before young adults were even finished their schooling. The "making it stop" would have been factored in. It was likely a simple procedure.

"Do you know what's going on, Saint Paul?" Darlene asked.

"It's pure speculation on our part and Dr. Sayer could give you a more technical explanation but what we've concluded is that you're fitted with an implant, probably at birth. You have a tiny scar behind your left ear. It either sends an impulse, releases an endorphin, or a bit of chemical. We're not sure which. It affects dopamine and serotonin levels in the brain like the antidepressants of four and five decades ago. That generation of mood altering drugs can be credited for your temperament. When SSRI's were all the rage, one of their benefits was they made people happy despite bad circumstances. Users of the drugs weren't inclined to make lousy situations better. It was also apparent that while under the influence of SSRIs, critical thinking vanished. No mental engagement meant everything looked marvelous. In much the same way as it does for you. That side effect proved useful in protecting the status quo. As conditions continued to deteriorate, rose-colored glasses were needed to keep everyone's spirits up so we would keep pretending and keep it all going. Or, at the very least, a procedure that made everything look rosy. That turned out to be the alternative of choice."

It struck Saint Paul as odd that such an elaborate program had been undertaken when there were plenty of examples demonstrating a majority of the population would willingly do to themselves what was now done surgically. We had proven time and again how content we were to overlook the obvious in favor of outlandish myths. In the face of compelling evidence to the contrary, we convinced ourselves we were a democratic republic, born again politicians don't lie, banksters aren't criminals, the stock market would provide retirement for millions, oil and gas resources are infinite, transporting trinkets twelve thousand miles is sustainable, and God (and technology) would save us because we are the chosen ones. And there was another fable that forced some to grow curious

145

and others to shrivel. On the morning of September 11, 2001 while four terrorist attacks occurred over an hour period, the most powerful military in the world was unable to get a single fighter jet off the ground.

He guessed there was a slight risk that the active-minded, a paltry two-percent of the population, would capture the imagination of the masses and they would rise up. It was so funny, though, that no one bothered to calculate how small this risk really was.

"So what are you saying? What's happening inside my head?"

"It sounds like your implant has started to malfunction."

"Will it ever start working again on its own?"

"Perhaps intermittently. I imagine you'll have to be operated on."

"And if I don't get anything done about it?"

"You're going to be an oddity and it will be hard for you to hide that fact."

A smile lit up her face. "I'm going to know more than everyone else."

"What you're going to have is a different reality from everyone else. Before you get too ecstatic about that prospect you might want to consider the downside."

"Downside?"

"You're not going to be able to let on what you know. We don't know how high up the chain of command it goes and who knows what. And we certainly don't know how a situation like yours will be handled. We do know, however, how a situation like ours was. You're going to feel isolated at best. At worst, you're going to be an outcast." Saint Paul was referring specifically to the relationship she had going with that doctor and how she would handle that. Chances were she would wish to extricate herself and that wouldn't be easy. Her life was about to get more complicated if this thing persisted. And he had a hunch Darlene wouldn't like it complicated.

So caught up in the newness of it all, she hadn't thought to be frightened. "But I can talk to all of you and you will tell me things, won't you? And I'll be able to understand some of what you say."

"Yes, we can try," he agreed. "But you could be too brainwashed to take much of it in," he continued as he began to think about how difficult it would be. "Chances are we would have to put you through a debriefing process to wipe the slate clean before you could begin to accept what we have to say."

He didn't know how to tell her that there was more than an implant that separated them. Her brain would likely never fire on all cylinders. Even if by chance it started to, there wasn't any valid information or experiences to draw from. She would always be closer in temperament to her coworkers at the Institution than her patients. And it was better for her that way. It really was. Darlene was yet to realize the obvious. Her patients weren't going to be around forever. She was more than forty years younger than the youngest of them. When that dawned on her she would come to her senses. Thinking was treacherous. All her patients agreed on that.

In the meantime, she wanted to be filled in on the rest of Saint Paul's story. Picking up where he left off with what happened after the Portland bookstore. That was what she was there for – the story.

He began by telling her how he took it upon himself to deliberately defy a church directive. When Paul got back to Topeka thinking one way, he found the Methodist Church had been thinking the opposite way. The tricky part of Paul's position in the church was that his wife, Janet, was also a Methodist minister. Hers was an administrative function as she oversaw the state of Kansas. More specifically, she was Paul's boss. She didn't waste any time informing him of the church's intention to get on board with the preaching practices of the Evangelicals. They were pulling away from the curb at the airport as he returned from his Portland trip, when she gave him his instructions.

After what he'd been reading and thinking about during his flight this was the kind of reality check that angered him. His response reflected this aggravation. "So does that mean I should start practicing my YEAHHHs, throwing my arms skyward, and resort to talking in terms of good and evil. That's not exactly my style."

"Now Paul, you know it isn't appropriate to make fun. This will address the dwindling numbers of Methodists and the expanding flock of Evangelical Christians. The leaders of the church have taken note of the trend and they think the public is attracted to that style. The older folks are passing on and this younger generation is seen as more zealous in their religious convictions. We want to be an option for them. If we don't provide it then you and I will both be out of work."

"We've talked about this before. I don't believe in the Bible in the literal sense and I certainly don't believe it's the word of God. It's a metaphor. You know that's what it is. How can you expect any intelligent human being to tell a congregation that if they don't follow it word for word they'll burn in the fires of Hell?"

"I've never agreed with you on that. If anything, I've indulged you too much over the years instead of telling you to quit with the doubts about our profession. If believing in a Heaven makes people more decent then there's no harm in it. Isn't that the most important thing? You have to give people what they want."

"Sure, like what people want is the gold standard. I might buy that if human wants weren't so self-serving and destructive. You know as well as I do that most people are greedy and selfish and not very smart."

"Paul, you're being awful," Janet scolded.

"No, I'm being truthful here. Anyone who is so morally bankrupt they have to be reminded weekly to be decent really has a problem. And they're the last ones who should be screaming about the immorality of others. Particularly, when a large portion of those others don't have to be told what it takes to be a good person. They figured it out when they were about ten years old. There is no correlation between church attendance and integrity. If a relationship exists it's likely an inverse one."

"Sure, Paul, I've heard it all from you before."

"You haven't heard what I've been thinking about since leaving Portland. I came across an author and now I'm reading one of his books and you know what I'm finding out, Janet? We know nothing. You and I are ignorant. And you know why that is? We keep concocting sermons based on the same book that we then recite once a week to the same people who wish to learn nothing new. The conclusion I've come to about the Good Book is that not only is it not the word of God but much of it was written by the worst kind of men. The kind that are in power today. The kind that benefit from the public remaining ignorant. The kind that wish the faithful to believe that the reason they're so rich and powerful is they've earned special favor from the One who bestows such gifts, so better go along with whatever they propose."

He didn't say it out loud but it only made sense to him that someone who believed in the story of religion was less likely to question authority and the command and control system. They were apt to defend and support it as vehemently as Christianity – a command and control system of epic proportions. A true believer was willing to live by His commandments and under His control in fear of screwing up and being denied a place in the kingdom of Heaven. That sounded as lopsided as the modern day workplace and Institutions of all kinds where questioning authority meant being denied the good life, or in other words, a viable place in the kingdom of human society.

"Settle down, Paul. You're going to blow a gasket."

"You know why brainwashing is so effective? Because no one thinks he is. We all believe we're acting on free will but if we don't *know* anything how could we be? Religion should be a stepping stone not an end game. There is more wisdom out there than what's written in the Ten Commandments. I want to learn more and then help others to acquire wisdom so we can all grow together and make informed choices. That's the direction I'd like to see the church take; moving away from the static and towards embracing human potential. And that means being fearless when it comes to reinventing ourselves, our relationship with other life, and our ultimate purpose. We must do this regardless of whether it conflicts with what we're preaching right now. Unless we're willing to grow beyond narrow religion, we have no business preaching."

They had pulled into the driveway and were sitting in the car with the engine running. Janet was looking at him warily, really hating the prospect of where all this was going to lead. Hoping also, that his interest would wane after a few days and he would be deterred from taking this new course. "You know," she said, "if you start down this rabbit hole it's going to change everything. It will tear down your entire belief system and all that you've accomplished thus far in life. You may end up with nothing, and I mean nothing."

She spoke as if it were a threat. And in a way it was. Janet did hold the keys to his current life and that included his career, children, and the conventional world. It was possible that she had been indulging him for years and would continue to do so as long as there was no risk to her personally. Pursuing an avenue of thought that was on a crash course with the church's doctrine and dogma was just the kind of catalyst to change all that.

Back then, when Paul tried to bring his congregation up to speed, he didn't know there were levels of personal development and that he was speaking to a group that was several stages below the one he was asking them to reach for. He hadn't yet delved into the eastern religions. He hadn't read about "Spiral Dynamics" for a better grasp of what he was up against. He believed that he could assist the incurious in finding something they weren't looking for. The congregation listening to him from the pews had no interest in obtaining a more expansive view of the world. Fully satisfied with their narrow inaccurate perceptions, it was affirmation they were seeking. Paul could have saved himself all the trouble if he had heeded the words of the columnist George Monbiot: "Tell people something they know already and they will thank you for it. Tell them something new and they will hate you for it."

The same held true for Paul's family. They wished to be left alone and left behind – content as prisoners of their minds. Minds that more and more gave the impression of imploding as he reached for more. The rift widened. Janet and his two teenage daughters were united against whatever it was he was trying to sell. They were not in the market for anything other than what mainstream was offering. He may as well have been an absentee father for all that he had impressed upon his children. This was another one of the dynamics he had failed to notice. His wife was not a parent. She was one of the girls reliving her youth through her daughters. Happy to revisit that block of time that included adolescence through early adulthood at least two more times, she was looking backward over her shoulder not forward into the unknown. Already, she and their eldest daughter were making plans for Mother-Daughter events at the sorority that Janet belonged to while she attended university – and the daughter was still a Junior in high school. The way his wife went on about it, she was breathlessly eyeing a sophomoric future when it was still three years out. No husband of hers was going to spoil this by making her think there were more weighty things to focus on than Homecoming and tailgate parties. She had a good job – a better paying one than his. She had her two girls. The girls had a mother who could afford to give them whatever they wanted without any questions asked. He was worse than superfluous. He was starting to spread ruin over all the fun.

They were thrilled when he went his separate way and they didn't pretend otherwise. This should have been a clue as to how the concept of a different kind of society, a dynamic shift in the way we live and think, would be received by the general public. But he wasn't able to see that yet. He believed those things he was reading about human potential and improving the human condition. He thought anyone with a functioning conscience, once in possession of the facts, would wish to live differently. It sounded so easy and doable, this awakening process. This information dissemination that everyone was eagerly waiting for. He explained away his family as anomalies and felt strongly that average folk all across the land were picking up the same books as he and were similarly inspired. Paul was slow to come to the conclusion that a specialized form of Agoraphobia was the greatest threat to humanity. The secure places we were afraid of leaving were not physical structures but mental constructs.

"Not long after leaving Kansas to live that independent life in the west I'd heard so much about, my new neighbors in Missoula, Montana reported me to Homeland Security," Saint Paul explained to Darlene.

"What did Homeland Security want with you? I thought they were mainly interested in foreign terrorist types?"

"Thanks to one of the Bills passed by Congress in 2007, their attention shifted to homegrown terrorism. In other words, engaging in mental activities that were in conflict with government policy. Preventive detention was the phrase used. Fortunately, it was before the Internment Camps were complete so I got let out. For a while, anyway," he explained to Darlene.

"So who were the camps for?" As the words were forming in her mouth the familiarity of this conversation made her tingle. It was Jerome Raines, of course, who once spoke to her of Internment Camps. In her new "enlightened" state, she recalled word for word what he said.

Terra Dime

"Do you know something peculiar that happened about thirty-five years ago? The U.S. Government started building Internment Camps. A contract for $385 million was awarded to the leading defense contractor. They happened to be well connected with the leaders and profited handsomely from any military adventures the government engaged in. But that's another story. It speaks to the fact that there were corruption issues. Each facility was to hold 5,000 people and it was rumored 700 were to be built. That was enough capacity to detain 3,500,000 people. Some of the numbers were pure speculation. The project was so secretive it was nearly impossible to access the facts. Here's something that isn't speculation though. When a corrupt regime takes over, especially one that is not democratic, one of the first courses of action it takes is either killing or incarcerating those who would oppose its policies. That usually means the smart, active-minded people. You have to wonder what a government that can survive only if it's surrounded by the lumpen public and a few elites has planned."

"Sounds like a bunch of hysterical paranoia to me. That sure is one thing all of you have in common."

"Really? Is that what our medical charts say or did you come to that conclusion on your own?"

"Next, you'll be telling me you spent time in one of those Internment Camps because you're so smart and all."

Darlene had used her ugliest tone with him to make sure she got her point across. And her point was that she didn't believe anything an old mentally ill cripple had to say. The memory brought with it a strange sense of shame. Another, in a long list of emotions, that was unfamiliar. It was not like her to have any twinge of regret for the things she had said.

"Then you would be wrong. I wouldn't waste my time trying to convince you of something as obvious as that." He said it almost in a whisper but then he often talked like that. The spoken word was not his preferred method of communication. It was as if his voice was shrill to his ears. As if he could hear himself the way his detractors did.

Saint Paul had begun speaking again and this snapped her back to the present. "They said to handle illegal immigrants from Mexico. There was a lack of facilities to hold them before they were sent back and the

The Institution

government wished to rectify the problem. Some people bought this story without considering how porous the southern border was and that the U.S. economy was dependent on illegals getting in. Others wondered what the government was getting ready for."

"What did you think they were for?"

He evaded the question and decided in favor of talking to Sunny before elaborating further. "Oh, I had my nose shoved so far into those books of mine, I didn't even know about them. At least, not then. But I found out soon enough," he said, expecting her to recognize the significance in that.

Instead she noticed the clock on the wall and realized she had overstayed. "Oh, I've got to get going," she groaned. "So what did you find out?" she asked placing her hand on the doorknob and preparing to leave.

"There isn't time to talk about it now. Why don't you ask Sunny when you see her? She can fill you in on the Camps."

"But I won't see Sunshine today. I'm not sure I should wait."

"Then see her after hours."

"That would be risky. I'm not sure I could get away with it. And Sunshine and I, well, we don't really hit it off."

He smiled at the thought of Sunny's honesty. It was tough to bear at times. "Not to worry. I'll let her know what's going on. Soften her up some. It's best coming from her because she was on the outside longer than I was."

He also wasn't sure about blurting out everything he knew when it was so unbelievable. As soon as the door clicked shut behind Darlene, Paul pulled the pages he'd been reading out from under the picture book and started in where he had left off. Later, when they got together over lunch in the dining room, he spoke to Sunny of the situation with Darlene. He had been so excited, the story came out in confusing fits and starts. If anyone was going to be perkier than a situation warranted it was bound to be Paul. Sunny listened politely and was interested in what had happened but doubted she would be as bowled over. They also had their differences of opinion on whether there was anything to be gained by filling the Nurse in. Sunny chose to reserve judgment until they had a chance to talk.

153

Terra Dime

BOOK THREE

THE LEFT BEHIND PARADOX

With Jerome gone, Sunny felt completely alone. There was no future, and because of this, history loomed way out of proportion. She kept playing it over and over again in her mind. What really drew her in was her paralyzing indecision. She had a habit of dwelling on that. What else did she have to do but make herself as crazy as the doctors said she was?

In retrospect, she was unable to get over why she didn't cut and run. It was difficult to break ranks and to abandon what everyone else considered normal. In hindsight it was easy, but at the moment, no. She should have been receptive early on to what Jerome was saying rather than clinging to mainstream like it was something she invented. It wasn't human nature to leave behind the things we should. She was proof of that. Mass delusion provides comfort. Fantasy feels good, when it's shared. That's what we aren't very good at articulating when we uncover the remains of failed civilizations – the collective deception that prevents citizens from fighting the mood of any moment throughout history, no matter how doomed.

Sunny now understood why past civilizations didn't respond to collapse in the ways that would have saved them. They didn't believe it was happening. Just as we didn't. Without prior experience, we couldn't assimilate collapse. That's the way it is the first time something abnormal happens to you. Brainwashing served to compound the disbelief. We were convinced a civilization as exceptional as ours couldn't collapse. That late in the game, by the time it was going down, the system was so corrupt none of the information floating around could be counted on. Those in charge tried to keep it going. Those who were well informed saw so many potential catastrophes coming at once they couldn't be certain which to fear most. Everyone else, tuned into entertainment spectacles of some sort, remained blissfully preoccupied while the real event unfolded.

The Institution

***

The bread dough was warm and squishy to the touch. Each time the heel of her hand pressed into it, olive oil and rosemary scented the kitchen. National Public Radio played loudly. At one time their programming had provided a way to make sense of what was going on in the world. Sunny used to feel it was the only community of like-minded people that she had. She went so far as to picture herself elderly, but not isolated or lonely, as long as she had her "Morning Edition" or "All Things Considered." But recently that had changed. NPR, along with many previously independent Institutions and individuals, had been neutered by the response to the September 11, 2001 terrorist attacks and the ignorance that caused that response. It was but another source of angst and it played now mainly to muffle the irritating drone coming from John's bedroom. Her husband's latest revelation – a room was insufferable without a television blaring 24/7 – had driven her to find another place to sleep. *That*, she suspected, was what he intended all along. She wished she could say this created a void in her life but it didn't.

In a matter of minutes, he would be leaving on an overnight backpacking trip in the company of the same outdoor group they had been with when the two of them met. She no longer participated. The Trekkers were not a group she ever related to on more than a superficial basis. For her, being an outdoor enthusiast translated into caring about the environment in a very special, personal way. But that wasn't the way they saw it. Nothing had a right to be simply for its own merit. Everything was there simply for human pleasure and enjoyment. It was a different kind of connection from the one she felt. They fell so short of her expectations she might as well be in the company of twenty little John clones and one was more than enough.

At one time so opinionated and comfortable with her stance on important issues, she rarely told anyone what she thought now. Least of all, that group. It had grown stilted and wearisome before she quit it all together. Hours upon hours playing games, discussing the trivial, and generally making sure nothing meaningful slipped from her lips in an unguarded moment. For Sunny, what wasn't mentioned was much larger than what was. A weekend in their company left her stunted and it would take days for her to come back to full health. There was trouble on the horizon – the whole system was in peril. Intelligent people should have been able to recognize this so why did no one wish to bring it up?

She was also secretly wishing that by giving John opportunity, and lots of it, he would find someone else. It was lame on her part but every time he returned from a weekend like this, she would hope that the first thing he would tell her when he walked through the door was that another woman had caught his eye. She could give herself the same pep talk over and over again. *It's not that bad to be married to a man like John.* But the trouble with that reasoning was it did matter to her. This was her life. And it was the life she swore she would never have.

She tried to be honest with herself about when things really started to deteriorate in her marriage. Was it before or after the World Trade Towers came tumbling down? In all fairness it was before. They weren't compatible. Marrying John was one of the few impulsive decisions she made in her life and it hadn't been a good one. The 2000 Election was a big clue as to what lie ahead for the two of them. She might have bailed then before "The War on Terror" drew attention to how far apart they were. The Iraq War only served to magnify it. Upcoming Middle East conflicts inflated their animosity to outrageous proportions. But it was Sunny's insistence that ecological collapse was the greatest problem we faced that had turned them into full-blown enemies. John didn't like to be told that instead of obsessing over the same silly-ass issues every election cycle it was high time we got to work on what mattered. Because the issues that kept getting carted out were the ones that mattered most to him and they hadn't been resolved to his liking.

On top of this, the leadership of the city of Silver Falls and the county had changed. They were in the hands of a gang of pro-business men who believed that clean air and water paled in importance to the growth spurt the region was currently experiencing. There was a feeling throughout the business community, particularly those connected with the construction industry, that it was their turn to make it big. Silver Falls had been known, and not always fondly so, for its lack of boom and bust cycles. The city had missed the boat in years past when comparable cities saw the kind of exponential growth that turned land speculators wealthy overnight.

This new breed of politician that had amassed power in the region was not going to let the growth that promised to double or triple the value of their real estate holdings get away this time. They had taken the first steps in a campaign that would decimate the environmental agencies they viewed as obstacles to the kind of unregulated growth the community deserved. All indications were that their initial target would be an easy one – the agency that monitored air quality. Air was not something you could see. Therefore, no one gave it much thought. The air in Silver Falls had just started to clear following a lengthy stint on the federal list of cities with serious air quality issues. It had been frequently visible in the form of a greasy, poisonous film you wished you couldn't see. However, those times were forgotten. Memories were short when it came to making a buck.

The prior day had been a day in the life of the city of Silver Falls that epitomized all the madness of the current paradigm. It was followed by an evening that brought those same horrors home when John forced himself away from the television long enough to ask, "What is up with that wacko over at the air quality agency? Why would anyone in his right mind wish to keep business out of Silver Falls? Falsifying reports, taking a hard line with the corporate types who make things happen around here. That guy needs to go."

"I strongly doubt that my counterpart over at Air has done anything wrong. It's obvious to me that these new County Commissioners have a specific agenda in mind. Anyone who gets in their way will be treated the same."

"Oooh, are you talking conspiracy theory?"

That was the current way of dealing with anyone who questioned those in power. Laugh at their intellectual curiosity. Then smugly label them a conspiracy theorist. It was John's answer to everything. It would be only a matter of time before she and the agency she headed up would be on the Hit List. It was this sense of foreboding that drove her out of bed early to enjoy the last bit of calm before facing what she knew was inevitable.

There was something else that had interrupted her sleep. The dreams were a part of her life. Sunny knew this and had resigned herself to the fact. It was the frequency and intensity with which she had them that concerned her. After twenty years, it was her mental health she now questioned. The dreams weren't as erotic as they once were. Now they were more about loss. There was something about the knowing she was dreaming while she was dreaming that was disconcerting. That, as well as not wishing to awaken and when she did she found herself crying. She couldn't stand to leave him, yet somehow, her subconscious knew that morning was upon her and she must wake up. When she tried to hold on tighter to sleep the pain became excruciating.

Alone in her kitchen that cool autumn morning she felt pressure on the small of her back gently steering her. But she wasn't sure where. That something kept taking her time and again alongside that same young man, to the same place in a line, waiting for a turn on a roller coaster was remarkable. What was this place she kept returning to? What was significant about that day?

While the inside of her home was chilly, the environment of Silver Falls wasn't. That past summer, the summer of 2007, was scorching hot. It was hot in a way that was hard to put into words. It wasn't the kind of heat that merely burned the skin. It was the kind of heat that got under the skin and made the blood boil. The fact that the entire region had endured another winter of below average snowfall made the situation frightening. At least for some. There were still the holdouts refusing to believe this was anything more than a passing dry spell. For the first time the residents of Silver Falls were forced to ration water. If it weren't for the large quantity of treated sewage being dumped into the river, compliments of a burgeoning population, there would be no flows at all. And that created another problem. Even with improvements in the quality of the treated waste, the city couldn't keep up. The phosphate levels kept increasing and the river continued to die. And still the new houses were built. The adjacent, newly incorporated bedroom community of Lost Lake was on track with its ambitious plans for new housing units within its boundaries and suburban sprawl was destined to extend to the prairie thirty miles east.

Many things separated the people who resided in this vast region that included urban centers, rural farmland, recreational property, heavily forested tracts, and wetlands. Notions of rugged individualism and white supremacy were tempered with equally strong commitments to technological salvation, gentrification and environmentalism. There were even odds that you could land up living next door to a "red neck" or a "yuppie." But the one thing everyone had in common was dependency on the aquifer. The underground river that ran under the bedrock of the Silver River was their water source. A study that took several years to complete and was meant to determine how much humanity the aquifer could support, as well as its health, provided more questions than answers and more wrangling over conflicting interpretations of the data. While the study was taking place, new housing developments kept marching up, over, and across the landscape as if it was of no consequence whether there was enough water for the newcomers as well as those who already lived in the region. Even when any sane person who didn't have an economic interest in building more homes could interpret the study as a resounding NO, the farmers kept selling off their land, the developers kept building subdivisions, the realtors continued to market homes, and the people kept moving in. The bottom line was no one had the imagination to come up with another plan. No one knew how to do anything except promote growth – external, not internal. Always external. It was the foundation of our whole culture, it was the lie we all believed in, and it was killing us.

Sunny didn't speak of these things. There was no one to speak with about any of it. But it was always there in the back of her mind how strange it was that we thought it was normal not to have productive farmland close to where people lived. That somehow we had come to believe that dependence on, not independence from agribusiness, oil imports, and foreign food supplies was sensible. And anyone who dared mention the problems with this kind of food system was made a laughingstock for his lack of understanding the value of this new way. That we saw food grabbed from supermarket shelves and freezer compartments as normal and crops close at hand growing in the soil as a harmful and indecent waste of land was worse than odd. It was stupid.

And it was this thoughtless march down the same road, the complete absence of meaningful dialogue anywhere in mainstream life, that was killing Sunny bit by bit. It would have been bearable if there had been someone at home who shared her frustration. What she had, though, was a spouse whose reality was growing more distant from hers with each passing day. Since he was so focused on becoming a citizen of the kingdom of Heaven and didn't give a damn about Planet Earth, she wished he would move there. The sooner, the better. Sunny wasn't ready to give up on this world. She loved this planet.

Election season was in full swing again and would continue to be for another year. The current candidates' platforms included the usual issues such as creating an ownership society – code for "doing away with any programs that didn't ensure those who already owned most everything, owned more." Then, of course, there was health care reform which translated into "making the general public think they would have access to cheaper health care when in reality they would pay more to get less." What about voting for "real change" in Washington DC? The "real change" candidates had in mind was never elaborated on nor understood and it never would be. Over the past two decades, we'd seen a great deal of "real change" in the form of wealth transfer from the middle-class to the rich. Wouldn't we just love to see more of that? Wresting power away from the non-elected oligarchs – the beneficiaries of government largess – would do much to improve the life of the average American. It was a safe bet that none of the candidates had a move like that up his sleeve. That was the kind of thinking that made men and women unfit to participate in politics.

The campaign promise Sunny continued to love the best was the one to make the country 20% oil independent by 2030. Did anyone remember that some form of this had been promised for the last thirty-five years? The goal just kept getting smaller and further into the future. The real story was that these politicians were able to promise this stuff with straight faces, the media reported on it for the millionth time, and the masses were able to listen without committing group suicide.

The replaying of worn out clichés, the endless controversy without the introduction of fresh perspectives and her own single-minded way of framing environmental battles had begun to wear on her. Was she simply getting old and losing her will? Possibly, but she felt it was more than that. She felt she was seeing things more clearly now. Her parents' activism and her own commitment to the environmental movement had not brought about the sweeping changes she had hoped. In recent years it was the opposite that was true. This twenty-five year ideological movement to the right had been successful in turning the general public against environmental sustainability. It was economic sustainability that was foremost in people's minds.

The host of "Weekend Edition" began interviewing an author. And that author just happened to be Jerome Raines. That seemed like too much of a coincidence since she had been thinking about him half the night and into the morning. She stopped working the dough to listen more closely. His recent book, *Crisis, What Crisis?*, explored the phenomenon she was mentally railing against.

News clips that drove his point home began to play. An announcer is referring to a Bill before Congress. Its purpose is to cap "frivolous" lawsuits so plaintiffs can no longer sue for pain and suffering. This item is immediately followed by the recent revelation that the maker of the most popular diet pill knew conclusively that there was a link between their drug and diminished mental capacity. They covered up the test results so the drug would not be taken off the market. There could be as many as ten million people with dementia as a result. He then goes on to report how many square miles of the Arctic ice cap has melted over the last five years and that this thaw is expected to open up a vast oil and gas region for drilling. Without missing a beat, he blandly states that this past summer over thirty-five thousand people died from the heat in Europe up from the thirty thousand that succumbed four summers ago. He finishes with a glowing economic report and forecast for the United States. This is followed by an announcement that a technology firm and the country's largest automobile maker are both laying off ten thousand workers apiece, a textile company is closing two of its three plants, and a wireless communications company is moving its customer support services overseas.

"How a news agency can string together a report like that without questioning why the pieces contradict one another is troubling because it is so Orwellian," Jerome said. "I can't speak for everyone, but it seems to me, if pharmaceutical companies are in the business of suppressing unfavorable test results in order to sell potentially lethal drugs, the last thing we should be doing is making it easier on them financially to pursue this way of doing business. What strikes me as odd is that not only are our leaders not making this connection, they are, in fact, coming to the opposite conclusion."

Sunny lifted the dough to her face and breathed in. The aroma of yeast was pleasing to her senses. Then she sprinkled more flour on the counter and began to knead some more.

"I know our society doesn't value critical thinking," he continued. "But what has happened to our basic survival skills?" Sunny paused and considered how twenty years ago, as an audience of one, she had heard this voice speak similar words.

"As far as the Arctic is concerned, to be applauding the destruction of our life-support system as a way to produce more of what is creating the loss of our life-support system takes backward thinking to a new level. People have been dying of the heat in Europe in increasing numbers. The most pessimistic of scientists did not anticipate this kind of widespread die off until the middle of the century. But yet we can't agree on a different course of action. It's the kind of event that should serve as an opening into a discussion about what we can do either to prevent this from worsening or prepare for the worst."

The host of the program responded, "History shows we have a great deal of success when we have confidence in what we're doing and stick with it. Willingness to do that, through thick and thin, is the mark of a strong survival instinct. Under most circumstances, there is more risk in abandoning the proven way and that's why we hesitate to do it. To most of us, questioning the long-term viability of the status quo and working to change it speaks to a low survival instinct. For me, that would amount to taking the biggest risk with my future and that of my children."

"What it really speaks to is natural selection dealing us a bad hand when it comes to dealing with the kind of difficulties we're facing today. The traits that made our ancestors successful in the survival game determine what we are today – sexually prolific, tribal, self-centered, and short-term thinkers. Those who were the most preoccupied by sex, as well as fertile, had the highest likelihood of being represented in the gene pool. Being tribal paid off because there was security and safety in numbers. If one wished to survive, being self-centered was also useful. And I can't overstate the importance of being a short-term thinker when enough food must be found just to get through the day or when there are predators lurking in the bushes. Having one's mind focused on making the world a better place wouldn't have paid large dividends in those days. In all honesty, it doesn't pay that well today either."

The Weekend Edition host laughed and so did Sunny. This got John's attention. She had forgotten he was there until he came storming into the kitchen. "What the fuck is so funny?" he asked.

She was not forced to explain, however, once John realized his wife was listening to that liberal trash of which she was so fond. He left the room as quickly as he had entered, slamming the door behind him to ensure none of that liberal poison polluted his mind.

Jerome's words came across as refreshing after the uninvited interruption. "It's important to understand why we're so set in our ways. If we fear truth because it would put some of the beliefs on which our civilization is based in jeopardy, then I don't know why we bother learning. When that kind of fear permeates a society the situation is hopeless. Knowledge could be put to good use in encouraging behavior adaptation. Obviously, there are some opportunities in that arena. I suppose it's possible that we'll still be debating issues such as Global Warming when there are two colonies of humans left – one at the north pole and one at the south pole," said the voice on the radio. "If that news report is any indication it's highly likely that will be the case."

Next, Jerome was asked what could be done about problems that are overwhelming to the average individual. She put down the box of cornmeal she had been sprinkling over the baking sheet and listened more intently. He went on to explain that this preoccupation we have with issues rather than an overall vision is debilitating. "This pandering by politicians to the most uninformed segments of the population has got to stop. We are facing ecological and economic disaster. We don't need any more leaders who are just like the average Joe – lacking in fiscal discipline and lacking in ideas about how to change the way we live. The system is crumbling and is going to have to be remade from the ground up. And I mean everything. We are going to have to look at ourselves differently, at what the human role is, how we interact with the planet, how we educate ourselves, how we work, how we get around, how we can become critical thinkers. Instead of patting ourselves on the back and telling ourselves how great we are, I suggest we expend some effort on truly being great. The problem with industrial civilization is that it does not evolve, it consumes. And it will eventually consume its way into a post-industrial Stone Age. Evolution is the answer – cultural and biological. It always has been and it always will be. We should seriously consider abandoning any Institutions that are an impediment to that."

"That was Jerome Raines and his new book is *Crisis, What Crisis? – How "Advanced" Civilization Bickers While Earth Burns*. As always, it's a pleasure to hear your point of view. Thanks for talking with us today."

"Another book," Sunny said to her ball of dough as she rolled it into a smooth round and covered it with a towel. What had happened in the two and a half years since Sunny became reacquainted with the man being interviewed on the radio? For all she knew this wasn't the only book he'd written since then. She hadn't followed up with her personal promise to broaden her perspective. She feared that alternative viewpoint more than complacency. Since being promoted to the top position of Director, she had more to lose should she venture forward. She was one of the liberal-minded that Karen alluded to back in February of 2005, someone who thought she was already sufficiently enlightened. Another two and a half years had been lost. She was ready to heed the nudging and prodding. Reaching behind her back she unfastened her apron, slipped it over her head and threw it down on the counter. She left the kitchen, entered the office, turned on the computer, and began to search.

She discovered that he had written four books. Four books and she had not read a one of them. But when she did, she was struck by how unfamiliar both the information and perspective were. She had either not been exposed or had failed to register anything new in many years. Taking this step changed all of that. The weeks spent discovering Jerome Raines rushed by in a whirlwind of expectation. Each time she saw his image on a jacket and then began to turn the pages to find what was inside she was a modern day explorer about to make a grand discovery. She forced herself to read them in the order they were written so that she could get a sense of being alongside him in the journey – in the Evolution of his mind. The information contained on those pages provided a way for her to reconnect

The Institution

with the world of ideas. A world she had come to believe was imagined. And she couldn't get enough of him.

Jerome's latest book ventured into environmental territory – her area of expertise. By coincidence, not long after picking up the book, Sunny learned of a conference in Seattle that related indirectly to her work and she decided to attend. All the talk in 2007 and 2008 shifted in the direction of Global Warming. That was the hot button issue that had moved to the forefront of every environmental discussion going on in the world and it was capturing the short attention spans of experts and laymen alike. The whole fascination with the problem could be attributed to that basic human belief that anything, no matter how devastating, could be fixed through technology. In the case of Global Warming, it was bio-fuel and carbon offset policies. Environmentalists had a large part to play in the conviction that bio-fuels would save the day. Evidently, no one in power had put a pencil and paper to the consequences.

Sunny found it peculiar that Jerome was invited to speak at this particular conference. In *Crisis, What Crisis?*, he referred to environmental, economic, health, and resource emergencies that were building up one on top of the other. Global warming was but one of them and he had not suggested that planting crops to feed a personal transportation habit was a viable solution. If the organizers of the conference had read his other books, they would have known it was unlikely he would endorse any kind of move to keep us moving unless it involved getting off our lazy asses and walking. The environmental movement had waited for their moment in the sun for a very long time. Their concerns were now a political priority. So ready to strut their stuff, they didn't anticipate criticism from one of their own. But Jerome wasn't one of them. He was an independent who called it the way he saw it. Even the most committed environmentalists couldn't wrap their minds around the bad news Jerome laid on them at that conference. His attempts to enlighten them about the unfeasibility of any environmental plan that paid homage to the automobile were not appreciated.

Sunny made sure she attended the session at which he was scheduled to speak. She had a hunch it wouldn't be like the others, and he didn't disappoint. It was funny to watch the group get something they hadn't bargained for. One of the many high points was when Jerome said, "We're going to have to kiss our cars good bye. You see, cars are hungrier than humans – about 1,500 times as hungry. Turning land for growing food for humans into food for cars is a really bad idea. Unless, of course, we're all willing to eat less than one meal per day and the population suddenly starts decreasing. Then we might be able to swing it."

That was right before he expressed disgust, instead of the admiration they were expecting, for their environmental efforts. "I'm more than a little disappointed with the lack of imagination being exhibited. All you can muster is an alternate way to fuel what's in place? You may be so pleased with what's been accomplished thus far that you don't believe there could be anything better, but I'm not that wowed. I think we can do better. Our civilization must be looked at as a work-in-progress. How about we at least make an effort to think outside the car, big house, food supply 1,500 miles away, pollution, chemicals, technofixes, and the lack of quality in just about everything we do? All of it has got to go. How about we quit worrying about moving around and consider moving forward? It's too late in the day to convert the oil economy in its current form to a bio-fuel economy."

While he was saying this, knowing he was really pissing some people off, he wondered whether it wasn't too late period. What could they logically do? What did lie beyond industrial civilization? Was it the space age future that had been the science fiction of his youth, the post-industrial Stone Age of the doomsday scenario, or was there another possibility? How might he tackle that?

"Now if we were talking about bio-fuels or hydrogen or solar to operate rail in place of automobiles and I mean right down the middle of where freeways, highways, and arterial roads are today, the discussion would be moving in a viable direction. But it would be perceived as going backwards and would be fought accordingly. In the first half of the 20th Century, when automobiles replaced rail, it was a case of a lower quality system replacing a more highly evolved one. The good of society should trump selfish individualism. However, it is no secret that automobiles speak very strongly to the latter. Ford's invention of the assembly line, along with the discovery of plentiful, cheap energy, was so effective in satisfying biological urges it led us away from the common good that it had taken centuries to achieve. It was one of many steps we've taken toward rewarding selfish, primitive behavior at the expense of a workable society, clean environment, and a healthy planet. When a civilization defines satisfying base desires as its ultimate goal, I don't know what it hopes to accomplish but I suspect the strides we're currently making provide a clue. Bigger vehicles, wider highways, more air flights, increased debt, larger homes and more second homes. Land development is currently outpacing population growth by seven times. Ever larger televisions located in more rooms of our homes and more public spaces – airports, restaurants, waiting rooms, offices. Higher calorie consumption from further up the food chain. And the mother of all accomplishments; education for the sole purpose of acquiring more of what I just listed.

"'If it feels good, do it' is not advanced thinking and it's not a slogan on which intelligent human beings should build a civilization with a future. It appears, however, to be the one on which carbon offset programs were designed. Another shameful solution concocted by the environmental community. We are resourceful when it comes to finding ways to continue bad behavior. The constructs we will invent to feel good about that same behavior are beyond belief. I suppose carbon offset programs are a pragmatic society's way of dealing with truth as defined by that society. Namely, what the developed world has to offer its citizens is a lot of goodies that are the very essence of modernity. To be denied access to them would be a giant leap backwards. No modern, advantaged person would do this voluntarily. Since it isn't feasible to stop behavior that industrial civilization has determined is essential to quality of life, some kind of mitigation measure must be employed. An indulgence tax is just the ticket to make educated, well-informed people comfortable with the damage they are reeking on the biosphere by planting a tree or two.

"If we were a rational, reasonable, or realistic society we might accept an actual truth, one we are currently incapable of seeing. We would conclude that many of the values on which western civilization was built aren't true at all. It's comical that we're unable to recognize their falseness. A rational society would say we're going to have to stop this nonsense. We're going to have to create lives that are meaningful on a daily basis, close to home, so that we don't feel compelled to escape our low quality existence. This means changing much about how human habitats operate, are designed, and how they feel. And it also means a shift in the way we feel about the definition of progress itself.

"The destiny of progress, the way it's currently defined, is to extinguish the planet's ability to sustain life. How can we be so enamored by such a thing? And how do we advance beyond the fascination with gewgaws and technofixes? Programs like carbon offsets reinforce bad behavior as something desirable to be done at any cost and ensure our dollars and efforts keep a bad system up and running. And that starves alternatives.

"The study of past Evolution is fascinating. But it is in the potential beyond the static state where the real magic lies. That evolutionary studies end with who, what, and where we are right now is telling. It points to an innate belief that we humans have achieved the ultimate in biological and cultural Evolution. This is a blind spot that may prevent man from becoming the link between ape and civilized human being. Further advancement? That will depend on whether we're willing to engage in a dynamic, higher quality relationship with a planetary system that holds the key to Evolution."

***

After that cheery speech access to Jerome was unfettered for the rest of the afternoon. The public agency folks were so stunned they didn't know what to say or think. On their way to the next session, they made a nice wide berth around this confused author. Sunny decided to take advantage of his pariah status. She purchased a Black Butte Porter at the Bar and joined him where he sat alone in a corner with a pint in one hand and a pen in the other. Engrossed in the notes he was taking, he did not notice her until she pulled out the stool across from him and sat down. It wasn't the first time that she wondered from whom or where he got his strength. Going against the flow like that, how did he do it?

"It's me again," she said. "Crazy, isn't it? Our paths don't cross once in eighteen years and now twice in under three."

"You're still speaking to me. There's hope for you yet."

The Institution

"You've got guts, Jerry. An environmental conference is an interesting choice of venues to say what you did. The least I can do is toast you and your lack of concern about your popularity." She clicked her beer glass against his.

"What are we drinking to? The mean green meme?" he asked.

"How about tough love. That's what you just dished out, isn't it?"

"I try to be honest. The way I see it we have some tough times ahead unless we're willing to let go of a few luxuries that we believe we must have. I get the crazy feeling that if we had the chance to do it all again, we would do it exactly the same way. And that is mind-boggling because it means we haven't learned a thing. We still believe that the way we're living has a future. Why is that?"

"It's all we've ever known. There's no one even alive today who was born before oil was discovered. And darn few who knew a time without cars and plastics and strawberries in January. Stone Age Man couldn't envision a world different from the one he lived in. He certainly didn't imagine what we have. You're expecting too much. You're wishing for the impossible."

"It's always been value-driven and self-fulfilling though. If we thought the most important need was something like leisure, we would have come up with a system that emphasized that. What if the force behind our civilization was something like quality? And not only the quality of individual lives but also the quality of the system. Would that not shape a very different future from the one our current beliefs will create? As it is, we're completely hung up on things like personal wealth, convenience, and tradition."

"You know what you're explaining with that quality stuff is very similar to environmental philosophy and the preservation of healthy ecosystems."

"I know it is. That's why I'm hard on the environmental community. They ought to get it. They ought to have the imagination to envision a human system based on those same principles. *You* ought to get it, Sunny."

"Jerry, environmentalists are not the enemy. Neither are individuals. Corporations are to blame. Corporations have fought it all from fuel economy standards to emissions controls. Under the current administration,

169

Terra Dime

they're too powerful. Once we get the right regulations in place, things will be better. I told you before once the Democrats are back in power we'll all begin to feel better about our circumstances, including you." She was thinking specifically about her employment prospects and her wish to see the County Commissioners, her bosses, ousted by Democrats. In Sunny's line of work, one of the challenges when it came to environmental continuity was whether a political party made it a priority or not. It had been "one step forward, two steps back" for as long as she could remember. What else could she do but hang her hopes on the Democratic Party? It was only when they were in office that any strides at all in her line of work came to pass.

"That's a terrible message – telling people all that is required is a change in leadership. Big government and big corporations are one and the same. Neither of those large Institutions is amenable to significant change or innovation. Change will have to come from another source. At what point do you and your cohorts intend to connect the dots and voice publicly that all the public agencies in the world can't regulate this system into feasibility?"

"Since we last spoke, I read all your books. I loved them. They're wonderful from a purely philosophical standpoint but reality is something else all together."

Sunny worked within that reality everyday. Jerome thought she wasn't doing enough. The Commissioners thought she was saying and doing too much about corporate polluters. Right now, while she was attending this conference, those wagons of theirs were circling. They were rallying around their political sponsors and plotting which of their methods to employ in order to remove her. If she had done what was ethical with regard to the health of the Silver River, she would have joined the ranks of the unemployed much sooner than she was going to. Ethics didn't pay. Greed and stupidity were lucrative though. She did not mention any of this. It continued to be Sunny's way to keep information about her grim personal circumstances to herself.

"Sunny, you're smarter than you're pretending to be. To see you shut down and hide behind the righteousness of an environmental agency under the control of politicians is not very impressive."

The Institution

She sat quietly, not knowing what to say. All the insults that had been hurled at her over the years didn't sting like the sensation he was losing all the good feelings he once held for her. Sunny's ego was in her throat. She could feel it there grabbing at her voice and trying to prevent her from saying what she really felt. Prior to that day, her ego consistently won the battle of wills. She reached across the table and placed her hand on his. He looked up from his beer, startled by the gesture.

"Jerry, I have so much to lose. More than I ever thought I'd have in terms of lifestyle and prestige. I wish I was like you, really I do. But I'm not. I'm too practical. I can live without many things but I can't live without my job. That's the ugly truth. I'd be nobody without it."

It may have been the most honest thing she had said in a decade and Jerome had mixed emotions about it. He was encouraged that she was being up front with him but also discouraged that she was more concerned with what she had than who she was. And he was reminded of Erich Fromm's book *To Have or to Be*. Sunny had chosen the former – assets and assimilation. The preference for those was so predictable that it was absurd for him to feel bad for her. But that was, in fact, how he felt. His fingers closed around hers, real and warm.

"Sometimes I forget how powerful the whole thing is. When I hear individuals defend their livelihoods the way you just did, I'm not sure who's doing the talking. I'm not sure you know either."

Jerome had this image he couldn't erase – each of us – daubs of paint taking up a small portion of a very large canvas. We did not recognize the narrow parameters for what they were. We had convinced ourselves there was nothing beyond that tiny place where we existed and that what we had gleaned from our time spent there was the important stuff.

"It's all about fitting in. You have to live in the village. At least I do. Creating a different one is too daunting. You can choose to live poorly or well. I chose the latter."

"Is that living well or living large?" The embarrassed look that flashed across her face told him which. "So it wouldn't matter to you how unethical or destructive the underlying village values were, you would still support and defend it and extract your reward? How far would you go? If not speaking out meant the planet would die, would you speak out then? Is there some line you have in your mind that you will not cross? Or is it possible to think in those terms when you've been programmed by the village?"

Sunny hated to think about their household footprint. It was huge. Carbon offset programs had been invented for people like her and John. He was on a plane half the time traveling to the other side of the world "streamlining production" of completely frivolous items. When he was home they led the active, successful lifestyle which involved travel to either the condo or the cabin. The shoulder seasons took them further afield. They had to keep busy. Their marriage depended on it. As an environmentalist, this was the thing she struggled with the most – the line between living in a sustainable fashion and enjoying life. But it was so much more than that. It meant incorporating being well-informed and vocal and proactive and not living large into her definition of the good life. It was understanding how every purchase she made left an environmental impact. Caring and consuming were mutually exclusive, no matter how it was packaged. It meant being more concerned about what the government was doing in her name than whose baby the latest pop star was having. And in this land, it wasn't a very sexy way to be. If the technology was available to do something and it was affordable, it was unreasonable to expect people not to use it, wasn't it? That was why carbon offsets were such a hit.

"I don't know what you're asking. It's not like I'm personally hurting anyone. I'm just doing my job."

He let go of her hand. "Really? And who do you think you work for?"

"If you mean do I know that I'm a public servant and that taxpayers ultimately pay my wages, of course I do. And there's something else I know. They don't want to know the truth. If I thought people wanted the whistle blown, it would make a difference and I would do it. But I've tried on a small scale, in the company of people who should trust me to be speaking the truth. Here, let me list some of what I've attempted to discuss.

"Wasteful Water Use – we can afford it, it's so cheap, and as long as it still flows from the tap there isn't a problem. Peak Oil – no such thing – we won't run out of oil for at least another hundred years. Alternative Fuels – we'll come up with something – the technofix is just around the corner.

The Institution

Pollution – our air and water are in better condition today than they were a hundred years ago. Population Control – that's taboo – besides population is leveling off so no need to worry about that. Fertilizers, Herbicides, Pesticides – got to have them on my crappy little lawn. Processed Food – I don't intend to spend my life in the kitchen.

"I can't even get my next door neighbors to consider cutting back on the Round-Up. Do you think I would have success if I stood up as a public servant and set off the alarm about the condition of our river and then had the audacity to lay out what it would take to make it right? My family and friends already think I'm an idiot. The general public would eat my lunch. I'm not willing to give up my 'large life' as you call it for a public that does not wish to know the truth. I won't do it."

It was depressing to think about the stilted conversations she had initiated. She couldn't get any traction. There was no easy way to get people who had spent a lifetime spinning their wheels up to speed in an instant. Because what you were really asking was whether it made sense to continue investing in a way of life that was verging on obsolescence. They had no point of view on that. It was futile to keep asking and yet that was the one question Jerome persisted in posing.

"Whoa," he said, surprised that all this pent-up passion of hers was coming to the surface. "I wasn't thinking in terms of your working for the general public. I was referring to the planet. That's your real boss – the one you're supposed to be working for. I didn't mean to imply that I hold you to a higher standard because you work for a public agency. Keeping the planet healthy is a responsibility we all share."

Sunny had been holding back for a long time and now she was ready to talk. "I don't understand why we don't do better. Why can't we stop? We're digging ourselves a hole. Does it have something to do with the way human beings are inclined to behave worse in a group than individually? I think that's key," she said. "It's why societies don't produce optimal results. Kind of like when guys get together and act like complete jerks resorting to behavior they don't personally condone. We are willing to be untrue to ourselves to fit in. That's how much we value it. We might ask ourselves in hindsight why we went along. But that wouldn't stop us from doing it again another time for the very same reason. Haven't you ever dated someone you thought was okay on a one-to-one basis and then when you saw her in a group, you were completely turned off by how superficial she became?"

"That sounds familiar."

"Humans are social creatures who want to please their peers."

"That's more of a commentary on the quality of our civilization don't you think?" Jerome responded. "Society brings the behavior of some individuals to a higher level but the bar is set such that it doesn't encourage the really exceptional. That's not to say we couldn't organize society to take that into account. We could choose to be a collective, conscious intelligence instead of the unconscious, non-intelligence we currently are. Unfortunately, the civilization we've created is one for babies. It's based on a set of immature principles. Think about it. The structure kind of resembles the parent/child model when it comes to our Institutions. On the job, we are paid for being told what to do and get raises when we perform in a compliant fashion. Our political system places a patriarchal figure at the very top and he chooses what we will value during his term. And to top it all off, we cannot seem to grow beyond a religion based on a set of beliefs that if followed without question will also deliver a reward from the big parent in the sky." He paused for a moment and let all that sink in. "Well, it sounds like you've been giving thought to some things. I'm glad to hear that."

"Maybe so. But you won't be glad to hear some of the other conclusions I've come to. Like fully understanding why I became an environmentalist in the first place. I would like to see some kind of life, other than human, left on this planet once we're gone. I'm not a humanitarian in the way that you are. I do not wish for the survival of mankind, the way you do. Not, if it comes at the expense of all other life. I can't get past how clueless we are to wish for our continued existence. I have tried to do my part to minimize our destruction of the ecosystem so that once we're gone, the deer and antelope still have a place to play. For me, that's what matters most."

"And I would agree with you on that. I don't believe humans have a claim on the universe. I wish to see life of all kinds continue on this planet. I'm not in love with humanity alone and I recognized a long time ago that satisfying our desires is not the most important goal. The only difference is you believe if the human being continues to exist, all other beings don't stand a chance. Therefore, you've come to the conclusion that it's time for man to go. At one level I know you're right and that what I'm thinking about is a lost cause, but I feel I have to try. I can't accept that where we're at right now is the best we can do. We have to find a way to move beyond this. It's time for man, as we currently know him, to go and a better quality of human being to take his place. Developing ourselves is a challenge we must take on because every problem stems from our shortcomings."

"Wake-up, Jerry. The majority of the population doesn't want to change a thing. They're happily rolling along enjoying the superficial goodies the modern world has to offer. They're tuned into it and loving it. If this whole thing collapses, they'll miss their fast food, cars, trinkets, weed whackers, NASCAR, and trips to Disneyland. How low we're going to go cannot be understood by those who didn't bother to read a single book while society was able to produce citizens who could write them. It is a small contingency who can grasp the seriousness of the situation and recognize the slide back into the Dark Ages for what it is. Most have completely missed out on the knowledge and wisdom at their disposal. And because they don't know we had the potential to be so much more they will be spared that loss. No one longs to be more than they are. That's why another way of being or seeing doesn't exist for most people. You're suffering disproportionately. And I don't understand why you would do that. Your fellow man isn't worth caring about."

"Present company excluded, of course," he said interrupting her in mid-sentence.

She shrugged her shoulders in response as if to say, *You tell me.*

"You fall into a trap when you group everyone together into one big screw-up. I try to think of people as individuals. I envision those I care about and what I would like to see in their future. Otherwise I'm bound to become prejudiced. Perhaps the same argument holds true for weighing the pros and cons of man's future as it does for capital punishment. 'It is better that ten guilty go free than one innocent suffer.'"

"Jerry, you're overlooking one important point. I am one big screw-up. I might be the biggest one of all because I should know better. You said so yourself."

"But still you have potential. I know you do." He laughed when he said it and on the surface made light of what she said, but he also saw the truth in it. His efforts were based on an underlying hope that man would survive. That with all the evidence to the contrary, man's survival was a worthwhile goal. He was also aware that everything he proposed relied on the improvement of the overall quality of the human species. Without that, not only was the possibility of survival unlikely but also the merit of the goal itself was called into question.

"You know what's odd about you, Jerry? You don't self-monitor depending on whose company you're in. Your internal self is consistent with your external. There aren't many people who can say that. That's why you gave the speech that you did instead of the speech that was expected. It catches people off guard. They don't know how to react. I think it's a good trait by the way, a quality one. That's why I'm not offended by what you say even when it's personal because it speaks to the part of me that dreams of what humanity might have been."

"Sunny, do you really feel that in the past tense?"

The beers they ordered were placed in front of them and the interruption forced them to look up as their empty glasses were removed from the table. For Sunny that meant confronting those eyes that haunted her adolescence and her dreams with what it meant to be human.

"Yes, I believe we're done. And, I believe it will happen in our lifetime." Jerome reached for her hand and curled his fingers under hers as if he thought anyone who admitted this should not do so unless they were holding fast to someone else.

She began to speak candidly. "Sometimes I think we're reading the whole political situation wrong. We're all screaming about unnecessary imperialistic wars and loss of freedoms, me included, but what's really being attended to is maintaining our lifestyles for whatever time we have left. And, as I demonstrated by my failure to engage even thoughtful individuals in meaningful discussions, our way of life is non-negotiable. It has occurred to me that our elected leaders are implicitly protecting what the average citizen wants them to protect. If we had guts and/or foresight, we would admit that keeping this going for as long as possible will take a lot of death and destruction."

From her, another genuine response. That made two, in a matter of minutes. He sensed it was only a beginning. Before responding, he brought her hand to his face and brushed the back of it across his cheek. The fondness he showed for her worked its way through her brittle exterior. It was becoming no easy task for someone as romantically impoverished as Sunny to continue giving the impression she was unaffected.

Jerome continued on with the thread of conversation she had dared to drag out into the open. "What I wonder, is how many times throughout human history two people have sat across from one another like this and pondered these same kinds of things? Are you right in assuming we will live to see the end? What are the chances that of all the humans who have existed we are in the final group? Are those chances greater or lesser than the odds that we would be born in the wealthiest time the species has ever known? Is the linking of those two odds more than a coincidence? My Aunt Joan used to scoff when I brought up dire predictions. She once told me that 'people have been predicting the end of time since the beginning of time so I shouldn't take any of it too seriously.' But some group of people is going to face it. It's just a matter of who."

"The one thing I do know," Sunny said, "is that it would have been just like this when it happened before. Pick a lost civilization. Say, the Mayans. There would have been those Mayans who thought everything was fine and didn't wish to be bothered by pessimistic thinking. There would have been the progressive Mayans who were convinced standards of living could keep rising indefinitely as long as a few minor adjustments were made. There would have been the earnest Mayans saying, 'No, no we have to make major changes otherwise we're doomed.' Inevitably, there would have been the pragmatic Mayans who were in the progressive camp at one time and then segued into the earnest one before finally settling into reality. Their mantra would be 'screw it.' The faster the whole thing goes down the better off it will be. Since no one intends to change one iota, full steam ahead is the best course of action. Get it over with as fast as possible and maybe, just maybe, there will be something left to salvage."

"Well, Sunny, thanks for that. You're a bigger downer than I am."

"I can't help it. I'm curious about details. Like what did different kinds of people think about and talk about when the collapse of their civilization was imminent? Now I know. And I can't say I'm particularly impressed. So now you and I have gone full circle. We're right where we started in 1986. We recognized the adjustments that needed to be made. However, most were neither noticed nor discussed," Sunny said sadly. "More than twenty years later we're a zoned out unconscious civilization that has given up pretending it has any notions about an ideal future or that it is pursuing 'The Good Society.' We're suffocating under the weight of keeping it all going and pretending we're enjoying it. So in a way, we're already suffering. The statistics on mental illness tell you that. The question is how long will the pain last and how excruciating will it become?"

Just as Jerome opened his mouth to speak a woman standing at the door to the Bar noticed them and approached their table. "Sorry for interrupting," she said. "Sarah, we'd like to be on the road in about thirty minutes. Can you swing that?" She tried to look away from her co-worker's hand holding, but couldn't quite manage it. "I didn't realize you two knew one another."

"Oh yes," Sunny replied nonchalantly. "We go back a long ways." Nothing else was offered. No one bothered with introductions. Sunny told her she'd be finished here in a minute and would be right up to the room to get her bags. The other woman left.

"That thing I said a few years ago when you were in Silver Falls. About not being attracted to you like I once was. That wasn't a true statement," the *real* Sunny felt compelled to tell him.

"No?" As far as Jerome was concerned these confessions of hers kept getting better. He tried to think of something else to say that would put her further at ease. "Well, that's a relief. I thought I'd lost my touch."

"Not with me you haven't. That's for sure." She let go of his hand and stood up. "I wish I could stay longer but it looks like it's time for me to head back across the mountains."

The Institution

"If ever you'd like to continue our discussion here's a card with my e-mail address," he said. His expression seemed to reflect a blend of optimism and sadness.

"Looks like you have a blog too," she commented after looking over his information.

"What else would you expect from an extremely opinionated author," he said when she started to leave.

She laughed as she turned her head for another look, "Great things," she said. "Really great things."

Those words stood in stark contrast to what she was treated to when she returned home. The County Commissioners had initiated their attack while she was out of town. In addition to sending her a memo, one of them, a real estate man prior to his appointment, had taken it upon himself to speak to the press about Sunny's attire. According to him, the Commissioners didn't like the way she dressed, too casual, not the image they wished for her to portray. This reproach succeeded in filling her with wonder at the smallness of elected officials. Even as she contemplated this petty complaint, she knew it was only the start. They would invent more substantial criticisms. This was a way to get her out there in a questionable light. More complaints would follow. After a while, hers would be a household name. Always in the paper, always shrouded in controversy until the citizens of Silver Falls would be relieved when she was finally removed.

The Commissioners next tried to nail Sunny with some ethical issues that weren't well thought out on their part. Once that tactic proved unsuccessful, they moved on to the epiphany that the Department did not have to be headed by a person who knew anything about environmental issues. It could be handled just as well by a layman, an administrator, or in other words a bureaucrat, acting as a liaison between them and the scientific staff. Preferably, someone who "dressed real good" and knew the "value of a robust economy." It would be optimal if this special someone wasn't concerned about the health of the environment.

While Sunny's life fizzled around her, she contemplated many things. The dedication she had exhibited towards her employment seemed pointless once she realized that its continuation was not based on performance. She thought about how inconsistent it all seemed. She was at the mercy of conservative politicians whose platforms revolved around personal independence and rugged individualism. Unfortunately, that did not extend beyond the abolition of social programs. This same leadership believed strongly in keeping lowly wage slaves in the most infantile state of dependency. Were whistleblowers who drew attention to the breaking of laws heralded for their independence? Hardly. Were those who questioned the stupid men in charge held in high regard? No. There were labels for those people. Labels like insubordinate, disgruntled, belligerent. They were not team players. If she spoke up, those labels would be attached to her name and there would be no shaking them. It was a hypocritical, demoralizing system that was all about towing the line and maintaining the status quo.

There were days when she came close to laying everything she knew out there on the line. She wanted to go on record about what a sham the whole environmental protection racket was. And she wanted to make sure that every last person in the city of Silver Falls knew that she wasn't fooled by the motives of the Commissioners and neither should they. She would be inches away from dishing out a large helping of truth, a plate full of tough love, the kind Jerome dealt in, when she would begin to feel guilty for questioning the command and control system. Everyone said she should accept it. It was that way for a good reason. We couldn't have attained a high standard of living without it. And yet, she had a hard time believing that mankind could not conceive of something more gratifying. How could anyone not be despondent about cronies who were worthless in their own right making their way to the top?

But that was all philosophical reflection on her part and not very productive given the hand she had been dealt. Circumstances on the ground were dire with respect to her job and where she was going to end up. Already the balance of power was shifting in her household. John blamed her for the mess she was in. According to him, she had never listened to reason from anyone and now it was going to cost the two of them big time. He told her they were going to have to start selling assets. The ski condo first, the cabin second. They'd be lucky if they could hold on to the house.

The Institution

She would never find another job that paid as well as the one she had. She would have to work two jobs, he told her, to make up for the shortfall.

In the interim, she tried to think and believe in the abstract. Once she returned from the conference in Seattle, she began letting out her lifeline in Jerome's direction a little at a time. Wishing to disconnect from what was going on around her, she had difficulty remaining frugal in her contact. Not when there was this persistent void that he filled so perfectly. He drew attention to what separated her from the people in her life she ought to be closest to and pushed her to another level of discontentment with her surroundings.

On Saturday mornings, Sunny slipped in front of the computer at home to read the latest posting on Jerome's blog. She did this with the kind of enthusiasm she hadn't felt since adolescence. When she read his stuff, she thought every sane person on the planet would want to jump on board. It made her feel less unusual as she read through the comments by ordinary people who were also dissatisfied with the current state of affairs. It heartened her to know that there were thoughtful intelligent people out there. But it also saddened her that they were spread so far and wide and not easy to hook up with. Within her circle of acquaintances these were not the kind of discussions that were taking place and she found herself less willing to settle for what her family and friends were offering.

What constituted a community anyway? Traditionally, it was those with whom one shared a physical place but what if that were all that was shared? How to reconcile the philosophical closeness of distant strangers with the mental desolation of those nearby? Why were so few asking whether we could do better? At the very least, all one had to do was extrapolate the current trends into a not very distant future, and come to the logical conclusion that it was not going to be pretty. This didn't appear to be done in the mainstream but it was something Jerome Raines did lucidly. What encouraged her most about his writing was that he did have ideas about how to improve our lives. His was neither a negative vision nor a painful transition. Instead of laying blame for our current situation, he indicated that what was appropriate in the past was no longer viable. It was a way of life that the Earth could not support. There were too many of us.

Terra Dime

For a while his blog and the people who visited it were more than enough, more than Sunny had dared to hope for, until she too began to comment frequently. It was a natural progression, to wish to be more than a lurker at his site. Before long, she was e-mailing him privately, at first occasionally and then regularly, until she had a good idea what he was working on, where he was going, and what he was thinking on a daily basis.

At that point she seriously considered seeking a divorce. But she knew if she did it then, under those circumstances, it would be because of Jerome. He had changed her expectations. She was honest with herself about that, as well as the fact that she didn't have much to bring to another relationship except a pile of financial baggage. She knew what was coming her way as far as employment was concerned. That wasn't to say she was without options. She could start up her own consulting firm or go to work for someone else who was already in the business. But she always felt sorry for those people because their services were often required by land developers in order to put an environmentally friendly spin on projects that weren't environmentally friendly at all. She didn't wish to compromise her principles to that degree. And she was sure Jerome wouldn't wish her to do that for the sake of money. The whole thing was so embarrassing that she wasn't able to bring herself to discuss it and give him the chance to mull it over.

She also knew she couldn't be objective when it came to Jerome. She hadn't been from the first second she saw him. It wasn't something she had ever told anyone. How she had been unable to forget what passed between two teenagers. She thought she would come across as silly trying to explain how a brief encounter had impacted her way beyond what the circumstances warranted. She decided to break the code of silence. She spoke of it twice – once, to a male colleague and another time, to the members of her book club. She didn't give any details but she did ask, in passing, how they felt about loving someone you didn't know that well. In both cases, almost all concerned thought whatever she was describing wasn't real. And most of them went on to relate a protracted courtship that ended in a marriage that was tolerable at best. All but Karen. From across the living room, at the home in which the book club met that night, she looked right through Sunny and knew exactly who and what this was about.

Not for a second did she believe this was a hypothetical question that Sunny was asking. Karen tried once again to help her. She suggested there were many factors to consider. Age, maturity, quality of the individuals, and what it was that was drawing the two people to one another. She implied that if Sunny asked herself those questions, she would have her answer, and with it, nothing to fear. But as far as Sunny was concerned, it was nine nays and one yea. She had another excuse not to make a change in her life.

***

A few months after the Seattle conference, a Sustainability Summit was held in Silver Falls giving Sunny another reason to see Jerome. It was the final event she would attend in her capacity as Director because she had been asked to resign. After so successfully predicting that outcome, she didn't have the stomach to speculate further on her future.

It was no chance meeting that brought them together. They had planned in advance of the Sustainability Summit to meet for a bike ride at noon on the final day. He decided to make a vacation out of it and brought his bike with him. Sunny often had her bike with her because she used it to get around as much as she could and that included to and from work. That was why her dress wasn't as impeccable as the Commissioners would have liked. Her preferred mode of transportation had also been a sore point with them. It wasn't unheard of for an environmental agency to promote alternative transportation, but not those dudes. It made her a freak in their eyes. A liberal one. The worst kind.

"How did you ever manage to stay single?" Sunny asked as they stood on the bridge overlooking the falls in the heart of downtown. She'd been thinking about it over the last couple of days as she watched the way women tried to get his attention. It was the same on the bike ride over from the Conference Center. He didn't slip by any females unnoticed. She wondered what caught their eye. Did they see what she saw? Or was he simply good looking? "I'm sure you've noticed this. Women stare at you."

"That's because I'm funny looking."

"No you're not."

"I've been too busy protesting. A guy like me does fine until I open my mouth. The women I've met want the conventional and they want stability. I can't provide either. Society has programmed them for that. There's nothing worse than a man who is not a good provider. There are many traits that can be overlooked but that doesn't happen to be one of them. It's acceptable to have an unhealthy relationship with your husband. Who cares if you have nothing to talk about? It's not even necessary to like your spouse as long as he has a job."

She felt sick inside at how close he had come to describing her marriage. "But you've written several books. You must make a decent living."

"I've had many lean years. Some of the time I barely scraped by. I lived in furnished basement suites, didn't have a car, never went out for dinner, had absolutely no possessions – only books. All I did was read and write and when I did talk it was about stuff most people hadn't heard of. Not exactly the catch of a lifetime."

"What about now?"

"I live on a sailboat in Gig Harbor. I don't have much in the way of assets. I've always had this burning need to be able to pick up and move on whenever I feel like it. Kind of nomadic, I guess. What about you, Sunny, are you happy?"

The bridge's top railing provided a place for her to lay her arms. She folded them across the metal edge and turned her head sideways so that her cheek was resting on the backs of her hands. Alongside of her, she noticed Jerome had done the same. When she looked at his face searching hers for the answer to that question, she lost track of it all. The last twenty years of her life gone. Even the great pounding of the falls dropped away.

"It's a crazy thing, the difference in people. How the really bright ones can recognize they have much to learn and the dimwits can be convinced they know it all. And those same dimwits are so good at making others feel foolish or naïve or evil for being curious. Eventually, everyone around them is forced into verbal and mental silence. When you talk of being able to move on, that's the kind of freedom I dream about. Freedom from idiots controlling the process."

"Something tells me you have first hand experience with this."

"Then you would be right. In both my personal and professional life."

"So is that the answer to my question?"

"Yes," she said, leaving it at that. As usual, she wasn't willing to elaborate. "Well, let's go for a ride instead of standing here gawking at one another. I packed us a lunch," she said pointing to her full backpack. "I thought we could head out towards the State Park and the Tempest in a Teapot."

"What's that?"

"It's a rock formation that creates a gorge in the river. It's worth seeing."

"Alright," he agreed, although he was enjoying gawking at her. "You lead the way."

They began riding again, leaving the urban park and heading west down Bridgeview Boulevard and into Valley Flats, an old neighborhood situated on the south side of the Silver River. They rode in silence until reaching the pedestrian crossing at Rock Creek that would take them to the north side. The river curved and headed downstream towards the golf course and the State Park. Sunny looked around at the distant plateaus heavily forested in ponderosa pine before getting off her bike and walking to the other side of the bridge. There, she took in the upriver view of the falls and the city. While she was doing that Jerome came up behind her.

"I want to tell you about a decision I've made. I've been spending far too much time traveling around trying to sell books. I'm going to quit attending conferences and giving speeches," he explained. "It's time to stop talking. Someone has got to start doing. For the next few years, all of my energy is going into two more books that I intend to use to advance a concept. Writing books that are nothing more than critiques isn't a solution. Ideas without implementation are worthless. They lie on a page, in a vacuum, and they fail to grow, much like people. There will be no more weekly blog either. The problem with writing and talking about current issues is it gives you the warm fuzzy feeling that you're doing something when really you're not. I could go years without commenting and if I returned to it, we would still be debating the same worn out topics. And we'd be doing it as if they were fresh and new and no one had ever made the exact same observations years, decades, or even centuries ago. I can't do it any more."

It was the first time he ever voiced this level of concern. A big emptiness began to settle over her at the thought of their no longer being able to communicate. This contact with him was all she had. Without it her life would be small again. "I've often wondered how you do it," she responded. "How you keep going without getting depressed because nothing changes, just as you say."

"There's something else too. I've never been scared like this before. But lately, when I'm writing, I can feel myself groping around the same way other authors who I respect, are doing right now. Unless there's some kind of progression, I don't think any of our thinking is going to advance. Every one of us is stagnating because we're trapped in the same philosophical void. Ideas eventually have to take flight. Some will fall flat. Others will soar to greater heights. It's the taking flight that is key though."

As if in response, a blue heron exploded in flight from a nearby pine tree. Its huge body and long legs curved away from them, out over the river, coasting effortlessly to another perch on the opposite bank.

"So what do you think about my changing course for a while?"

"You have to put your efforts into what you believe is important, I guess. I can't be objective about it because I look forward too much to reading your stuff. I like to know what's going on inside your head and I'm sure I'm not the only one of your fans who feels that way. My concern would be that unless I reminded people every day by commenting on what's going on, I'd be forgotten. You know how short attention spans are. Also, there is some merit in using the Internet as a network. It is quite the tool for distributing complex intelligence. That is what has struck me since I've started reading your blog and getting linked to other sites. There are some really smart people that no one has heard of who don't get recognition for their insight. Mainstream conversations, the whole political system for that matter, is so bleak it's easy to lose sight of that."

They started riding again. Once over the bridge they left the paved path and followed the river downstream until the trail climbed steeply up the bank and terminated on the road above. They then biked past heritage homes lining the rim before descending a steep hill that took them back alongside the river. They entered Silver Falls State Park. Almost immediately, the silence was broken by the crack of a ball being struck followed by a soft thud when it landed on the adjacent fairway. Further along, the river provided white noise as it sped over rapids.

After they rode for a few more miles, Sunny made a left turn off the road and stopped at a bench. "If you're hungry, we could have lunch here. There's a viewpoint right over there that looks out on the Tempest in a Teapot. Or we could go into the campsite below where there are picnic tables. If neither of those options sounds good, we can cross the river and get onto the trails, ride for a while, and eat later."

"I'm pretty hungry," he said. "This bench right here is fine with me."

"The water's still high so the view should be good. What do you think the temperature is, about 95°? Cool spring days aren't what they used to be. We ought to have the place to ourselves. No one in his right mind would be out exercising on a day like this." Sunny unzipped her backpack and handed him a packet. "Grilled vegetables on foccacia and there's also a tabbouleh salad and some fruit. I also took it upon myself to throw in a few cold ones. Would you like one?"

"Did you say beer? I love beer."

"An IPA or an Amber?" she said holding one in each hand so he could check out the labels.

He reached for the IPA, twisted off the cap, and took a long thirsty drink. "Does that ever taste good."

"Somehow I thought you might see it that way," she said.

"I have been known to drown my sorrows in a pint or two."

"Haven't we all," she responded softly as they sat side by side silently sipping their beers, sticky with sweat and drowsy in the heat.

It was such a long time before either of them spoke his voice sounded out of place when he found it again. "The other reason I want to bow out of what I've been doing lately is I'm caught up in this concept of developing people. And I think that can only happen with different living arrangements. I'm trying to come up with this concept – a life-time spa is the closest description I've been able to come up with – that is structured in such a way that it incorporates much of what is missing in our current system. I'm talking about a mixture of liberal arts education, meaningful work, healthy food, quality accommodations, leisure and recreation, and no debt. A movement away from the traditional workplace, financial Institutions, marketplace, and a learning process that stops once a degree's been attained. Time's running out. The issues we're focused on are a waste of time because the proposed fixes aren't going to help. We've got to come up with another model."

"What you think about amazes me. You know that, don't you? It's not that I'm complaining. It's that I find it overwhelming."

"I guess I don't know how to be any other way. And you're selling yourself short. If you invested as much time as I have in thinking critically about the way the whole system works, you'd come up with ways of seeing that I'll never think of. You said something earlier about being a fan and looking forward to what I write. I don't want to be some kind of personal guru who you think has all the answers. I'm more interested in the sharing of ideas. I don't want you to feed off of me. I want you to challenge me. Way back when, I wasn't attracted to you just because you were cute, although, you are that. It had more to do with our both being aware enough to have doubts about our culture. You know the Zen Maxim – 'Great Doubt: great awakening. Little Doubt: little awakening. No Doubt: no awakening.'"

She continued to pry at the lid of the salad she had prepared long after it had given up its seal. "Do you need help with that?" he asked after watching her flounder away.

"No, what I need help with is understanding the variations in the human species. How can men resemble one another and yet not be the same at all? How can one have the desire to be extraordinary and another shameless about being nothing more than his material demands. That's what I need help with. Because it has to be more than personality, environment, education, intelligence, or any of the other justifications we've come up with to explain it away. Is there a theory that explains…it," she finally said. What she was thinking was that it seemed to be a minority versus assholes like the County Commissioners, Conrad Tilton, and the President and his inner sanctum. The list went on and on culminating in her husband who was a one-man wrecking ball. When they were together she would will him not to speak. *Please don't talk*, she would think to herself knowing that if he did she would end up more saddened by the minds of men. And she wasn't sure she could bear the added disappointment.

"The libraries are full of theories. They don't change anything. We're obsessed with finding the words to explain away the human condition. If only we were as focused on improving the root of the condition – our minds. All the theories ever conceived won't change the fact that we're at an impasse. That includes you and I, by the way. I wish I were wrong but I don't think so."

Sunny put the sandwich back in its wrapper and finished off her beer. She looked down at her feet and shrugged her shoulders, not wanting to consider for even one minute what might have been. Not to herself and certainly not out loud. She had never forgiven herself for the marriage she was in. As a young woman she made so many promises about the kind of life she would have. She had been a poster child for the working girl lie of the 1980s and 1990s which promised that if you got a degree and got a good paying job you would be forever satisfied, independent, and happy. Except for pursuing a career in environmental stewardship and being a faithful wife she had failed in all the areas she wished to excel. And now those, her only two successes, were both in questionable territory.

As she had that thought she wondered what was worse, being unfaithful with her body or with her heart and mind. Her subconscious inability to picture herself happy with anyone other than this casual acquaintance seated beside her must have taken a toll. It occurred to her that John knew he had never been the love of her life and never would be, and that he had given up trying. When she wished to wallow in guilt, this was how she saw the situation. But then in more lucid moments she determined she was assigning feelings and intuition where they did not belong. The likely scenario was the more he got to know his wife the less he liked her. He traveled a great deal. He had a good job – the kind that impressed women. She suspected that while he was out of town, he found many of them that were more to his liking. John was the kind of guy that would be emboldened by such success. Recognizing the ease with which he could find a replacement was what kept him cocky and inflexible.

What tied Sunny to John were debts and, more recently, her employment situation. Her impotence in controlling the family debt problem blew her away. Since being married she had managed to go from being debt-free to being completely maxed out on credit. Their combined incomes were barely enough to cover the minimum payments on various mortgages, vehicles, and credit cards. Prior to discovering that his wife would most likely lose her job, John had been looking seriously at the latest model One-Ton Turbo-Charged Super-Duty Extended-Cab Pickup. She had expected him to go ahead with the purchase while she was still employed. The reason being that they could qualify for the loan. Even the prospect of paying for it on one income might not be enough to dissuade him. Owning a big rig was the biggest dream of his life. John was not the type to suck up a disappointment of this magnitude gracefully. She found there was nothing to be gained in pointing out the emptiness of a life that revolves around possessions to someone whose life revolves around possessions. Forget about mentioning the incremental loss of freedom that was sneaking up on them with every purchase they didn't have the resources to pay for. It wasn't worth it to her, but it was to him. The concept of being a free agent instead of a slave to a house, a job, and a whole culture didn't resonate. She came off sounding shrill and insensitive to what he needed if he were to realize his full stature as a man.

John's begrudging suggestion to sell some assets would not help. He suffered from an inflationary mindset that saw only one way for the value of their possessions to go and that was up. John was sold on the economic principle of greed. His schooling had taught him debt was good and interest payments a necessary part of the formula to get ahead. He was a believer in the investor society and a willing participant who anticipated his stock portfolio would grow exponentially over time. No actual value had to be added, only time, and its worth miraculously would multiply. They had taken out a $100,000 home equity line-of-credit to remodel the kitchen and enlarge the garage. Soon, they would be moving on to improve the other rooms in the house. They had a second mortgage on the cabin. After gutting the whole thing, it was now a nice little retreat worthy of the six weekends per year they spent there. Sunny had done the math. If they sold everything except two vehicles they would still owe $200,000. That was a hundred thou apiece. And from that dubious position they would be starting over again with zip. She would be burdened with the added distinction of being back at square one in her career. No, neither one of them was going anywhere. It was an economic impossibility.

Her present circumstances were dreary and insurmountable. The past had determined where she was today just as what she chose to do now, with respect to her life, would determine the future. It was no different with civilization as a whole. All it really amounted to were billions of individuals making personal choices every day that when added together determined the direction of the entire species. In the end, it would all come down to the "sunk cost effect." That would provide the single biggest influence in Sunny's future as well as the future of the world. It had already proven its mettle in keeping everyone moving on a predictable course.

While Sunny turned this stuff over in her head, Jerome continued to look at her profile. He wondered what she wanted from him. An affair? That wasn't something he wanted and he doubted it was her style. "Why are you so quiet?" he asked.

She picked up her sandwich again. It had been sitting in her lap, more a diversion to stare at than to eat. "Oh, I was thinking about Expo '86 and that first time we met. I can't help but think about it whenever I see you. I wonder whether we'd be in a different place, you and I, if we had met up the second time at Expo. Or has it taken on greater importance than it should have?"

"Well, I've given some thought to that. Left no stone unturned, analyzed it from all angles as you might expect, and this is what I've come up with," he said, sliding closer as he took her hand and held it against his thigh. Against that same muscular leg that caught her attention with a vengeance when it pressed against her all those years ago. That was when she knew the boy thing had potential. Now, she sat inches away from having it all. And she already knew she was too afraid to make it happen.

"We were both shy but I think I would have had the nerve to hold your hand just like I'm doing now," he explained, giving her hand a squeeze as he lifted it towards his mouth and brushed his lips against her fingers. "And we would have kissed goodbye." He said this with such certainty, as if indeed it was something he had taken the time to consider over the years. "There's no need to put so much pressure on yourself. Let's pretend that it's twenty years ago, that we're two teenagers with absolutely no romantic experience, and let's do what we would have done had we met up that afternoon. Chances are we would have sat just like this. We might have kissed a time or two, told each other how much we liked one another and we would have been happy with that. Ecstatic, even. So why can't it be the same now?"

"Since we're not going to do anything more than neck can we quit wasting time and get right to it?" she blurted out.

"Now, Sunny, you're cheating. I don't believe you would have said that at fourteen."

"I might not have said it but I would have been thinking it."

"You see, I was right. I could tell just by looking at you that you were a good catch. Then, I would have suggested we exchange addresses and write to one another. That's assuming the kiss was a pleasant experience. I have no reason to believe it wouldn't have been. Whether we would have been able to continue a long distance relationship for any length of time, I don't know. It's likely we would have fallen victim to the 'there's no way you could have met the right person at your young age' rant and given each other up. It seems no matter how well-intentioned you begin, conventional wisdom is destined to get you in the end."

"You're forgetting something though, my hippie parents. They would have been the wild card. I don't believe they would have discouraged us. They'd have had you spend the summers with us. They'd have let us sleep together."

Jerome stood up and faced her. "How cool that would have been. A teen age libido with parent-approved twenty-four hour access. I might have died from exhaustion. It makes me all tingly just thinking about it," he said, hamming up his words. Both his face and body language turned into expressions of pure delight at the prospect.

She started to giggle watching his antics. It was something Sunny didn't do all that much. She was increasingly aware of how she had lost her sense of humor. It had to do with living in unfunny times but it was also about not speaking the language of those times. A language was more than words, it was mutual interpretation of what was going on.

He reached for both her hands, lifting her to her feet and without thinking too much about it he kissed her casually, like they'd been doing it for years. "Just as I suspected. Very pleasant," he said. He kissed her again. "Even better the second time."

Sunny's self-restraint evaporated. Her arms went around his neck and she clung to him in a way that said more than she intended. Jerome was a large, athletic guy. His size was not something most people missed but Sunny tended to overlook it because she thought his personality more remarkable. Until he had his arms around her. She settled into him, slipping away and out of sight, surrendering to a sensation that was intensely satisfying. She was overwhelmed by intuition. There really was a repository of untapped joy so full and promising it was limitless. Each of us was capable of accessing it. It was only a matter of putting aside one's small self. Choosing not to do so, how could that be natural? And yet, that was the decision Sunny kept making.

He whispered in her ear. "If we'd done this back in 1986 and it felt this good, no one could have kept me away. The only downside I can see is we wouldn't have appreciated how lucky we were. We would have grown up failing to know the pain of a bad fit." He ran his hands over her back while he explained. "With you around, I would have been so content I wouldn't have been able to write a word. Then what would I be doing for a living? I might be a civil engineer, wasting my days working on grading plans for new subdivision developments."

"Oh come on, I wouldn't have turned you into something as awful as that," she protested. She removed her arms from around his neck, looked into his eyes, and felt fuller still. "What do you say we take a closer look at the river and its famous rock formation?" she suggested in a half-hearted attempt to prevent this from going any further.

He agreed and when they reached the rock outcropping high above the river he stood behind her and pointed to the footbridge below. "Does the park extend to the other side of the river as well?"

"Oh yes, there's a parkway on both sides. It goes for miles."

He placed his hands on her shoulders and his lips on her neck. "Looks like some nice territory to explore," he said, kissing her in several places.

It was better than imagined. Even this much contact was pure bliss. She kept talking and tried to ignore how he made her feel. "There's something else I've often wondered. Why, when I stepped beside you to wait for the roller coaster, did you tell me your thoughts? You could have asked me my name or what sports I played or where I was from. Any number of questions that would begin a regular conversation but instead you launched into a dissertation on the intellectual transportation void of the World's Fair. It didn't strike me as odd at the time, but later on it did."

"I had a hunch that you weren't a small talk person and I wanted to hear what you had to say. I wanted to impress you, too, and I had only a limited amount of time to do it so I told you what was really going on inside my head. You would either be put off or turned on by my abnormal choice of conversation. It's a waste of time to start with small talk only to find out that's the extent of a person's range. I guess that sounds antisocial but the world would do just fine, better even, with fewer small talkers. I pretended that what you had to say was no big deal but I was thinking that I'd hit the mother lode. Because we didn't meet up, the rest of that summer I was miserable."

"You and me both. I'm feeling that way right now thinking that you and I aren't going to communicate via e-mail any more. Are you intending to cut me off too?"

His hands moved down to her waist. "No, I didn't mean to imply that," he said pulling her to him. He could feel how relieved she was to hear him say that.

"Do you head back home tomorrow?" Sunny asked.

"I was planning on it...but if you ask me to stay longer I will."

She placed her arms over his and treasured the feel of his skin beneath hers knowing it was fleeting. "I don't think I should do that. I'm not in a position to be hanging out with you."

"That brings me to another question. Why am I here with you like this? What are you looking for from me?"

"It's tough to explain," she said. "When I'm with you I can see that there's a way of being that isn't demoralizing. I want to believe in that. What I'm experiencing can't be all man is capable of. It can't be. There has to be more to us than that."

The Institution

"What's going on?" he asked.

She told him that she intended to step down next week and how her career difficulties had come about. He wasn't surprised though. "That's something we're going to see more of," he said. "There will be many casualties. There has to be when we depend on finite natural resources to satisfy the insatiable. Environmental concerns and those who champion them will be some of the first to go. Economic growth is right at the top of the current hierarchy of needs, instead of something that makes sense, like environmental health. It's like you said in Seattle, our leaders are doing exactly what the general public wants them to do. They're keeping it all going for as long as possible in lieu of our having to make any of those non-negotiable lifestyle changes."

"Because of having to find another job, I've been thinking about the future of environmentalism. If it has a future, that is. It must represent one of the biggest arenas of human delusion that exists, don't you think? If polled, 90% of the population would say the environment was very important to them. And then, you look at what they're driving and buying and how often and at what speed. That such a disconnect exists isn't very encouraging. I think I'm employed in a twilight industry."

His grip on her lightened and he turned her around in his arms until she was facing him. He kissed her eyelids, the tip of her nose, the corners of her mouth. He couldn't help himself. It was what he always felt like doing whenever he was close to her.

"When you do that you make me crazy. Being touched like that is not something I'm used to."

He held her face in his hands and looked at her as if he knew he wouldn't see her again for a very long time. "Why wouldn't any man in his right mind not want to love you to death?" he asked.

"Perhaps it's because I'm funny looking too…or something?" was her awkward response.

"Or something…I think that's the better explanation. Any ideas about what you're going to do?"

"Move to China for a couple of years. Don't look at me like that. I'm not joking. My husband has come up with the perfect solution. He's taking a foreign assignment with his employer. That way he'll get paid a much higher salary, our living expenses will be covered, and we'll be able to keep all our real estate. Plus, he'll learn more about the manufacturing operations and that will make him eligible for promotion, maybe to CEO one day. John's very ambitious, you know. At least, in the conventional sense of the word. Now that I'm soon to be unemployed I don't have any excuses not to go. As a matter of fact, we're leaving next month."

"So how do you feel about making a move like that?"

"Horrible. If you knew about my life, you wouldn't think very much of me so I won't tell you about it. You're just going to have to accept that I don't have a choice. I've thought it through and I'm trapped. But the prospect of living in a foreign land isolated from everyone except John has got me freaked out. That's why I wanted to see you so badly before we go and why I was hoping we could keep in touch through e-mail."

They moved away from the overlook back to where their bikes and the remains of their lunch awaited. He sat down beside her on the bench, reached for the backpack and said, "You got any more beer in here? I believe we're going to need it." When she said she did, he reached in and pulled out a couple. He moved closer until they were touching from knee to shoulder and put his arm around her. She buried her face under his chin so that she could nuzzle there. He felt her breath against his throat. How quickly he had grown used to the idea of her being around. Expectations that had been building up inside began deflating. He wanted to offer her another option but she had all but said not to.

"At the very least, I do my best work when I'm low and you've given me something to be really down about," he joked, trying to make light of the situation.

"You too? Hopefully something good will come out of this then," she said, wistfully wishing that things were not about to turn darker. "I can't quite put my finger on what it is right now but you never know…" Her words became muffled, kind of dying against him.

They sat like that until dusk. The bike ride forgotten. Finally he suggested that it was time to start back. There was not much light left and he thought her husband would be worried and wondering where she was. Sunny did not bother to correct him on this. She would not say how much

The Institution

she hated going home. It had been like that her entire marriage. Home was not where John was. Home was a metaphysical place, where he wasn't.

When they parted, Jerome tried to be brave because he had always been so, but he wasn't sure what he thought about life without her. He did not wish to dwell on it, but she had ruined something for him. That inner equilibrium it had taken years to perfect didn't feel quite so solid as it once had.

And Sunny slipped back into the darkness of her life. Back to the place she had left that morning, realizing that over a few short hours, the whole scene had grown more inadequate. Coming up Jefferson Street at dusk, she looked into other homes. The family on the corner, out on their side deck finishing dinner, sipping the last of their wine. They lived with gusto, never missing an opportunity to dine al fresco during the spring and summer months. Further up the street, the young man who shared the duplex with his girlfriend was in the chair at the window reading. Small glimpses of their life, a cat curled in his lap, a tower of books beside him, flames dancing in the fireplace, made Sunny envy that gal. A block later, she braced herself for the back of John's head and the frenetic blue light that was visible from the street. The big flat screen with Sensoround dominated their living room and their lives. All of John's meals and salty snacks were eaten in front of that forty-inch TV and everything he believed was gleaned from it. As long as Fox remained on the air and continued to assign the label of fascist to everyone except those who deserved the moniker, she would not be missed.

***

When Dr. Marsh knocked at Darlene's door in the early evening, it surprised her. She suspected a visit was imminent but in her memory it had never occurred at such an early hour. The last time he had shown up in the wee hours of the morning, she convinced him she was ill. Once Darlene shared how she had been vomiting all night, he didn't hang around. Since that time, they had not seen each other in the course of their duties. He was anxious to get together with her so sure was he that by this time she would be missing him and eager to prove just how much so. He was hoping the night would be long and fruitful.

Darlene readied herself to greet him in a way she never had before. The door was barely closed behind him and he had her in a bear hug. "Have I ever missed you," he said squeezing her still tighter. "It's not nice of you to keep Dr. Doug waiting. You know how much I look forward to us getting together," he cooed. "We have some lost time to make up for."

He fully expected her to start undressing him and herself at the same time and then fall upon him in a panting display of lust. He knew how much she liked it when he played the roll of lovesick sap. On this occasion he was ready to oblige and to his surprise she was slow to catch on. He had his eyes closed waiting to feel the reward, the scratching of fast moving fingers having their way with the buttons of his shirt. It was true about absence making the heart grow fonder. Thanks to the erectile dysfunction drugs he had loaded up on prior to leaving his apartment, he could feel that fondness spreading to where it would be put to the highest and best use. He was waiting, waiting when suddenly he felt her wiggle out of his embrace and step away from him.

"I'm not comfortable with the way this whole relationship of ours is going," she said. "When we first started seeing each other, I was sure that by this time we would either be married and living in family housing or you would have gone back into private practice and we'd be living together in our own house."

"Oh Darlene, why do you have to bring that up now? You know how hard I'm trying to get ahead so we can have a nice life together. You know how my first wife cleaned me out, bankrupted me really, and ruined my practice. This arrangement I have here is the best way for me to get back on my feet again. You know how it is, Darlene. Please be patient."

"It's been two years, Doug. I don't want to wait any longer because I don't think you're being straight with me."

"Straight with you about what? What are you saying?"

"That I'm not the only one you're telling this story to. I've heard other nurses talking. You've got something going with several others. I know you do."

"No baby, you're wrong. It's just you and me."

The Institution

"I think you're lying. The very fact that I feel that way tells me there's something not quite right between the two of us."

Dr. Marsh searched her eyes as if looking for clues. "What's wrong with you? Are you having breakthrough qualms?" he wondered out loud.

"What are breakthrough qualms?" she asked innocently, not letting on she knew exactly what they were.

"Never mind," he said. "It's a clinical term."

"Not one that I was ever taught," she responded before she could stop herself from showing an inordinate amount of curiosity.

"Forget I said anything." All pretense of kindness forgotten. "Why weren't you watching a program when I got here. You're always watching programs. I think you need to get in for a check-up. I'd like to run a few tests on you."

"What? Why the interrogation? I was tired and didn't feel like watching TV. Just because I don't want to be your lover anymore you think there's something wrong with me. That's ridiculous."

"It's not your losing interest in me that's the problem. A short attention span is to be expected. It's your interest in the truth that has me concerned."

Darlene had to change tactics fast and go to Plan B – the one Mrs. Holmes had recommended. "Like that would ever happen. Look, I didn't want to tell you but you've forced me into it. There's someone else I've been seeing and I think he's a better choice for me. Monogamy is important. Anything else is a sin. We both know that."

"You're screwing around on me with someone else at this facility? I could get you fired for that," he threatened. All civility vanished from the conversation. He turned into a menacing figure. "I could make sure you never worked anywhere ever again."

There was nothing to be done except smooth Dr. Marsh's ruffled feathers. She had hoped to avoid this. "I wish you wouldn't do that," she pleaded. "We had many good nights together. Can't we leave it at that? No hard feelings. Two mature people moving on."

Next, she was going to have to turn the whole thing into his idea. Also, Mrs. Holmes' suggestion. Break-ups had been her specialty. "I've noticed lately that you haven't really been into it with me anyway. I think

199

you've been coming to my apartment out of habit and that it's really you who have wanted to call it off. You just haven't been able to tell me and so now I'm making it easy for you. I'll miss you more than you will me."

She stood before him with her head bowed waiting for him to take the bait and mentally preparing for what would surely come next. Mrs. Holmes had warned her as well about the most likely, albeit, unpleasant outcome of Plan C.

He sought to regain the upper hand. "You're right. It hasn't been great between us for a while now. I haven't wanted to hurt you. Believe me, I wish it could have worked out because at the start it was very good," he said, in complete control now. If he were forced to give a true reckoning of their relationship, it was her breasts that pleased him the most. They were nothing short of amazing. He wolfishly looked at them straining against her blouse. God, he loved the way the fabric between the tips of both nipples pulled and puckered and was never quite up to the task of making her look respectable. The front of his trousers began to look strained at the thought of them lying there waiting for his ministrations. His outstretched fingers unbuttoned her uniform, slipped the garment off her shoulders, and freed those big babies into his hungry hands. Losing access to these – that was what pained him dearly. He thought about the rest of the staff. Was there another nurse, technician, secretary even who could furnish an adequate replacement? There were two or three possibilities but he would have to work on them later. For now, that huge nipple he had just slipped into his mouth had his undivided attention.

"Absolutely fantastic," he gushed going for the other one that looked so forlorn without his tongue on it. "You know what I'm thinking?"

"I think I'm getting the drift," she said with resolve as she watched his mouth ravage her breasts in front and from behind felt his hands reach up under her panties and squeeze her bare cheeks.

"I think some farewell sex is in order before we call it quits. You know, two mature people enjoying what the other has to offer, and then, no hard feelings. What do you say to that?" he groaned as he ground his groin into hers.

There was nothing to say. It was a question that wouldn't be answered with words.

The Institution

***

Darlene's curiosity about Jerome had gotten the best of her. He was all she wanted to hear about and she insisted that Heather tell her more.

"Are you sure you don't want to hear about my first husband, Robert? We haven't talked much about him. Where's that album of mine? I'll show you his picture. That will get you interested for sure."

"No, I don't want to hear about that stuff. I want to know about Jerome Raines, the author. I want to know what he was like and why he was so disappointed. I could never figure out what it was he wanted." Darlene found it more gratifying to talk about Jerome now that he was dead. His presence, a disconcerting combination of physical illness and mental strength, had proven too much of an obstacle for her to overcome.

"Okay, we can talk about him some more. Do you remember where we were?"

"Sure I do. He had just walked with you from the beach back to your tent. And then you got all dreamy-eyed."

Heather looked sharply at Darlene. "An act, in order to keep you interested. Obviously I did a good job of it or you wouldn't be sitting here begging for more."

"Sure Mrs. Holmes. It was an act, nothing more. What else could it be?"

"If you're finished with your rather transparent speculating, then I'll continue. Later that same day he stopped by where I was staying. I had told him I'd like to read something he'd written and so he brought me a copy of one of his books. He placed it outside, on the patio table, and meant to leave without my seeing him, but I caught him. And I made him autograph it. And then I asked him to join me for a glass of wine and so he was forced to spend more time with me."

"Which book did he bring?"

"It was his latest one at the time – *In Praise of Climate Change*. Although it had not received very good reviews and had not sold many copies, he said that it was the one he liked the best. For Jerome, it was the poor response that made it a bellwether book. It told him that self-knowledge, which was key to any personal or societal change, was in short

201

supply. That critics and readers alike could not see their own sensibilities revealed in the pages of that book and allow that knowledge to sink in, was an 'ah ha' moment for him.

"He felt that seeing our behavior for what it was and recognizing where it was leading would ultimately make us more aware. But first we had to be willing to open our minds. Unless we were able to do that, he didn't know what could be gained through education, reading, experience, wealth, hardship, anything. If exposure to acknowledged mediums of change was not powerful enough to spur introspection, then we were in a world of hurt. That's what prompted him to begin working on his last book. It wasn't vague when it came to our options.

"While he was sitting there with me, he said something funny. He hoped I would read *In Praise of Climate Change* because I was an average woman and he would like to know what I got out of it. Of course, my face registered bemusement when he called me 'average.' He quickly pointed out that given the fact I was able to afford the $10,000 per week it cost to stay at the Spa, I wasn't average in a financial sense. What he meant to say was that I had a conventional view of American life. I didn't seem troubled by what purpose our efforts served. And it would be helpful to know what a person like me thought he was trying to say. It was very funny, you see, because he wanted the same thing as every other man I'd ever known. He wanted to 'know' the bimbo. In his case, he wished to get acquainted with the inner workings of my small mind. Becoming intimately familiar with my more obvious attributes did not intrigue him at all. Talk about the consummate insult. He had no idea what he'd said. Jerome was focused on writing a good book and intended to use all the information at his disposal to do just that.

"After he left, I hunkered down with his book. I read like a demon day and night hoping I could finish it before the week was over and discuss it with him in person. By week's end I was done but when I went looking for him, I found that he had gone home. I was so disappointed. I had tagged the book with notes and questions and really wracked my brain so that I would come across as intelligent in his eyes. I went to all that trouble just to have the opportunity to talk to him again. He saw things from a different perspective. Incorporating that perspective into my life changed

The Institution

everything. All the old baggage fell away. The things I had dwelled on for decades seemed trivial. I realized it wasn't all about me. There was a larger world with which I longed to feel a connection. I began to see with a certain kind of clarity.

"It made me wonder why I had been so convinced the fundamentals of the system under which we lived were sound. Those were what we never questioned. We might support regime change but not *thought* change and without that there would be no meaningful improvement. I was the perfect example of this. I kept either overthrowing a spouse or being overthrown by one but never advanced my thinking, so that I would make a better choice the next time around. The system was stagnant and so was I. Everything rolls into everything else. It's easy to see how individual micro visions are duplicated many times over at every level. The macro version perfectly reflects the maturity of the individuals who make up a nation. It's called 'cult'-ure. No matter how much we wish to blame a leader or a political party, we are responsible. If we were more, we would demand something better. Simple as that. Now that's self-knowledge and that's why Jerome's book either wasn't understood or wasn't appreciated.

"When I e-mailed him with a message to that effect; do you know how he responded? *'It was wrong of me to assume you were average or conventional or anything else I may have assumed. You are one, of I hope many, who are living well beneath your potential.'* It was the best thing anyone ever said to me."

Heather had hoped to come back from the Eco Spa free of ill feelings toward her husband and the latest love of his life. What she hadn't anticipated was coming back liberated from the whole catastrophe. She could still remember the trip from the airport to her home in Beverly Hills. The sterile sameness of the freeway with its overpasses and ON & OFF ramps. *ON & OFF ramps to where?* That is what she asked herself. *What the hell are we all doing? Where do we think we're going?*

Everything she saw brought something like that to mind. There was an endless supply of material in the crappy environment we had created for ourselves, and she couldn't stop herself from reacting. Every third SUV sported a magnetic ribbon in support of the troops in the Middle East on a mission with a purpose very few wanted to understand. Because if they did,

203

she suspected they wouldn't be so proud of their allegiance. It was likely they'd be cramming those ridiculous ribbons into a drawer somewhere and then shutting-up about the whole thing. The "Baby on Board" bumper stickers were as telling. Talk about "the prison of individual existence." That was the best example out there. What did those parents think? That you were not supposed to tailgate your usual two feet off the bumper? Or when passing, you were to take that extra special care and not clip the front end on the way by, the way you did with other vehicles that didn't have such precious cargo? Had they ever stopped to consider that there were babies on board the whole planet and not just of the human variety? How about if every one of us expanded our focus beyond that one piece of cargo and took some care with the entire planet and the load it was carrying?

Yeah, like that was going to happen. Where would one start to try to change things? First and foremost, it meant changing people. Where did the momentum come from for something like that? What could this author she ran across purely by chance offer up that would be a hedge against financial, environmental, and civilization collapse? The cars whizzed by at high speed. At that velocity, was there any chance the guy in the next lane over had ever given a moment's thought to where in the life of a civilization we were. He would laugh in your face if you told him summer had ended in the 18th Century. Autumn had sped by over about a two hundred-year period and now we were in the throes of winter.

He would say, *"What you talking about man,"* as he fiddled frenetically with his BlackBerry, *"We got technology, dude."* He would not understand that inventions and innovations such as those were distractions that had little to do with our civilization's direction. That was the thing about technology – it tricked people into thinking civilization was advancing. Instant communication satisfied personal egotistical needs and that was about it. Regardless of whether it was stem sell research, DNA sequencing, cloning, or nuclear technology, each was potentially harmful if made available to us at our current level of development. At some point we were going to have to ask ourselves, when do we start developing people? What were we waiting for? It was already winter. If we waited much longer the final season would be over. But Heather wondered how to convince everybody what season it was. They wouldn't believe you. They never had before.

Fed up with the whole Hollywood scene, she was careful not to get involved with any men just for the sake of having one. The tabloid pictures of Ricky and Sonja screamed from the supermarket checkouts and she felt nothing about the two of them. Only the awareness of time that could have been better spent, but she was attending to that. She shed her famous juvenile look and went about her business freely once no one recognized her as The Heather Holmes. Not remaining stuck at thirty enabled her to slip into a different set of ways and that included getting up to speed on some issues.

About eighteen months later Heather received a copy of Jerome's manuscript, *Turning on the 'digm,* and a note asking her to review it. The manuscript was broken into three sections. The first, the typical bleak accounting of our circumstances that was common during those years coupled with a forecast of systemic collapse. Intellectual intolerance, the abuse of faith, and the obsession with pleasure, possession, and power were identified as the common elements of every civilization before decline. If that didn't strike a chord of familiarity with everyone who read those words then it was time to start paying attention.

The second part tackled some of the "progressive" thinking of the day that proposed operating the existing system with a minor modification or two in the direction of renewable energy sources, more social programs, and wealth redistribution. Those solutions assumed there was nothing inherently wrong with the commission or the quality of our lives, it was only the type of fuel and the way financial resources were concentrated that were the problem. Jerome saw some major flaws in both that assessment and the solutions. We must be realistic with regards to our dependency on oil if we were to prepare for a post oil civilization. Oil drove our expectations for both the present and future. Debating this was silly but for the sake of proving his point, the manuscript outlined a week in the life of a modern western human in case there was anyone out there who didn't understand how dependent we were on a single resource. We were doing ourselves a disservice by not accepting that when oil was removed from the equation our expectations would be markedly different. An even larger population, operating with a less powerful energy source, could not live as we do. Oil was the glue that held our society together. Without oil, it would disintegrate. Other than engaging in war to maintain access to the richest reserves, we had not planned, conserved, or engaged in an intelligent discussion about how best to use the remaining reserves. We continued to squander the resource on trashy products, services, and modes of transportation and couldn't anticipate the reverse science fiction future we were working towards. One in which we looked backwards from the vantage point of a primitive future and see the present not as quaint and old-fashioned but as the extravagant, blissful "high-point."

While oil's legacy was one of power and material progress, it was also one of waste in the literal sense and in terms of a future. It was a story about arrested Evolution and the regression of society. Too much power at our disposal made us stupid. Instead of what was appropriate, we chose what was expedient. We poured resources into furthering comforts and conveniences and neglected investing in the universal qualities that strengthen civilizations. Once basic needs are met, those richer components must be addressed. As long as we lived by a model based on excess, critical questions wouldn't be asked and the necessary adjustments would not be made. It was time to tackle the fundamentals of what it takes to be a quality human being, society, and steward of the planet.

The third segment of the book was the lengthiest. It discussed investing in different living arrangements. *Turning on the 'digm* attempted to explain the inexplicable, as in changing the predominant thought of the day. This was no easy task. When citizens of modern society looked around nothing seemed too terribly amiss. When they flipped switches things turned on. Gasoline flowed from the nozzle at the fueling station. Professional athletes jetted around from venue to venue where they performed at super human levels. The stores were so full of stuff it appeared there was an endless supply of money and materials to meet our every need. The number of material choices produced an intoxicating side effect that numbed us to the low quality of our day-to-day existence.

Turning on the 'digm explained the two paradigms under which humans had lived. The first lasted for millions of years. It was the small tribe, egalitarian, nomadic, hunter and gatherer system. The second major

The Institution

paradigm came about 10,000 years ago and continued to be the one under which we operated. Because it was agriculture based, it led to stationary communities, the growth of large cities, and the creation of and dependency on a marketplace. Under those conditions, the hierarchical, command and control system was born. The third paradigm would come about for reasons similar to the second – most likely as a response to burgeoning population, climate change, and destruction of the ecosystem. So far, our response to problems of this kind was to increase our food supply through unsustainable agricultural practices or spread our impact over a larger portion of the earth's surface. How we coped with deteriorating conditions – both in practice and in theory – were second paradigm in nature. We hadn't considered giving up on the current paradigm. However, its day was done.

Other than suggestions on the fringes about permaculture augmenting conventional agriculture or building community, meaningful discussion was nowhere in evidence. The important questions weren't on many people's radar. Questions such as: Did it make sense to go into work at the office everyday? What were the ramifications of obtaining college training in order to be employable in a job that kept the whole thing going exactly as is? We continued to believe being tied geographically to one group of people and one place for most of our lives was ideal. Community, in the form currently envisioned, was another vestige of the current paradigm. The hierarchical system did not appear to be under siege either. Most people thought that government and the Constitution as the founding fathers envisioned them were the greatest. As far as the marketplace, it was sacred. We couldn't conceive of another way to obtain even the basics. Barter and local currencies had been bounced around but the fact remained that without money for food and shelter, living a quality life on a planet with seven billion other people was not possible.

The manuscript referenced how difficult it was going to be to get the largest group of all time, who were fully invested in promises of material progress, to accept that it wasn't going to deliver. The developed world was fully committed from an education, debt, and financial investment standpoint. We were all working at building and maintaining empire. Did we really need to be employed this way? Why were we so sure that competition was essential in order to get ahead? And what did getting ahead mean other than amassing wealth for retirement, purchasing consumer items, and putting children through college so they could get jobs, enter the workforce, and repeat the whole cycle of the mindless mainstream? We spent our lives paying for these things. That's what consumed the citizens of our "advanced" civilization. Although we were free in many respects, specific expectations, timelines, and structure prevented us from being very nimble. In order to welcome another way, we must accept that the future wasn't getting progressively better under this system. Then, it was a matter of determining how to live in the face of environmental overshoot. As it stood right now, there was no counterbalance, no sanity, and no easy way to get off the wheel even though the system had peaked. The signs were everywhere. *Peak Everything* was another way of describing the complexity that preceded all collapsed societies. Chances were that every civilization that collapsed had its own *Peak Everything* phase. Without a paradigm shift, ours would self-destruct in much the same way.

Turning on the 'digm questioned whether the satisfying of human wants as opposed to needs was indeed a noble goal. And what it meant when this was the basis of progress. It hinted at how the general belief that human beings were constantly improving, getting stronger, becoming smarter, and living longer was another great lie swallowed by the public. Cumulative knowledge and modern technology masked some glaring declines in individual performance. But we continued to measure progress in material terms. The most virtuous work we engaged in was ensuring that a higher material standard of living spread to a greater number of people. The thought being that once this was achieved, and only then, was the human being inclined to improve himself through education and the arts. The facts told a different story. They seemed to indicate the more people had the more they wanted until there was a blurring of wants and needs. Individuals couldn't be satiated. Living in 2,000 square feet made one long for 3,000 square feet. A $20,000 car made one desirous of a $40,000 set of wheels. And hence that long-awaited improvement in oneself never came to pass. In fact, all the emphasis on the material seemed to make the human being a little smaller, less interesting, and not very bright. One had only to look at the list of top leisure activities to see our propensity for personal improvement and enlightenment was not what motivated us. Dull minds did not seem to grasp the extent of their dimness. And they never would at this rate. We needed sharp minds that were not preoccupied by narrow self-interest but focused on the scope of the global predicament. We had to accept that our refusal to consider a way to measure progress in anything other than human terms was disastrous. The future depended upon food, housing, and employment arrangements that complemented – rather than tore down – the complexity of the planetary system.

We knew enough about Evolution to recognize that different environments encouraged certain characteristics. Given a set of living conditions, adaptations took place to ensure survival. These adaptations could be losses or gains depending on the energy required to maintain a trait that was no longer required. Birds on the Galapagos Islands became flightless in the absence of predators. Horses lost their toes in favor of hooves because a hoof was a better foot for crossing the plains. Evolution did not always take species to greater levels of complexity. It was important to be aware of this when we developed technologies that shaped our future.

Turning on the 'digm was a call to start brainstorming – a summons particularly to those who gave a damn. *All* the sentient members of society should be talking about meaningful change. Turn off the television and the other diversions that prevent us from thinking and caring. Focus on one question. If we had the chance to restart civilization, what type of system would we create? Pretend that the conditions under which we currently live aren't sacred. Accept that some of our values are illogical and destructive. If we found a way to do that then possibilities would begin to emerge. Knowing all that we do today, what must be discarded and what should be saved? What would we teach in schools? Would we continue to be hung up on ownership and personal property rights? What about religion? Would we wage wars, manufacture semi-automatic rifles, and handguns? Would we think differently about mobility and transportation? Would our cities look as they do now? Would we purchase food and other essentials in the way we currently do? Would there still be a Wall Street, a Main Street, and a traditional marketplace? If we can accept that it's either change or extinction, what do we change? This is a world war but in this war our way of life is the enemy. What do we do to cut down that enemy before it snuffs out all life?

The manuscript attacked the way the system was currently configured and suggested that in addition to being unsustainable, it didn't promote physical and mental health. A concept that incorporated those elements should not be considered radical, although it wasn't acceptable in modern parlance to discuss any structure other than the one we had. There seemed to be a general consensus that everything had been settled for the best. All ideas had been exhausted and all possible combinations tried. We had everything invested in one way of living. And if it failed, which appeared likely, civilization failed. We were operating within a closed circle where education, the marketplace, corporatism, and the financial markets all fed into one another. A noose that tightened with every life move bound us to defending the status quo. We must accept that the middle class "investor society" was a myth and a distraction that deluded its followers into believing a luxurious retirement was their birthright. The system implied that something for nothing – another term for inflation – was a viable investment strategy. As long as that carrot dangled out there, we scoffed at investing in anything else. We weren't investing in a civilization with a future because the immediate monetary return on that could not be measured in dollars and cents.

The first thing to do was accept that Wall Street or the concept of Wall Street had scammed us. A few big players had been paid handsomely for a Ponzi scheme that netted them millions and in some cases billions. We should applaud the magnitude of their greed and ability to manipulate the average man. And then we should get over it, cut the funding, and ask ourselves another couple of questions. If "get rich quick schemes" aren't in our future and it isn't realistic to expect twenty years of do-nothing retirement with a pot load of cash at our disposal, then what kind of system would we prefer and what types of people would we wish to be surrounded by? How about we begin to work towards *that* type of return on investment, instead of the usurious or inflationary kind?

Irish monasteries preserved much of the literature and knowledge that was in danger of being lost after the fall of the Roman Empire. When the Dark Ages settled over Europe, a marked decline in the quality of thought

The Institution

ensued. A similar decline was underway in our age. Before we headed over the cliff into an equally bleak period, *Turning on the 'digm* suggested getting to work on a "scholastic option" that revolved around living arrangements we could realistically achieve and maintain for long periods of time. A hedging of our collective bet in favor of a less energy-intensive, sustainable model was what the manuscript advocated. After taking into account what was missing in the current system, *Turning on the 'digm* proposed a solution that addressed issues of usury, lack of quality, consumption, static lives, overspecialization, unhealthy lifestyles, leisure shortage, energy dependence, personal stagnation, and loss of connection.

There were many possibilities but this was the one Jerome offered up in his manuscript. The concept was the culmination of years of research and study. It incorporated the recurring elements of a dynamic environment and eliminated the stifling characteristics of a stagnant one. He envisioned a bank that operated like a club and did not charge or pay interest. The bank would be in the business of creating sustainable places where people lived, learned, worked, and played. Some would be in rural settings. Others would redevelop properties in existing neighborhoods. The idea was to establish a network of private but cooperatively owned Paradigm Clubs open to the public. Much the same way as private golf clubs with public access operated. This was an attempt to move from a "possess to an access" way of life and to gain independence in the process. Meals, on-site living quarters, health care, a stipend for incidentals, and access to the assets of the club would be provided to working members – partners if you will – in exchange for twenty hours of labor per week.

Assets and opportunities would vary from club to club. The emphasis was on quality, not quantity. All of them would be well-constructed and furnished with a restaurant that served spa cuisine of excellent quality. The scale of each kitchen/restaurant would be important. It had to be a creative and enjoyable place for both guests and for those who worked. Some properties might be outdoor recreation oriented. Others would be centered around permaculture, the arts, or the pursuit of wisdom. Life-long learning in the art and science of living well would be the keystone of each property. Dynamic living arrangements like these were key in improving the quality of thought and advancing beyond fixed beliefs.

Terra Dime

The level of access available to members providing capital would be contingent upon the timing and amount of their capital contribution. And when space was available, the general public would have access to lodging and/or meals for a fair price. Unlike the current paradigm, the goal was not to have any empty space or to have mountains of food rotting on the supermarket shelves waiting for someone to purchase it. The intention was to operate more efficiently than the traditional marketplace where shopkeepers, innkeepers, waiters, and office workers waited around for someone to require their services. The emphasis would be on wholesome local food, a prix fixe format, and no waste. A network of locations would enable people to be somewhat nomadic. This would eliminate the staleness that comes from being settled in one spot. The constant influx of guests, scholars, and members of nearby communities for meals, education, or a weekend get-a-way would serve to keep things interesting and vibrant. It took into account sustainability with its emphasis on food grown mainly on the property or at nearby farms and gardens. Since meals would be enjoyed in on-site restaurants with European-style dining, personal kitchens could be eliminated and as a result, living quarters could be smaller.

The Paradigm Club combined the excitement of a vacation resort, the comfort of a club, the dynamic learning environment of a campus, and the health benefits of a spa. It was a complete way of living as opposed to the current arrangements that were fragmented, inflexible, and of low quality. More importantly, it offered an alternative. The existing modes of living did not accommodate those who were conscientious and aware.

Once a sufficient number of aware people realized that current living arrangements were a dead end, it would be easy to begin transitioning. A portion of the members would invest time, another segment capital. The capital commitment would vary depending on level of interest, resources, and leisure time. Experimenting with small-scale locations would allow for fine-tuning of the product. Because the majority of the investment would be in tangible assets, like land and improvements, the risk would be minimal. In addition, risk would be lowered further as a result of the assets not being encumbered by debt.

A couple of ways to begin building up this new bank account to finance the Paradigm Club were also recommended. One was through the carbon offset programs already in place, albeit in a meaningless configuration. Instead of sending funds to schemes that paid for rinky-dink tree-growing projects, individuals could begin building their investment in a system that addressed our carbon footprint over the long-term. The same went for the purchase of Jerome's book and others that were offered for sale at his website. The net proceeds would be credited to the purchaser and there was no reason that other authors, who wished for more than words, could not do the same. In this way, when individuals made an investment in personal development through the purchase of books that expanded their base of knowledge, they were also providing capital for real change. He also believed foundations that existed to promote social, environmental, or personal awareness could be enlisted to aid in a transition. Establishing a working relationship with Land Trusts, both rural and in existing urban areas, might be another way to move the transition forward.

This inability to imagine ourselves in something other than the current model was preventing us from creating a pleasant built environment. It was also getting in the way of our thinking outside the inefficiencies, boredom, and lack of stimulation that were inherent in the traditional marketplace. While the model envisioned by Jerome did not involve taking away existing freedoms, it did provide new freedoms that were comprehensive. Our options did not have to be so limited. Why we persisted in clinging to a bad system was inexplicable. We were textbook examples of how difficult it was, when stuck in the middle of something really bad, to see how good it could be.

"Once I read the manuscript I thought about it for days before responding. The simplicity of what Jerome proposed contrasted sharply with the complicated mess we saw as normal," Heather explained to Darlene. "We were committed to a freeway frenzy that got us to jobs where we waited around for somebody to want whatever it was we were peddling. More and more crap kept getting built, more lanes were required to connect it all, and we couldn't see what was missing. We had long ago quit giving any thought to the journey. Our way of life didn't encourage that. It was the destination on which we were focused. It began with education, then a job, a house, family, and finally what supposedly made it all worth while, retirement, before the ultimate destination. We couldn't weigh in on the ugliness because we were attuned only to the next little thrill, milestone, or event. The inability to see civilization itself as a journey instead of a destination was the bigger tragedy. This left us disinclined to rework the basic structure.

"During those years there were all these 'think' tanks popping up everywhere. There was so much discussion from specialists who wished to weigh in on every debate, defending the same positions over and over again. It went round and round and we always ended up back where we started because we didn't consider changing the relationship between ownership, education, employment, and leisure. Comprehensively combining them would do more to improve lives and decrease footprints than anything I'd seen proposed. Still, Jerome was right to be concerned about how he'd be perceived if he published. This concept of his was based on the premise that man wished to know more and be more, not have more. Why he believed this to be true confounded me."

From what Heather had seen, people didn't feel strongly enough about anything except material wealth to make changes that were perceived to be inconvenient or uncomfortable. That's why any ideas that were bounced around always involved some kind of legislation or monetary penalty. Massive improvements in our hearts and minds would have to take place before there was voluntary anything. And the current structure didn't exactly lead to a whole lot of that. It was a chicken and egg thing. Without a different structure, it was unlikely we would ever have the good sense to know we were in desperate need of a new structure.

Heather also saw what he had tried to come up with. And that was access to a high-quality physical destination that bypassed the thirty-to-forty years of beating ourselves up competing for it. With that pressure out of the way, we would be free to focus on the journey. The journey towards species maturity was the most critical trip on which each of us could embark. And yet, its existence and importance was known to so few. This was what was unusual about Jerome. He had the ability to see everyday life from the perspective of an observer, not through the fleeting fears of a human life span. It was an unusual trait that had the potential to be very unpopular.

The Institution

Engaging a population that was asleep at the wheel was a real challenge. That was the tragedy, the irony, and the double bind. We were aware of the hollowness and we attributed it to a lack of community. We tried to create community. We wanted to feel something, call it a connection, with those who were occupying the planet at the same time. But we did not like many people for legitimate reasons. What was there to like? We were empty-headed, self-worshiping consumers, who went out of our way to avoid looking at one another when we met on the street. So what exactly were we lamenting? Was it a lack of connection? Or was it the lack of wonderful human beings to connect with? Beautiful places in which to live could be built for us but turning the mind into a fertile, delightful spot was an individual responsibility.

This was the motivation behind Jerome's words and knowing it pained Heather. How were people like him going to take it when it crumbled? Would he go easily from believing in man's potential to preparing for the slide back into a state of primitivism? His book pulled her into a reality we all knew existed. Raw in its pleading honesty, it was difficult to read but more difficult to forget. Every day we shared in human triumphs and failures. There was no single hero or lone villain. We, as well as a long line before us, had all contributed. We were products of an historical process. Our beliefs had been shaped over time by all the human history that had gone before. How we comported ourselves in our daily lives was of grave importance. The present values of a nation, including all its successes and failures, were destined to become part of an evolving human code so we must choose wisely. That meant introducing and incorporating the wisdom to create quality living arrangements superior to the ones we were so reluctant to abandon. There would be many denials of the unflattering portrait the book painted. Critics would say he was being too harsh. The general public would say it was too depressing to think about and political pundits would make the case that what was being proposed was unrealistic. It wasn't capitalistic enough. It wouldn't provide enough in the way of riches to the few. All "progress" would stop. There is no changing the blessed system.

In spite of all this, Heather believed it was a book that should be published. It was an unusual time, unlike anything she'd experienced.

Terra Dime

There was this sense of urgency within the scientific and intellectual communities that we were about to bump up against the edge of something. Uncaring, cruel, and harsh, more omnipotent than mankind, it lurked in the shadows preparing to pounce. There were a great many names for this malicious phantom – Global Warming, peak oil, flu pandemic, pollution, drought, overpopulation, economic collapse – and a shortage of strategies for battling such a shadowy enemy.

The groping around for a solution to the human predicament was everywhere. And yet all the books, conferences, documentaries, and speeches dedicated to the subject never amounted to more than a pitiful bit of fumbling. The sheer inability to improve the quality of the human species in the face of overwhelming evidence that it was imperative; this was the phantom's true form. The one we couldn't single out and struggled to name. Without progress of that kind there would be no long-term plan and hence no future. And that would most certainly lead to the end of our history. But we did not have the wherewithal to make arrangements to stave off that eventuality. Everything we believed had been learned within the system. It was all we had. It was all we knew. And it was leading us to its logical end. *The End of History and the Last Man* indeed.

A traditional marketplace that worshiped ownership could not provide a solution to what ailed us. Not as long as it could make a buck off of it. Destruction paid too well. All kinds – air, water, soil, human health, other species, war. "From possess to access." It had a nice ring to it. And Heather was willing to accept that the continual carving up of the planet for human ownership didn't look promising. Jerome had identified one model for change. Perhaps, there were others out there who'd been thinking along the same lines and would speak up once the dialogue got started. But someone had to get it going.

After she read the last page of the manuscript, Heather recalled looking up at the vaulted ceilings of her Great Room and over at the granite fireplace. It was one of four in an enormous house she occupied alone. The kitchen was large enough to dance in. It was fully appointed with a commercial stove, wood pizza oven, walk-in cooler, and was the most underutilized room of many that vied for that distinction. One of her everyday place settings cost $400. She had twelve of them. And one of her fine china special occasion settings cost a cool $700. She had twenty-four of those. She considered all the homes and apartments out there in consumerland. Each of them was a completely self-contained unit with more appliances, crockery, knick-knacks, bedrooms, and linens than was logical. It was a lot of shit. Most of the time, the rooms sat empty. All but a few essentials untouched, forgotten. Empty space everywhere. Empty minds everywhere. A tragedy.

If "the invisible hand of the marketplace" was so just and responsive, why did it keep producing and why did we keep buying? The invisible hand? It operated more like an iron fist poised above our heads. Its nimbleness did not extend beyond getting the latest consumer items on the shelf. Would we ever cease to associate freedom with consumer goods and the subsequent destruction of nature? We didn't come equipped with a self-regulating shut off valve that clicked into position when we were about to acquire more than was reasonable. If education failed to fill in the gap and furnish each of us with the wisdom to make simple connections, then what other tools were available to us?

Heather saw how she could contribute in a meaningful way. Other than donating to the environmental causes her mother championed, she hadn't thought much about the future. But that felt like ancient history. She owned acreage in south central British Columbia on which she intended to build yet another dream home, possibly log with a horse setup, where she would spend a week or two out of every year basking alone in her considerable wealth. That land could be put to better use. It was fertile, actually bordered the Similkameen River, and was located in wine country. Seventeen hundred acres of rolling hills covered with the perfect mix of meadow, conifers, and shrubs – all adjacent to a wilderness area. Included in Heather's comments to Jerome regarding the manuscript was the offer of this land and her name to help generate interest.

When he read her e-mail he was blown away by her willingness to do such a thing. And then he was uncomfortable with the prospect of owing a huge debt of gratitude when he wasn't sure of the spirit in which she was bequeathing the property. He vacillated between the fear of being forever in her debt and the importance of getting the concept up and running. Once he settled on being honest, he wrote to her about his concerns.

She responded by explaining that mentally she had already moved from "possess to access." It was ridiculous for humans to believe they owned the land. It was to be shared by a whole succession and procession of life. That had become so obvious to her, she no longer saw any piece of property as belonging to her alone. We were all borrowers – from an insect that stayed for a matter of weeks to a mature cedar that survived for a thousand years. Possession implied boundaries that were limiting. She was willing to embrace the borrower philosophy, so he did not need to worry about where her heart was. The challenge would be in turning humanity into something other than a lousy neighbor. Poor habitat sharing practices were a big part of the human community. She was uncertain there was any way to rectify that.

She also told him that as scary as that first step was, he had to start somewhere. The first step for him might be in trusting that she wished to make this gesture for no other motive than it was ethically worthwhile. That, and she could see herself living in places he described. She couldn't say the same for where she currently lived, or for any of the conventional real estate for that matter, regardless of how expensive it was. She knew she could donate money to charity but then she would have to wonder how much went to the cause as opposed to the salaries of the administrators and the whole hierarchical system. She no longer believed that was the answer. She agreed with him that it was the infrastructure that needed to be fixed. He was going to have to trust her when she said that she was suffocating too.

"And so with that out of the way, we decided to proceed," Heather explained.

"You?" Darlene asked. "You helped him like that?" she said, incredulous as well as convinced Mrs. Holmes was lying to her. "I can't believe you were that involved with the likes of him. You always seemed so normal to me."

"You forget what I am, an actress, and a reasonably good one. Everything you think you know about me is what I wanted you to believe. No more, no less. Anyway, I didn't do him any favors by getting involved. I was from Hollywood after all, so that made me a representative of Satan. At least in some groups' eyes. If anything, my participation was a hindrance. At the start of the new millennium there were many small-minded folks mouthing off every chance they got. The Constitution was sacred and it supported individual property rights. Everybody knew that. What people didn't accept was property rights were important to the founding fathers because owning land meant eking out agricultural subsistence. They wished to create the means for personal independence. They didn't believe a Democracy could survive without it. A far cry from the debt and wage slaves we became. Working at mind-numbing jobs in order to hang on to a plastic house and a chem-lawn behind a vinyl fence. Jerome's Paradigm Club was more in line with the independent agrarian vision on which the country was founded. But somehow the vision got lost in translation – and indoctrination."

The concept of ever having survived off the land was completely foreign to Darlene. It was an "urban legend" she wasn't sure could be taken seriously. It was the kind of thing your friends might laugh themselves silly over if they found out you believed it.

"'From possess to access' didn't have as pure a ring to the Conrad Tilton's of the world as it did to me. Conrad Tilton had Jerome back in his sights in the time it took to say 'Ready, Aim, FIRE,' or maybe he had never let Jerome out of his sights. And this time he had the added bonus of me, the immoral Hollywood accomplice, and the titillating speculation about the nature of our relationship. It was plain as day to ole' Conrad that there was only one thing a woman of my tastes could be getting from a man twelve years my junior in return for my endorsement. He went so far as to ponder what an intellectual snob purported to have an IQ in the 160 range could even discuss with a woman with about 50% the horsepower. Or whether he bothered to grunt out a greeting before he and I jumped in the sack. It was awful. It was humiliating. It got under my skin. I had a history but it was nothing to do with Jerome. We didn't have that kind of relationship. That's not to say Jerome wasn't a passionate guy because he was. He was in love with a great many things. But it wasn't a kind of passion I fully understood."

Heather quit talking again, not wishing to share all of her feelings. There had been something intense about Jerome. At times, she wanted to attach like a leech, and do everything Conrad said they were doing.

Somehow, though, she never got around to it. For Jerome, the sexual speculation was not the worst part of being trashed by Conrad Tilton. It was being made to look a fool by a fool. Majority opinion has a way of messing with your mind. Even with the mind of someone thoughtful. There had to be moments when Jerome was overcome by doubt. However, he was adept at hiding those doubts. Still, it couldn't be easy to speak out against what your fellow citizens were building their lives around.

She drifted back to that occasion when Jerome did offer an official response to Conrad Tilton's firm belief that the system we were living under was practically perfect. By that time there was desperation in the air, at least from certain quarters. So Heather guessed that Jerome figured he had nothing to lose by confronting that ridiculous man.

"After much introspection and soul searching (thanks to you I now believe I have one), I have decided that you are absolutely 100% correct. I am a fool for daring to hope that we could avoid making the same mistakes that other civilizations that collapsed before us made. With so much accumulated, conventional wisdom such as yours on our side telling us what's what, we should definitely stick with a system that:
- *discourages critical thinking*
- *confuses the fouling of the nest for progress*
- *excludes anyone of average means from the political process but yet deems average ideas a worthy prerequisite*
- *concentrates wealth and power in the hands of a few*
- *is so opaque and convoluted that how it really operates is understood by very few*
- *encourages its citizens to invest against their own best interests*
- *requires its citizens to spend three quarters of their lives in debt, enriching the lives of the wealthy*
- *wages wars because they are profitable*
- *discourages any other way of living or thinking*
- *reinforces through advertising, education, and other forms of brainwashing that this is the best we could possibly do*

- *promises its uninformed masses they will be rewarded in Heaven for their ignorance*
- *is an enabler of belligerent, uninformed talk show hosts who in their blatant disregard for the truth prevent positive change from becoming reality.*

And then, we should all pray. Every last, stinking one of us. Because if we don't choose to take intelligent action, it's likely we'll all end up addicted to painkilling drugs. Good luck, good night, and God bless America (and Conrad Tilton for helping me to see the light.)"

After that, Heather deduced that hers was not the only skin Conrad Tilton got under. Jerome wasn't one to use satire so it was surprising when that was how he responded. A majority couldn't tell that he was joking. She had to admit that by that time we were so stupefied by mushy-headed leadership, it wasn't easy to know if someone was serious or not.

Darlene began talking again. And in doing so, Heather was forced to return to the here and now. "I still don't understand what Jerome wanted. He seemed to want everyone to do something. But what exactly?"

"Accept that life as we knew it couldn't continue. It was the end. We had to do this before we would start building something else. He wanted to begin transitioning painlessly while we still could rather than later when it was forced on us through disaster and shortages. He thought if we could mentally abandon the monster of a system under which we lived, we would see how unsustainable it was and consider other ways. At the very least, we would give ourselves the opportunity to grow wiser."

"Wiser than what or who, exactly?" Darlene asked, unable to make head or tail of what Heather was saying. We were what we were because around six thousand years ago, God created us this way. There was no way to be anything else.

They were at a verbal impasse. What Jerome feared most was that Darlene would be the person of the future. Everything he worked on throughout his life had been to prevent someone like her from being representative of humanity. Despite his good intentions, here they were. Heather wasn't cruel enough to say it. There was a part of her that still wished to be popular with everyone. That was why she had done so well in life. It would be left to Sunny to speak that particular truth.

BOOK FOUR

CRISIS, WHAT CRISIS?

How "Advanced" Civilization Bickers While Earth Burns

John's two-year assignment in China stretched into another year in India and then it was on to Thailand where Precious Pieces also had a manufacturing/distribution facility. Sales remained robust for the products John's company produced. They made a good choice marketing something as frivolous as fine china to infants. It was the wish of parents of a certain socioeconomic level that their children have their own patterns. As the gap between the rich and the poor continued to widen "the haves" kept dreaming up ways to increase their sense of wellbeing. There seemed to be no end to the list of entitlements and essentials that were necessary to achieve this feeling.

What made it really perfect was there were more women of childbearing age on the planet than at any other time. After decades of the population rate declining in the developed world, it began to increase. The younger generations weren't satisfied with two or fewer children. A pious self-centered group, who believed in Creationism and Manifest Destiny, they knew better than science when it came to environmental issues. God would continue to provide. All they had to do was believe and have babies. They were bound and determined to procreate civilization out of its troubles. It was Albert Einstein who said, "The world will not evolve past its current state of crisis by using the same thinking that created the situation." But they believed themselves to be smarter than Einstein if, on the off chance, they knew who Einstein was.

Given these attitudes, Sunny couldn't overstate the career wisdom of John's decision to spend those years outside of the United States. He was on a fast track to success. After receiving two previous promotions, he was offered the position of President of Overseas Operations. He had made

Officer. He was feeling good and in control. And he believed wholeheartedly that his wife in her subservient role needed something to do. Producing offspring was what immediately came to mind. The contribution of a meager two spawn from a man of his merit wasn't nearly enough. It wasn't something Sunny anticipated. After years of John's mind being the most rigid part of his anatomy when it came to her, in her worst nightmares she hadn't seen him hot for her crotch again. If he thought he was going to impregnate her, he was one crazy fucker.

"I'm not having a baby. I told you that when we first met. Because you already had two children you were okay with that. How many offspring do you feel you need?"

"You are so selfish, Sarah. You're not very sympathetic to other people. I don't think you even have a heart."

"Oh really? Like having babies when the world is already grossly overpopulated isn't the most selfish thing a person could do."

"Why do you have to be so analytical about everything? That's not an attractive trait in a woman. But then, you're not really a whole woman anyway. A woman who doesn't have a child will never be more than half a woman."

"Who gave you that idea? Some preacher or something? You know, John, you're half a man for suggesting such a thing. You have some crazy idea that you're the only one in this marriage who's not satisfied. You think you make me happy? Have you ever considered the possibility that you're not perfect? A little effort on your part wouldn't hurt."

"No one could make you happy. I have no idea what you want but it's not a man."

For once John was right. Sunny didn't want a man. At least not as defined by conventional standards. The kind civilization or empire or whatever you wished to call it was pumping out. And it showed no signs of changing. She had thought the equality movement would make young men and women more compatible. And with that, more and more couples would have the kind of relationship that eluded her. But that wasn't coming to pass either. Religion was back in vogue. That never translated into egalitarian circumstances for women. None of it was going the way she thought it would.

The Institution

"Why is it," she asked, "that we always seem to be moving in the opposite direction? We're both living through identical circumstances, inhabiting the same planet at the same time but we're not moving in sync."

He had no idea what she was asking. "You mean like why is my career going great guns while yours is on the skids? Why am I more successful as every year goes by and you less? I don't know but it's starting to get embarrassing when business associates ask about what you do."

Because John hadn't understood the question, he also wasn't cognizant of inadvertently giving exactly the answer she was looking for. "Interesting, isn't it? Selling trinkets is a highly respected profession but protecting the environment is so superfluous I'm unemployable. That speaks more to what our society is than your merit as a man."

He started to disagree but she stopped him. "Please, before you launch into another round of patting yourself on the back, why don't you give that a moment's thought? I bet even you have enough wisdom to recognize that what you're doing may pay well but it's absolutely meaningless." But she was wrong in that assessment. Again, giving credit where it wasn't due. He would never be able to see something like that. Monetary award was the only measure of a man that counted. And she was not giving him the respect he had earned.

Their relationship deteriorated further after that and he lost interest in her again. He accepted the futility of convincing her how wonderful it would be to have a baby. Sex with his wife would never be anything more than recreational. It normally took place after she consumed a great deal of alcohol and seemed to be confused as to who he was. But Sunny could see where this new found success of her husband's would lead eventually. To a third wife, a trophy bride, so he could go around again rather than going forward. Once his wallet got a little fatter, he would join the ranks of men over fifty years old with young children in tow. The largest contingency of this kind, ever. They were being rewarded in flesh for their monetary worth. Their sophomoric genes were contributing disproportionately to the future pool.

It was the degree of separation, though, that stood out and again struck Sunny as odd. She may have been out of the country and isolated, but that did not mean she did nothing but wait for John to come home from work, the way he believed. The future of environmentalism was something that nagged at her. The fact that very little of what humans did on a daily basis was environmentally benign confirmed Jerome's opinion that environmentalists were ineffective. She, and many others who professed to care, were missing the whole point.

Reading the statistics on the increased toxins children born after 1980 had been exposed to shocked her. It drew attention to the disturbing fact that anyone born after that year was not going to live longer or have a healthier time of it. The deck kept getting stacked higher and higher against us. The chemical poisons were everywhere. They remained in the food chain. It was little more than wishful thinking to believe being prudent about the food ingested and the products used made one immune. We were all in this thing together. We were part of a gigantic interconnected natural system that circulated, not only around us, but also through us. What we fouled up didn't go away never to be seen again. Instead it drifted and spread. The toxic tendrils stretched far and wide and always resurfaced somewhere.

Continuing to introduce poisonous gas into a sealed room would eventually kill the inhabitants. This was not disputable. And yet, with all the education that passed down through the ages we were either unwilling or unable to apply that principle on a larger scale. Post-secondary education prepared us for employment in which we were obsessed with the little picture. We learned how to produce products, package, and distribute them but we did not receive the kind of education that encouraged us to ask whether a product was good or bad for our health and the health of the ecosystem. We slapped up whole tracts of housing units and marketed them. But it wasn't in anyone's job description or his financial interest to inquire what the building materials exposed us to.

A chemical engineer's primary concern wasn't how products that contained his chemical components were eventually disposed of. His interest revolved around the production process. And if it didn't, then he wouldn't be as effective at doing what he was doing. He'd be weighing in the pros and cons and when he got through calculating the long-term planetary costs, he might question whether certain products were essential enough to be developed in the first place. And that would mean fewer products to sell. The marketplace didn't respond favorably to foregoing products. It thrived on the latest innovation. That's how wealth was created. Nobody got rich on what wasn't produced and so we were deadlocked.

There was no will to change the education system. Young people went to school so that when they got out they could get a job, preferably a high paying one. There was no reason to go to college other than that. It wasn't as if the public – highly-educated and uneducated alike – thought their minds needed improving. We believed the human species was getting smarter under the current structure. Each of us saw ourselves as a prime example of this. The facts, however, were more ambiguous than individual perception. Domestication translated into smaller brains. The rules were the same for us as they were for farm animals and koala bears. It was but one more disturbing trend we were in denial about.

What we needed was the kind of education that produced critical thinkers who formulated the arguments for not doing what we were doing. An educated living force that could see what we really are – slaves to a system that would eventually extinguish all hope of survival. If we knew more, there was the distinct possibility we would wish for less of what our current system was giving and more of what it wasn't. What did we do instead? We created more areas of expertise such as environmental studies. And this was broken down into narrower specialties because air was separate from water. One dealt in particulate matter, the other parts per million. Fresh water issues were of one kind, salt water of another. And what happened on the land – in the forests, underground, on hillsides, to the tops of mountains – was broken down into smaller areas of expertise. Playing off against one another, the environmentalists needed the bad living practices we engaged in to survive and the rest of us needed the environmentalists to make sure there was something left to destroy tomorrow or else how could we keep our economy and population growing. And then where would we be? Just like human health, environmental health was a misnomer. It was about sickness brought about by a sick system and was concerned only with mitigating damage. Human activities were systematically destroying everything.

Terra Dime

Sunny spent her time during those overseas years studying and working on a paper dealing with the future of environmentalism. The more she read the more she realized that environmentally we were close to the point when the natural system on which all life depends quits functioning. Ecologically, we could be looking at a decade or less. The facts and figures clearly supported shifting to a new economic and social system that was not based on consumption. No one seemed to have a clear vision of what that might be. It meant we had to turn the system upside down so environmental wellbeing drove lifestyle decisions because bleeding nature to satisfy insatiable material desires wasn't prudent.

This was why it surprised Sunny that while all of this was foremost in her thoughts, for her spouse, producing more offspring was all his mind could muster. The lack of concern amongst people who were alive during the greatest holocaust of all time was unbelievable. Whenever she brought up anything that had an environmental collapse component to it John would become livid. He would tell her that he had been hoping that since she was no longer in the business, she would forget about that stuff. What he didn't understand was that being out of the game made her able to see the game clearly. She had time – glorious time – to read, to think, and to develop an informed opinion.

Many studies pointed to 1986 as the drop-dead year when we should have gotten serious about our ecological footprint. There had been some advancement over the previous decade before the loss of momentum took over. That's what Sunny and Jerome had picked up on at the supposed Transportation Expo – an exposition that had an air of irrelevance because it was in the business of providing what was wanted, instead of what was needed. Fuel usage per mile, vehicle size, miles traveled, home sizes, food choices, and all manner of consumption increased in the years that followed. In hindsight, 1986 was the Eleventh Hour. Rather than getting serious about environmental issues we purchased SUVs, accumulated airline miles, and then sat back and ignored how our impact was growing. More than twenty years of overshoot meant we had arrived at the Twelfth Hour. It was going to take more than a technofix to prevent catastrophe. It was going to take heroic effort on the part of regular individuals. But most of all, it was going to take the wisdom to grow up.

The Institution

The sense of foreboding Sunny felt while she was in those developing countries as they strove to better themselves overshadowed everything. Everyone was so earnest in his wish to rise out of poverty and live like Americans. And so sincere in his belief that he could do it better than the Americans had. And so delusional. The way of life they were striving to achieve was not environmentally sustainable. Never had been, never would be. Not for the millions of people who currently enjoyed it and certainly not for the additional billions who wished to. She was rendered speechless at the imagery of western civilization dominating the east, especially in the face of their then deteriorating ecological conditions. The water table was dropping from year to year in places like India, and not by small amounts, but by hundreds of feet. Farmers knew this and they also knew that it couldn't go on indefinitely. One day they would be unable to draw the water to the surface where it was needed to keep the rice crops alive. Scientists worked feverishly on test plots of genetically altered rice that could grow without flooded fields as if the Green Revolution mentality could solve the problem it created. In the deltas, where much of the world's agriculture took place, salt water was working its way further inland foreshadowing the difficulties that were yet to come.

And when the sea level did in fact rise by five feet it cost the wealthy countries billions of dollars and millions of lives everywhere else. Between the drought in the north of China and the swollen rivers and flooding in the south, the number of its citizens malnourished and in danger of starvation increased exponentially. This did not stem the tide of food being exported by this poor country to the wealthy ones. Feeding its own people before everyone else was not the way of the world. It *was* true that he with the most money and biggest guns wins. Sunny found the whole experience to be a textbook study in macroeconomics and empire. There was famine throughout the world with more starving to death than at any other time in the history of humankind. While this was going on, the consumers of her country blissfully ate Central American beef grazed on land that had been stripped of its rainforest, continued to buy trinkets manufactured in sweatshops, and filled their cars with ethanol grown all over the globe.

Sunny quit sharing her concerns with John. It was more gratifying to write a little piece or send an e-mail to Jerome asking his opinion. They communicated frequently. She branched out into subjects beyond her area of expertise. Evolution, systems theory, economics, financial markets, the Green Revolution, agribusiness, politics both current and historical, and civilization collapse were the kinds of things she studied. And although she reached a similar conclusion to Jerome about how dire were our circumstances, when it came to why we were in this situation and our prospects for bettering the human condition, this was where they parted company.

The way Sunny interpreted the data, western civilization was based on a linear view of progress. It was flawed because it ignored the cyclical nature of the seasons of life. We were bound by the same natural laws as the rest of the planet. We ebbed and flowed and because of this our manmade systems rose, boomed, and busted without fail. The cycles arrived on schedule and depending on when in the life of the cycle we were born, we acted in predictable ways. It was a pattern that replayed itself just as surely as spring turned to summer then to autumn and finally winter. A linear viewpoint was flawed in much the same way as Jerome's belief in the possibility of continuous renewal. That would be analogous to perpetual spring.

Sunny liked the whole seasonal analogy of human systems. It explained so much about why we behaved irrationally. At some level we wished to bring about winter. Without it, there would not be another spring. The evidence was all around that we could no more shun the cyclical nature of the earth that is in our blood than a caterpillar could expect to remain in a cocoon. While much of Jerome's philosophy was based on fact, this was a reality he ignored and that made him as naïve as a linearist. She believed we all had a blind spot and she told him so. Idealism was his.

It didn't surprise Jerome that Sunny was pessimistic about the human prospect. It was in character. What impressed him was that she would go to such lengths to find material that backed up her point of view. In his opinion, and he told her so, her own propensity for intellectual improvement kind of blew the whole theory. She was acting like a person infatuated by intellectual spring, rather than moving on to a staid summer or waning autumn mindset. And those latter seasons would be more appropriate for her chronological age. She got a big laugh out of that even though it meant he got in the last word, as usual.

He encouraged her to send her paper to some journals for publication and offered suggestions as to likely takers. Before her scheduled arrival back in Washington State, a periodical did agree to publish the article. A mainstream publisher told her that because of her ability to explain complex concepts, she could write science books in the style of James Gleick. She was ecstatic. Soon she would be going home and with the means to live without John.

While Jerome was writing *Turning on the 'digm*, Sunny helped with the accuracy of the environmental aspects and, in return, incorporated into her work his ideas regarding societal change. She also issued a challenge for others to comment on how we might be more sustainable. She knew the direction Jerome wished to take and wondered what others envisioned. Was there only one way to proceed? Were there many ways? Were there none? While she was getting desperate about the narrowing window of opportunity, the machine kept rolling along. The ocean dead zones grew larger, extinctions accelerated, ice caps melted, sea levels rose, the earth warmed and dried, and none of this tugged at the average human heart. Addiction to speed and power usurped all other passion. And then, as if to punctuate obsession, we the people decided the Fraser River had outlived its usefulness as a free flowing marvel of nature.

In the autumn of 2012, a month before she was to get on a plane and return to the States, Sunny received a message from Jerome that was not as innocuous as his others. He gave her the lowdown on the Fraser River hydroelectric project and indicated he would be attending a protest that was being held. He thought he was done with the whole activism scene but felt the dams would lead to devastation on a grand scale. As a consequence, it couldn't be ignored.

Surely, no one seriously believed that once the North American Union combined Canada, the United States, and Mexico into one big "Security & Prosperity Partnership," Canada's natural resources would not be put to better use. The formation of the North American Union meant the Amero. It was a much stronger currency thanks to the vast water, timber, mineral, and oil reserves of the north, cheap labor from the south, and a wealthy elite backed by the military industrial complex in the middle.

For a natural resource like the Fraser River to lie untapped when it could be supplying power, water, and recreation – while lowering our carbon footprint all at the same time – was criminal. The dam promoters began presenting their case. Anyone who opposed it was labeled anti-human and given the moniker "human-hater." The building of five dams was a project of such magnitude it would provide employment for twenty years and with great swaths of wilderness made accessible, summer homes on the newly minted lakes would follow. Brand spanking new towns were sure to spring up where they hadn't been viable before. The road construction alone would keep the British Columbian Province of the Americas' economy rolling along nicely into the future. As a bonus, it would guarantee fast and easy access from the cities of Vancouver and Calgary. There was no end in sight to the growth of those two metropolitan areas. It was backward thinking to expect their residents to do without more places to recreate. World-class cities must provide world-class access to the great outdoors.

Capturing and diverting that fresh water was what really sealed the deal. The southwestern United States wanted it so they could continue building houses and growing crops in the desert. Vancouver, so that the paving of the entire Fraser Valley could continue uninterrupted. Calgary and Edmonton because Alberta had the oil sands. Extracting that oil may have contaminated all the watersheds east of the Rocky Mountains but that didn't mean the rest of Canada should hold it against them. Alberta was an industrious province. And because of this, at least one of the other provinces owed them a new source of fresh water. Rapid shrinkage of the glaciers had contributed to lower flows in the Bow and Saskatchewan Rivers on which much of Alberta's population depended. The water had to come from somewhere if they were to continue marching along the path that had brought so much success. Watershed destruction was a small price to pay. Besides, the earth was covered with water. There would always be another source to tap. Humans were smart. We would think of something. That, in a nutshell, passed for wisdom in our day.

The Institution

Among the more disturbing bits of information Jerome passed on was the chilly reception *Turning on the 'digm* was getting in the west. He had been worried about being branded a socialist, not a lunatic. That was before his discomfort with the cultural status quo turned into a rant against the whole model and that made him certifiable. Like a body exposed to disease, culture looked for a way to destroy anything that threatened its viability. The speculation on the state of his mental health spread from the usual suspects into the mainstream and even progressive arenas. All but a few fringe thinkers got busy writing him off publicly as a very sick man.

"The reality check of this whole situation is good for me though," he e-mailed to Sunny. *"Sometimes you get so caught up in what you've discovered that you forget there is very little discovery going on around you. There is not a collective realization that we are on the wrong path. Actually, we aren't on a path at all but stuck in a roundabout and we can't see we're going in circles. We are committed to maintaining the lawn instead of recognizing that other seeds must be planted. It is gardeners that must step up – not mowers, whackers, and blowers. I think I failed to stay in tune with the kind of thinking that has been going on around me. I should have recognized the escalation of commitment that permeates every move we make. When people are dependent on a dysfunctional, immature economic and social system to provide a standard of living that pleases them, it only stands to reason they will become increasingly dysfunctional and immature themselves. They have to, in order to believe in and defend – against foes like me – what is logically unsupportable. That belief I've always had that the bar could be raised and our circumstances improved is fading. My philosophy on humanity is undergoing a major transformation."*

When Sunny received this message, she wondered who was above being marginalized the way Jerome had been? Economic and social change needed a spokesperson. Someone respected, considered wise, unbiased, constant, and true. Who might that person be? Was there any messenger out there who wouldn't be compromised for daring to deliver it? Or was the message too toxic to be conveyed?

The character assassination Jerome received for trying to advance the discussion beyond the mundane convinced him there was no overcoming modern man's mental paralysis. It looked more and more as if we would not choose the easy way. Complete collapse was what it would take to wake us up. And that meant billions served up on a platter, dead. The question for him had changed from *whether* it would happen, to *what* would happen first – environmental or economic disaster? He was hoping for a financial breakdown. It wouldn't be as final and it might give some breathing room to environmental health.

He went on to explain that although he had intended to invest most of his money in making the Paradigm Club of his book a reality, his commitment was waning. If the concept didn't click with a certain portion of the population there was no point in proceeding. Getting working members/partners wouldn't be that difficult. There were plenty of disenchanted youth who were beginning to realize that if all the bad news they were hearing was true, there wasn't going to be anything left for them. It was impossible, though, to convince the one or two generations that were materially successful to leave something for future generations. They justified their unwillingness to do this by telling themselves they were well-off because they were smarter and had worked harder than their children and grandchildren. They didn't credit natural resources, the source of all wealth, which had once been in abundant supply. The fantastic store of energy in the form of oil that was extracted during their lifetimes was not relevant either. In their minds, it was because of a superior work ethic and frugality during their early years. And now, there was no need for them to hedge their bets because it was all going to last long enough for them. What that translated into was using up whatever was available without caring about tomorrow. Future generations would make do with what little was left.

Feeling the way he did, Jerome thought he should be careful about going forward with something that looked destined to fail. His thoughts were turning more selfish and in the direction of personal survival. Sunny would see why he had grown more apprehensive once she was back in the country. He wanted the two of them to talk seriously about their options as soon as she returned. For him, this meant figuring out a way they could be together. There were no messages after that.

***

The Institution

They were heading west toward the Fraser River. Heather had flown into Kamloops early in the morning. That was where Jerome picked her up. It was the closest airport to Lillooet, home of Moran Canyon, the site of the first dam to be constructed on the main trunk of the Fraser. It was also where the protests over the coming weekend were to be held. She had not intended to come to British Columbia for this purpose but because Jerome felt compelled to participate she agreed to tag along.

Originally, what had been planned for this week was a trip to the Similkameen River property so they could look it over and decide whether to proceed. She had been so excited about that prospect when the Fraser River protest thing came up, she found a way to work around it. Heather did not delve into her personal reasons for being filled with expectation about the trip. Twenty-eight years later it was no different. The losses sustained on that clear fall day were painful enough.

He hadn't recognized her when she stepped from the Concourse into the baggage claim area. She was practically on top of him waving her arms before it registered. "Yo, Jerome. I'm over here," she said.

"It took me months to figure out who you were and now you don't look like you. Are you in disguise or what?"

"No disguise. I decided to lose 'The Look.' Kind of shocking, isn't it? Ages me about ten years. Oh well, you can't stay young forever."

"Any baggage?"

"Plenty of it. But I didn't bring it on this trip. I decided to leave it behind."

Always quick with the one-liners, it didn't surprise him that Heather was popular. She was fun to be around. "I meant *checked* baggage," he laughed. "Though I am glad to hear you left the worst of it in Southern California."

"No, this is it," she said indicating the satchel slung over her shoulder.

Less than thirty minutes later, they were above Kamloops Lake, which was just a wide spot in the Thompson River. Semi-arid desert all around. "It's so barren out here," she said. "It shocks me. When I think of British Columbia, I think lush and green."

"The interior portion of the Province is extremely dry but it looks worse than it did even five years ago when the Mountain Pine Beetle

Terra Dime

trashed about 40% of the ponderosa pine in the Province. And then the Spruce Budworm piggybacked on top of that."

"Forty percent? Isn't that an awful lot of trees?"

"It's only the start. All the boreal forests of the north will be gone within our lifetimes."

"Climate change?"

"That's a big factor. The forests are under siege from many sources. Over cutting, weakened trees because of drought, beetles that no longer perish because the winters are too mild, beetles that have mutated and grown stronger probably because of insecticide use, and reforestation practices that create a monoculture not a forest. All the trees are the same size and species. And beetles like that. It's all either climate or human related. Although, there would be a number of people who would argue that. The bigger problem is that we can't slow down. Our way of life won't allow it. The situation is dire. It requires immediate attention but we aren't nimble enough to respond. It would be too harmful to the 'just in time' economy."

"How odd it looks," she said. "Such a pretty bit of water in all this desolation. I assume it at least has some fish in it."

"You wouldn't believe how many. In case you didn't know, the Thompson is a tributary of the Fraser. Less than a month ago it would have been full of spawning salmon making their way to the Adams River. I believe it's one of the largest spawning grounds on the planet." He pointed above them to the other side of the river. "See those stretches of a disintegrating wooden flume up there?"

"Who put them there?"

"The British Columbia Development Association. It was a London-based investment syndicate that purchased 6,000 acres here in 1908 and 1909. A 'horticultural colony' by the name of Walhachin was built and it thrived briefly before WWI drained away the manpower. The colony lasted until 1922 when it was abandoned due to economic unfeasibility."

"Been reading up have you?"

"I had a few extra hours so I did a little research. Didn't want to be a boring travel guide. If you look closely, you can still see a few old fruit trees. Stragglers, a hundred years old and still hanging on. They've made their peace. They're part of this land now. It's relevant anyway, this diversion project of the past. The current dam scheme we're here to investigate isn't the only one that's been tried. It's been an endless series of successes and failures."

"Jerome?"

"Yes," he answered when she didn't say anything more.

"I want you to know that I feel really bad about how your name has been out there getting trashed by Conrad Tilton. I didn't mean for that to happen. When you're in the limelight the way I've been you get used to that sort of thing, at least to a certain degree. But I'm sure it's not something that you're very comfortable with. He was particularly cruel this time around, even for him. At least that's what I thought. I didn't think it through very well when I let it be known that you and I are acquainted. I'm sorry for setting you up like that. When my intentions are good, I can be so naïve."

He looked over at her kind of holding her breath. Her clear blue eyes stared straight ahead. "There's no need for you to apologize. His speculation about our being romantically involved wasn't the part that bothered me. It was the other stuff. Making love to you, let's face it, I could do worse than that."

She turned his way and smiled. Her head fall back against the headrest. "I'm glad you can live with that," she said in relief, while inside she wished that what they'd been accused of was more than an allegation.

"The damage Conrad Tilton does is much greater than to one person's reputation. I don't know if he's truly unaware of who has the power in this country or not. What he succeeds in doing is preventing much of what is wrong with the system from being exposed. Many good people who listen to him are duped into voting against their best interests. He's a great enabler of the powerful because he stops the discussion from going to the next level. And he does it under the guise of doing the right thing. He represents himself as the great wise man exposing bad ideas that are sure to put everyone at risk when what he's really doing is denouncing the learned, alternative view. He and his followers are so ill-informed about what's pressing."

They began to travel away from the Thompson. The river took a route further to the south well below the level of the highway. Hay fields fanned out across the bench on which they were driving. When a cluster of road signs appeared Heather asked, "Cache Creek, is that a town? Because if it is, I'd like to get something to eat?"

"I did pack some food. It's in the cooler in the back seat. I didn't know whether you'd want to stop given the possibility you could be mobbed by a bunch of guys. I wasn't sure how to handle that. From what I've come to understand, I'm the only guy in the whole western world who wouldn't know who you are."

"I guess it's good for me to meet a man who wouldn't give anything to get into my pants." He was startled when she said it wondering if she was expecting him to say something about that not being so. Thankfully, she kept on talking. "So what do you have for us? If it's decent, I'd just as soon not go in anywhere."

"Usual picnic stuff – bread, cheese, fruit, some of those little carrots, pea pods."

"Ahhh, healthy stuff."

"Well, there is some chocolate. Dark, 72% cacao, loaded with antioxidants. I guess that's healthy too."

She released her seat belt and reached into the back seat to check out the contents of the cooler. "So what would you like?"

"Just an apple for now." She handed that to him while she layered several slices of Swiss cheese on a roll and broke open the sugar pea bag.

He slowed to make a left hand turn off the highway onto a secondary road. "Obviously, we're not going that far but if we followed this road all the way through it would take us to Whistler. Have you ever been there?"

"Really, to the ski resort? Sure I've been. You'd expect that I've hit all the high points, now wouldn't you? I'll bet that's a beautiful trip. So how much further is it to where we're going?"

"About fifty miles."

They rode along in silence while she ate the bread and cheese. When that was finished, she broke off chunks of chocolate for both of them and they tied into those. "So tell me something about yourself, Jerome."

"There's nothing to tell. You already know the interesting stuff."

The Institution

"I was thinking about something more personal."

"Oh," he groaned. "I don't really like to talk about me." But she kept looking at him in a persistent, hopeful sort of way.

"Okay," he acquiesced. "When I was twenty, my mom, dad, and sister were killed in a car accident. They were on their way to visit me at the university I attended. Because of their deaths I got some money – mainly from insurance and the sale of the house. It wasn't much, but that money enabled me to do what I wanted instead of the conventional. I've always felt guilty about that. Knowing my life took a turn for the better on account of their dying." He quit talking.

"So, is that personal enough for you?" he added, when she had nothing to say.

"That's awful, Jerome. That wasn't what I was expecting from you. Well, at least you didn't blow the money. You turned it into something productive."

"Did I? Some would say writing books is the least productive thing a person could do and that a society can't afford to have very many of its citizens employed that way. It's narcissistic when you think about it. Believing your words are so important they should be read by others. Hoping for celebrity status so you can travel around like a star knowing people want to hear you speak. Building up a fan base that can't wait for your next book to be published."

"That's very unflattering. I'm not sure I agree with you. It's not like you're a Conrad Tilton or something."

"But that's where you're wrong. We're different sides of the same coin. The similarities can't be overlooked."

"Doesn't society need someone like you to write about what's really happening? Where would we be if it weren't for people who are willing to speak out?"

"In exactly the same place."

"No way. Things would be worse. I know they would be."

"Heather, I wish you were right, but you're not. All I'm doing is providing comfort to those people who already feel as I do and who likely know as much as well. Affirmation, it's all anyone seeks. The reason I'm able to provide this service is I'm part of the hierarchy. That's why my

239

books get published and another writer, who is lesser known or doesn't have credentials, but might have better ideas, doesn't. I wish words had the power to change the place we're heading, but they don't. They might slow down our arrival by a few years but that's it.

"No matter how hard I try, I don't understand the way we live. Even going to the grocery store makes no sense to me. I do my best to limit my exposure because everything about the system screams inefficiency and waste. We have this food delivery system that requires the burning of fossil fuels at every point in the process. In addition, it generates an obscene amount of packaging we can't figure out how to dispose of but that's not for want of trying because that's what we spend our time on. What we should be questioning is whether purchasing food in this manner makes any sense at all. There are so many ways in which this system is a failure.

"This whole Fraser River dam thing, you know how long engineers have been dreaming of performing this feat? Eventually, they'll get it done. I've not seen any evidence that we've grown wiser about such things. Have you been anywhere where the human footprint has grown smaller and we're using up less of the land base? Population pressure and energy prices are such that more dams in this part of the world now make good economic sense. The river and surrounding land will disappear under a lake stretching for possibly 150 miles, all the way to Quesnel. It will produce so much power that population will bust its seams expanding outward. Possibly another aluminum plant will be built to harness all that spare capacity and meet the demands of growing numbers of people. Or more likely, the one further north will be expanded. That's easy enough to do. Punch a few more holes in the rock and reverse the flows of one of the Fraser's tributaries. There are plans out there to bore tunnels through the mountains and divert water to the Peace River and the Columbia and pipe the excess to drought-ridden California. Now that all of this is part of the North American Union, it's going to happen."

"So if that's the case what are we doing? Why are we here?"

"To try to slow down the inevitable. To give the salmon a few more years. A small accomplishment in the whole scheme of things."

"I didn't realize you were so conflicted."

The Institution

"I'm getting more that way all the time. There are too many battles to fight. This late in the game they're coming from so many directions it's hard to know which are the ones we even have a chance of winning. And the problem with all these little skirmishes is they are distractions from the really cool stuff we could be working on. Every time I get caught up in a battle like this, I get mad. Mainly I'm mad that we still haven't moved forward but I'm also scared that the luxury of time to do so is running out. And those who control the political process, the purse strings, and just about everything else don't seem to be struck by this same sense of urgency. So here we are out here burning up resources we can ill afford, spreading our own big footprints across the land. For what? It irritates me because I'm being forced to compromise what I believe in – which is a small personal footprint – because a majority of the population believes it is their right to leave a really big one. Let's add it up. You got on a plane and flew 2,000 miles. I jumped into this vehicle and drove 400 miles for this. And how many others are going to do the same this weekend to make the point that we shouldn't be consuming so many resources. Strange way to do it if you ask me.

"What kills me is that this is what my fellow man prefers. Driving, flying, sitting in a cubicle, living in crowded conditions, eating genetically modified food that's covered with poison. I don't get it. If I were in charge of designing the human habitat, it wouldn't look anything like what we have. I'd be trying to figure out how to restore the earth back to the spa it was before humanity took it upon itself to turn it into a dump. All we have to do is want that. Why do we like asphalt highways better than footpaths? What is so great about neon lights that we choose them over the moon and stars? Why wouldn't someone prefer to be surrounded by gardens rather than stores? The roar of commerce speaks to us and we don't hear the pulse of the planet. How could we, when we'd rather be chasing the next deal instead of finding peace of mind?"

The scenery through the windshield was splendid as it whizzed by. His words heightened her awareness of the beauty of it all. And they underscored with every mile that passed what we should have seen. They were there, but not really so. This disassociation – wasn't that the human narrative? These were the kind of thoughts that made Heather panicky.

Terra Dime

She asked him to pull off up ahead. She had seen a sign for a rest area where they could get off the road for a few minutes.

Once the truck came to a stop and he turned off the engine, she sat there looking out at the lake, mountains rising sharply from the far shore. The golden mix of tamarack and birch amongst the evergreens was a beautiful sight. It was a perfect day. She couldn't remember a bluer sky or a lake mirroring its surroundings as well as this one. As she got out of the truck and walked to the edge of the small lake, she had that strange sense of seeing the world for the first time. All of it so crisp and bright she felt overwhelmed as she stood there opening up, letting it soak in. But the sensation was more than she could hang on to for long. The razor sharp edges had already begun to soften when she turned at the sound of his step on the gravel path.

"It's nice here," she said. "The lay of the land, the vegetation, the sky, the quality of the light. There's something about it that agrees with me. Do you know what I'm talking about?"

"Yes, I do." And then, as if he read her mind, "Sometimes the human world can get in the way of that. I didn't mean to upset you. Every now and again, it gets to me. It's not always easy to stay upbeat. Nevertheless, it's wrong not to be enjoying moments like these. I do know that much."

"Does this mean you don't want to go forward with the Paradigm Club idea? If you don't want to take the trip over to look at the acreage just tell me."

"We'll go. We have to. We told that guy we'd meet him there. Once we're there looking at the place, maybe something will come to us. Another way to proceed, possibly. I don't know."

"What's changed, Jerome? A year ago, we thought there was an opportunity to generate some enthusiasm. I'm not crazy, am I? We really thought there was a chance, didn't we? You wrote six books that were optimistic. Then what?"

"Daniel Quinn, the author, has something to say about all of this. He says, 'there is a secret plan in place. It's a secret plan that we don't talk about because, well, it's a secret, and we want to keep the secret. That's what we've been taught to do.' Heather, do you know what the secret plan is?"

The Institution

"Do I want to know?" she asked.

"According to Quinn, this is the secret plan: 'We are going to continue on this way until we can't anymore.'"

"That doesn't sound like a very good plan."

"No, it doesn't and that's why everyone keeps quiet about it. It's also why I don't believe in the potential of the human species any more. That's why I'm struggling. I'm not sure where to go from here. I've been focused like this since I was fifteen years old and now I can see it was for nothing and I'm going to have to let go. We're all going to have to let go. Mankind overplayed its hand and will continue to do so until the last day. You and I both know what that means."

"I've been doing a lot of listening and observing lately and I'm not liking the signs. Ever since we met, I've been preparing myself for something but I didn't know what. Now I see that you're doing the same and I admit I'm kind of scared. I made an outrageous amount of money in such a stupid occupation. At the time it seemed normal for someone to get rich that way. It seemed normal for skills such as mine to be in high demand. But now I'm thinking it was nothing more than a freak of timing. That was one of the books I read, *The Winner-Take-All Society*, and I think we've had our day, us non-producers."

"You're right to be scared. We all should be. Everything we've relied on and thought would be the same tomorrow isn't going to be. Just because we don't have the imagination to see anything other than the present duplicated decade after decade, doesn't mean that's the way it will be. It was an illusion we were able to maintain as long as energy production kept ahead of population growth. It's the creaking and groaning you're hearing that's making you uneasy. We are about to be paid back for the way we've controlled and manipulated."

"All my instincts are telling me to bail out. And that means slipping away to a remote corner somewhere with someone I trust. I'm not sure at this point whether to go with my instincts. I'm still weighing the odds. Would you be willing to take that big of step?"

Right away he thought about Sunny and the prospect of letting her go. It would be the sane thing to do, but when had he ever been that. He knew

Terra Dime

what Heather was really asking but he didn't let on. "I'm not sure I'm ready," he answered.

"But there will come a time won't there, when you quit? When you give up trying to change the world and instead start drinking in what's left? Set up house in a little cabin on a lake like this and hunker down. Have dinner by candlelight, make love in front of the fire, watch the snow fly. Is any of that in the cards?"

"I'm not as quick a study as you, but yeah I think that time is approaching."

Heather wanted to ask who she was. She could see that now. There was someone who he couldn't imagine living without. He was already doing without, though, so that meant she must be married or something. He seemed smarter than that.

"After we're finished here today, what are we going to do?" Heather asked as they pulled out of the rest area and back onto the two-lane road that would take them to the Canyon.

"I booked us into a Bed & Breakfast Inn for tonight and tomorrow night. On Sunday morning, we'll drive to the property. The B&B, it's up the road a little way. Right around the next corner I think. Yeah, see it up there. The old brick farmhouse. I hope that's okay with you. I know I didn't ask but I thought we should get reservations somewhere and it was better if you were somewhere out of the way where there weren't as many people to fawn over you."

"I love places like that. Can we go up there and take a look now?"

"Check-in isn't until mid-afternoon so we better not. It is someone's private home. They might not appreciate our showing up early. We're not that far now from the site."

Before long they were working their way across a high desert plateau sliced into two sections by the river flowing far below. The steep walls of the Fraser Canyon rose to meet emerald fields of hay on a narrow swath of arable land, only to rise higher still into what was native to this place, sandy slopes dotted with sage. They began to descend and eventually crossed the river downstream from Moran Canyon. They then headed back north. After passing through the town of Lillooet, they traveled along the west side of the Fraser until they came to a pullout.

The Institution

"I think this is the place," he said as they rolled to a stop in a field of scrub.

"Are you sure?" Heather asked. "If there's supposed to be some big protest out here tomorrow, shouldn't there be someone out here setting up?"

"You would think. I'm sure about the location though. I checked it out thoroughly. Let's take a closer look." He pointed to a narrow dirt path that ran along the edge of the plateau for a distance before dropping out of sight. "We can walk down that trail and at least see if we can get a view of the Canyon."

They had been on foot only a few minutes. Once over the lip and working their way down a precarious stretch of scoured sand, they heard a vehicle above them. The engine idled a minute or so and then shut off. Next, there was the sound of two car doors closing in quick succession. Heather was in front and she looked back at Jerome but he indicated they should keep moving forward. The next time she looked back she could see two men gaining on them. One of them was waving his arms angrily, at least that was how Heather read the body language. "Jerome, I think those guys behind us are serious about letting them catch up."

He looked around. "Stop over there beside that big rock," he said.

"What do you think they want?"

"I don't know but something about the look of them makes me think this isn't going to be pleasant. They look like they're in the Service or something. Some kind of Law Enforcement, maybe. And I'll bet you ten bucks they're not Canadian. Those boys are a couple of our countrymen."

"You can't tell that from here."

"Want to bet?"

And sure enough, as soon as they opened their mouths, she caught the drawl. "You folks know yo trespassin'?"

"I called the First Nations Tribal Office to ask for permission to access their land and they said it was fine," Jerome responded. "The guy I spoke with said if anyone asked to tell them that Mannie had given us the go ahead."

The two men looked scornful at this inadequate explanation. "This ain't Injun land no mo," the one who seemed to be pulling rank and doing all the talking said.

Terra Dime

"It's not? That's news to me. Since when?" Jerome added.

"Since the Union happened buddy. Ain't you bin payin' 'tention to the news? Them Injuns may have had a 'greement with the Canadian Guvmint but not the Union. All this belongs to the No'th Amer'can Union Guvmint now. As I said befo' this here's private prop'ty and yo trespassin'."

"We're only here because of the rally that's taking place tomorrow."

"There ain't gonna be no ralli I can assure ya o' that," he snorted, his eyes hidden behind dark glasses. "Yo name is Jerome Raines ain't it? We've bin ordered to take y'all in."

He pulled out some kind of badge and waved it in front of Jerome's face but Heather was too far away to see what department they worked for. And whatever it was Jerome saw, he didn't like. "On what charges?" he asked.

"Terrorism, sedition. There's more if y'all'd like to hear 'em." He removed a folded document from his breast pocket.

"Leave yo hands where we can see 'em," the less senior of the two piped up when he saw Jerome reaching into his jacket pocket.

"I was just getting the keys to the truck to give to her so that she can go and get some help."

"Well ya see that's a probl'm now, ain't it? You wasn't supposed to have anyone with ya. Seein's that ya do, we're gonna have to take ya both in. Now the both of ya, put yo hands on your head and march back up that hill o'er there."

That confirmed to Jerome that these two representatives of the security firm that worked as a mercenary army for the U.S Government were not here by chance. He had been set up. Lured here, to get him alone where he could be quietly taken away. There wasn't going to be a public protest against the dam. That's why there was no evidence of it where they parked. He looked over at Heather where she stood waiting and looking confused. He motioned her over. "We're not going anywhere with them. We've got to get back in sight of the road as quickly as possible," he said.

She stepped around the two men and began making her way up the hill. It wasn't easy going. The path was narrow and steep and barely negotiable at a walk let alone at a run. But somehow she managed to get within sight of the top. The roof of the pickup was just coming into view when she heard Jerome, right on her heels, yell out. She turned around to see one of the two men holding a stun gun in his hand; the electrical charge striking Jerome with tremendous force. His body convulsed and he fell sideways down the mountain remaining mostly airborne until landing heavily on a rock spire rising from a shelf that jutted out over the river. That scrap of ledge stopped him from making it all the way to the turbulent waters below. He was lying on his back impaled in a grotesque, tortured way but he was still alive. He was trying to break free, to roll his broken body into the river where it raged its way through a narrow slot. And he was screaming. His suffering tore through rock, beat against the canyon walls, and exploded over the land.

***

"Saint Paul, Dr. Sayer says what happened to Mr. Raines wasn't an accident. Someone did that to him intentionally."

"Someone, like the authorities, maybe?"

Darlene looked scornful when he said this. "Why would someone do that?"

"This is what I know first hand. He was one of my favorite authors and he was writing about things that weren't being written about elsewhere and I wanted to hear more. I contacted him thinking I might be able to help get something going and we agreed to meet in southern British Columbia. He never showed."

"Why not?"

Paul looked at her in that peculiar way of his. He peered over the top of his glasses as if questioning whether she was being disingenuous. "He told me he planned to attend the Fraser River dam protests prior to meeting up with me. He seemed to disappear there. Another word of his never appeared in print. A couple of years later, I went back to that piece of land where we were supposed to meet. It was unchanged. No one had set foot there."

"What I want to know is what *you* think happened to him and why," Darlene asked, hoping that of all of her patients he was the one who would tell her what she wanted to hear.

"Again, as far as first hand knowledge, his was the first disappearance of which I was personally aware, although there were many others."

Darlene looked bewildered. "So how did you finally meet up with Mr. Raines?"

"In here, of course. When oxygen levels began to plummet, the religious right said it was the start of Tribulation being brought down upon us by the Godless members of the community. Certain people were singled out for lynching and burning and tying to pickup truck bumpers so they could be dragged to their deaths. Because I was vocal in my opposition, I was seized and put away. I guess I should be thankful I wasn't burned at the stake."

"Why were you so against it? That was the proper analysis. It was the start of Tribulation and that is what we're living through right now. The sinners were doomed anyway. No reason to try to save them. Any day it will be over. Jesus will return and we will know Heaven on earth."

"That may be what you were taught and I know most people alive today believe that to be true, but I don't. According to scripture, Tribulation wasn't supposed to last more than seven years. It's been over fifteen. There is another way of looking at what happened to the earth. There is another explanation for why we can no longer go outside without respirators. There is another reason for why the forests vanished along with everything else."

"I don't know of another explanation. Sunshine has tried to tell me crazy stories about ecological collapse but I don't hear her out. It's a sin to listen to such tales."

"I'm sure it's a sin for you to listen to this too. But, you see, all of us in here, we suffer from the same affliction. And it's incurable. Dissidence often is."

"I don't believe you. I've read through all of your medical records. Every one of you has severe mental issues. You're a danger to yourselves and society."

The Institution

"You've got one part of that right. We were a danger to a certain kind of society, a deluded one. I'm getting kind of frustrated here. Can't you try a little harder to understand?" Darlene refused to pick up speed that was for sure. She seemed to fluctuate between a wee speck of horsepower and none at all. Paul suspected that either that implant of hers was still spitting out a little juice, or it was like he feared it would be for her. There was nothing to draw from a well of deception.

Darlene ignored his need to berate her. She liked him better before he had begun resorting to this kind of behavior. "But if what you're saying is true then what kind of place is this – a mental Institution or a detention facility?"

"You know what it is. I believe Jerome tried very hard to clue you in."

"Mr. Raines must have resisted when they tried to help him with his mental problems. Otherwise, the rest of you would have been harmed as well. And you weren't."

"I don't think they left him a paraplegic intentionally. They planned to incapacitate him temporarily before bringing him in. And you're right, he didn't like the idea of being detained for telling the truth. As it was he needed extensive medical attention. A doctor had to be involved. And I doubt they expected anyone to be with him at the time so that meant a witness and another person, a high-profile one, to institutionalize."

"Someone was with him? Someone saw what happened? Who?"

"Why, Heather, of course. You didn't know that she was there? She saw the whole thing."

"Mrs. Holmes did? Why didn't she ever tell me?"

"You'll have to ask her for yourself. I doubt she thought you would believe her. Based on the looks you're giving me now, I think that was a good assumption on her part. Heather was always one to cut her losses early."

"Aren't you appreciative, though, that you haven't been mistreated? We're helping you even. All of us, we are motivated by the One True God, that's why. We have goodness in our hearts."

"I thought you simply had to believe in your righteousness to feel secure about a place after 'The End Times.' Isn't that why Dr. Marsh convinces himself that for a man of his standing, access to a harem of nurses is not a sin? And why you have found a way to believe that you are his only lover and that he intends to marry you? And that our charts are not fabrications because the medical profession is above reproach even though you are going through an odd experience that might make you question the integrity of medicine? Putting away your enemies and then saying to yourselves 'see we could have killed these people but we didn't' is just more self-righteous denial. That you firmly believe Christ will deal with us harshly during 'The Second Coming' is the biggest factor in your benevolence. Whatever mental manipulation you've chosen, it isn't based on altruism."

"You've told me why you think you were rounded up but what about Mr. Raines? If he weren't insane, which I don't believe for a minute, then what was he guilty of?"

"You know, that was the thing I didn't understand at the time. He wasn't that powerful of a figure and yet he was one of the first to go. Sure, he had openly denounced religion at a time when we were moving towards a Theocracy. But his reputation had already been undermined so what was to be gained by removing him. It wasn't until those Fraser River dams were pumping out power and greening up desert that I realized the importance of silencing contrary opinions. A nation grows into surplus energy. It plants itself on the full teat of expanded power capacity and sucks with all its might growing ever larger and bloated and frivolous in its ways of waste. It dreams up ways to be less energy efficient for more hours in a day and becomes convinced it wouldn't be living any other way. The ruling class made a decision to keep it all going until the environment collapsed completely under our weight. It would be too disruptive to do otherwise. They also saw the potential for a little more upside to their portfolios before the planet ceased to cooperate. Who knows? That alone may have been enough incentive to extract every last resource. Once it was decided that leaving the planet smoldering was in everyone's best interests, it was simply a matter of silencing the opposition. That was why the RAH RAH voices, the proponents of progress, were the only ones heard after 2012.

"The other thing Jerome did was dare to bring up the unmentionable – that there was something beyond this civilization we accepted as normal.

The Institution

That there was life after empire. Empire wielded a big stick that shook furiously whenever its existence was questioned. We were all supposed to be of one mind. There was western civilization or there was primitivism. The latter was a step backward 10,000 years. Not many were going to sign up for that. Presented in those terms, our civilization was safe. But what if people began to think there was a better way? Something other than progressive programs, tax incentives, or policy changes. What if consumers began to question whether the traditional marketplace was the most effective way to meet basic needs? And what if they went a step further and asked whether creating competition between human beings for scarce resources was a good environment in which to flourish? What if they were then compelled to ask the ultimate question: Was our civilization capable of preventing the potential catastrophes that appeared to be accelerating in speed, strength, and number?"

What also fingered Jerome as a dangerous figure was something he couldn't begin to explain to this hapless nurse who couldn't calculate a 5% return on an investment let alone what a negative return meant. Jerome's critique of Wall Street, the macro marketplace, and his conviction that the common man who invested in it was a luckless patsy was radical. He didn't write about this as if it might be so. He wrote about it as if it were so self-evident it fell within the realm of scientifically proven. The rich and powerful didn't want that same common man to panic because that would ruin everything. Having the masses count on stock appreciation in order to retire was the closing of the circle.

Paul could remember way back to 2007 and how over the course of a few months, there were a half dozen oil spills in different parts of the world. They barely made the news. In Japan, an earthquake caused the release of radioactive material at the world's largest nuclear power plant. First, the severity of the accident was underreported. After a few days, it wasn't reported on at all. The change in attitude was really something. We no longer cared about environmental damage – particularly when doing so would jeopardize the size of our portfolios. Everyone had become a defender of the status quo regardless of the societal cost. Social safety nets were abandoned both monetarily and ideologically. Whole communities became dependents of the large and the homogeneous. The guys who dreamed up "the investor society" were the smartest, richest guys in the room. And they got a whole lot richer. All that money earmarked for The Street every payday. All those wannabes convinced they were getting richer by the minute. All those defined benefit pension plans believing they would be adequately funded when more was being drawn out than was going in. All the rules that were in place prevented investors from taking their money out of the market in a downturn. Trapped by the tax codes, they had to ride the wave into the depths of the trough. It seemed as if the architects of "the investor society" planned it this way. Did they know the majority who invested in this fashion would lose their principal as well as their appreciation? It appeared to be designed to make the middle class believe that down the road something grand would come their way. Meanwhile, the fat cats at the top were being rewarded in real time. The income disparity of that period was no coincidence. Jerome never doubted for a minute that these were the smartest guys in the room.

This was the one part of Jerome's writing that made Paul uncomfortable. Jerome alluded to a cabal of wealthy powerful men pulling the strings and Paul didn't believe it. He, like millions of others born into the system, got nervous at the mention of a non-level playing field. If he was dumping on Capitalism then what was he, a Communist? We had been taught that the system we lived under wasn't perfect but it was the best humans could expect to do. The story line went that everyone had the same opportunities. If someone else was doing better then it was because he was smarter or had worked harder. We didn't go to school for nothing. We went to learn our lessons well.

And it was easy for Paul to believe in the goodness and decency of it all when he didn't know anything. Once he started delving in, a pattern emerged. It was all bad. The way we grew our crops, the way we tortured animals, our blatant disregard for natural systems, how we got around, our jobs, our health, building practices, education, entertainment, our urban centers. The consistency of how bad it was, was shocking. The more digging, the more dismay until he came to the realization that it was rotten to the core. All the conspiracy theories and stories of greed and corruption and manipulation that he dismissed over the years as paranoid were true. So he began to ask himself why he was defending this thing. It was kind of

like wishing not to be left out of Heaven. The kingdoms ⸍
empire were very much alike. Not many people had thoug..
they operated or what a day in either one entailed. Yet, they were ↶
that both were places they wished to be.

    Paul made that comparison because it seemed odd to him that as a minister no one ever asked him what Heaven would be like. The people who attended church weren't curious enough to ask that question. And then he realized, once he parted company with the church, that people weren't asking any better questions in the larger community. At some point we were going to have to address what needed to be done. We were going to have to do what had never been expected of us. In fact, we were going to have to do what we had been trained not to do. We were going to have to consider a different way to live. And the new arrangements would have to address the need to develop people because under the current conditions we had stalled. What we needed was going to have to take precedence over what we wanted, or at least, what we had been indoctrinated to believe we wanted. He didn't see how we were going to make the leap. Being warped and small and not particularly adept at recognizing our shortcomings was a huge obstacle.

    Jerome's thoughts on living arrangements turned how to effect change upside down. His approach was an analytical, systems one. We'd been fixated on people becoming more aware. Raising consciousness was a favorite buzz-phrase because that was sure to improve the human predicament. Well, modern civilization wasn't exactly conducive to personal growth. It was a major impediment. Jerome had come to the conclusion that sitting around waiting for people to remove their blinders in a society that discouraged a move like that was the same as doing nothing. A dynamic living system that encouraged thought as well as mental and physical health would be a better first step. We had to begin living in a way that helped us transition. As long as we had only one choice, we were bound to stick with it. And by sticking with it, we prolonged its survival. Jerome wasn't interested in accepting what was probable. He was captivated by what was possible. He clung to that with all his might. He tried to entice others to do the same because if we didn't give at least equal attention to that, the probable would be a self-fulfilling prophecy.

like wishing not to be left out of Heaven. The kingdoms of Heaven and of empire were very much alike. Not many people had thought through how they operated or what a day in either one entailed. Yet, they were certain that both were places they wished to be.

Paul made that comparison because it seemed odd to him that as a minister no one ever asked him what Heaven would be like. The people who attended church weren't curious enough to ask that question. And then he realized, once he parted company with the church, that people weren't asking any better questions in the larger community. At some point we were going to have to address what needed to be done. We were going to have to do what had never been expected of us. In fact, we were going to have to do what we had been trained not to do. We were going to have to consider a different way to live. And the new arrangements would have to address the need to develop people because under the current conditions we had stalled. What we needed was going to have to take precedence over what we wanted, or at least, what we had been indoctrinated to believe we wanted. He didn't see how we were going to make the leap. Being warped and small and not particularly adept at recognizing our shortcomings was a huge obstacle.

Jerome's thoughts on living arrangements turned how to effect change upside down. His approach was an analytical, systems one. We'd been fixated on people becoming more aware. Raising consciousness was a favorite buzz-phrase because that was sure to improve the human predicament. Well, modern civilization wasn't exactly conducive to personal growth. It was a major impediment. Jerome had come to the conclusion that sitting around waiting for people to remove their blinders in a society that discouraged a move like that was the same as doing nothing. A dynamic living system that encouraged thought as well as mental and physical health would be a better first step. We had to begin living in a way that helped us transition. As long as we had only one choice, we were bound to stick with it. And by sticking with it, we prolonged its survival. Jerome wasn't interested in accepting what was probable. He was captivated by what was possible. He clung to that with all his might. He tried to entice others to do the same because if we didn't give at least equal attention to that, the probable would be a self-fulfilling prophecy.

Terra Dime

The reactions to the prospect of living any other way were disappointing. It was like we had all drunk the Kool-Aid. And in a way we had because the Kool-Aid was everywhere. As children it had been lovingly administered by our parents, in the classroom it was our teachers' stock in trade, in the workplace employers force-fed it for our own good, and politicians shoved it down our throats. We opened wide for it so often we weren't aware of gulping it down. We were so full of Kool-Aid it bubbled out of our lips when we spoke and yet we were unaware of how it soiled our words. So well-schooled in how to react at the mention of an alternative, we didn't realize we weren't thinking. We were reciting lines that had been fed to us over a lifetime. Lines we were able to recall with remarkable speed and clarity when the moment dictated. Parents turned against their children, children against their parents, if one of them dared to question the story they supported. The story of empire. The power of the beast. The machine we were supposed to give way to. The Institution.

Paul was living proof of where loyalties lie. His wife and children wanted everything to do with the system they believed in and nothing to do with him. His daughters wanted the same predictable lives their friends had and they thought it cruel of him not to comply. They found it disconcerting to hear from him. To know how he spent his days annoyed them. They expected their father to call on their birthdays, eat turkey at Thanksgiving, and send presents at Christmas. He was despised for not doing these things.

Paul felt bad about how out of step he was with his family so he began looking to join an intentional community of like-minded individuals. It was a fringe way of coping, still tied to the conventional workplace, possibly more static and homogenous than mainstream. It was a solution that could be embraced because it did not threaten the larger system. After being involved with several failed intentional communities he was bewildered by why they didn't work. He would be so sick of his so-called community in a matter of months that he would go out of his way to avoid contact. He would take to hiding in his house or sneaking around after dark. And Paul was a social guy so he didn't find this behavior overly gratifying. These places were plagued with the same issues that were prevalent elsewhere. Oftentimes, the participants weren't particularly enlightened or able to resolve conflict or concerned about their place in the larger world. In some instances, it was concern with their own survival that caused them to seek out the safety and security of a small tribe. He could see this wasn't a step in the right direction. But he didn't know what was. He was looking for a viable alternative that would be embraced by a greater number of people. Each of us finding the means to be more selfish and concerned with our personal existence wasn't it. It embarrassed him to be connected with this type of thing.

Paul had grown more animated as he related what he knew. He had a way of speaking that served him well when he was in the pulpit. In view of what he was saying, his delivery made Darlene increasingly uncomfortable. "When I read *Turning on the 'digm* I jumped on it. Reading something that wasn't written with ink that was 100% Kool-Aid was shocking. I wasn't used to the truth. It didn't read like anything else. It affected me profoundly. Living differently scared me too. Don't think that it didn't. But I knew if we didn't, the toughest times imaginable lay ahead and that scared me more.

"There were signs all around that a catastrophe was imminent. Something major's afoot when middle-aged white guys start talking collapse and the end of the world as we know it. People were daring to utter the word. And it wasn't one kind, like financial. There was a consensus that everything was maxed out so hold onto your hats it was all downhill from here. More than anything else we needed a course of action. It was ridiculous for advanced people not to try transitioning towards a new way. We were marching along fully aware of the human predicament that we had turned into a planetary predicament because we hadn't faced how destructive our way of life was. And we still wouldn't step out of line. We refused to be mature about our options. All indications were we intended to ride this thing right off the cliff as if that were an excellent choice or something.

"Then at some point I quit being angry with my fellow man and became sad. We were all pathetic. Most of us were stuck at a level of development that would enable us to know we were facing extinction but not developed enough to do anything about it. We would eventually pay the ultimate price for failing to evolve beyond dysfunction.

Terra Dime

"I couldn't understand why we were all sitting around waiting and what exactly we were waiting for. I was *so* ready for a new improved vision for humanity that would translate into some kind of future, I couldn't bear to listen any more to the political promises of perpetual economic growth that would somehow, someday, be coupled with a voluntary decline in greenhouse gas emissions. The talking heads had nothing new to say. It was time for the usual players who dominated the discussion to shut up and listen for a change. When one is fresh out of ideas it's only proper that he pass the talking stick. And don't tell me I'm crazy for thinking this."

That was the last thing he needed to worry about. Darlene was so freaked out after listening to that diatribe she wasn't going to tell him anything. What flowed from this man's mouth was so foreign to Darlene she couldn't put a label on it. Saint Paul's levelheadedness had evaporated at the mention of Jerome Raines. It was obvious to her *that* was why the author had been sent away. It wasn't for what he said. It was for what he had been able to stir. Mr. Raines turned normal people insane. Someone with that ability couldn't be running around on the loose.

The truth was something she had been taught to avoid at all cost. These were the words of a politician who held office at the turn of the current century. She couldn't remember his name, but for a politician he was a down to earth guy. He had given a common sense version of the value of truth. And so useful was his message, it had become part of the high school curriculum.

It went, *"The truth is useless. You can't deposit the truth in a bank. You can't buy groceries with the truth. You can't pay rent with the truth. The truth is a useless commodity that will hang around your neck like an albatross all the way to the homeless shelter."*

Darlene was fond of that quote. So fond of it, that she quoted it one time from memory for Mr. Raines, in order to prove a point. She should have known he wouldn't be as gaga over the spirit of the thing in the way she was. He was such a smart-ass who was never without a contrary opinion. He had a couple of quotes about truth that resonated with him.

"There was a man named Albert Einstein who was also alive during the last century," Jerome explained. *"A very smart man. Ever heard of him?"*

She shook her head to indicate she hadn't.

The Institution

"He had something to say about truth as well. Mr. Einstein said, 'Unthinking respect for authority is the greatest enemy of truth.' He thought the truth did matter and so do I. You might ask yourself: If the system you live under is fair and just, why is the truth so objectionable? The very fact that what you just recited has been passed off as wisdom should tell you much about the culture you were born into.

"Here's something else to consider. George Bernard Shaw said that 'All great truths begin as blasphemies.' Do you think there could be any truth to that?"

That both Mr. Raines and Saint Paul subscribed to vices known to be destructive opened a window into the past and filled Darlene with confidence about the present. The olden days were looking increasingly harmful and troublesome. A great deal of time had elapsed since these people were her age. Humans had learned so much since then and were much smarter. Anyone could see that. All she was getting out of this was a splitting headache. Mr. Raines always had that effect on her and now Saint Paul was bringing about the same discomfort. Her head was being overloaded with useless analysis and cloudy facts. The patients never tired of talking. Once they got started it was impossible to disengage. The listening was exacting a heavy toll on her peace of mind.

***

During the time Sunny was out of the country she heard rumors about the direction America was headed. Jerome often alluded to them. The country was experiencing more pain. Crime rates were on the rise again, infrastructure was failing, foreclosures were at an all time high, homelessness was rampant, and consumer spending – the pastime by which the country lived and died – was in the doldrums. And the culprit responsible for this misery was the rising cost of oil. Over the previous four years, the President had failed to get the price under control. Expensive oil had little to do with that particular President. He was a scapegoat, nothing more. Someone had to be setup to take the fall in order to ensure the successor would be a man with a tough talking way about him. A strong-arm type to get the country back on track – a pious track. That would solve everything. Pray more and when that didn't work kill your resource competitors, also known in "noble lie" terms as thy enemies.

The world reached Peak Oil. There was bound to be fall-out associated with that. When you were the number one consumer of oil in the world it only stood to reason that the shock waves of demand exceeding supply would reverberate more through your society than other less dependent societies. Anyone who was in the know about the financial condition of the country kept waiting for Wall Street to register these realities. They expected a crash along the lines of 1929. But they also knew that as long as the stock market kept chugging along and the boys at the investment banks kept being rewarded with big fat bonuses, the citizenry would be satisfied that all was well. But Wall Street hadn't been in touch with real value for quite some time. Without inflation, its numbers would not be nearly as impressive. It responded favorably to rising oil costs and was ecstatic when one of "the masters of the universe" brought another tool for financial manipulation to the table. The Street was the last to recognize real misery and failures in real production. Even when Wall Street was shuttered once and for all, the average person remained resolute that the market would deliver. Delusion ran deep. It would take years for people to drop their lofty investment expectations. We then went rapidly from high expectations to wanting nothing more than the lights and heat to stay on.

In the autumn of 2012 Sunny made sure she was able to vote absentee. John told her not to waste her time, as her candidate did not stand a chance against his shoe-in candidate. That he turned out to be right on this matter was revolting. It was the scariest election of her lifetime for all indications were that unless something in the order of a real miracle happened, the Christian Conservative Party would govern the North American Union. The two-party system was finally broken, sadly enough, by something worse.

The CCP had only three talking points during the campaign and they were criminalizing abortion, returning prayer to the public school curriculum, and ensuring homosexuals had no rights. The polling that was done indicated that they were well in the lead. That proved we were in a heap of trouble. The really big problems, the ones that were going to take

The Institution

us down, didn't exist for them. A 1,700-year old text would be the one and only guide of this Administration – complete with all the scientific ignorance and abuse of rights that were seen as divinely arranged. Unless, of course, when it came to a biblical passage like, "If someone strikes you on the right cheek, turn to him the other also." That didn't resonate with the party faithful, seeing they liked weaponry in a really big way and were itching to kick some ass, especially Muslim ass, or the ass of non-believers.

The problem with the Holy Bible was it didn't address issues like environmental degradation nor did it have a plan for seven billion human beings. "Be fruitful, and multiply, and replenish the Earth, and subdue it: and have dominion over the fish of the sea, and over the fowl of the air, and over every living thing that moveth upon the Earth." That didn't really cut it in the year 2012 as a strategy that was destined to work. Not when your dominion thus far had mopped out most of the wild fish stocks, introduced bird flu to migratory birds, and caused mass extinction of everything else. *Be prudent with the resources that are left and quit breeding.* That had some teeth.

The religious fanatics won anyway. It was the morning after Election Day when Sunny flew into Seattle. It was a deja-vu moment. The 2004 Election brought with it a not-so-subtle shift amongst the population. A movement away from thinking in terms of a future to doing the math in one's head as to how long civil society would last. No one wanted to live long enough to experience what was coming. With the 2012 Christian Conservative Party victory, the odds of being spared fell further. Their policies would be swift and severe. Sunny's gender and values were their primary targets.

At her side, John was glued to the election returns on satellite television and ecstatic. He was counting on the Christian Conservative Party to save the day. The flight was painful. As the night wore on, the CCP was well in the lead. Ideological brotherhood had John reacting as if it were he who was winning the race. When the results became certain he whooped and hollered like he alone had completed the performance of a lifetime. He went in search of congratulations from his fellow first-class passengers. That section of the plane was awash with the wordless acknowledgment that life was going to get even better for those folks. It hardly seemed possible.

John was out of his seat stalking the aisle shaking hands with the men, embracing the Asian stewardesses as if they too must share in his joy. He kept repeating himself over and over again, "What a relief. Now we're really going to get the country back on track. You mark my words. Ours is going to be a great nation again." Everyone acted as if this were profound analysis they were hearing for the very first time. Never mind, that this was the victorious party's campaign slogan and her spouse had uttered it thirty times in fifteen minutes.

Sunny stared sullenly out the window and tried to block the whole business out but there was no escaping this. The euphoric winner-take-all mentality wouldn't be going anywhere anytime soon. He slammed his body into the seat beside her and bellowed as one of the stewardesses passed. "How about some champagne for everyone."

The stewardess stopped and leaned towards him for the details of his request. With their faces practically touching he whispered in her ear. His eyes were at the bottom of their sockets straining to see down her blouse. She replied with something flirtatious that Sunny couldn't make out. "Oh my, aren't you sassy," John said loud enough to be heard for several rows. "You need a good spanking."

The stewardess giggled agreeably and for a horrifying moment Sunny thought he was going to lay her across his knee and let her have it. As she swayed back up the aisle to satisfy his request he leaned ever so slightly in his seat, his eyes never leaving that retreating bottom that was so in need of a good sound smack. "Cute girl, don't you think?" he remarked approvingly.

John was enamored with Asian women. They presented a compliant front that was irresistible to John even when Sunny sat no more than six inches away. How he behaved when she was nowhere in sight would be enough to make her wish for the ground to open up and swallow her whole. And if these objects of his interest knew him better they would wish for the same thing. She began to panic. It had been five weeks since she heard from Jerome. Where was he? The better question, though, was why was she still married to someone she found so repulsive. As the emerald waters of Elliot Bay came into view below she was struck by the weight of what she should have done years ago while she had the chance and the terror that it was now too late.

Terra Dime

BOOK FIVE

IN PRAISE OF CLIMATE CHANGE

The changes were perceptible even before the new government took office. The periodical that agreed to purchase Sunny's article asked for a picture and a personal biography. When they discovered Sunny was a woman's name, rather than a man's, they reneged on their promise. That wasn't the reason they gave for their decision, but gender was the determining factor in the irrelevance of her point-of-view. When she wrote to Jerome about this – no response.

By that time it was December and she felt an effort to locate him had to be made. When e-mails sent to the regulars who used to comment on his blog netted no answers, Sunny planned a trip to the west coast and more specifically to Gig Harbor. John was pleased when she told him she was going to Seattle for Christmas shopping and to search for new furniture to redecorate their home. For him, this had the ring of "normal" behavior for a woman and he was glad to hear of it. He was optimistic that she would come around and adopt a proper way of thinking.

On the trip over, it came to her attention that it was becoming inappropriate for a woman to be traveling alone. Everywhere she stopped, she was met with the same suspicious look that translated into her being one of those loose, free-thinking kinds. A more opportunistic woman would have pulled out the cell phone, dialed up her stockbroker, and had him purchase shares in a company that manufactured berkas and bonnets. And then, when her net worth increased, congratulate herself for capitalizing on a dismal trend.

The traffic had been bumper-to-bumper since she reached the outskirts of Pierce County. That was 2 ½ hours earlier and it continued to crawl along on yet another rough road through the once tiny village of Gig Harbor. It was dusk when she arrived but she was able to make out the same development pattern that appeared everywhere. No town or village

The Institution

with a shred of character had escaped the real estate boom of the first decade of the 21st Century. Ubiquitous luxury town homes and the hulking shadows of single-family trophy homes perched high upon the hills overwhelmed the tiny downtown. All the private wealth stood in stark contrast to the pot-holed pavement and other tired infrastructure. There was no money to maintain the public realm. The names of birds, trees, and vistas on street signs and entry statements were all that remained of what brought newcomers to this quaint place. That loss would go unnoticed as it had in thousands of homogeneous developments. The light of day was not necessary for that depressing reality.

At the Marina, she found visitor parking and explained to the guard who she was there to visit. Sunny walked along the docks in the direction Jerome had once described – his hope being that she would drop by sometime. Light spilled from the brightly colored houseboats of different sizes and styles. Many sported rooftop gardens or outdoor patios with remnants of the summer's potted plants. Muted conversations from around dinner tables drifted in the air as she passed. It was the antithesis of suburban housing developments, the breeder boxes that had been the mainstay as long as she had been alive. This little village on the water had the feel of a permanent vacation about it, a lifelong sabbatical from what was happening out there on the land. She was sure it was an illusion though. What was happening on the seas was equally as dire. But still, she longed all her life for snowstorms and power outages, unplanned interruptions that brought variety to our bland existences. Harmless slowdown buttons that she wished it were within her power to push. How else to nudge us towards a different pace we might come to like?

When she stepped onto Jerome's stretch of dock and saw the sailboat glowing on the black water, her heart leapt a little in anticipation of his being there. Then she saw the source of the light were temporary solar lamps that had been placed around a seating area in the stern. It had been a clear December day with sufficient light to charge their cells. The cabin was all darkness. Her heart felt weighted down again the way it had for weeks on end. She climbed on board, placing her bag of groceries on a deck chair and searching for the pot of thyme to which the key would be affixed. The kitchen herbs were in desperate need of water. That, along

263

with the patio furniture he had not stored away made her think he didn't intend to be gone this long. Inside, the condition of the fridge's contents further confirmed what she wasn't ready to face.

Looking around the cabin she compared the size of this space to the one in which she lived. There was a forward sleeping bunk, a bench seat that folded out, a dining booth that would have to double as a desk, galley kitchen, and a head that was utilitarian and unlikely to satisfy the bathroom needs of the average McMansion occupant. Sure, when she factored in the outdoor space sailing the boat would provide access to, it was very large. But was her inner life rich enough to find this gratifying? Without the constant distractions she had grown accustomed to would she be bored silly within minutes? She wasn't sure how she would fare under these arrangements today. As a young woman too much time on her hands caused her to see John as husband material. She liked to think she would do better than that today but wasn't convinced of her ability to make good choices.

She craved a way of thinking and living that ought to be intrinsic. The inability to capture this saddened her through and through because she suspected it was the root cause of all our misery. This was what had prevented her from jumping off the whole cobbled-together mess and joining Jerome where he physically and mentally existed. It had kept him just beyond her reach. She couldn't think of how to go about making herself feel differently and yet she knew this was key. It was what had to happen at the personal level of many of us if we were to improve the quality of our civilization.

Sunny knew the impenetrable cage around her was partially self-imposed. The simple surroundings in which Jerome lived screamed loudly and clearly that he saw her way of life as one without a future. And more than that, he had outgrown the belief in it and the need for it. She also saw why some of the environmental/political/social activists and non-profits were ineffective at bringing about the changes they said we desperately needed. They made no meaningful changes in their lives or the structure of their organizations. Rather than questioning the investment system, they were inclined to invest in questionable Institutions as long as they were money makers. These various causes also weren't interested in measuring

The Institution

the effectiveness of their efforts because they liked the lifestyle too much. It was all about "partnering" and getting together for conferences – lovefests – with like-minded specialists who weren't inclined to ponder the system as a whole. They hadn't accepted that high consumption must become obsolete. That was what their behavior communicated. It was a powerful message, more clearly understood than a song or a Powerpoint presentation. Until the public saw high profile advocates tell the truth about what needed to be done and then do it, their messages would have the ring of deception.

Stepping back outside to retrieve the groceries Sunny was startled by two figures silhouetted on the dock peering at her expectantly. A woman spoke and there was disappointment in her voice, "Oh, who are you?" she said bluntly. "We were expecting someone else."

"I'm Sar...," she almost said and then decided in favor of the name Jerome knew her by. "Sunny Day," she said extending her hand to first one and then the other. "A friend of Jerry's. Do you have any idea where he is?"

"I'm Linda, by the way, and this is my husband, Dave. And your name is Sunny Day," she said, grinning as if she didn't quite believe it. "Well I never would have guessed."

Dave cut in. "In answer to your question. No we don't. When we saw the lights come on inside we were hoping you were him."

"Oh I see," Sunny said. And she could hear resignation fill the early evening air. It had such a disquieting quality to it.

"We were about to sit down to a glass of wine before dinner. Would you like to join us? Then perhaps we could talk comfortably out of the cold," Dave suggested.

"Sure, that sounds good. I bought a bottle of wine on my way over today. Would you like me to bring it?"

"Oh no, that's not necessary. We have plenty of beer and wine and any other beverages you might like to give a try. Jerome spent many evenings on our boat sampling the contents of our bar."

Sunny followed them kitty-corner across the dock to a tug that had been converted into a floating house. "I love your boat," she said appreciating the soothing feel of the vessel with its wooden hull and walls, stainless surfaces, and shiny brass fixtures. "Does she stay at the dock or do you travel in her?"

"Thanks," Dave said. "We think she's a real beauty too. Usually, we'd be on our way south by now. But this year we're late getting started." He hesitated a moment before finishing the thought. "On account of Jerome not returning from what was supposed to be a five-day trip and the whole political mess. Both those things have got us so worried and upset we can't seem to get enthusiastic about going."

"Before Dave gets on a roll, what would you like to drink dear – a Chardonnay or a Syrah?"

"The white sounds good. Thank you. It seems like I'm here for the same reason you haven't left," Sunny said as Linda handed her a glass and then took a seat on the other end of the couch.

Dave looked suspiciously at Sunny and asked, "How long have you and Jerome known each other? You've never been here before have you?"

"For heaven's sake Dave, do you have to interrogate everyone? It's none of our business how they know one another."

"Well you have to admit it is a little odd her just showing up like this," he said out loud, talking as if she had left the room.

Linda shook her head at her husband. "Surely you're not questioning that they know one another. Dave, her name is Sunny Day A-K-A 'Dia de Sol.' Get it?"

There was a second or two of hesitation. "Oh, I see what you mean," he said before opening his mouth to say something else and then deciding against it. Both of them looked over at Sunny who decided it was time to re-enter the conversation even though she had no idea what they were talking about.

"Jerry and I met briefly for the first time in 1986. It's only been in recent years that we ran across one another again. And then up until last month I was out of the country. Unfortunately, most of our contact has been via e-mail. And since October we haven't even had that. Where do you think he is?"

"I think they got him."

"Who?"

The Institution

"Some government-sponsored enforcement agency. I don't know which one exactly. There's been a systematic silencing of dissident voices, either by discrediting or removing them. At least the most vocal ones. Maybe you don't know this, because you've been out of the country, but that actress gal who was backing him, she went missing too. I believe they were together at the time. Kind of stupid on their part to grab her since she's so well known. Her equally famous brother was up in arms for a while looking for information as to where she was. And then you know what? She reportedly called him to say that she was fine. According to him, she said she was in a remote part of British Columbia and was 'dropping out' for a while. She agreed to make contact with him regularly, but other than that, she wished to be left alone. I'm guessing that wasn't what she wished to say. I'm guessing she made a deal to keep someone else alive."

"You don't think he and Heather Holmes could have taken off together? Isn't it possible they're lovers?" Sunny had read all the speculation about the two of them. While overseas she hadn't missed their faces on the tabloid covers.

"Without letting anyone know? I thought you knew him?"

"Not THAT well. He's a man. She's a beautiful, rich woman. Their being romantically involved does not take that big a leap of faith." She hadn't wanted to think too much about this most likely explanation but now by giving voice to it, it had become real.

"You don't understand. That just isn't his style. He's a serious guy."

"Well maybe he got sick of his style and being so serious. Maybe he wanted to have some fun for a change."

"Wow, you really don't know about him do you? He was having fun every day. He loved what he was doing. The life he had here on this boat – writing, sailing, kayaking – was by design. He wasn't biding his time waiting for something better to come along."

"I don't understand how you can be so sure. Why do you believe such a farfetched explanation instead of the obvious one?" Sunny asked. Unintentionally, she found herself calling Dave's credibility into question. She was assigning the conspiracy theorist label in much the same way as her husband did with her.

"There's something else too. Normally, I wouldn't tell you what Jerome and I discussed in confidence, but in this case I'm going to. I asked him about her, you know, because she is – like you said – good looking and wealthy to boot. He told me that she had more going for her than that but there wasn't anything going on between the two of them. And it wasn't because he found Heather Holmes unappealing. He was hung up on someone else. And knowing that, it wouldn't be right to start something with her. He wasn't good at that kind of thing. There was no way he could hide it from her. So you see, it's not like you think. He wouldn't lie about something like that. Believe me, wherever he is he's not there of his own free will."

Sunny felt momentarily elated at this bit of gossip. Much to her embarrassment, she had been struggling with jealousy over a situation she'd brought upon herself. The relief evaporated when the likelihood that something ominous had happened surfaced instead. She was ready to delve into that possibility.

"You talk as if you believe they're alive though. Why is that? Do you have some ideas as to where they might be?"

"They could be in one of many places. A detention facility for sure. All kinds have been built in places as far apart as Alaska and Indiana. Most of them were done as renovations to existing structures. It was easier to keep it secret that way. Many are on military bases. Some were constructed under the guise of mental Institutions, which is really funny if you think about it. It's been government policy for quite some time to put mentally ill people out on the streets. In more remote areas of the country, really large facilities will house the renowned dissidents – the types who have made names for themselves. From those locations, it's unlikely a detainee will ever leave. In one of those, that's where Jerome is. He'll spend the rest of his life there."

Sunny couldn't believe they were having this conversation. It was true that for a matter of weeks, she had been filled with dread. It was what had brought her in search of Jerome. Until now, she had no idea why she was so unsettled. "But why would the current government do this now? They're about to leave office. A new political party is taking over. It doesn't make any sense. Maybe next year, but not now."

The Institution

Dave thought for a moment before he replied. "Most people don't realize how dedicated those in power are to preserving the status quo. Jerome, and a few others who dared to challenge that, had to be silenced – regardless of the party in power. While you and I may be more comfortable with the rhetoric of the outgoing party, it's important to remember that there is at most 'two degrees of separation.'

"It should also be noted that the CCP are not a new party. They're the same party we had four years ago dressed up in new clothes. The players are all the same. That old sneering VEEP who was a lunatic during the prime of his life is an old fool now. You know what they say about old fools. And he continues to call the shots. He so enriched himself during the Iraq War that he is now all powerful on three fronts – corporate, military, and political. That guy's got nothing other than misery in his bag of tricks."

Linda interrupted Dave. Something she had become adept at when he got going like this. "Sunny, any time you can't bear to hear any more you tell him to shut-up. He misses Jerome you see. He hasn't had anyone to rant with of late. Some more wine?" she asked and Sunny extended her glass when she brought the bottle over.

"No, I need to get up to speed on what's going on. Ever since I've been back I feel like a foreigner in a strange land. I get this feeling we're on the brink of something. I don't think it's my imagination that people are gearing up for some major changes."

"A fascist Theocracy. That's what we're gearing up for. Remember that Republican PR guy – the brains behind The Idiot President – how his goal was to see the country under fifty years of conservative hegemony. Well his dream is coming true. Why anyone would wish for something like that is too awful to think about. He kept adding fuel to the religious wacko fire. Future politicians were being educated by religious fundamentalist Institutions to infiltrate the various branches of government. Television stations helped stoke it. While immoral programming played on one station, another of their stations demonized the liberal left's control of the media as responsible for the vile content. It all drew attention away from the fact that the media had been consolidated into the hands of a few

269

corporate players who had ceased to deliver anything that was edgy and intelligent because it was in the best interests of their owners not to.

"You know what else was happening back in the second term of that disastrous Idiot Presidency? He was able to put into effect laws that gave the President dictatorial power in the case of a 'catastrophic emergency.' This meant any incident regardless of location. It didn't even have to occur on U.S. soil. And guess who got to decide whether an incident met the definition of 'catastrophic emergency?' The President, without oversight from any of the other branches of government. At the same time, the Supreme Court was being stacked to act in favor of Institutions over individuals and the Executive Branch was busy taking away a citizen's right to public assembly. Any act of civil disobedience and the President could enact Marshall Law. That, in conjunction with the building of all the Internment Camps, ought to have been cause for concern. On a grander scale, the Pentagon changed the rules of military engagement to ones that permitted this country to engage in preemptive nuclear strikes. This passed without fanfare and with no reporting by the mainstream media. While we were sleeping, a President with an approval rating in the 30% range was busy amassing power. The question I kept asking myself was why would a political party do that when it looked as if losing control of the White House was a done deal. They wouldn't wish to load up their political rivals with that much power. That would be kind of magnanimous for those boys. So my guess is they knew they weren't going to lose control for long. How could they have known that unless they controlled the voting process? You would think people would wish to know what was going on but nothing could be further from the truth. When I tried to point these things out to family and friends they got mad at me. They had adopted the stance that if it wasn't on the news, it wasn't true. Before long I either quit bringing it up or I found new friends.

"Anyway, that same PR guy is still orchestrating behind the scenes, launching whisper campaigns to destroy political rivals, controlling what issues are debated to ensure they are morally charged so the electorate remains mesmerized by the trivial and votes against its own interests. And when that doesn't work, votes are changed electronically. All the same characters have been in control in some form or fashion since about 1980. Why doesn't 'the liberal media' report on that appalling lack of diversity?"

"What's the motivation?" she asked, unable to comprehend why anyone would work for over thirty years to achieve this brand of policy success. "What do they envision will come out of all of this and why does it look so good to them and so bad to me?"

"That's easy. The 1950s prior to the counter culture movement. Back to a time when we were focused on working, warring, praying, and procreating. Red meat, in other words."

"They believe if we relive those times everything will be fine? That's ridiculous. You can't pick a particular historical period and freeze everything in place and say that is the best we can ever be. The dreams of idealists and visionaries would disappear. No one really wants to live that way, do they? It is so defeatist, so anti-evolution, so static, and so creationist..."

"Remember, this is the religious right we're talking about."

"Wow, that whole 1960s anti-establishment, hippie protesting thing must have really left a mark on those dudes. To blame all of our problems on that movement is to ignore some glaring flaws in our belief system. Why can't we simply have a dialogue about what was good about the 1950s and 1960s and what was bad and then get over it. Surely we can come to an agreement that civil rights and environmental awareness were positive outcomes. We might even get consensus on the merits of getting out of Vietnam. And I think there are many people who suspect the drug culture and sexual promiscuity that took root during that time aren't to be applauded. But we don't want to cut off options for anyone but white Christian males. That would be creepy."

Even as Sunny said it she knew that was exactly what "we" were planning and that there wasn't a consensus on the issues she mentioned. Nor would there ever be. Those who identified with the political party about to take power were still wishing death to environmentalists, believed firmly in the inferiority of women and minorities, and held fast to the notion that if we stayed the course in Vietnam, victory would have been ours. The other side continued to sing the praises of recreational drug use and felt moral values were unnecessary. Her face registered this realization and Linda picked up on the fear.

"There may be tough times ahead especially for free-thinkers and women. Do you have someone you can trust who will not become crazy with power? If not, I have heard of single women setting up group living arrangements so they can depend on one another when the going gets rough. Strength in numbers kind of thinking. Dave and I, we plan to head for international waters."

Sunny's situation did not take long to sum up. She had John, a card-carrying member of the Christian Conservative Party. Her mother was capable only of "happy talk" thanks to the legal drug trade. Her stepfather was a wealthy businessman without sufficient intelligence to grasp how unsustainable a system that handsomely rewarded men like him had to be. That left her grandparents. No doubt they'd be eager to take her back into the fold. They hadn't spoken a dozen words to her since the UVic days. They were the only Canadians she knew of who were pleased by the creation of the North American Union. It was a miserable assortment. It occurred to Sunny that the real reason she had made this trip was to get away from all of them. Without admitting it to herself, she had made a choice that she could now see was a lost option. And she had no other alternatives.

"Do you know how to sail, Sunny?" Dave asked.

"No, I'm afraid I don't."

"Well that's too bad, because if you did you could take the 'Dia de Sol' and sail off into the sunset."

"The 'Dia de Sol'?"

"Yeah, Jerome's boat. She's a lovely vessel, so sleek. Moves through the water beautifully. I doubt he'll be returning for it. After your coming here like this I'm certain of it. I believe Linda and I will go forward with our plans and leave, although I hate to go this late in the season when the storms can be so bad."

Sunny was half-listening at this point. She and a boat shared the same name. She couldn't help but smile at that. She finished off the last of her wine and stood up. "Thanks for the drink and the conversation, but I'm

The Institution

famished," she said, ready to be alone so she could begin processing all this new information.

"You're welcome to stay for dinner," Dave offered.

"No thanks, I brought some food and plan to stay overnight on Jerry's boat. It's too late to head back to Silver Falls at this hour. We can talk again in the morning," Sunny said as she left the tug and stepped on board the 'Dia de Sol'. By comparison, it was silent as a tomb and just as cold. But once the pasta water was going and the vegetables sautéing it felt much cozier. The bottle of Cabernet helped too.

That night, while she was getting acquainted with Jerome's numerous books, she found a hand-written page in a notebook. It was an epilogue to *Turning on the 'digm*. At the top of the page was a comment referring to how he had consistently thought in "bottom up" solutions alone. He preferred to believe that individually we had the capacity to see what was wrong as well as the wish to improve what's ailing us. He was wrong. Clearly, we had wasted our time fighting over the truth. If each of us were in possession of the facts, we would change nothing because we have the way of life that is analogous with what we are. Although a citizen-led movement was the most palatable way to proceed, it was impossible because the majority cannot conceive of anything dearer than what we have. In retrospect, he should have given more thought to a "top down" solution like the following:

I am coming to the conclusion that it is unrealistic to expect the general public to make a move without their leaders telling them to do so. We haven't been programmed that way. In fact, the Constitution prohibits it. What I'm suggesting acknowledges, and challenges, the ruling class. If there is to be meaningful change those who really hold power will have to be the instigators. This is also a course of action that might wake people up. It would draw attention to the grimness of our circumstances and how imperative it is that we act.

At this juncture, it is up to the powerful to save our asses by suggesting that society take a "jubilee" from doctrine, dogma, and specialization. Except for essential services, daily life as we know it would be transformed into a twenty-four hour, seven days a week opening of all public and private libraries for a period of at least six months. No one would go into the classroom, the office, or any other workplace. Those who do not currently "labor" would be required to help those who provide essential services. All payments that are due during this period would be added to the end of whatever payment schedule exists. All of us – religious persons, professors, professionals, and producers – would take the time to find out how our little slice of pie fits into the whole. We would do this purposefully with an eye towards developing ourselves into higher quality human beings and transitioning to a mature, advanced civilization. As a society we could potentially leap forward into a more comprehensive age.

Even in the face of how rapidly things are deteriorating it won't be easy though. I'm not sure how to get the talking heads, the think tanks, the political pundits, and all the other so-called experts to quit leading their followers down this dead end we call the American Dream. The American Dream is an ecological nightmare. The Enlightenment principles on which this liberal democracy was founded are based on material growth in a land of plenty. The founding fathers neither foresaw nor made provision for scarcity. Did they suffer from what University of Colorado professor Albert Bartlett calls the greatest shortcoming of the human race – our inability to understand the exponential function? Is that why they never asked, what happens when we run out of the land and resources that provide the means with which to expand? Because our political/economic system is flawed at the core, once the material peak was realized the failure of this democracy was a given. Promising perpetual abundance through the conquest of nature and the tyranny of property rights may have looked like a sound plan at one time. That was before consumer demands and retirement expectations exceeded our society's capacity to provide them without bankrupting the nation. Now that economic gains can no longer be delivered, what do we do? It seems to me, we might entertain basing our political system on something other than selfish individualism.

In order to overcome the flaws of the current paradigm, four considerations stand out – ecological continuity, consciousness, personal virtue/ethics, and a form of governance that ensures our stated goals are met. These must be at the foundation of whatever we conceive. Perhaps we could look to ecological principles for answers. A climax forest would be a good place to start searching for clues as to what works over the long haul.

In that environment many species committed to quality growth efficiently use the available energy to lead long, complex, symbiotic life cycles.

When Sunny read this she was reminded of how much he cared about humanity. The species was failing. Anyone who didn't have his head up his ass could see that. Jerome felt it personally. Sunny didn't. It bothered him so much that he thought and wrote about it all the time. Reading through his notes, she felt like Jerome was close at hand, still trying to figure out how to fix the human predicament.

She kept fighting the notion that anything bad had happened to him. The conclusions Dave and Linda had come to felt like an overreaction to the events so far. Possibly they, and Jerome himself, had read too much into the political situation. She didn't want to start believing in the whole notion of conspiracy. Once a person started down that road, there were villains everywhere. She felt herself too smart for that. Her mind danced away from Dave's speculations – unwilling and unable to imagine where it would lead. As if in refusing to entertain such an unbecoming assumption, nothing would come of it. Sunny remained focused on the looming environmental calamities. Those were what would eventually take us down regardless of whether we were in the grip of fascism, world war, or a one-world government.

She told herself repeatedly not to succumb to paranoia. However, her paranoia seemed justified when she found Jerome's laptop tucked away in a drawer. He would not have left it if he intended to be gone for so long. This increased the probability that Dave's speculations were well founded. If Jerome wasn't somewhere of his own volition then he was lost to her, to everyone, forever. By the time she climbed into the berth, she was overcome with grief. The boat was such a small, tight space. It oozed Jerome. The hull creaked when it moved ever so slightly in the shifting tide, just as it would have when it was he who was lying here tired and craving sleep, but kept awake by a mind that wouldn't rest. And where was he now? She turned her face into the pillow, caught the scent of his hair, and had to hold her breath to keep from sobbing out loud. Crying was the only option left to deal with how badly she had screwed up. While she was out of the country, Jerome had been on board this vessel trying to find the words that would inspire. She couldn't stand the thought that he was paying for a way of being we ought to applaud. The injustice of it was that she was okay because she'd stayed with John and gone along willingly on a fool's errand. What kind of person felt relief for being that malleable?

Finally, at a time when all the odds were stacked against her, a desperate desire to be free took hold. The thought of remaining silent and in place was painful. She brooded over how she could break away to start a new life on her own. One possible means of escape stood out from the others. She could drive into Seattle tomorrow and check into the hotel where she was supposed to be staying, call John, and let him know how well the shopping was going. And then she could explain how she had run across a couple of classmates from the University of Victoria who were in town to attend a concert. She could tell him how much she wished to go with them but it meant staying in Seattle through the weekend.

While John thought she was catching up with old friends, she could begin systematically to take cash advances on each of their credit cards, enough to get her through a few months. It would take a couple of weeks for him to find out. Sunny was the one who paid the bills and she did it on-line. John would not think to check right away. When she didn't return as scheduled and he realized that something was wrong, there would be confusion. The nature of the crime would be questionable. Had she run or been snatched? The car would have to be abandoned, somewhere like Whidbey Island so it might occur to everyone that she had gotten on a couple of ferries and made her way to Victoria. If John suspected that she had run, the British Columbian Province of the Americas is where he would expect her to go. She could easily work her way back to Gig Harbor via public transit, lie low for a while, and begin searching for other women who were in similar situations. In the New Year, there would be women seeking anonymity in droves. They would have to be looking for places to live and work without intervention.

All night long she worked this over in her mind looking for flaws in her logic, getting used to the idea, hoping that come morning she would be more comfortable with the prospect of abandoning her existing life than sticking with it. When she awoke she attempted to summon up the nerve to flee. By the light of day, she began to question if making a fugitive of oneself over the belief that something bad was going to happen was insane.

Fear settled in. She began to shiver as it emptied her of everything else. She was no match for the kinds of people who removed Jerome. She had no idea how to go about living on the run, obtaining fake ID, being paid under the table, and living under the radar. That scared her more than anything John could dish out. Awareness of her dependency solidified. She was going back where she belonged. Driven by her love of comfort and convenience but motivated mostly by fear. There were no alternatives to the system in which John had found a starring role. The human race had surrendered its freedom in favor of domestication a long time ago. What little freedom we had was an illusion. Indeed, Conrad Tilton's stock-in-trade was centered on this illusion of freedom. During the hard times that lie ahead, the boundaries of the cage would continue to shrink. They might become stifling enough for all but the dimmest to sense.

***

"Paul says I should tell you everything. I disagree. I won't convince you of anything. Besides, there is no definite beginning or end to this parable. Insanity has a way of being endless when you are trapped by beliefs a five-year old should be able to see are doomed. Utter madness all around and hardly anyone could see it for what it was. For what it still is, as a matter of fact."

Sunny's reasons for not wishing to relive the whole thing were numerous. There were parts of it that she chose to skip over in her mind as a way to forget what it was like to see her darkest ecological fears realized. The personal losses of freedom were a teeny, tiny part of the story. To watch it all die right before her eyes and not see anything in terms of an appropriate sense of responsibility for the carnage had filled her with the most profound hatred of her species. In view of the sorry fact that humans were about all that had endured, nothing was left for her to love.

"I'm not going to talk to you because it's the right thing to do. And I don't intend to tell you everything because I'm the one who will suffer. I'm going to talk to you because you have something I want." Her face was to the window, the way it always was. She did not turn around to address Darlene.

Darlene looked at the back of Sunshine's head in alarm. "And what is that?"

"A way out. I want to make a deal with you. Once I tell you the way things really are, regardless of whether you believe me or not, you'll let me out of here. You'll unlatch the door, give me the code to the gate, and let me – and anyone else who wishes to – leave."

"But your body will be starved for oxygen. You'll die out there. It's a sin to assist a patient in committing suicide. I took an oath."

"Don't lay that crap about sin on me. Your religion saw the mopping out of all life other than human as a step toward 'The Promised Land.' If you were willing to face up to that, you'd be so ashamed you'd do the right thing and kill yourself too. If you don't help me get out then you can count on my telling your superiors that you're not like them any more. That something has changed. That you know the *truth* – the very thing you all fear the most."

Darlene gasped. "You're evil. You're mean and awful."

"Good, I'm glad to hear you feel that way because if I'm so *evil* then I deserve to die."

"That's not the way it works. I'm supposed to forgive those who trespass against me. The Bible is quite clear on that."

"This isn't about you. This is about me and I'm dying in here. I wish to escape this phony world we created. I need the real thing. I want to go back to the earth where I belong. It's a small thing to ask. It always was."

"I don't understand why this means so much to you. Really I don't. But if you feel that strongly about it, okay, I agree to let you leave."

Sunny wasted no time in fulfilling her end of the bargain once she had been granted a reprieve from the Institution. "You know something, humans like their little stories. That tendency to believe in religious and cultural fables might be our greatest flaw. You would have thought by now we could have turned that tendency into a positive force. Surely, if we can get children to believe myths they carry with them into adulthood and throughout their lives, we could convince them of another story. One a little closer to reality, let's say. We prefer tall tales of heroes who performed noble deeds. Every victory accepted without question. Because 'right makes might' there is no need to question. Not to have any regrets seems odd to me on a personal basis but evidently not for the culture as a whole. Could it really be that every choice we ever made was the right one? I suppose it doesn't matter if there's a fallback position. When the signs are everywhere that we are screwed, we look to a story based on a myth to explain it all away. And provide us with a happy ending too. A moral, righteous lie makes the hideous fate we created for ourselves look tolerable. So what do you think? Do you think what you're living is a happy ending? Have you ever wondered even for a nanosecond where the road not taken may have led? Or, are you certain you're on the way to Nirvana and humanity couldn't do any better than that?"

Darlene knew she shouldn't give the pat answer that was the first to come to her lips. That made her so flustered she couldn't speak. This patient terrified her in much the same way as Mr. Raines had. The connection they had to a feral world made them larger-than-life figures. They saw beyond the human story and Darlene considered whether it was something she should try to understand. If she was going to grasp anything Sunny Day had to say, she would have to let go of her faith and she wasn't prepared to do that. She was prepared to test her faith, however, just as God tested our belief in Creation and the age of the planet by creating and burying dinosaur bones. That hadn't discouraged the truly pious, just as whatever Sunshine had to say wouldn't dissuade Darlene spiritually. Her faith was that strong.

The whole non-believer thing was an anomaly from another age. Not that far back in terms of years, it was eons removed ideologically. During Darlene's lifetime religious belief was not questioned at all. She didn't think that it was a matter of not being permitted. It was more a matter of no one being silly enough to debate something that had gone through rigorous scientific testing and been proven beyond a shadow of a doubt. Well, maybe not quite as conclusively as other scientific theories, but faith was different in some way. She couldn't think of why that was exactly but she knew she had learned it some time along the way. The rule to remember was 'religion good, no religion evil.' It had been made simple. But Darlene had an inkling that wasn't what Sunshine wanted her to say.

Sunny remained facing the window but Darlene could see her face from the side and the way her cheeks squeezed into a smile. She was laughing at her inability to come up with an answer. "Forget it," she offered eventually. "You don't have to answer that question right now. Possibly, you'll think of something in a few days, once we're through."

Over the course of those days Sunny told of what it was like to be alive when the planet supported such an abundance of life it was a feast for the senses. She told of how she met Jerome, just as the other patients had. Although Sunny really tried to explain about him, it was in the telling of this part of her life that she was the biggest failure. Her actions with regards to him had never spoken as loudly as her thoughts. An inconsistency she couldn't wrap her mind around; it was ridiculous to expect it of someone else. She gave her version of his disappearance and the events that followed once she returned to Silver Falls.

The face of the nation changed once the Christian Conservative Party took power. Babies began to appear in numbers Sunny couldn't begin to count. Births per woman in the U.S. more than doubled. Small families became a thing of the past as did women in slacks or shorts. Nothing but dresses was acceptable for the weaker sex. The new President, Vice-President, and Supreme Court appointee all set the standard for the nation. They were powerful men in dark suits. Their wives wore frumpy dresses. Their daughters were sweet in ruffles and lace and black patent. Their sons, who represented the future, appeared in short pants and blazers and oxfords. It wasn't enough to adopt the family sizes and clothing of a bygone era; the attitudes had to be embraced as well. Before she could say, "No way, it will never happen," the colleges and the workforce were no place for women. It was the Lord's way or the highway.

Other strange little things happened. Sunny couldn't find anything to eat. Food began to take on a bland, meat and potatoes quality. 'Ethical eating' was out the window. There were no longer vegetarian options on menus and organic or local produce could not be found in the stores. The message seemed to be "we're a meat eating, pesticide using, GMO, agribusiness kind of nation – either conform or die." It was a concerted effort to rid the country of any of the so-called progressive thinking that emerged in the 1960s.

There was no more lamenting the looming costs of an aging population. The demographics were changing in favor of young full-family

The Institution

households and meeting a nouveau collection of insatiable demands. We moved back into full production like we hadn't seen since the end of World War II. Bereft of environmental concerns, political policies no longer had to pay lip service to sustainability. There was no sense of uneasiness about burgeoning impacts or loss of open space. There were no fringe groups and no passionate nay-sayers. Not a one. It was eerie. Like we were engaged in a war, one that felt just and good, one we all believed in. To speak out against it would have been an act of treason. All discussion about the environment and the inevitability of collapse if we carried on this way vanished. For the majority, the specter of collapse hadn't existed anyway but all mention of it disappeared along with those who once raised the possibility.

These new, old 'tudes were effective in jump-starting an economy that had been in the grip of a depression over the previous three years. Economic sustainability reigned supreme. "Quantity of life" issues were carted out the way "quality of life" issues were in prior decades. It was a return to the baby boom, post war era of the previous century. It was socially engineered to be so. Instead of McCarthyism style witch hunts, we engaged in religious campaigns to rid the nation of the Godless, the stated enemy. The Godless fell into three categories – lacking in religious conviction, environmentally sensitive, or sympathetic to equality and individual rights issues. No amount of urging from friends and former colleagues could convince Sunny this new/old worldview was going to deliver the human race to a better place. She was unable to engage in another "Great Forgetting" that demonized the learned view of our relationship with the planet. She had difficulty pretending she believed.

It was up to the Canadian Provinces of the Americas to accommodate the migrations from the heavily populated low-lying coastal areas and drought-stricken regions of the United States. With a large percentage of the world's fresh water and a landmass that was virtually unpopulated, the Canadian regions were up to the task. And what an economic boon the whole sea-level rise thing created. Homes and churches were constructed in unison all over the place. A House of Worship nearby was the main drawing card when it came to attracting potential homebuyers. The new era subdivisions borrowed heavily from medieval principles except, sadly, when it came to charm. Once a prospective site was cleansed of its trees, the bulldozers shoved everything out of the way, and the graders flattened what was left into a wasteland of biblical proportions. Work then began on the big box church that looked remarkably similar to a big box store. It was similarly surrounded by a parking lot large enough to land a Boeing Dreamliner. Next came the wide sweeping streets and looping cul-de-sacs. Predictably, three-car garages with houses attached rounded out the complete living package. "Righteous Ridges" took over all remaining high pieces of land lording over the valleys below and as a final insult, ruining the view. It was the church on the hill all over again, providing strength and comfort, and safety from reality. Always back, never forward.

Everyone jumped on the new bandwagon with reckless abandon. It didn't matter your age, gender, education, or socioeconomic profile. Like every other bad idea that had come before it in America, we were one nation smug in our collective belief that we had the best system and knew the one right way to live. That we were smarter and better than everyone else was self-evident. We were living proof of Manifest Destiny.

"The thing people fail to understand about requiring everyone to live by a set of irrational beliefs is that if you don't wish to participate there is nothing for you," Sunny tried to make clear to Darlene. "For a while there was still access to alternative ideas on the Internet or in the libraries, but once some of the government's covert plans were made public and had to be abandoned due to on-line chatter, censors were put in place. Whole websites were shut down and search engines no longer delivered the desired results. I began to notice the non-fiction section of the library kept shrinking and the racks of new offerings kept displaying less of what interested me. There was only one book worth reading and that was The Good Book. I am sure that you are familiar with the concept.

"I didn't know whether this was a local, regional, national, or world wide phenomenon. Once your communication is cut off or filtered you lose touch. You know only what's happening to you."

"And what was happening to you that was so bad?" Darlene asked, unable to hide her sarcasm.

The Institution

"I hesitate to mention it because under the circumstances you accept as normal you wouldn't find it particularly distressing. Like I told Jerome many years ago, people don't exactly clamor for a new perspective."

"But if what you say is true, some did. Aren't you proof of that?"

"That's because I had access to cumulative wisdom which is something that should never be taken for granted. Singularly, we are as uninformed as the first man was. It's up to each of us to seek out what has been learned, discovered, remembered, written down. That's not to say that the lion's share of humanity chose to draw upon those years of stored wisdom when it was available. And it showed. But when it wasn't available, we shrunk all the more. With nothing other than culturally acceptable propaganda to read and no one intelligent to talk to, I felt myself getting smaller with each passing day. It's different now, for you, I mean. Propaganda is all you've been exposed to. But to know that everything being chosen for you to watch and read is pre-rational baby talk and the goal is a society of infants that believes whatever it's told, was painful. For a while I was able to turn to nature for peace and intelligence until there wasn't even that.

"That's how a slave religion operates. It reinforces that each of its followers is a special little lamb in no need of mental improvement. All one's troubles fall squarely on someone else's shoulders. That the flock's lack of curiosity may have contributed to the misery is never considered. I'm not referring only to religious faith. If a belief system is so threatened by the truth that it does not welcome facts, it's a myth. Unquestioning faith in anything, be it cultural values, material progress, the government, a political party, a profession, all fall under the same umbrella. That was why ethical and environmental issues at odds with the predominant set of beliefs were explained away as a hoax. Questioning population and lifestyle and how those played a roll in the destruction of the planet was the stuff of conspiracies.

"It seems to me that what we really want, what we've always wanted, is to continue doing whatever it is we're doing because we crave the comfort of both mental and physical routine. And we will fight any idea that could break us of our habits. We will and we did. We fought all suggestions about how we might reconfigure our civilization in the face of natural limits. We denied there were any. We convinced ourselves it was normal for whole forests to succumb, fresh water to become scarce, and the oceans to rise and turn acidic. These things came to pass and no alarm was sounded. We were too busy doing what we do best – working, warring, praying, and procreating."

Darlene tried to change the subject. She was already tiring of Sunny's cynical point-of-view. "What about your husband? What was he doing all this time? What is he like? You never talk about him, you know?"

"He had me committed. That should tell you everything you need to know except for maybe this; he was a non-entity. He didn't exist in anything other than the most basic physical sense. There was no there, there."

"You speak about him as if he is dead. He's still alive isn't he?"

"Not as far as I'm concerned."

"It's terrible to harbor such ill feelings. He made many sacrifices caring for you all those years."

Sunny spun around and looked directly at Darlene, realizing immediately why she had chosen those particular words. "Is that what he said when he called the men in the white coats to take me away? You must have gleaned that tragic tale of John's sacrifice from my records."

"All indications are he was sincere. He is your husband after all."

"I don't need to be reminded of that. I can assure you he reminded me of our relationship and his rights time and time again. I never doubted for one minute of any day as long as he was around, what they were."

Sunny preferred to omit John from her life story. Of course, he would be the thing Darlene found most interesting. In much the same way as Darlene, he also had a humorous side. He and her mother packed Sunny into the car three times a week and dragged her off to one of those big box churches. They were sure that one fine day, among the swaying and chanting, she would see the light. Their certitude was priceless. When Sunny's mother started to fret over her daughter's soul, high drama came to their household and spilled over into the church where she played out her fears to a sympathetic congregation and a caring pastor who insisted a baptism would save the day. Order was restored once tap water was

The Institution

splashed on Sunny's forehead and the whole nutty group was convinced she had become one of them.

What Sunny didn't find equally amusing was how the pastor insisted on his congregation being sexually profligate. Babies and more babies. That's what it was all about. How anyone with a brain in his or her head could even think to bring another child on board the poor beleaguered planet was irrational. That was the key phrase: "with a brain in his or her head." During a time when it was illegal to obtain birth control, this presented a home remedy challenge that kept Sunny fully occupied. John was all fired up once again about his conjugal rights. Wishing to do his part, he would mount up religiously every morning and every night. He would sow his seed and she would work to ensure crop failure. It went on this way for more than a decade until she was put away in the Institution.

"I wish you'd let me help you Sunshine. One of our goals here at the Institution is to rid you of your anger."

"I don't want your help," Sunny responded. "My anger is warranted. My anger is all I have. Billions of people should have been angry – not just a few thousand. There are times when anger is an appropriate response."

"Not in a healthy mind. No way. That's not what I was taught."

"I don't wish to argue with you about this. Because you received special training in the area of psychiatry you feel you're an expert on the subject. Unless you know about many other things and are able to tie your training into the larger context, I don't believe you are. That's what I'm trying to provide for you, the larger context. Now if you don't wish to continue with this, we can stop anytime. It was my understanding, though, that you wanted to know."

"I do. I get uncomfortable when you speak badly of my religion, calling it a slave religion and all. You're wrong about that. We're not slaves. We have 'free will.'"

"Well, no, actually you don't, because you're not critical enough to exercise it. For decades, man-made calamities were either misrepresented as biblical revelations or ignored. If you're unwilling to open your mind and let in a little real light, there's no point in continuing. Because you're going to hear about the destruction of the planet, and after that, we're going to talk about extinction. So I suggest you get over your hurt feelings."

Darlene stared at Sunny with profound dread. "I can't do any more of this today," she said. "I need time to absorb what I've already heard. Right now I'm feeling defensive and not very receptive. When I'm more prepared we'll talk again."

"Unless you're willing to exhibit some of that 'free will' of yours, you will never be more prepared to hear what I have to say. The library adjacent to the resident dining room would be a good place to start, don't you think?" Sunny offered. "Exercising some of that 'free will,' I mean."

"But that's for the patients' use only. It's off limits to me."

"Gaining access to real information, it's not your natural inclination. Why do you think that is anyway?" It was a question that remained unanswered when Darlene left the room. It wasn't something she had ever thought about. Nor was it something she ever would. That was why she was unable to comprehend the significance of her lack of curiosity.

BOOK SIX

TURNING ON THE 'DIGM

What Sunny told Darlene about environmental concerns disappearing from the mix wasn't entirely true. For a time, carbon sequestration was sold as an environmental solution when the new coal fired power plants came on line in a big way. Carbon sequestration meant coal could be sold as 'clean.' Anything with the label 'clean' must be environmentally friendly. As if taking down whole mountains could ever be anything other than ecological suicide. The thing with air was everyone relied on it and that included the wealthiest men on the planet. It wasn't within their power to stop the wind from blowing and to keep polluted air from spreading to where they lived. Nor had they been able to keep the sea level from rising or the rivers from running dry. It became increasingly difficult for even the most conservative amongst them to deny there were some climate issues when the waves were lapping up over the balustrades of their beach front properties. That was why the whole notion of burying carbon was bothered with at all. Although important businessmen were quick to dispute publicly that Global Warming was human caused; privately they were concerned. It was easy for them to escape living next to those excavated – formerly coal-bearing – mountainsides and mountaintops, but they couldn't escape living on the same planet as the rest of us, much as they wished they could.

Sunny didn't know whether anyone really believed another technofix would save the day. It was hard to know, what with our failing to recognize that every other technofix we had come up with had been a disaster that led to another technofix more devastating than the last. She assumed people thought about such things, weighing the pros and cons, before proceeding. Although there was no evidence to suggest that was the way it worked. We needed more energy to grow the economy. Wealth creation was at a standstill without it. Coal was there. Coal was quick. Coal was easy. The ground beneath the surface of the earth was lying there empty, waiting to suck up the carbon dioxide that we couldn't let seep into the atmosphere. Whenever Sunny saw plans like carbon sequestration carted out, it was a no-brainer how to proceed. Don't go for it. We didn't need another technofix imposed on us. What we needed was to deal with the moral issue of economic growth itself. But big industry meant good-paying jobs. When anything more than ten jobs was promised, politicians gave up on trying to understand the larger issues. No need to, when no one would ever be held accountable for technology run amok. The bottom line was that sequestration didn't live up to the hype.

Washington State had a lot of basalt. Basalt was billed as a substance that when carbon was injected into it, the carbon would be rendered inert. In addition to prodigious amounts of basalt, Washington also had many lakes. This was where the CO_2 exited. Nasty business. Killed everything in the lakes and everything on the land and in the air for a twenty-mile radius of each and every one. It wasn't as if Washington State was the only place that opted for the economic and environmental rewards of carbon sequestration. There were many other sites in North America and other parts of the world that were similarly unlucky. It seemed to be the tipping point though. All that carbon dioxide, years worth, escaping up into the atmosphere in one giant poof. Or, it may have been just a coincidence. According to some climatologists there would be a twenty-five year delay from when CO_2 entered the atmosphere and when it started impacting climate. Possibly by 2020, we were feeling the effects of the SUV phase of our energy gobbling, 20,000 miles per year per vehicle existence and that was what delivered the big smack up the side of the head. A temperature spike of 3°F in a single year definitely got our attention.

With all the environmental time bombs we had planted, it wasn't easy to know which one was delivering the death knell. There were so many likely candidates. We had the time bomb of genetically modified crops ticking away in the fields spreading their noxious seeds. Plus we had the depleted uranium and nuclear waste. The government, in its wisdom, had determined that these lethal substances would be best disposed of by spreading them far and wide. As a battlefield component in the form of shells and armor during the Iraq Wars, depleted uranium circled the globe for all to enjoy. Also mixed surreptitiously into fertilizer, it had been

The Institution

spread evenly over the entire planet where it eventually found its way into everyone and everything.

But we continued to love technofixes. We were very adept at coming up with them and putting them into play. There was never a review of the technofixes that had been employed in the past to conclude whether they were successes or failures. Because we weren't prone to measuring the damage each had wrought, no person or corporation was held responsible for bad technology. Quality was not one of the criteria in determining the merit of a technological 'advancement.' Technofixes always got a pass because proponents claimed their purpose was to improve human lives even when they didn't. No one went back and reprimanded those scientists who genetically altered corn and soy beans before they knew how genes operated and then sold them commercially as if they knew exactly how it all worked. Untested and unproven frankenseeds were blowing in the wind so they might cross with other seeds and exact a deadly toll. The most fundamental fact of seed biology overlooked. The Conglomerates who introduced these monsters were not run out of town. They remained all-powerful industry leaders and controlled the universities with their big money and their big plans ensuring we continued on with the same brand of lucrative manipulation.

Before most people had acknowledged the probability, the reality of declining oil reserves hit. It really happened. We started running out of oil. An event as life altering as Peak Oil slipped by in the first couple decades of the 21st Century – barely noticed and rarely discussed. The aftermath, the downside of the curve had sharp, steep claws that threatened to tear modern civilization to shreds. As a substitute for oil and natural gas, nuclear, hydrogen, wind, and solar were implemented only at the margins. Coal-fired power plants and hydroelectric were the predominant sources of energy. Because we had not prepared, we had no choice but to rely on existing technology.

Dams popped up not only on the Fraser River but also on every free-flowing river in North America. When the most plentiful, high quality, and easy to extract oil reserves in poor countries began to fail and high exploration costs did not result in big discoveries, we were forced to rely on less conventional oil in first world countries. And that was expensive. It drove oil profits down and the price up to the point where it didn't make sense to be using oil for all the purposes we had found for it. Plastic packaging, baby toys, vinyl siding, and driving, for that matter. Driving was the toughest sell by a long shot. But faced with going electric or not going at all, people came around.

Electric cars had been in existence for at least a hundred years. Contrary to what forty years of paralysis may have led us to believe, it wasn't that big of a deal to bring them back. It wasn't necessarily any better, it just wasn't that difficult. Other than building dams and power plants, the basic infrastructure and delivery systems remained the same. Oil and natural gas reserves were used where there were no viable alternatives – military, air travel, agriculture, chemicals, and pharmaceuticals. We weren't forced to change or give up anything, certainly nothing as sacred as the car or any other part of our living arrangements.

Most of us, if forced to place a bet, would put our money on nuclear holocaust as the best way to destroy the life of this planet. Continuing business as usual – that didn't sound very spectacular. Slow but steady poisoning turned out to be more than enough. Sunny noticed the leaves first of all. Their colors turned pale and watery. It was as if the process by which chlorophyll was made had partially shut down. She suspected it had something to do with CO_2 or oxygen levels but there was never any serious discussion that took place. She asked a biologist friend about it. He got mad at her for being so pessimistic all the time. He said he hadn't heard anything about it. His sole source of news had not reported on the phenomena so therefore she must be wrong. She couldn't get him to entertain the idea on a purely hypothetical basis. He'd already made up his mind that it wasn't happening.

When Sunny's tomatoes produced a small number of fruit in a summer that had been long and hot and her purple plum tree did not overwhelm with its usual bumper crop, she began to wonder. She read many years back about how rising CO_2 levels would also lead to an increase of ozone gas in the atmosphere and that would have an impact on crop yields. A thirty-percent reduction had been the prediction. Out in the park near her home the ponderosa pines were also showing signs of something having gone wrong. She called it their aura – a glossy shine they had when their needles pulsed with life. They didn't have it anymore. She stood there and looked up at all the trees and it was the same with every one. Flat and lifeless. Then she thought back to earlier in the year when the pines blossomed. Usually she took note of the deep red pine flowers dotting the trees because she was slightly allergic, but she hadn't had a problem that year. Nor could she remember the yellow pollen blanketing everything like dust. She should have noticed those things. Not that it would have made any difference, but she should have been aware. She would have been more prepared for what happened the following spring.

She was still running then. She wasn't supposed to be. Women exercising was frowned upon, especially out in public in mixed company and certainly not in skimpy clothing. So she slipped out before dusk, got on an old trail that hooked up with the Silver Falls State Park trail system, and after removing her loose-fitting pants and long-sleeved shirt, she ran, as she had all her life. As the trail began to rise up towards a high plateau it grew steeper with each step. She used to love that part of the run. She liked to feel her heart pumping strength and stamina to her legs. Out in the woods like that, working it, was the most alive she ever felt. But there had been a decline in her performance. Some lightheadedness – a little pain even – accompanied this part of the climb. So on that evening she approached it with resolve, trying to block out her apprehension. She kept pushing and pushing long after she should have given in and stopped. One quarter of the way up, she was gasping so hard for breath she sounded like a broken-down engine. Halfway up the slope, her burning legs turned rubbery until she was no longer running, but staggering. As she approached the top, she was light-headed. Her mind became a muddle that kept breaking up into incomplete thoughts. Finally, her body, with a will of its own, made her stop. She knelt down by the side of the trail and continued to gasp for breath. Her stomach was in a full, roiling boil. She kept swallowing saliva thinking the feeling would pass but she couldn't stop herself from throwing up and she kept on retching violently long after her stomach was empty. She assumed she was seriously ill. As she walked back home under the stars it never once occurred to her that she wasn't the one who was sick and dying.

Terra Dime

That experience was not one she recovered from very quickly. She was so concerned about having a repeat of it she laid off of running but still didn't feel that well. She was short of breath all the time and convinced she had lung cancer or something. That was until she realized that everyone was having difficulty breathing. Even the neighbor's dog couldn't chase after a stick without huffing and puffing and then falling at her feet. It seemed that everywhere she went she was met with the rattling of lungs. The sound of the human animal gasping for air was the new noise pollution plaguing them day and night.

It wasn't as if we didn't have plenty of early warning signals. We ignored them or pretended they had nothing to do with us. The oceans were turning acidic so rapidly that the shells of some types of marine life were being eaten off their backs. They couldn't evolve fast enough to survive. It was the same with human children and their lungs. Over the previous three decades we had seen asthma in children reach epidemic proportions. They weren't adapting quickly enough to the man-made degradation of the environment. Sunny's guess was that if oxygen levels were dropping that rapidly the oceans must be in serious trouble. Possibly the plankton had been wiped out. If it had ceased to fulfill its role in producing a majority of the earth's oxygen, we were in deep trouble. She reasoned that it could also be the tropical rainforests. We might have cut enough of them that the earth had reached a tipping point. There was also the chance that it was both.

Back on the land close to home, once the pines lost their life force, the end came quickly. Needles, dried and brown, rained down into mounds dotting the hillsides like graves. And then they just fell over. Whole forests of one hundred-year-old trees gone in a matter of months. It happened so fast there wasn't time to adjust to the loss. The cleanup crews came around in big trucks and scooped up the remains of wildlife where they fell. For a period of time their deaths provided steady work. Birds dropped from the sky in mid-flight. They littered the streets, yards, rooftops even. Eventually we got what we had been working towards all along. A planet populated with nothing other than people, pets, farm animals, and domesticated plants. Any living thing that was not under domination and control vanished.

The Institution

While she still could, she would go down and sit by the river she had been paid to protect. The Arrowleaf Balsamroot that typically softened and transformed the region with saffron blossoms in April and May never bloomed again. On those slogs down barren sandy slopes, she would get on her hands and knees and sift through the dirt for a native plant, a beetle, a blade of grass. No sign of life anywhere. Where Rock Creek and the Silver River met was a muddy torrent. One hundred miles of sand from the sloughing of upstream slopes had altered the composition of the river. The water no longer ran clear over a rocky bottom. It would widen and flatten and flows eventually dwindled. For then, at least, the water still flowed. Whether it could sustain life or how pure it was – these things already seemed like silly pie-in-the-sky dreams from a distant past.

In the face of all this destruction, we were quick to respond to the lack of oxygen problem. Technophilia came to the rescue. The government immediately launched the *Oxygen Enhancement Program* which had several components. All were big boons to the economy, since it was approached in much the same way as the war effort of the 1940s. Instead of manufacturing guns and ammo and planes and tanks, we churned out respirators and oxygen-producing apparatus that attached to existing HVAC systems in our homes and automobiles.

Modifying agribusiness presented the greatest opportunity. Structures had to be designed to house livestock. Crops had to be genetically modified either to perform in a reduced oxygen, increased ozone environment or be grown indoors. The latter method ended up being the only thing that worked. That wasn't determined, however, until the chemical companies pocketed billions before coming to the understanding that life on Planet Earth needs oxygen.

The whole indoor crop thing worked so well because we were able to create a super-enriched environment where crops flourished all year round. There were only two major hiccups in the whole program. Like the A-bomb effort of WWII, the program had the greatest minds working on it, in what were touted as the worthiest occupations of the day. The numbers of livestock required to fulfill our dietary expectations could not be met indoors. Cows were big and they took too long to mature. They consumed too much on their way to becoming slaughterhouse size even with the growth hormones we loaded them up with. It was a dilemma. We had to find a way to ratchet up their growth another notch or two or in the euphemism of the day 'condense maturity into a shorter timeframe.' It was called *Accelerated Development And Maturation* or *ADAM* for short and no expense was spared on its successful outcome. A way forward was found by genetically altering the bovine pituitary gland. The technology produced the same adverse side effects that accompanied growth hormone therapy, only more pronounced. It was nice, though, that biotechnology finally had its day in the sun after promising innovations of miraculous proportions for so long. The wealthiest people in the world not having to cut back. It didn't get any more wonderful than that.

The second hurdle came during this transition period. Before we could get our agriculture program fully 'enhanced' there was the threat of a few lean seasons. The situation was so dire that our food shipments to other countries were suspended. When China attempted to make this their policy as well, we were up in arms, literally. The rules were always different for us than for everyone else. We were forced to obtain their grain by force, preemptively. There were weapons of mass destruction involved. No doubt nuclear. There weren't any reliable sources of information to know exactly what happened. We were told whatever the government felt was necessary. The stakes surrounding nuclear warfare were not as great at that point. We had already destroyed most of the flora and fauna. Humans couldn't survive outdoors in an uncontrolled environment anyway so what was the harm in adding a little more nuclear fallout to the stew. The deterrent had been in fouling our own nest and since we had already accomplished that, there was nothing to hold us back.

That was one of the downsides of a social system based on self-love. Sympathy doesn't generally make the leap to empathy and extend beyond whatever boundary one has set for oneself. Whether that boundary was biological, ethnic, religious, or nationalist, it rarely included people from other countries and certainly not those who looked different. And when it came to the family of life, all the little live things we considered separate from us, not a chance. So the North American Union dropped a bomb or two on a bunch of people who looked different and worshiped a different God – not "The One True God." The bombs likely killed a couple billion people along with everything else that was clinging to life. The grain that was sought probably perished as well. There was precedent for military failures of that magnitude. As far as the bombing campaign itself, in no way was this a violation of God's law. The Good Book's warnings about the "slanty-eyed, yellow-skinned people" were prescient. What were the effects of the increased radiation circling the globe and contaminating the air, soil, and water? Most everything was either dead or so degraded we couldn't measure the impact.

And there Sunny was, still afraid of what would come of her if she objected. She was no different from the people who participated gleefully every day of their lives. It made no difference where her heart was if she failed to act. Convincing herself otherwise was a mental manipulation that didn't hold up to scrutiny. When given a taste of society minus those who were willing to speak out, she didn't like it much. Many members of the community of life who didn't have a way to voice their disgust had died and she wondered what she, who had a voice, was waiting for.

Living through the doomsday scenario proved to be something she wasn't psychologically prepared for. Unlike those who believed the stories that were being touted, Sunny knew what was happening when the building became unstable and began to fall. That was key, the knowing. She was actually born on the top floor. There would never be anything built above her. It didn't seem possible. There had always been the promise of another level of progress. The elevator wasn't supposed to stop without warning and then vanish without leaving provision for a slow, measured descent. There was no getting out. The building was sealed tight as a drum. All of us – who happened to be alive – were meant to sit bravely waiting while it became increasingly unstable. Until we were buried alive in the rubble.

Sunny knew she could talk about this until both she and the Nurse were exhausted. She could wrack her brains trying to come up with the words that would move Darlene and would not be able to convey the insanity of our civilization. Not then, not now. Sunny had watched the planet go through its death throes. She did not have the distance of time to act as a salve on the ecological wounds. They bled large and grisly right before her eyes. And they festered after that until there was nothing left but scar tissue as far as the eye could see. It was unforgettable. It took a certain kind of mental flexibility – or powerful meds – to ignore or defend what was happening all around.

Nothing in our upbringing or education prepared us for that type of event. Thinking back on it she realized she was in shock, utterly lost, and unable to function. The clinical diagnosis would have been Post-Traumatic Stress Disorder. How could she not be suffering from it? Our home was taken from us and she wasn't talking about the one with four walls, she was talking our big home. The only one any of us will ever have. John and her mother said she was severely depressed and should seek medical attention when she began to ask where certain high profile people had gone. Friends and neighbors said she was exaggerating when she began to speak of how bleak it all was. Later, they ran the other way when they saw her coming. And still later, they complained amongst themselves, to John, and to their pastor who contacted the authorities. Once she was warned, she protested more vigorously. She posted her opinions on signs, placed them in their front yard, and made everyone uncomfortable. She wrote letters to the elected officials. John told her she was being ridiculous. He pointed out that the citizenry didn't protest any more. It was an indulgence from the past. It was silly and immature and would get her into trouble. And he was right once again. She was something from another time and she didn't belong.

No one came out of the woodwork to express how similarly he felt. She didn't ferret out a single compadre who had been lying low waiting for someone else to express what he was feeling. If there had been only one she would have been consoled. She hung around in the front yard waiting for someone to engage with her. When she referred to the circumstances under which we were living, not a single person cared enough to hear her out. That's what made her lose it. She folded up into the fetal position right there in the yard and retreated so far into herself she was no longer of this world. That was her final reaction to living amongst aliens who relied on a life support system so different from hers she couldn't communicate at the most basic level.

She stopped eating and allowing herself to be screwed after that. She didn't know for sure which strike got her the most attention. The sex thing resonated with John's pastor and ensured John didn't want her back, but it was the refusal to eat that meant she must be committed. Suicide was not an acceptable out. Sunny's mother was called to the rescue and swept in like Florence Nightingale, intent on being her daughter's salvation. The truth of it was she wished to be rid of both John and her mother and if dying would accomplish this she was all for it. All she could remember after that was waking up in a place where she was fed intravenously. She continued to refuse food, fearing she would be sent back to John. When one of the attendants encouraged her to begin eating so that she could leave the Intensive Care Unit and be placed in a permanent room, she perked up. She took the chance that they had no intention of sending her home and became curious enough to stay alive a while longer.

***

The library at The Faith is Truth Institution was for the sole use of the patients. It was not locked. It did not need to be. It was the thing Sunny noticed that first day she ventured out of her room. A sign was posted indicating the space was off limits to staff and that was it. A sign was the only barrier between those employed by the Institution and volumes of information. And it was respected not out of reverence for the rule but because there was so much that was more titillating and easily available. That was the funny thing. It was all there. The real story. All the pieces to put the puzzle together but no one bothered to try just as the censors who allowed the library to be filled with differing opinions knew they wouldn't.

Jared Diamond's *Collapse: How Societies Choose to Fail or Succeed* was among the library's offerings but it didn't hold quite the fascination it once had now that Sunny had lived through the real thing. All of Jerome's books were there. She ran her fingers down the spine of every one and felt weak-kneed at the recollection. As she became reacquainted with all her favorites, she began to feel calmer. She pulled Richard Heinberg's *Peak Everything: Waking up to the Century of Declines* from the shelf. She had meant to read this book but it had been published while she was out of the country and when she returned to the U.S. events escalated so quickly she hadn't got around to it. It was so weird to read a book that was predicting the future, in the future. The subtext when it came to the *Peak Everything* theory was the shadow of peak population. If all the support systems were in an engorged state, it followed that our numbers had reached a maximum as well. That was another one of those big gorillas in the room. If we had peak food and water, peak energy, and peak technology, we also had peak population and we were about to head back down the same slope we had climbed so successfully. The question had always been how the die-off would occur – through attrition or annihilation.

For a few hours she sat and read undisturbed until she became aware of movement in the room next to the library. Through a glass wall panel she saw people arriving, finding chairs at tables, and settling in for a meal. She opened the door quietly and looked around guessing that these were the other patients. A quick estimate told her there were about two hundred. She gave them little more than a glance so intent was she on finding a way to get past without being seen. There were many conversations going on. She caught snippets of them as she hugged the wall on her way to the exit. So used to avoiding banal discussion, it didn't connect with her that these were conversations in which she might like to participate.

"Any news from the outside?" someone said.

"They brought my grandson to visit yesterday. Odd kid. I asked if he was okay and not strange in the head. Everyone assured me he was fine. Something about kids not being the same as they were in my day and I best get used to it. Like what was there to get used to. It was like he was dead."

And then, from a different section of the room, "Did you read that article about the explosion in Washington State. In the 'Carbon Sequestration Region,' whatever that is."

"Region? Like it's a small part of the State. Try about half the State."

"It was one of those propaganda pieces to dispel fear because the basalt that captured the carbon is beginning to blow sky high. The State will be reduced to rubble when all is said and done. How do you break that to people gently without lying?"

The voices of yet two more strangers drifted to her ears. "The CCP just gave notice about their intent to embark on another 'Keep the North American Union Working' campaign."

"Oh no, not again. What is it this time?"

"They intend to 'give the land back to the people.'"

The Institution

"What does that mean?"

"They're deeding the national parks, state parks, and public lands to private interests for development. It will be a nice construction boom while it lasts. A lot of salvage timber too. Remember, it's all good."

"How could we possibly need to build more houses?"

"There's a population explosion going on in the North American Union. The *Mandatory Many Children* policy has worked wonders. Why just the other day the President called a special conference specifically to congratulate the country on 'keeping the American Dream alive by lifting the birthrate and ensuring prosperity for generations to come.' It's best to keep everybody busy though, don't you think?"

"I don't know. We humans have been busy enough for quite some time now."

A woman spoke as if to herself. "What do you think is going on in the rest of the world? How do you think other nations are faring? Jerome, did you hear me? Jerome?"

It was the sound of his name, and out of the corner of her eye a head turning her way, that caught Sunny's attention. She was almost to the door. She stopped then and picked him out of the crowd. His eyes were so soft and warm and full of love she felt exposed. And then he took stock of himself. The look wilted and turned to desperation. She took a step in his direction and panic engulfed him. Something wasn't quite right. She could see he wasn't well. She saw the wheelchair and wanted to ask, "What happened to you?" but his hand went up defensively in a gesture meant to stop her. His eyes pleaded with her not to have this encounter here on these terms. Understanding this, she went back to what she had been attempting a moment before and slipped out of the room to wait in solitude for him to come to her.

In the silence before Jerome's arrival she did her best to prepare herself. A barrage of humbling emotions confronted her. It had been twenty years since they had any kind of physical contact. The dreams she had once had about yielding under him had evaporated. The time had been ill spent. It had left her poorly prepared for bearing the weight of his pain. All his beliefs, dreams, desires unfulfilled. Stripped down to the core, who would he be? He would be expecting something from her, something more than philosophical banter. She didn't want to disappoint him but by then Sunny knew herself well. She had been consistent in not providing anyone or anything with what was needed.

"Tell me," she said, as soon as the door was closed and it was just the two of them. And so he did. His words had her internalizing everything she was hearing and everything she had seen. She started holding herself accountable for all the horrors that had been built into the system. The shame of it was more than she could bear. Sunny found herself backed up against the wall of her room. She had been moving away from him while he spoke and now they were as distant as they could be in a confined space.

"Jerry, why did we make all this bad stuff happen? Why didn't we stop?"

"I'm not sure Sunny. Arrogance? I think there was a consensus that when things got bad enough then we would make a move. With disaster imminent, we would work hard to solve the problems. And we would do so in the nick of time."

"Just like I did with you?" she asked, choking on the words, the imagery, and the familiarity of it all. Why had she been so weak? She was as big a disgrace as the system she lived under. Why did we cripple everything we came in contact with and accept none of the blame?

"I'm not accusing you of anything, Sunny," he said when he realized she was distraught. "Sunny?" he repeated when there was still no response.

All she could think about was how once upon a time, through his eyes, she caught sight of the love humans were capable of. How it could wrap around a person like a warm, full breeze saturated with the mystery of the universe. Had we let that wash over us it might have had the power to transform, to make us whole.

"What are you thinking?" Jerome asked when she failed to respond in her usual way that was levelheaded and strong.

"That I should have said or done something. We all should have joined in the fight. Under the circumstances I should have made my stand and fought for all I was worth. Of all the battles that were worth waging the one for the life of the planet was the one to show up for. I didn't do that, Jerry. I didn't have the courage to fight for the two things I loved more than anything – you and Planet Earth." With that said, she crumpled. The length of her body slid down the wall. Holding her face in her hands, her elbows rested on bony knees that were drawn inward to protect her from blows that no one physically administered.

"It was bigger than any one person. Everyone of us in here feels like a failure." He turned the wheelchair around and inched closer to the door, his back to her now.

She lifted her head. "Don't go," she pleaded when she thought he intended to slip away. "Please, don't leave me. I couldn't stand it if we were separated again."

She saw his shoulders were shaking and she quit talking and waited for the pain to subside. Her feelings for Jerome were as strong as they'd ever been. She got up, went over to where he was, and touched him. Cautiously at first, because she was fearful that she was only dreaming and that reaching for him would confirm he wasn't really there.

"I can't believe it," she said, tightening her grip on his shoulders. "I didn't think I would ever see you again." Her arms went around him. She ran her hands down his arms and over his fingers while her lips brushed the back of his neck. For once she knew and delivered.

"You have no idea how good that feels," he said.

Sunny accepted his appreciation with mixed emotions. Nothing she did now would ever make up for what he had suffered. She saw the parallel between Jerome and the planet. The human animal really had a knack for destroying what was splendid. She walked around so that she could face him and knelt down. She placed her hands against his chest, looked into his eyes, and kissed him. He told her he liked that too, which wasn't necessary as she felt his heart pounding away.

"What you said about loving me. I feel the same about you. I don't know why I didn't think to tell you that before." He was bewildered by how he could have overlooked a detail like that.

"I knew how you felt. Even before I found out that you named your boat after me. If you'd told me, it wouldn't have made any difference. I was too stupid to listen."

She leaned back to get a better look at him. "Don't look too closely," he said. "I'm kind of a mess."

Terra Dime

And she thought about those she had been surrounded by for the better part of her life. Jerome could never be a mess in the way they were. In a way that was thoughtless and destructive. How many times had she listened to a fanatical spouse rave about being saved from this cesspool of a planet? It would never occur to him that it was minds like his that had made the mess. The smaller the mind, the bigger the ego. What a dreadful combination.

***

Breaking the rules to gain access to the library terrified Darlene. It was an incredible risk to take in order to seek affirmation. If she were caught in that library there would be no way to explain it away. Her desire to go in there would be an irrefutable verdict on her state of mind. She had hoped to get quickly in and out but deciding what she wanted out of such a large collection of books was not easy. Finding the ones that were recommended was a lengthy process. Prior to this, she had not set foot in a library. She had to admit this appalling omission to Dr. Sayer so he could explain how books were catalogued. She went to him because he was always talking about books and offering up advice, but it had been awkward.

At first he was against her going in. He said it was too dangerous and that he could tell her anything she wished to know. Books could not be removed. An alarm would sound so that meant she would have to read them there in that vulnerable position. It wasn't worth the risk. But Darlene wanted to see the books for herself. She wanted to see the number of books, the years they were written, the pictures and credentials of the authors, and get an overall sense of a time she hadn't lived through.

Some of the author's names and faces, albeit a lot younger, were known to her. She hadn't expected this. She knew Jerome Raines' books would be on the shelves, but not the writings of at least thirty other residents of the Institution. None of those others had been her patients, so she did not know anything of them, but she recognized familiar names when she saw them on the spines. These she jotted down, along with the titles, and compared them against the patient roster. For that many authors to go off the rails and have to be institutionalized was quite a coincidence even by Darlene's standards. The fact they had all been questioning different parts of the same system was the common thread that ran through their writings. Some expressed their concerns about the future from an ecological standpoint. Others had been up in arms about economic and democratic collapse due to corruption. Still others foresaw a complete breakdown of human civilization.

On subsequent nocturnal visits to the library, she began to get a feel for the amount of literature that had been devoted to systemic catastrophe during the first decade of the 21st Century. And she noticed how the tone became more urgent and to the point as the decade came to the close. After 2012, nothing. Whatever had produced such an outpouring of concern ended. The Year 2012 was significant for a couple of reasons. Darlene knew from her history classes, why that was. It was when the Christian Conservative Party came to power and it was the last year of strife of any kind, especially economic. The *Real Deal* was signed into law and with that, the North American Union became stronger, gaining the economic status and Superpower might that was its due.

There was a lesser-known fact relating to that year. It was the year in which the Institution was established. Darlene was reminded of it every time she ventured into the lobby and looked at the official plaque with its powerful symbol of the Union affixed to the base of a statue of the important man who made this Institution and others like it a reality. He was the guy with the famous quote about the truth being useless. She still couldn't remember his name. She had known it at one time but his name wasn't important anyway. It was what he said that stuck with her, stuck with a lot of people in fact. She wasn't sure whether his words or the Faith is Truth Institution had any bearing on why there was a change in course, but there it was.

***

"So, if thirty patients on this roster are published authors, then what are the others? Why were they committed?" Darlene asked as she held out the list for Dr. Sayer's review.

Terra Dime

Dr. Sayer handed the list back to her and asked, "Are you asking me what they did for jobs? Why does it matter?"

"I'm trying to establish credibility here. You're telling me that the patients in this Institution are here because they disputed the authorities. And I'm asking you what credentials did they have to do such a thing? It all goes back to credibility. If they had neither credentials nor proof then what right did they have to go against the flow? And without those, who would listen to them anyway so why would they be considered a threat? Ordinary people who question their superiors – those people who know better than they do – are nuts. Without special training or education, no one is equipped to comment on what's right. Anyone with half a brain knows this."

"So you're saying that unless a person is an 'expert' they have no business commenting on anything of consequence. And if they take it upon themselves to do so they should expect to be carted away to the loony bin for crossing a line that everyone knows to be sacred?"

"Exactly. I'm not going to take the word of a couple of hundred lay people who couldn't possibly understand what goes into making a nation as great as this one function. It would be wrong for me to do so."

"You don't think being an artist, a chef, a craftsman, or a citizen of the planet for fifty years or so qualifies you to comment on its behalf? It's not as if the 'lay people' as you seem to be calling us are disputing the 'experts' who you don't have issue with because they were published."

"All I'm saying is it doesn't matter what you say. There are only about thirty people in here out of a possible two hundred or so who are qualified to speak on this subject. That's not enough to convince me. The rest of you all have agendas of some kind. Look at you. You have a grudge against the medical profession that has left you jaded. I don't know, possibly you got passed up for promotion or something. Sunshine is an environmentalist. Everyone knows they're extremists. And besides, she is the most bitter, unhappy woman I've ever known. She is not to be taken seriously. Poor Saint Paul. Who knows what happened to him other than running across Mr. Raines ruined his life. He caused him to lose faith in his faith and that destroyed his career and his family. Not much wonder he had a breakdown. None of you are very honest with yourselves about your mental and emotional states. You've indulged yourselves so long in persecution ideations you're no longer in touch with reality. I know I'm acquainted with only a small cross-section of the patient population but I would bet money that a larger sampling would net the same results."

"Quit talking to me in clinical mumbo jumbo. You're not saying anything different from what you said before you had access to new information. The whole reason you embarked on this journey was you said you wanted to know."

"I was wrong. I don't wish to know. I would hate what the knowing would do to me. It would depress me. I wouldn't be perky all the time. I wouldn't have any fun. Worst of all, I wouldn't have any lovers. And, I wouldn't feel as good about eating those nice big juicy ADAM Rib Eyes if I came to believe they were tortured meat. Desserts wouldn't taste as sweet if I were convinced I'm fat. And for the life of me, I don't know how anyone can get through a single day not believing in the Lord, the goodness of man, and in Heaven. Searching for truth, why that's not enough."

"So what are you going to do?"

"I'll keep my promise to Sunshine, if that's what you mean. After that, I'm going to get right to work on becoming the old Darlene."

***

"And so who was he?" Darlene asked. "Who was Jerome Raines after fifteen years of being certifiable?"

"Just what I should have expected," Sunny answered. "The real thing."

"And what exactly does that mean?"

"He had found a way to balance the parts of civilization that made us a higher quality being with our natural traits that tie us to the earth. He had it in just the right measure. It was rare."

"But man doesn't need nature. We've proven that once and for all."

"Whenever I talk to you I'm reminded of how we live under a system that relies on its citizens being blind, deaf, and dumb. I didn't think it could get any worse but it did. You comprehend less than my generation and ten years from now, if anyone has survived under these conditions, they'll know less still. None of it could function any other way. Thinking remains the great enemy. The whole system is so incomprehensible it would breakdown in a heartbeat if anyone dared to think about what he was doing and why he was doing it.

"All Jerome ever wanted was for humanity to be the best it could be. There is no good reason why that should have made anyone uncomfortable. At least no honorable, good reason. It's tragic how we can believe unequivocally in the wholeness of a religious figure but not in a comparable potential that exists within each of us. So, what do you think...Is this the best we could have done? Any uneasiness about where we're heading?"

Darlene knew the answers to Sunshine's questions – had always known – as a matter of fact. She was ready to reassert her authority with this patient. "It's a lot of work trying to figure out what the truth is and I don't think it's worth the effort. Truth is what the majority believes. Anything else is bound to make people uncomfortable and for little reward. If there's no guarantee that others are going to join you then what's the point in isolating yourself. That sounds so sad and lonely. In fact, that's how I feel when I think of you locked up in here. You are so sad and lonely. It would have been easy for you to pretend you loved your husband. Or, look the other way when a corporation that, overall, was doing more good than harm dumped something extra into the Silver River. And you could have said you believed in God even if you secretly didn't. Sometimes if you pretend things long enough, you can start believing them. I don't think you ever gave that a try. You have a negative attitude, Sunshine. That's your biggest problem. Instead of recognizing how lucky you are to be alive and thanking the government for providing a nice, warm place to sleep and accepting that if it weren't for agribusiness you would have starved long ago, you dwell on what's missing. It's not very constructive. You may think me unworldly but at least I know enough to count my blessings.

"I don't want to be like any of you, even Mr. Raines. That's what he wasn't smart enough to figure out on his own. Why would anyone wish to focus on such uncertain rewards when there is so much that is tangible right there for the taking? All of you could have enjoyed the hand you were dealt and the times you were born into instead of lamenting a few innocuous side

The Institution

effects. Now honestly, in retrospect, don't you wish that's what you'd been about?"

"It's hard to argue against such logic as yours," Sunny said agreeably. "That's why we're where we are today. No closer to understanding what we've lost, and why, or coming to terms with what's going to become of us."

"Oh no, that's where you're totally wrong. We are very close to knowing what is going to become of us. Very soon the earth will be restored to its original beauty and some of us will get to enjoy it, in all its splendor, for another thousand years. Others won't be as fortunate but it's not as if everyone didn't have his chance. People like me just going about the business of living aren't responsible for Tribulation. No way, we wouldn't do that. Only God and sinners are capable of such awesome trouble as that. So when I look out the window the way you do, I don't see the end and I don't bear any responsibility. I see this as an essential step towards a new beginning. I'm really excited about that."

As Darlene talked about human beings not being capable of inflicting grave damage, she remembered something else Mr. Raines told her. It made her mad that it would come to her like this and she swore it would be the last time she ever thought about anything he said.

"Here's another peculiar thing. I heard this guy being interviewed on the radio – a scientific specialist of some kind. It doesn't matter of which variety because those guys are remarkably similar when it comes to limited scope. Anyway, he was looking for evidence to prove our human ancestors were not responsible for the extinction of large mammals that once occupied North America – like the Woolly mammoth and Giant sloth. Evidence had pointed in recent years to the possibility that when humans crossed the land bridge that is now the Bering Strait they managed to hunt the large animals that were here until there was not a one left. He was determined to prove it was an asteroid that created runaway climate change that led to the massive die-off. The fact that this scientist was living smack dab in the middle of a period in which human beings were responsible for extinction in the neighborhood of 200 species per day didn't register. Those statistics didn't assist him in wrapping his mind around the idea that we are capable of being one dangerous, destructive creature. The conditions he goes on to explain

307

that contributed to the massive die-off are so similar to the ones we were experiencing, namely Global Warming, I kept expecting him to say so. But making connections wasn't this guy's strong suit. This scientist then alludes to how terrifying it is to find evidence that in recent history (10,000 years or so ago) something as devastating as an asteroid capable of taking out major species struck the earth, causing it to warm, and creating intolerable conditions on the planet. I don't believe we have to look back 10,000 years for evidence of something this destructive. Just ask the passenger pigeons, blue whales, gorillas, black panthers, and Indian Elephants. I felt like screaming at him, the Homo sapien sapien asteroid, ever heard of it?"

"You and Mr. Raines read too much into things. You twist facts around to fit your view in the most peculiar way."

Sunny ignored Darlene. She had heard it all before and in this way was reduced to an observer who had let it go. She was speaking from way inside now. "The night Jerome died he told me he couldn't take the pain any longer. He had been getting progressively worse. I think his organs were failing. We had been hoarding painkillers and sleeping pills for him in case things got really bad. He didn't wish to be more of a burden than he already was.

"He felt that he had done enough. He thought it was his job as a citizen of the planet to inform, particularly those who didn't have the knowledge, or the brainpower, or the motivation to find out what was really happening. He thought everyone would welcome the information and he had paid a high price for believing he could change minds. He said he never lost his idealism and he never quit trying – but he failed. He had big crazy plans for life on this planet but now it was over. There were a few planetary details that needed to be worked out but he didn't wish to stick around to see when and how the end would come.

"He had been working on a final manuscript. I'm sure you didn't know that. You're not exactly astute. I had planned to let you read it to see how it affected you but in view of how you've responded to the spoken word, it seems ridiculous to bother with the written. He told me that with it finished there was nothing more for him to do or say. He wanted me to be the first to read it but he warned me that I might be surprised by the tone of the whole thing. He had broken all the rules. It took all the emotions he had ever known to tell the story of Planet Earth on the verge of going dark. The shame and sadness overwhelmed the words giving them a life of their own. He was glad in a way, how it turned out, because if someone were alive in the future to read it, the sincerity would ring true.

"Jerome didn't want a bunch of fanfare around his dying. He didn't wish to bother with individual good-byes. The manuscript was a huge farewell and once everyone read it they would understand. He realized it was a selfish request in view of the fact that he was intending to desert me, but he wanted me to touch him and talk to him until he quit breathing and he wanted to go ahead with it right then and there. Somehow I kept myself from becoming weepy because I knew he didn't want to waste time with that. I helped to lift him up onto the bed. Usually he didn't need help but he had given himself over completely. He began swallowing pills, many, many pills. I crawled up alongside him and we looked at one another for the longest time. We felt so strongly about one another, we didn't know where the one ended and the other began. And it felt right our not being separate. What we spoke of in that final hour was greater than the wisdom of the human world. It was more than Jerome's lifeless body I embraced. It was the remains of a dying planet. I wish with all my heart I could breathe life back into both."

Darlene was suspicious of this unusually intimate story from a patient who up until that day had told her nothing nearly as personal. "Why are you telling me this?" she asked.

"Because I want you to recognize that I'm not the one who is impoverished. You may be pleased with yourself for the daily access you have to so many physical and material pleasures. And I'm guessing you think that because you believe in God and know all about good and evil and are certain there's a place for you in Heaven, you have a rich spiritual life. As if that's all there is to it – believing – no personal development required. Good and evil couched in such narrow terms. What human beings did to the planet was evil. What's happening to those animals out there in the livestock building is evil. So is the system that created and condoned it. Ever consider that?"

"I have," she stated proudly, "and then I saw the light and I said to myself, they're only animals so it's okay."

Sunny was no longer in the room. There was nothing for her there. "There's an unfathomable depth to the planet, or at least there was, of which you haven't the tiniest comprehension. Without an awareness of that, you can't possibly know your true place, and hence you have no spirituality. What you have is a construct that reinforces your self-absorption. I wish you'd all get over yourselves. No, what I wish is that you would set me free tonight so that I won't be forced to have another conversation like the one I had with you today ever again. I can't bear knowing what you're all thinking."

Darlene was relieved. The patient was changing the subject. "No one wishes to go with you. Dr. Sayer considered it and then came to his senses."

Sunny had thought it through. There was no way she intended to be the last one alive in this place. That would be a do-over of life on the outside. If Heather were younger she suspected she would go for the quick, easy end. As it was, she didn't expect to live much longer. Her heart was so bad she doubted she had the strength to make it to the river.

"Now, I need a promise from you that if I let you out the gate you won't try to make contact with anyone on the outside. That would be a disaster. You'll stick to your original promise and go back to the earth or whatever it was you said you intended to do. But please don't give me any details. I prefer not to know."

"Why does that not surprise me?" Sunny said with the kind of resignation that was complete. "Weren't you listening just now? Of course I'm not going to try to make contact with anyone. I prefer death over having to talk to one of you."

***

"Isn't there a part of the story you've omitted?" Darlene asked. "Like the part about how you were with Mr. Raines when he had his fall. I'd like to hear about that."

"It's not something I wish to tell you," Heather replied.

"Come on. You've told me more personal stuff than that. What's the big deal?"

The Institution

"No, I haven't. Most of what we've talked about didn't mean anything to me. I refuse to try to convince someone who's been brainwashed about what happened twenty-eight years ago. I tried at the time with a whole bunch of people including the pilot and attendants who airlifted him, the emergency room staff, and the police. All brain dead just like you. The whole country is brain dead. I saw it happen. He was only a couple of feet from me. Dr. Sayer was the only one who accepted the story and not because it came from me but because Jerome told him, probably in between pleas to let him die. I'm sick of telling it. I'm sick *from* the telling of it," Heather said angrily, becoming more agitated and confused when Darlene pressed her.

Darlene attempted to soothe the patient from the waves of madness that were sweeping over her. Mrs. Holmes' strength waned before her eyes. Her demeanor lost its sparkle. A speck of frayed yarn took hold of her. The starlet looked feeble as she began picking frenetically at a flaw on the front of her sweater.

"Mrs. Holmes, can I get you anything? How about a cookie or a nice cup of tea?" she offered.

"No, I don't want anything except to rest and forget." And then softer still, at a level Darlene could just barely make out. "But that's not possible, is it? Not as long as I'm alive."

Darlene caught the shadow crossing her face. There was no doubt what that look of life exhaustion signaled. Mrs. Holmes fell asleep. Sitting opposite, Darlene watched her disappear into a dream world and wondered what those old eyes turned inside remembered. She was twitching and muttering and grasping invisible objects out of the air. Darlene pulled a throw off the end of the bed and positioned it around the older woman, tucking the sides and corners in snugly so it wouldn't slip off in her restlessness. She lifted her legs, light as feathers, and stretched them out on the sofa. Then she gently arranged her head and upper body into a horizontal position wishing while she worked that she could leap over the void to that place Mrs. Holmes inhabited. She wished it only with this patient, not the others. But she didn't fool herself. The chasm was as wide between the two of them as it was with the rest. Perhaps wider, because it was impossible to tell when she was acting or playing it straight or whether

her own interest was genuine or driven by the fact that Heather Holmes had been "a somebody." It was kind of endearing – her wish to take her best kept secrets with her knowing they would never measure up to the fantasies her fans preferred. The ones about charisma or star quality or whatever it was she had that was more captivating than reality. As Darlene stepped out into the hall she looked back at what had once been a sex symbol, head thrown back, still mumbling away, channeling a world dead to her now.

And in that world Heather was screaming at the two goons who were surveying the damage below, the one still holding the "non-lethal" taser in his hand. As they neared, she made the phone call. And by the time they were within earshot, she had her brother on the line and was explaining where she was and that she was involved in a situation and that if he didn't hear from her again where he should start looking. While she had her brother as a witness, she told the two men who she was and spelled out their limited options just in case they hadn't understood. And one of those options included getting help for Jerome.

Once the helicopter arrived to remove him from the Canyon, she flew with them to Vancouver. He died three times on that flight. She watched him go and she saw them bring him back. Each time, her pain grew more acute as she feared they would not be able to shock the life back into him.

Heather roused a bit then from her dream to realize she wasn't in the helicopter at his side and it wasn't Jerome's heart that wished to end the nightmare. It was hers. Her feet had grown cold and the sensation was spreading through her legs. She looked down at the blanket covering her eighty-one year old body and the buzzer she was meant to push at times like this and she didn't reach for it. Instead she reached back to that day, the worst of all possible days when her heart was full and strong. She ached all over again with the sensation of watching him die. His pain tore at her chest. Waiting for lungs to fill with air, breath to catch, a heart to beat again. How quiet it had become. Listening for the waves to return and lap against her ears. Searching in the silence for the familiar hum of a living being. But there was nothing to hear.

***

The Institution

Darkness was settling over the grounds when Darlene opened the door for the runaway. She watched for a moment while Sunny opened the gate, hoping to register something telling in her movements. The way she turned without hesitation, purposely, a direction in mind, refusing to look back. Even in this, she remained a fluke of human nature. The night so quickly swallowed her it was as if she had been a fabrication all along. It was at this late hour Sunny wished to get on her way. Sure her absence wouldn't be noticed until the following morning, she would have about a twelve-hour head start. The one thing she wished to avoid was being captured and having to carry on.

Darlene went in search of her alibi for the night. Dr. Marsh was a creature of habit. She knew he spent his off-duty time in the staff lounge drinking whiskey and watching action movies. When Darlene found him only two others were in the room and they were so absorbed in the on-screen excitement they didn't notice her motioning to one of their colleagues. Doug looked surprised that she would venture into his domain. It was not something she had ever done before so he knew it must be important.

"Dr. Marsh, can I have a word with you?" she said in an official tone.

He stepped into the hall where they could not be seen from the lounge. "What is it?" he said. "Is something wrong? You're not pregnant are you?" That would be so inconvenient.

"Oh no, nothing like that. I've been thinking about what you said. About my needing a check-up and I think you're right. I've definitely not been myself lately."

"In what way?"

"Well, I've been having the craziest thoughts. I guess you could call them ideations."

"About what?"

"About what we're doing here. About what The Faith is Truth Institution is for. That kind of thing. It's starting to make me very uncomfortable." She was sincere when she said this. She wanted to get that implant of hers working again in the worst way. She'd had a rough time of it trying to hold on to sound judgment.

"I can imagine," he said. "That sounds terrible. I have an idea what might be causing it. We can get you fixed up and feeling better in no time."

"There's something else too," she said in a best attempt to sound coy.

"Yes," he responded encouragingly already anticipating what it might be.

"I feel bad about what happened between the two of us. I wouldn't have done that if I were in my right mind. Obviously, I'm not," she pleaded her case while closing the gap between the two of them so that when he looked down at her there was nothing but cleavage in his field of vision.

"What about that other guy you're seeing?"

"There is no other guy. I just said that because I'm not quite right, I tell you."

"Have you missed me?"

"You know I have. Do you have any idea how badly I want you?"

"I'd like to find out...but not here," he said stopping himself in mid-grab. "How about in your room in thirty minutes?"

"I don't think I can wait that long," she giggled. "Let's make it fifteen."

"That sounds even better," he agreed.

"I'm really going to be ready," she promised to his retreating back.

***

Finally, she was moving forward. Along the driveway, over the road, down the embankment, across the lengthy stretch of beach to the river's edge. She stepped right in as if there was no time to waste. Slipping beneath the surface, Sunny felt the water soak through to her scalp. She rolled onto her back and lolled around relishing the feeling of being buoyant. She looked over in the direction from which she had come and could barely make out the low flat structure. From this vantage she could see how isolated the facility had grown. Desolation all around. Other than a stretch of road that meandered along the shore terminating at the Institution, there was nothing out this way. This was the end of the road in every sense of the word.

The Institution

What was striking was how the city that once huddled along the east side of the river was abandoned. There was not a light to be seen from that direction. Neglected buildings, relics really, their hard edges crumbling into the sand. This city founded on timber and cattle was now an artifact. She wondered how and where this number of people had been relocated. There had been something of them here when she arrived. But thirteen years was a long time in terms of collapse. She had been absent from the more advanced stages.

She moved into the channel where the current was swiftest and started swimming. The population had to be concentrated in the large cities downstream. There was no survival without access to services. But what were those places like? Was everyone still racing back and forth to jobs, clueless about the severity of the circumstances? Were people still having children? Did they think their offspring would live to see better days? Did they hold their babies to their breasts, look out on the shattered world, and believe? The theologian, Thomas Berry, felt it was the great diversity of plant and animal species, geography, and geology that led to humanity's advanced state of Evolution. He believed if we lived on a moonscape there would not be the vast number of things to name, of complicated systems to comprehend. He mused that destroying the life of this planet would take us to a lower level of complexity. So, if he happened to be right, what would the children born today be like tomorrow?

Nothing moved on the bridge that connected the east with the west. No headlights blazing in the night, no roaring traffic to contend with. It was an ugly structure, the most utilitarian in design, that no longer had any utility whatsoever. There had been a beautiful historic bridge in Silver Falls that was a favorite with jumpers. Its suicidal popularity soared in the early part of the 21st Century when those who scraped by during the relative 'good' times realized their lives would be intolerable in the years that lie ahead. The lost ones of society who hesitated before taking the plunge got more attention in the last few minutes of their lives than they received in all the previous years combined.

She could sense more than see the deserted waterfront homes. Distant docks that were high and dry – embedded in hard pan – no chance of even a rogue wave reaching them now. A day at the beach extinguished, like everything else. On this wide shore all kinds of watercraft once landed. The owners of those craft had been in agreement when it came to the irrelevance of a salmon's need to access rivers and streams. They were all for having large reservoirs on which to recreate. When talk of draw downs or dam removal surfaced they were up in arms over the decline in property values and recreational activities that would ensue. They were similarly irrational in the face of environmental breakdown.

Skies without birds, soil without vegetation, rivers without fish, air without oxygen. It was a land turned inside out. And she doubted it got any better, further along, in the distance. Up ahead was a long stretch that had been spared from development. The water ran swifter through there. The walls were steep. The trees once plentiful. Animals had cut trails that zigzagged back and forth across the hills. But it had been a long time since four-legged critters leapt or crept or scurried about their business.

The river narrowed. She could feel the temperature change as the rocky cliffs rose higher, sheltering her, closing her in. And the sound. To hear something that wasn't human after so many years of hearing nothing else. The voice of a river surging and fading, flowing around the rocks, and tugging her along to its ultimate destination. And that was a few hundred miles away where the river drained into the Pacific. Years ago, near the mouth, an oil tanker left scars on the base of a pier supporting a much larger bridge than the one at her back. Attempting to meet an urgent delivery deadline, the fully loaded vessel rammed into it. The resulting spill meant death for the few remaining salmon that were being captured and ferried over the dams so they might spawn. All along the banks for miles, bedraggled birds and fish flapped around in the goo. Beset upon by unnatural forces far removed from the life force of this river.

She began to feel light-headed. While she had her wits about her she moved out of the current and swam to shore. A dozen strong strokes took her to a large flat rock that was partially submerged. She pulled herself up and perched there with her upper body out in the midnight air, hands clinging tightly to her landing spot, legs moving with the river's flow. She needed to rest. The exhaustion of swimming was taking its toll. She sucked in big lungfuls of air but there was not much in the mix to satisfy her body. Things weren't as they used to be.

The Institution

Time passed. She took in the high-tension lines cutting a swath over the hills to the west. Their hulking shapes silhouetted in the tepid moonlight. Still functioning they were. Providing a lifeline to The Faith is Truth Institution, no doubt. She was taken aback by a lone pine on the highest peak above her and immediately began speculating on how it might have survived. Further observation revealed the size and shape wasn't quite right. Then it occurred to her what it was and the hilarity of it struck her. A stealth tower – a cellular tower camouflaged as a tree so that it wouldn't be conspicuous in what had been a forest. That made her think about how the river would bring her within sight of what had been a popular winter ski resort. She suspected the runs still scarred the peak. No doubt it would be the same with the lifts. Chairs, dangling from sagging cables over slopes devoid of snow, would have endured. But not the seasons of the earth. They no longer arrived like clockwork. With that thought, she slid down the smooth surface and was weightless again.

An affinity for water – how could that have eluded us? A substance essential for life that also lent itself to boating, swimming, skating, and skiing should have had our full respect. But for humanity in general, water was an expedient dumping ground for waste too onerous to face on a personal basis. Out of sight, out of mind. We could never get past this flush-it-away stage and develop into something more meaningful. What was wrong with us? It was something she had asked herself time and again. Why couldn't we wrap ourselves in the elements and appreciate them for what they were? Why couldn't we feel the air working its way into our lungs, sweet water running down our throats, and know that without these, we were nothing. A guy Sunny worked with once told her that the elements that sustained life on Planet Earth were not that complex. After all, they boiled down to just four: air, water, soil, and sunlight. He found her awe of such humble things the mark of a simpleton. She explained why it was that he did not think they were special. It was because we had them all and in perfect proportion. There was no wisdom that she could see in being cavalier about undoing the balance. What would he say now? She liked to think he had learned enough to be sufficiently humiliated but that was too much to expect. More likely, he was the honorary member of some "think" tank making his living debunking the obvious. Were there still "think" tanks? Were "smart" dudes to this day putting a positive spin on this shit?

She swore out loud and her voice echoed in the darkness. "I've got to make it further. A little further," she screamed when she felt herself beginning to fail. "I have to keep going," she cried to an empty world.

Riding the river but a fraction of its length was all she could do. The obstacles to making it to the ocean were set in concrete. The dam she had in her sights was the last constructed on this incredibly damaged body of water. Squeezing out that last scrap of hydroelectricity meant we were able to have what we were entitled to a while longer. But it wasn't long before years of drought led to water levels insufficient to power the turbines and it had to be mothballed. She was not sure she would make it that far before becoming incapacitated. She was going to do her best though. When the big immovable object loomed she would take a deep breath, turn around, dive in, and swim upstream against the current for as long as she could. She would fight and die before coming up against one more senseless impediment laid down by man.

She had been doing the breaststroke prior to turning on her back and stretching her arms over her head in smooth fluid strokes. She concentrated on her chest rising and falling and the wake from her legs fluttering just below the surface while searching for other memories that might keep her afloat but they were fading in an oxygen deficient world. It was crazy to look to the past anyway because there was only her, the river, and a limited future that was terrifying. Not surprisingly, a part of Sunny wished to stay, in place, treading water indefinitely.

A slight flicker in the eastern sky forced her to look up. In her delirium, she strained to recall what it was. The sun forsaking us? Had it thought about shining and then turned away as if in disbelief, dismay, disdain? She couldn't be sure. She did not know the language of the sun or its sensibilities. But what was there to shine on? What was the point in bothering with such a wretched place? Its energy would be better spent searching for greener planets. Better to shine its light somewhere with a future. Better to leave this place to wither in the dark.

When the last living thing
Has died on account of us,
How poetical it would be
If Earth could say,
In a voice floating up
Perhaps
From the floor
Of the Grand Canyon,
"It is done.
People did not like it here."

— Kurt Vonnegut

Made in the USA